COVEN KING I

Virgil Knightley, Edgar Riggs

Copyright © 2024 by Virgil Knightley

All rights reserved.

No portion of this book may be reproduced in any form without written permission from the publisher or author, except as permitted by U.S. copyright law. Exclusive publication rights have been granted by the copyright holder to Royal Guard Publishing for ebook, paperback, and audiobook editions of this book. If you find this book anywhere other than in these places and in these formats, please contact virgilknightley@gmail.com.

From Virgil to Edgar, my coauthor on this book: We did it, and for what it's worth, I think *you* did a fucking awesome job, bud. I'm proud to have my name on this one alongside yours. Keep up the good work.

CONTENTS

1. Chapter 1   1
2. Chapter 2   23
3. Chapter 3   49
4. Chapter 4   78
5. Chapter 5   101
6. Chapter 6   130
7. Chapter 7   152
8. Chapter 8   178
9. Chapter 9   204
10. Chapter 10   226
11. Chapter 11   245

12.	Chapter 12	266
13.	Chapter 13	288
14.	Chapter 14	309
15.	Chapter 15	338
16.	Chapter 16	363
17.	Chapter 17	384
18.	Chapter 18	408
19.	Chapter 19	433
20.	Chapter 20	451
21.	Chapter 21	474
22.	Chapter 22	491
23.	Chapter 23	517
24.	Chapter 24	536
25.	Chapter 25	558
26.	Chapter 26	583
27.	Epilogue	606
28.	Links to Follow	640

CHAPTER 1

Extra Cash

"Thanks, Mister—uhh—Morse, right?" the balding gentleman said as I handed him his package. He had leaned in closer than I would have liked so he could examine my name tag. In the end, he still got it wrong. *Morrison. Logan Morrison. Is it really that hard?* I grumbled internally. I forced a genial smile and offered an equally friendly wave back at him as I returned to my delivery van.

I wasn't sure why I needed a name tag to begin with, and even more unsure of why some people felt the need to make an effort to call me by my name when we'd almost certainly never see each other again. Still, I was a little impressed—this guy was a living paradox. If he couldn't even read my big, bold name tag, then how was he supposed to read the book in that package I just handed him? "Dude needs new glasses," I grumpily mumbled as I climbed into the driver's seat.

With a sigh, I rested my head against the steering wheel. "It's not his fault," I said to no one but myself. "I'm just frustrated and broke again." I had to remember not to let the stress overwhelm me. I wasn't a full-time student anymore, and being forced into working to pay for the rest of my schooling out of pocket was my own problem.

I always knew things would be harder once I ran out of money. Sure, I could have taken out a loan and put myself into debt to finish school without interruption. Then I'd have that cushy life on campus surrounded by friends and cute coeds for at least one more year. But, alas, no.

I'd seen how debt chained people down and forced them into jobs and lives that they didn't want. No way. When I did graduate, I'd do it with work experience and entirely debt-free. I enjoyed my freedom and refused to spend years enslaved to financial aid repayments just to have one more year taking it easy. That was my choice, and I hoped it'd be worth it in the long term.

Putting the van in drive, I saw the balding man with the outdated lens prescription still standing at the door with a smile. He noticed me looking and waved one last time before heading inside. I waved back, grinning at him in spite of myself. I enjoyed polite people, but at the end of the day, Spartan didn't pay me by the hour. Instead, they paid me by the package. So when polite people held me up with pointless interactions or small talk, it only made my life a little bit harder. But they didn't know that, and it wasn't their job to know that, so it's not like I could blame them, and I sure as hell wasn't going to punish their friendliness.

You'd think that working for the largest online store in the world would mean you get paid a nice salary, right? Wrong. The only benefits were that I could make a full-time minimum wage without spending the full forty hours a week to earn it, and the fulfillment warehouse was within walking distance from my apartment near campus. The faster I could finish up my load, the faster I could get back to my studies and prepare for my part-time night classes.

That's why I was feeling so frustrated. I was broke after paying rent and tuition at the local state college again. I couldn't let the stress get the better of me. I couldn't allow myself to think about other guys my age who already had families and jobs, paying for everything themselves. I had no family. Not even parents. Life wasn't fair, and I learned at a very young age that I would have to take what I could get and work for everything I wanted.

This week looks like it's going to be nothing but PB&J and Easy Mac again, I silently seethed inside my head. *Maybe I just need to skip the meal and go straight to bed.*

• ♥ • ♥ • ♥ • ♥ • ♥ •

After wrapping up my last delivery and parking the van at the Spartan hub, I pocketed my name tag and headed over to the Student Union on campus. I always seized every chance to save a little cash, so grabbing a couple of complimentary bottled waters and a pre-study coffee from the common area each night was a no-brainer. Yeah, I could settle for tap water, but if I was stuck with mostly water to drink, I might as well aim for the best, right? Even if it was just some generic bottled brand.

"Probably came from someone's tap, too," I muttered with a sigh.

Scanning the room, I eyed the bulletin board adjacent to the corridor leading to one of the cafeterias. Sometimes it had something worthwhile. Most times, it was just student activities

I had no time for. I turned away from the board to head to the cooler. Or at least, I tried to.

But there it was—a piece of paper on the board, seemingly calling out to me amidst the sea of mundane notices. It was...odd. It beckoned me, almost like it was lit up in neon yellow, though it was just plain white. Even from a distance, I couldn't look away. Strangely, I didn't find it unsettling, though looking back on it, that must have been part of its magic, too.

With no other option, I approached the board. The closer I got, the stronger the urge to read it became—as if I were famished, and only the contents of that note could satiate me. "What the?" I whispered to myself. The words were like a magnet, pulling me in until I was a breath away from the paper, reading the message written in quirky handwriting adorned with black hearts dotting the i's and bat-wings crossing the t's.

It read, "Hey there, stranger! If anyone's free, I'm looking for someone to help tutor me in general mathematics. I've got a big test tomorrow and I really need to cram. I'm not picky, so I'll take any help I can get. I'll pay $20 an hour. Look for me on the second floor of the Student Union. I'll be at the table by the painting of that old bald guy in the tacky suit waiting for someone until at least eight in the evening. If you see this note on the bulletin board, it means I'm still there. —Cherry Cola."

The strange allure of the paper faded once I'd read it. It was like a hypnotic trance suddenly coming to an abrupt end. Shaking my head to clear it, I muttered, "Damn, I must be more tired than I thought."

A pleasant scent reached my nose. I leaned closer, sniffing the note. *Did she spray perfume on it? It smells amazing.* I pocketed the paper, deciding to investigate.

This was a golden opportunity for me. I mean, I aced calculus, so tutoring in gen ed math? Easy-peasy. Glancing at the offered pay, I couldn't help but imagine treating myself to a burger or maybe even a small pizza when this was over. The mere thought made my mouth water. But as I reread her name, I paused. *Unique name, probably a nickname.* Glancing at the clock, I cursed. "Shit, it's almost eight."

Before investigating any further, I went ahead and grabbed a plain black coffee. Lucky for me that I liked it that way since all the sweeteners and cream were gone. I decided to save the bottled water for later and headed upstairs. It only hit me as I ascended the stairs that I might already be too late. Who knew? Maybe someone was already tutoring her, or perhaps the notice was from yesterday and she forgot to take it down. *Only one way to find out.* I quickened my pace, careful not to spill my coffee.

• ♥ • ♥ • ♥ • ♥ • ♥ •

Reaching the top of the stairs, I let out a sigh of relief. Only one person was up there, which was odd because the Student Union was normally full of students studying around this time. *In fact, I haven't seen anyone since I came into the building*, I suddenly realized. Across the room near the wall, just under the painting of a bald alumnus, was a girl who I assumed was Cherry Cola.

I chuckled to myself. *That fucking name, though.*

I couldn't see every detail yet, but from what I could make out, she was cute. Like, super cute. She spotted me, put one hand high in the air to wave me down, and smiled.

I smiled back and began that long awkward walk. You know the one—where you and the person you're meeting are both looking at each other from across the room but you're too far away to say anything without shouting, so you just walk forward until you're finally close enough that you can talk at a socially acceptable volume. Interestingly, it seemed that she didn't understand the basic etiquette of this walk because she shouted at me almost right away.

"Heya! Are you here to tutor me?" She asked before launching an unexpected wink at me.

I had to admit that despite her wink not making any situational sense at the end of that question, it gave her a kind of quirky charm. What's more, her shout surprisingly made that walk's awkwardness disappear. Then again, maybe I was only thinking that because as I got closer, I realized just how hot she was. And when I say hot, I mean she was so hot that she was lucky she hadn't set her study materials on fire because of proximity alone.

Cherry was short and petite—not a classic supermodel physique, by any means, but certainly an attractive one. She had pale skin, a dark brown or black French bob cut, and red, kissable lips. She seemed to be wearing red colored contacts, too. Everything about her was attractive—the slenderness of her waist, the flatness of her tummy, the perfect yet not overbearing slope of her breasts—everything. Even under her tight hoodie I could make out those details. She seemed like a natural beauty too. I didn't detect a ton of makeup on her, and even the subtle rosy color on her cheeks looked oddly natural.

It's not that I have an issue with girls who wear makeup or anything—when done right, makeup can add a lot to a look, no doubt about it. Cherry, however, just looked like one of those girls that you could wake up next to after a long night of sweaty sex and she'd still make you gawk at how amazingly cute she looked. *And if I'm really lucky, maybe I'll find out how true that is*, I thought, daring to dream.

Her dark hoodie hid a lot of her figure, but her black miniskirt exposed enough of her legs for me to instantly think about them being wrapped around my waist.

After my eyes finished the elevator trip, I shouted back and waved. "Hi. You must be Cherry Cola?" I asked as I held up her request note.

"I am! And you must be my professor tonight," she said. A wink would have worked much better here, but she didn't think to try it.

"I guess I am. I'm Logan. You need help with math, right?" I clarified with a friendly smile as I finally reached the table.

"Mhm. That's right," she confirmed with another misplaced wink. Dammit. Was she trying to do them wrong?

I almost laughed. Instead, I smiled a little wider and offered her my hand. "It's a pleasure to meet you, Cherry."

She took my hand and gave it a small shake. "Mmm," she began as she deliberately looked me up and down while licking her lips. "I think the pleasure is going to be all mine, Logan."

I won't lie. It always felt great to be complimented by pretty girls, but to be flirted with so aggressively by a girl this gorgeous felt particularly flattering. "You're not so bad yourself," I said as I took my seat. "So, what exactly are you having trouble with?" I eyed the book to see what page it was on to get an idea of what I'd need to help her with.

Cherry closed the book without looking away from me. "We can get to that in a few minutes.

First, I want to hear more about you," she said. "You seem very interesting."

Don't get me wrong—I would much rather sit and chat with her all night. Well, not all night, maybe, because I'd rather be doing *other* things with her for a while too if it were up to me. Still, I felt it was important to get the business out of the way first. "Before we get to that, I'd like to ask—" She stopped me by answering my question before I could finish it.

"No need to worry. You're on the clock." She ran her fingertips across the back of my hand. "I just want to get my money's worth." Her tone had gone sultry.

I shook my head ruefully to try and disguise the shivers she sent down my spine. For the briefest of moments, I thought I saw her eyes flash or glow, but it was easy to chalk up to my lack of sleep and food and a trick of the lamps overhead. *It had to just be the light reflecting off her eyes,* I reasoned. "Okay. I'll answer one question that isn't related to your math. So you'd better choose wisely," I said, grinning at her despite the businesslike tone I struck.

She put on a frustrated pout. "Ten questions!" She demanded, holding up ten fingers.

I shook my head. "Two."

"Seven!"

"Three, and that's my final offer," I said as I grinned at her.

"Fine," Cherry begrudgingly agreed, huffing and puffing as she leaned back in her seat. She narrowed her eyes and tapped one finger against her pursed lips as she thought about it. "Okay, I've got one. Do you go visit family on the holidays or do you stay around campus?" She asked.

It wasn't a question I expected, but not one that bothered me anymore. I'd had my whole life to toughen up around this topic. "No, I don't. I don't have any family. Never have," I said honestly.

"Oh! I'm sorry. I didn't mean to hit a sore spot," Cherry replied with a slight frown.

"Nah. It doesn't bother me. Don't worry about it," I said.

As if she'd never been concerned at all, Cherry perked right up. "Great! So that means if you just up and disappeared no one would come looking for you?" She asked with a grin and a wink. This time, the wink felt oddly appropriate.

It was a dark joke, but I didn't mind. "Nope. They wouldn't." I chuckled. "And that's your second question."

Cherry gasped. "But—That's not fair!" She complained, puffing up her cheeks and shaking a fist in my face. A bracelet around her wrist jingled a bit, drawing my gaze and getting a smirk out of me.

"You've only got one more, then we get to work," I said as I pointed at the textbook.

She shook her head stubbornly. "I'm gonna save it."

I was totally into her, and I was sure she was into me, but she was paying me for a job, and I wouldn't feel right if I didn't at least help her figure out some of this stuff before her quiz the next day. Since she wasn't opening her book, I took her hand, which made her smile, but then placed it on the book, only for her to frown again. I laughed. "C'mon, let's get the work done, and then you can have me all to yourself, for as long as you want. You don't want to fail, right?"

"I never fail." That question specifically seemed to get her motivated, but something about the look in her eye told me she wasn't talking about her quiz. She was a bit all over the place so far, but failure seemed to be something that was off the table for Cherry.

She opened the book and flipped a few of the pages before pointing. "This stuff. All the shapes. It's more of a refresher quiz, except that I don't remember a lot of it," she said. "Can you help me?" She batted her eyelashes with a pleading look in her eyes.

It took me a moment to realize I was staring with a goofy smile on my face. *She's just so damn cute*, I thought, unable to help myself. I finally broke out of my stupor with a start. "Oh! Right, geometry? That's pretty easy stuff for me, no worries. I can definitely help you."

"You're sooo smart," Cherry said with a wink, then bit her lip as she leaned on her elbows on the table, cradling her chin in her hands.

I coughed to cover up a laugh. "It's mainly length, width, height, and pi stuff," I said as I flipped through a couple of the pages. "I'll have you ready to ace that quiz in no time."

Cherry's boot began rubbing against my ankle under the table. "Oh yeah? I hear it's the girth that matters most," she said with a naughty grin.

Fuck. I was trying not to give in to her flirting because I really wanted to help her out, but she was making it hard—literally. "Okay, let's start with some basics. You probably remember rectangles and squares well enough—length multiplied by height. So let's go over circles. That's where you start working with pi," I explained.

"Does that pi have cream in it?" Cherry asked as she pointed at the Greek letter on the page.

I chuckled. "No. That's the one you multiply by the radius squared."

Cherry licked her lips. "Wish you and I would multiply already."

I felt the side of her leg creeping higher up mine. I didn't want to encourage her by acknowledging it so I pretended not to notice—or I tried to. My throat was getting dry so I took a sip of my coffee. My voice came out a little higher than intended when I continued. "Alright, let's just move on to some 3D shapes. Let's take this glass for example. We can find out how much fluid is in it," I said as I pointed to a glass on the page.

She put one finger to her lips as if in thought. "Instead of a glass, what if I wanted to use a nice, *thick sausage?*" she asked with waggling brows.

With a playful sigh, I lowered my head. "Well, with a glass you'll have more liquid to measure. You won't find much fluid in a sausage," I said.

Cherry smirked. "You'll get plenty out of one if you do it right." Then she abruptly stood. "I'm hot. I'm gonna take my hoodie off," she said. And then she did.

She pulled it up slowly, and my eyes locked onto her thin waist just above her skirt. My gaze followed her motions to her cute belly button and flat stomach. *Damn, she really is petite—and fucking perfect.*

She kept going, and I thought for a moment she was topless under the bulky garment as more and more skin went on display, but instead, I barely caught the edge of her crop top underneath. My breathing deepened as it lifted, showing me a hint of the red lacy bra beneath. Without the hoodie hiding the rest of her shape from me, I found it even harder to look away.

She saw me staring, and her smile widened. "I'm *sorry*," she said exaggeratedly. "Were you saying something... about the glass?"

She was cleverer than I gave her credit for. I had been saying something about the glass on the page, and therefore I couldn't count that as her third question. "Yes. Yes, I was," I said. "I was just going over how you can use this formula to find out how much you can fit into the glass."

Cherry bit her red lips. "You're funny. Why would you want to know how much you can fill it up when you could just fill it until it's overflowing and dripping wet over the floor?" She asked coyly.

I grinned. "Are we still talking about math?" I asked.

"In the sense that I want to see what 'you plus me' equals, sure. But I'm not trying to *skirt* the rules." Cherry said as she slowly pulled her skirt up, exposing a little more of her thigh. She made sure I got a good look at the extra skin before lowering it, taking her seat, and leaning in closer. She rested her chin on her hand, and her eyes never left mine.

"I guess you're not," I said. Dammit, I held off longer than most could have, but in the end, I was only a man. I leaned in as well, putting our faces only a foot apart, the table our only barrier. Her hand rested atop my own. Being this close, I could smell that intoxicating perfume she wore. It was the same as what I smelled on the paper that got me this little job. My eyes looked into hers before flicking down to her lips and back.

I saw her eyes do the same as she looked at my lips before licking her own. She moved in a little closer. "I'm ready for my last question," she said softly.

My breathing quickened. We were only a few inches apart. "What's that?" I closed my eyes as I leaned in just a little closer. Then I felt her tongue run up my jawline before flicking my earlobe.

"Do you wanna come back to my place?" She whispered in my ear.

The warmth of her breath and the sensation of her slick tongue sent waves of anticipation through my body. I wanted to say yes instantly, but then all the strange things I'd seen came back to me. First, the letter on the board that I couldn't look away from, then the odd question followed up with one about me disappearing forever, and finally, that momentary flash of red in her eyes all came back to me. On the other hand, I hadn't been laid in weeks, and she was easily the sexiest chick I'd met in...maybe ever. In the end, I decided that I needed this—bad. What were the odds that she was some kind of evil satanist harvesting my organs? Probably low. Right?

"Hell yeah," I said, taking the bait. "Let's go."

CHAPTER 2

A Taste of Cherry

Cherry sprang off my lap in a heartbeat, skipping towards the stairs. "Alright! Let's go!"

Observing that she only grabbed her purse, leaving her hoodie on the floor and her study materials on the table, I wondered if she expected me to carry it all. Not that I'd mind. Spending more time with Cherry was worth it. Still, a little respect wouldn't hurt. I stood and gestured at her things. "Hey! What about your stuff?"

Cherry halted, slowly turned, and flashed a wry smile. "Right... *My stuff.*" She hurried back to the table and swiftly gathered her belongings. "I don't know how I forgot," she chuckled nervously, winking. Tucking everything under her arm, she headed for the stairs again.

Shaking my head with a grin, I offered, "I can carry it for you if you need me to."

"It's fine," she said. Her next response was unexpected, yet not unwelcome. Sticking out her tongue, she flipped up the back of her skirt and swayed her hips, revealing the enticing sight of her thong and tight ass. "Don't fall... *behind*," she teased before giggling and dashing down the stairs.

Unable to resist, I laughed and chased after her, undeterred by her growing quirkiness. Taking the stairs two or three at a time, I completely forgot about the water I meant to take with me. When I caught up to her, I decided to be bold and pinched her ass.

Startled, she jumped and covered her butt with one hand, "Eek!" Spinning around to face me, she continued walking backward. "Hey now," she mock scolded, wagging a finger at me, "No touchy-touchy until we get back to my place, *Professor Morrison*." Then she turned around and resumed skipping, each bounce causing her skirt to flutter and tease me with a hint of cheek.

I slowed for a moment, my mischievous grin fading. I couldn't recall telling her my last name. *Did I? This evening so far has all been a horny blur.* I couldn't decide if I did or didn't mention it, but what I could decide was that I wanted to get my hands on that body of hers. "Forget it," I said as I jogged to catch up. "Worst case scenario, I'm down one kidney."

It turned out that Cherry didn't live far from the Student Union. Once I caught up, she took me by the hand and led me to her apartment. She pulled me along as I trailed slightly behind her, trying to keep up. "C'mon, slowpoke! I can't wait to get you home and *make you mine*."

Normally, that would have been a sexy line—especially coming out of a solid ten out of ten like her. But something about the way she said it seemed a little too possessive or aggressive. I wasn't sure, but I knew it felt off. Before I could work out if I even wanted to question it, we reached the front door of her pad. I stopped next to her. "Hang on, I just need to unlock the door. Then we're gonna have a night you'll *never* forget," she said, grinning wickedly.

Again, something seemed off about all of this. My eyes strayed from checking out her cleavage and noticed that her purse, which I could now see down into, was empty. There was literally nothing in it but the key she'd removed. I furrowed my brow and opened my mouth to ask about that fact, but she stopped me when she opened the door and pulled me in by the wrist. *Damn! She's stronger than she looks.*

Once I stepped into the apartment, things got even weirder. Everything was perfect. And I don't mean that it was clean and tidy. I mean it was perfect. It didn't look lived in at all. The books on the bookshelf were too straight, the table in the open dining area was set for four, and there wasn't a single stain of any kind on the white carpet. The coffee table was neatly organized, tasteful paintings hung on the blue walls, and not a hint of personal items of any kind were out in the open. *This just went from weird to almost Stepford Wives levels of creepy.*

If I didn't know any better, I would've guessed it had been set up by a realtor to be shown on the real estate market, with an open house in its immediate future. Everything about it was way too normal, like it was going out of its way not to be suspicious. That only made it *extremely* suspicious, of course. I knew something was definitely wrong here. The foreboding sound of the lock turning behind me sent my mind running.

I began adding up all of the little things that had been bugging me through the night. It started with Cherry and her flawless body and face—literally too perfect to be real. Sure, there are gorgeous college girls, but they all have something that stops them from meeting that impossible mark of perfection. Some wear a bit too much makeup, some have acne scars, few truly possess ideal figures, and others have their miscellaneous minor flaws. None of it was something that would make you think they were anything less than breathtaking, maybe. But Cherry... She was perfect in every way that I could see.

Before I could think about it any further, Cherry tossed her purse on the floor, wrapped her arms around my neck, and went up on her tiptoes to kiss me. The moment her lips met mine, it was on. Adrenaline blazed through me like I'd been shot with a taser. There were no light pecks, gently probing tongues, or chaste kisses. It was instant full-throttle passion. Her lips pressed hard against mine, and our tongues were frenzied as they explored each other's mouths.

Cherry's passion was intense, and her scent was intoxicating. With every kiss, I felt my priorities shifting as one head was taking control over the other. All of my suspicions were becoming less and less important by the second.

I quickly realized that I wanted her more than I wanted to know what was up with her. *Whatever. I'm sure it's just my lack of sleep getting to me*, I thought.

I let my hands explore her body. After a minute or so, she broke the kiss and bit my bottom lip, pulling on it with alarmingly sharp teeth. She let it go as she dropped from her tiptoes and giggled. "Tasty boy," she cooed as she pushed my back against the door as she backed up, and she grinned at me. "You like my flavor?"

Cherry wasn't even winded, but I had to catch my breath a little. "Fuck yeah," I said, "I should've known you'd taste like cherries."

"Good, because you haven't tasted *anything* yet." Cherry's suggestive words hung in the air as she sauntered into the living room, her hips swaying seductively. She leaned forward, placing her hands on the back of the couch. "I hope you're ready for another sample," she teased, shooting me a playful wink over her shoulder.

Her wink was perfectly timed this time, sparking a mischievous grin to life on my face. Closing the distance between us, I dropped to my knees behind her, and eagerly lifted her skirt, sliding her thong down past her boots. I could have easily left it on, but I was on a mission and didn't want any distractions in my way.

As my hands explored her flawless curves, Cherry wiggled and giggled, taunting me with her playful banter. "I know I've got a cute booty, but if you take a picture it'll last longer," she teased.

I couldn't resist teasing back. With a smirk, I whipped out my phone, pretending to snap a photo of her ass, instead taking one of the floor. Though I wouldn't dare photograph her without permission, the sound of the camera's click was enough to catch her off guard.

Her gasp of surprise only fueled my desire as I slipped a finger between her pussy lips, teasing her with slow, deliberate strokes. She moaned in response, unable to resist the new sensation thrumming through her. "*Professor Morrison*, you're so naughty," she murmured, playing along with our student-teacher fantasy. "You had me for a second there—but I wouldn't really mind if you did film me. Fuck! Oh—that feels good! Ahh!"

Encouraged by her sexy squeals of pleasure, I continued my exploration, swapping out my fingers for my mouth and reveling in the taste of Cherry Cola on my tongue as I delved deeper. She squirmed, driving back against me, unable to contain her pleasure as I ate her out from behind. "Ah! Fuck! H—how are you so good at this?!" she gasped, her voice laced with lust.

I liked to think I had decent manners, and I knew it was rude to talk with my mouth full, so I said nothing. My tongue continued to explore her depths while my hand came up to massage her pearl.

Cherry pressed her perfect ass into me as I ate her out. "Holy shit! Logan, don't stop! Don't stop! I—I'm gonna—AH!"

It didn't take long before her juices were covering my tongue and chin as she came. *Fuck*, maybe it was only because I skipped dinner, but this woman tasted so good. I kept my steady pace as I felt her body shudder in my grip. I didn't stop until I was sure her orgasm had passed.

Now that I had her warmed up, I was unable to help myself. As I stood, I paused briefly to wipe my mouth and chin on my sleeve. She panted with ragged breaths, her ass still jutting out toward me. I caught her looking at me over her shoulder, trying to catch a peek as I pulled my pants down.

Cherry grinned and licked her lips. "Are you gonna fuck me, baby?" she asked with an unnecessary wink. I would have sighed if I weren't about to be dick-deep in the most beautiful girl I'd ever had the pleasure of meeting. Instead, I said nothing and winked back at her while I lined my tip up with her dripping center. I kept my eyes locked on hers as I pressed into her.

"Yup."

At the moment of our collision, her eyes went wide and her mouth fell open. Holy *shit* she was tight—so tight that I had to take my time and slowly work my way in. Also, I met a little unexpected resistance with the first push—almost like she still had a hymen, but with the confidence and sex appeal she had, I was willing to chalk it up to my imagination.

She clenched her teeth. "Fuck, Logan. You're too big! Take it easy, baby—ahhhh!"

I paced myself so as not to hurt her. After a couple of inches, I slowly thrust in and out in a rhythm. Taking my time so she could adjust to my size. Cautiously, I pushed in further, testing the waters each time until, finally, I hilted myself inside Cherry.

She covered her mouth and squealed like a piglet, her eyes rolling back as she tried to look at me over her shoulder. With a feral moan, she tightened her grip on the nearby couch and struggled to get out her next words, "F-F-Fuck! I feel so full. It's almost too much! Just, go slow for now."

I sat there for a while until I noticed her starting to relax. Then, I gently fucked her with slow, smooth strokes. Her pussy clung to me as if begging my cock not to leave.

"Mmmm...yeah, that's nice," she groaned, grinding back against me. Her moans were long and low and I could tell she was finally ready when she continued with her fantasy. "Ohh—God yes, Professor Morrison! Teach me how to get fucked by a big cock like yours! Ah–ungh!"

I decided I'd play along this time. "I'd be happy to show you, Ms. Cola. If you're good, maybe I'll give you opportunities to earn extra credit."

That seemed to do the trick for her because she started pushing her hips harder into me. I stopped thrusting and held myself still, allowing her to fuck herself on my cock. "Ah! More! I need more!" she said.

Fuck, being inside Cherry felt incredible. She moaned and dropped her head low when I grabbed her hips and picked up the pace. It wasn't long before my balls were slapping against her thighs and the wonderful sound of her squelching pussy being fucked joined her groans and squeals of delight. She was a goddess, her pussy a quality lock that perfectly fit my cock-key.

I heard something in the couch snap and she threw her head back, "Fuck yes! I'm gonna... I'm gonna—I'm *gonna cum my brains out—ah*! Nyah! Logan, fuck, baby, shit! Shiiit!"

I felt her walls clenching down on my shaft as her orgasm rocked her body, covering her in a glossy sheen of sweat and making her heartbeat noticeably throb even inside her cunt. I couldn't contain myself anymore. It was only with a blessed last-second thought that I remembered I didn't have protection and hadn't asked about it beforehand. It was definitely too late to ask now. So I pulled out and jerked myself as my orgasm hit me. I growled as rope after rope of my cum covered her lower back, skirt, and ass.

Cherry looked back at me as I was catching my breath and uttering curses. She whined. "Duuude! You got it all over! Why didn't you just cum inside me?" She stepped forward and pulled off her crop top. She passed it over her shoulder to me. "The least you can do is clean me up."

I caught the shirt and wiped down her back and ass. I eyed her slender back and shook my head. She caught me staring and raised a questioning brow. "How are you so perfect?" I asked her.

Cherry giggled impishly, wiggling her fingers. "Magic."

"I'm serious, though," I muttered. "You're literally flawless. The more I look at you, the uncannier it is."

She pulled her skirt down and started walking away. Her strapless bra went next, falling to the floor behind her. "Follow me and you'll find out by morning, I promise."

I didn't hesitate. I shucked off my pants the rest of the way and let my shirt join the rest of the discarded clothing on the floor. I caught up quickly. There was only one door left open in the hall so I went in.

Cherry stood next to the bed in all of her naked glory. Well, *almost* all of her naked glory. She still had her boots on. It was kinda weird, but honestly, it was also kinda hot.

She caught me eying her boots. "The boots stay on for now. Can't risk finding out you have a foot fetish and making things weird—I have the hottest feet in the world, so you'd never stop worshiping my little piggies. And I'm much too ticklish for that," she said with a rather serious expression, despite her brightly blushing cheeks.

It almost seemed like she'd been reading my mind when I reflected on her boots just then, but with her nude perfection in front of me I didn't give it a second thought. I laughed and walked up to Cherry, admiring her incredibly perky breasts and little pink pierced nipples before I placed my hands on her hips and kissed her.

After a passionate but short kiss, she twisted and tossed me on the bed. For the second time,

I was amazed at how much strength she held in that small and sexy frame.

Normally it would take me at least fifteen minutes after blowing my load to recover. But Cherry had me so aroused that my dick never lost its erection in the first place.

Cherry crawled on the bed with wide hungry eyes as she finally got a closer look at my length. She looked up at me with a mischievous smile. "Is it your turn to taste?" I asked.

She answered by licking my cock from base to tip, then said, "I just want to see how my cum tastes on you." Her lips parted and she wrapped them around my shaft. I groaned and watched her keep going until my cock had disappeared completely. Only Cherry's gorgeous face remained as she took me all the way into her throat. She stared me down as her cheeks hollowed while she pulled away, making sure that none of her juices were left on my shaft.

I groaned in bliss.

She blessed me with a wicked grin. "Fuck, my pussy juice tastes so good. You're fucking welcome."

I laughed as I lay propped up by my elbows on my back, "Such a bad girl. Do I need to keep you after class?"

She giggled and got to her knees to straddle me. "That depends. Will I get to ride this big cock on your desk?" she asked with a thoughtless wink. At this point, I didn't even care about the poor wink execution.

"Uh, sure," I muttered, losing the roleplay in a moment of extreme arousal.

She sat on my thighs, held my shaft against her pelvis, and examined it with disbelief, "Wow! I can't believe you actually fit that inside little ol' me."

I smiled and dropped onto my back, resting my arms behind my head. "You took it like a champ. But, if you're too scared to do it again..." I shrugged. "I could just go," I teased.

Her head shot up and her expression turned serious, "Fuck you. There's no way I'm ever letting you out of here."

My brows furrowed, but before I could give that response the kind of thought it deserved, she lifted herself and aimed my cock at her center. She didn't bother toying with me or going slow. My mind was suddenly enraptured with bliss when I slid inside and her tight walls engulfed my member, and I forgot all about her ominous comment.

She did not disappoint. She rode me fast and dirty. I held onto her hips and tried to meet her pace with my own thrusts. I enjoyed the show as Cherry pinched and played with her nipple piercings while her ass continued rapidly slapping my thighs. "Y-Yes Your fffucking dick is so—Ah!"

After already cumming recently, I had a bit more stamina than usual, so I redoubled my efforts and started fucking her even faster. Cherry's eyes crossed and her tongue lolled out. I could have sworn that for a moment I saw fangs, but I threw that thought aside right away. If I was having sex so good that I was hallucinating then that was alright by me, and if she was a secret monster, well at this point, I was in too deep to be bothered. Literally.

Cherry's arms went limp, leaving her perfect tits to freely bounce as I continued to have my way with her. Stil, she kept riding me and begging for more, "P-Please! Please! Logan! I—I—mmm fuck! More! More! More! Don't stop, baby!"

You'll be happy to know that I didn't stop. Cherry hit a point where she could barely bounce on her own as she became lost in ecstasy. I continued to jackhammer her from below, keeping things moving forward. Eventually, I felt my own end in sight as Cherry started convulsing and screaming incoherently, "Fu—I, Logaah! Yeah! I'm cu—Fuck! AHH!"

Her pussy started milking me, and as I recalled Cherry's permission in the living room, I lost it. I buried myself in her. She collapsed on my chest, breathing heavily, moaning, and shuddering as I filled her pussy with my seed. With each thrust, more of my warmth filled her, and Cherry's body spasmed with each burst. "More. I—Fuck. Fill me more," she said between breaths.

I lay there holding Cherry as I finished pumping the last of my cum into her. We panted while we held each other. She felt incredible in my arms. After a few moments, Cherry lifted her head and kissed me hard on the lips before sitting up with energy that seemed to come from nowhere.

She patted me twice on the chest and ground her hips, making me twitch inside of her. "You've got another round in you. I can feel it. Let's go take a shower and maybe I'll let you put that round in me instead," she said with a wink.

"Fuck *me*," I groaned as she nailed it again. My cock was already growing hard inside of her. I didn't know where this stamina was coming from, but I wasn't going to complain. *Who'd have thought I could go not only twice after the long day I had but three times with no break?!*

"Fuck you? Uh, pretty sure that's what I was just doing," she giggled before climbing off of me and leading me by the hand to the shower.

She was hesitant about taking her boots off but finally relented. Her feet really were cute. We took our time washing each other. I fucked Cherry one more time in the shower. Then I scrubbed her down with the loofah, and she scrubbed me with her body. It was more intimate and less efficient than what I expected, but it was more than welcome. After that, my little guy was spent. He wasn't the only one either.

I had just come off a full day's work, a tutoring session, and three rounds of the most intense and hottest sex of my life. Saying I was exhausted was an understatement. I started toward the living room to get my clothes so I could dress. "I'd better get going. I have class in the morning. Can I get your number? I'd love to take you out sometime on a real date," I said.

Cherry was having none of it. She tossed me my boxers. She narrowed her eyes before her expression softened. "You're not going *anywhere*. You're exhausted. Plus, you wouldn't make love to a girl and leave her without cuddles, would you?" she asked while batting her lashes.

I put on my boxers and smiled. She had a point; it was rude of me to make love and run, and a lay this good definitely deserved some aftercare. "You're right. I'd love to snuggle a bit and crash here. You know, you're pretty amazing, and I don't just mean your body."

She froze for a moment as she donned her black bra and thong. I wondered why she didn't just grab clean clothes from her dresser, but I was too tired to care. Cherry blushed and smiled. "Obviously," she said.

I laughed, and she led me back to the bedroom. I took my place on the bed, and she lay down in front of me, being my little spoon for the night, "Logan," she asked quietly, "don't sneak away in the middle of the night, okay?"

A small part of me tried to tell myself that I should be concerned by that question. But she was so vulnerable at that moment that I couldn't see why I should be. I kissed her gently on her neck, "Don't worry, I'm not going anywhere." She didn't say anything in response, but I was sure that I could feel her heart beating faster. I felt like I was in heaven as I held this flawless, chaotic, quirky woman in my arms, and it didn't take long before I fell asleep.

・♥・♥・♥・♥・♥・

I was startled back to consciousness probably hours later, but the room was still pretty dark. "Huh?" I rubbed my eyes and tried to make sense of my surroundings and the new sensations I was feeling. For a moment, I thought maybe Cherry wasn't real and I dreamed up the whole thing. But no, I knew that wasn't true. Cherry was very real and *very* hot. A smile split my face at the memories from the night before.

I stretched out on the comfortable bed as my eyes slowly opened. Then my newly adopted smile disappeared. "What the hell?!" I shouted as I realized my right arm didn't come down after my stretch. I looked up to see I was handcuffed to the bedpost. *I know we had some intense sessions the night before, but we never got this kinky,* I thought.

I looked around the room and saw that *everything* had changed. The biggest change? Cherry was gone. I wrestled with the cuffs, trying to pull my hand free but making no progress.

A sultry voice from outside the open door pulled my attention. "It looks like you're having a bit of trouble there, big boy," Cherry purred.

My eyes fell on Cherry as she sauntered in. Her crimson lips curled into a wicked smile. She was wearing a pair of black booty shorts and another crop top. This one was black, sleeveless, and had a white bat across her bosom. My eyes went wide when I realized that Cherry was different. She was still just as gorgeous, just as perfect, but there was more going on with her than before. She grinned at me, glowing red eyes and actual fangs on full display. My eyes widened in fear at the realization that I wasn't hallucinating the night before when I thought I noticed those things.

I gritted my teeth. "Uh! Cherry?! What the hell is going on?! Why am I cuffed to the bed?!"

Cherry's laughter sent shivers of fear through my body. "Logan, baby, don't be so dramatic. I told you I was going to make you mine, and I'm just making good on that promise. I needed some insurance so that you wouldn't run off on me before we made things official."

Fear and anger gripped my heart in equal measure. "What are you talking about? Do you think this is funny?"

Cherry giggled. "A little. But, listen, big boy, I've got a few things to take care of before we get down to business. Do me a favor and stay put, mmkay? I'll be back soon with some friends," she said with a wink before turning and walking right back out of the bedroom. "Like you so much, baby!"

My head dropped back onto the pillow and I stared at the ceiling. *Is this really happen-*

ing? I wondered. What gave her the right? This was kidnapping, wasn't it? I didn't care if she might have been wearing contacts and doing some cosplay stuff, or that the friends she was bringing might be part of some kinky fantasy she had.

Okay, I may have cared if she was bringing friends for a kinky fantasy, but that was beside the point. I couldn't just lay there in a stranger's home—not one who chained me to the bed while I slept. In that moment an old saying came back to me. *If she's too good to be true, then she probably is. This is what I get for going after the "perfect" girl.*

CHAPTER 3

The Great Escape

"Damn it!" I swore under my breath. With Cherry gone, my anger had subsided, replaced by panic and despair. Here I was, cuffed to a bedpost by a random hot stranger whom I tutored for a total of $40 that she never even paid me—and at this point, I doubted she ever would. Hunger gripped my growling stomach at the thought. *There goes my freaking burger,* I lamented. And, to top it all off, it looked like I was going to miss my morning class too. That would be a waste of my hard-earned money.

I didn't let the despair grip me for long. Despite growing up in conditions that made many others give up, I never did. And if I didn't quit when I was alone on the street, then I wouldn't quit now when I was alone in a hot girl's bed. All I needed to do was find a way out, and there was *always* a way out if you looked for it hard enough.

I knew I couldn't wait around for Cherry and her friends to show up. Who knew what kind of crazy stuff they had in mind? A part of me thought that crazy stuff might not be so bad if it was anything like last night. I shook my head. "No, I'm getting out of here," I told myself. "Thinking with my dick is what got me into this mess in the first place."

I needed to stop and assess my situation. Pulling my wrists out of the cuffs wasn't going to work. In fact, it would leave me with nothing but a sore wrist and a lot of regret. Thoughts of my former life on the streets came back to me.

It was a time in my life before I decided to stop fooling around and make something of myself. There were plenty of times I found myself in precarious situations after getting involved with less-than-savory individuals. It was then that I recalled a skill that I'd honed out of necessity, but hadn't used in a few years.

I scanned the room for anything that might work. Then I spotted it—like a lighthouse signaling the shore to a lost sailor at night, a shiny hairpin on the floor gleamed almost as bright. It was a little far but I thought I could manage. Climbing off the bed, I got down on the floor. I extended my body as far as I could and stretched out my foot like the manliest, most heroic ballerina the world had ever seen. "Just a little farther..." After a bit more effort, I finally snagged the instrument of my potential liberation with my big toe.

Like a warrior prepared for battle, I held up my little sword with determined excitement in my eyes and wasted no time in freeing myself. "Yes! Time to get the hell—OW!" The moment the hairpin entered the lock, the cuffs glowed brightly and a searing pain shot through my wrist. "Shit! What the hell is going on?!" I rubbed my wrist, which thankfully seemed to have sustained no real damage.

I leaned in to examine the handcuffs. There were small glowing shapes on the metal that looked almost like runes. I had no clue what they actually were, but I sure as shit knew that normal handcuffs didn't have them. Checking over the rest of the cuffs didn't reveal any kind of electrical power source that would explain how they caused me so much pain.

Deciding that maybe I had only injured my wrist by pulling on the cuffs too suddenly, I tried again. "Mother FU—Ah!" I gritted my teeth and tensed my muscles. The second time was worse than the first by a lot. Anger filled me as I threw the hairpin across the room. "Okay! I get it! No picking your stupid magical cuffs!"

The events of the night before kept playing over in my mind. It started with a simple note on the bulletin board with a magnetic effect on me. Then, it gave way to a seemingly harmless tutoring session that was filled with flirting and banter. I was unable to resist because of how impossibly sexy and charming she was.

Cherry had been far more interested in me from the start than she was in her studies. I'd always been able to pull chicks with ease at parties, so I didn't find it as suspicious as I maybe should have. More things followed, the flash of red in her eyes, the fangs, the overly perfect apartment, the empty purse, and her comments about making me hers and my never leaving... And now, the cuffs had some strange power that was almost like... *Magic*.

A chill ran down my spine as I connected the dots. *What the hell is she—some kind of Vampire Witch?! Is that it? Is she a real bona fide witch with real magic at her disposal?!* Normally, I'd think I was going crazy, but suddenly it seemed to be in the realm of possibility. *Wait—Am I gonna be sacrificed in some fucking blood ritual?!*

Growing up I'd seen plenty of cases in the news of people disappearing, never to be heard from again. And last night she specifically asked me if anyone would come looking for me. I had said no. *Why did I say no one would come looking for me?* I learned a long time ago that you always make sure people know someone is looking for you, even if it's not true. But I let my guard down after years of playing things straight, ignoring my instincts, all because of how hot she was, how hungry I was, and...I don't even know what. I swore not to make that mistake ever again. I guess a part of me thought something like this could never happen in Fresco City, WI.

Adrenaline surged in my body and I firmed my resolve. Grabbing hold of one arm with the other—I pulled. Nothing came from that effort but more pain in my wrist. I swapped my grip to use both hands on the chain and put one foot on the wall, and I pulled and pushed with all I had. The bedpost groaned and I was shocked to see that the bed itself refused to move. But, with a final desperate effort I used every ounce of strength I had left and tried again. *SNAP!* Just like that, the bedpost broke in half and I slipped the cuffs free. I would have to worry about getting it off of my wrist later.

I paused, straining my ears to listen. I wasn't sure if Cherry actually left, or if she was just on the phone and in another room while she waited for her friends to show up. An eerie silence filled the space around me. The loud snap of the bedpost should have drawn some attention if anyone was still around. With no sign of anyone coming to investigate the noise, I cautiously stepped into the hall.

Still wearing nothing but my boxers, I made my way into the next room. My goals were simple: recover my clothes, phone, and wallet, then leave. The last thing I wanted to do was leave a trail that would make it easy for them to find me. Calling the police felt out of the question. What was I supposed to say? "Excuse me officer, but can you please come arrest this insanely hot woman who cuffed me to the bed after a night of hot sex? I think she's a witch." Yeah... I was pretty sure I knew enough about the law enforcement system in town to be certain that wouldn't yield any positive results.

Stepping into the living room I found it was nothing like the night before. The too-perfect decor was gone. Instead, I was met by a room full of occult paraphernalia. Grimoires and books on the occult lined the shelves along with black, white, and red partially burned candles everywhere. They weren't the new age kind that anyone could find on *spartan.com* either. The flawless white carpet was gone, replaced by a wooden floor. And, to my horror, a large menacing pentagram adorned the center of it, carved into the floorboards. The sight sent shivers of fear down my spine. *Yup, she's definitely a witch.*

I spotted a desk across the room with the computer still on. Not seeing my clothes anywhere, I decided to check it out. As I made my way over to it, I ensured that I went around the outside of the pentagram. "Better safe than sorry," I muttered to myself. A cauldron coffee mug that said 'Witch's Brew' on it sat next to the monitor. "Figures that a woman with obvious Daddy issues like her would love dad jokes," I grunted before I examined the group chat that was still open on the computer. There appeared to be a conversation going between Cherry Cola and two friends: Halo Kitty and Alpha.

· ♥ · ♥ · ♥ · ♥ · ♥ ·

Halo: And then I top it off with strawberries and whipped cream. Goodness, it's so tasty!

Cherry: Hey babes! Guess who has a man in her bed?

Halo: Golly! The GF Potential?? That Logan guy? That's amazing! How did it go? Can we come home now, then?

Alpha: Good job. We'll head back soon. Halo, please stop using the chat to share your waffle recipes.

Halo: How about I just make everyone some waffles when we're all home, Alpha?

Alpha: Yeah, fine. Whatever. But, put extra whipped cream on mine. And bacon on the side. Do we have bacon in the fridge?

Alpha: No, wait. Let's focus. Cherry. You still there? Did he try to get away? Did he fight you at all?

Cherry: If by 'fight me' you mean rocked my fucking world? Then yes.

Cherry: Halo, Make me some pancakes too! But make mine chocolate chip!

Halo: Sure! But first, spill the tea! We need details!

Cherry: All it took was a few of my sexy winks and he was all mine.

Alpha: Cherry, your winks are so not sexy.

Cherry: Yes they are! Tell her, Halo! Tell her my winks are sexy!

Halo: Sometimes they are very cute.

Cherry: See! I'm sticking my tongue out at you right now! Just so you know. Wait. Here's a selfie. See it?

Halo: Why didn't you just use an emoji?

Cherry: I couldn't find the stupid emoji...

Alpha: And I'm sighing. Girls, focus. Cherry, tell us how you captured him.

Cherry: My bad. It went great. I tricked him into tutoring me like we said. He's a student at the nearby university, conveniently enough, so I just laid a trap and he followed me home like a lost puppy.

Alpha: And?

Cherry: So I got him back to my place, and oh my god can that man fuck! He literally fucked me senseless. Filled me up twice and everything. I think I came... three or four times? Hell of a way to pop my cherry. You girls have NO IDEA. Anyway, he's cuffed to the bed right now. I used a spell so there's no way he can get free.

Alpha: He what?! You mean you actually had sex with him?

Cherry: Mhm. I totally did, and it was amazing! It's not a big deal since he'll be ours soon anyway. Girls, there was something special about him.

Alpha: Cherry, that's reckless! If we don't end up bonding him, you'll lose your powers! You can't sacrifice your virginity before the contract is finalized!

Cherry: Don't even worry. We're basically in love. He won't go anywhere. And when he realizes his job includes having sex with not just me but the two of you as well, do you really think any man would back down? Besides—there are spells to restore my virginity if we really had to go that route.

Alpha: Costly spells! Risky spells! Spells that might not work for restoring your powers, too!

Halo: Jeepers, Cherry, are you sure about this? Alpha and I haven't even vetted him ourselves. All we know is he's a powerful candidate for being a coven's Greater Familiar. That's...literally it. He might be a total psycho.

Cherry: He's not like that! He's a good guy. You'll love him, just wait and see. He's special.

Alpha: I see... wait, what do you mean special? You're not talking about his...

Cherry: Well, that was special too, but no, I'm talking about something else. I'll have to explain in person. Let's just say you found a good one, Alpha.

Alpha: Cherry... You've got me pulling out my hair here.

Halo: Do you think he'll want some waffles? I'll make him some waffles. What flavor do you think he wants?

Alpha: He doesn't need any waffles. He's our prisoner. You can feed him, fuck him, and spoil him all you want once he's our pet.

Halo: Do you think he'll agree to the binding right away, or will we have to convince him?

Cherry: I don't know why he wouldn't agree. I mean, what guy wouldn't want to be bound to three hotties like us? Especially when he sees what we have planned for him. *wink wink*

Halo: Well, not everyone is okay with being basically enslaved.

Alpha: That's why we don't tell him he has a choice in the matter. We need him to do as he's told, so make him think he's being compelled, don't even let him know he can back out. He's going to be our familiar, remember? How many covens do you see with rebellious Greater Familiars?

Halo: What if he runs away or refuses to sign the contract?

Alpha: It's not like he can hide from us. I can find him anywhere he goes. If he agrees without running, we can give him a much nicer deal than if he pisses me off and tries to escape. If Cherry ends up losing her powers for good because of him, I don't know what I'll do. Probably have to kill him.

Cherry: Don't kill him! He'll be such a good pet. Like a community husband, really. You know, we're the first coven in centuries that found a human that's compatible with being a Greater Familiar! At least I think so.

Halo: Gosh, I thought you said that if he dies then we'd be in a real pickle? Isn't he our only shot at this?

Alpha: Yeah, I said that, and it is true, but he doesn't know that, so we'll threaten as much as we have to. Human men with witch bloodlines are so rare now. This really is our only shot if we want to avoid being strong armed into joining a bigger coven. If he won't be ours, or he dies, we lose our chance forever and we'll have to take a weaker option for our Greater Familiar or join up with someone stronger than us. Anyway... We'll head home soon. Stay focused girls, we can't screw this up.

Cherry: On my way back now too. I just stepped out for coffee and a few extra supplies for the ritual, just to be safe. *Talk to you later, babes!*

Halo: Are we still on for the gaming session?

Alpha: Priorities, Halo. But, yeah—maybe after the ritual.

• ♥ • ♥ • ♥ • ♥ • ♥ •

I blinked. There was a lot of information to digest in there. It turned out that not only was Cherry definitely a witch, but so were her friends. Not only that, but they wanted to bind me and use me like some kind of pet or servant—or husband. It sounded like not only would I be their servant, but also their sex slave. But the most troubling revelation was that running wouldn't make a difference. The only bright side was that they weren't likely to kill me.

The terrifying reality started to set in. I trudged my way back to the bedroom and slipped that damn cuff back onto the bedpost. I did my best to position the wood so the crack was barely visible. My mind spun as I lay on the bed staring at the ceiling. I knew I couldn't get away, and I didn't doubt that if I left them no other choice, they would kill me. A strong desire to put up a fight burned in my soul, but I instinctively knew that I'd be no match for the three of them.

Their determination was evident, and I had no illusions that they'd ever let me go free. It sounded like Cherry got herself into a real bind with me, and she was convinced that I would gladly accept my new role as her lover. Aside from the prospect of getting to have more sex with Cherry *and* her friends, my future was looking bleak, and my options were limited. If nothing else, I had to hear them out and exploit what little information I had; they needed me alive, and despite whatever they were going to tell me, I did have the ability to refuse. So, with a dour expression, I waited.

A while later, the silence was broken by the sound of the front door opening. Muffled voices slowly found clarity as they grew closer. Two of the voices were unfamiliar. The trio must have made it to the living room because the words started making sense and I caught snippets of their conversation mid-sentence.

"...waffles on the table, or take them to the room with us?" asked a rather chipper voice.

"We'll eat them at the table. But don't make them yet. We have more important things to do first," said a tomboyish but feminine voice. "He's in your room?"

"Yup! He's still cuffed to the bed. Poor fella doesn't stand a chance," said Cherry.

"That's kinky," said the voice I now knew was Halo with a giggle. "Is he a cutie?"

"He's *so* handsome. I like him so much... You're gonna like him, too," said Cherry.

"Awesomesauce! Do you think he'll go along with our plan?" Halo said.

"He doesn't have a choice, remember?" asked who I assumed was Alpha. "Don't give him an inkling otherwise."

"That's right. Once he buys into that assumption, he'll behave like a good little pet," Cherry said.

"Let's go. It's time he learned his place," Alpha grunted.

Cherry's voice spoke up much louder as they entered the hall. She must have assumed I was unable to hear their conversation. I almost laughed when she spoke as if she never left, and had been awaiting their arrival all along. But I was not in a laughing mood.

"Hey, babes! It's great to see you. Come with me, he's in here," Cherry shouted.

The door swung open, and Cherry immediately noticed the cracked bedpost beside me. She smirked, cluing me in that she'd clocked my little escape attempt. But she kept quiet about it, much to my relief. She breezed in with two babes in tow, their beauty matching Cherry's own. She led the pack, followed by a blonde and a redhead. I couldn't help but give them the once-over as they sauntered into the room.

The blonde rocked long pigtails, blue peepers, and a bod that could give Cherry a run for her money. On her head, she wore a plastic looking hair band with pink cat ears. Clad in a black midriff tank top, she flaunted a generous view of her assets, paired with a black miniskirt. Her bare thighs peeked out from her knee-high black socks and sneakers. But what really caught my eye was her snow-white, feathery wings. Like an angel.

The redhead's mane wasn't your standard orange; it was fire-engine red, down to her back, with side-swept bangs grazing past her captivating yellow gaze. She sported a white sports bra showcasing her impressive chest and muscular but tight physique. Her tight black hotpants drew attention before my gaze trailed down legs that seemed to go for days. And like the rest, she had her own quirks. Two triangular furry red ears with black edges were perched atop her head, while a fluffy red tail swayed behind her.

What the fuck.

Cherry stole my attention back with an obvious fake cough. "Ahem! Eyes up here, you're looking at your new, loving mistresses! Doesn't that make you excited? I bet that makes you excited," she said with a wink that mostly made sense. "Say hello to my wonderful friends! This is Halo, and this is Alpha," she said as she pointed from one friend to another.

Halo smiled and waved at me. "Hi there! It's nice to meet you. I hope we don't have to hurt you. I look forward to our many adventures together!"

She was so damn upbeat that, despite the circumstances and her apparent threat, I found myself waving back at her.

Alpha smirked, "I bet you'd like to know why you're here?"

I hesitantly nodded. I already had a pretty good idea of why I was there, but that didn't mean I shouldn't hear her out—or should let them know what I knew.

She smiled at what she must have decided was a display of obedience, rather than the simple acknowledgment that it was. "Good boy. So, here's the deal. You're special. You have a rare magical bloodline. Don't get your hopes up, though; you can't use magic on your own. That's a witch's domain, and witches are women. In fact, without our help, your blood is basically useless."

"Except as a snack," Cherry quipped. "But, lucky for you, we need a pet."

I frowned, narrowing my eyes. "What do you mean 'magical bloodline'? What makes it rare, and why is it useless without the three of you?"

Cherry giggled. "Oh, look at him! He's so tough and collected." I was pretty sure she was gushing sincerely, trying to sell how cool I was to her friends. I wasn't sure if I appreciated it or not.

Halo chimed in helpfully, "We don't know everything about it yet, but your bloodline sure feels strong to us."

"Your bloodline means that your body can use our attunements to become more powerful than a normal familiar. Why it's rare doesn't matter. All that matters is that you have it, and we have you," Alpha said with a grin.

I swallowed nervously. "I'm not sure about this whole bloodline thing. Sounds like I'm in a bit over my head, here, and I doubt I'll be much use to you all. I'm just a street punk trying to work my way through uni—I'm not some cool magical guy who can be your ticket to power. How about you three let me go, and I won't call the police, and we call it square. We'll never have to see one another again. I promise," I said, hoping that they might see some reason.

Halo covered a giggle with her hand. Despite how sweet it sounded, it didn't make me feel any better. "I like him," she said. "He's pretty calm and rational, all things considered. And the longer I'm close to him, I can feel his potential, too."

Cherry's lips bent into a frown, though. "What are you saying? I thought you and I had something special last night, Logan? Now I'm offering you the deal of a lifetime, and you want to 'never see each other again'?" She sounded genuinely hurt. Why the fuck did that make me feel a bit guilty?

Alpha frowned, too. "It doesn't matter if you believe in your potential or not. What matters is that we know the truth and we aren't here to waste anyone's time. And no, you're never getting out of this. The sooner you realize it, the better it is for everyone."

"I... See," I said. I held back my panic while quickly trying to come up with a solution. They only saw a pet when they looked at me so far. There was a power imbalance that wasn't really working for me here—but I could maybe make it work. I could gradually earn their respect and dependence on me—and more importantly, if I played my cards right, maybe I could negotiate a better deal that would make me more than just a pet or a slave. I needed to buy time to think about this—meanwhile, I needed to probe each of the girls for weaknesses or opportunities that I could use to push my own interests.

"So, I know a bit about Cherry already, why don't you two tell me a little about yourselves? Since you want us to work together, then maybe it would be a good idea if we broke the ice?"

Halo perked right up at the suggestion. "Wow! That's a wonderful idea! I enjoy—"

Alpha put a hand up to stop the blonde beauty. "Halo, focus, remember?"

An adorable pout fell on Halo's face, and she nodded.

Alpha wore a scowl with her hands on her hips. Her frustration seemed to be increasing quickly. "Listen, *Logan*, I don't need to get to know you. You're a familiar, a tool to be used to fulfill our goals. Here's what you need to understand. You're going to be bound to us by a magical contract, you're going to do what we tell you to when we tell you to do it, and there's not a damn thing you can do about it. If you don't cooperate, then we'll have to go find a new pet. You don't want that. Trust me."

I gulped. If I hadn't seen the chat on the computer then I'd have really believed that I had no choice. I had to admit that not everything about the situation I found myself in sounded all bad. Like Cherry said in her chat, 'What guy wouldn't want to be bound to three hotties?' But, my freedom was more important than satisfying my libido. So, I took a deep breath, and gathered my courage. "Ladies, I apologize, but I'm afraid I'm going to have to decline your offer."

Yellow eyes widened. "Excuse me?" Alpha growled.

Halo pouted. "You don't want to be bound to us? I thought we could all be friends."

Alpha wore a mask of incredulity. "What part of, 'you don't have a choice' do you not understand?"

To my surprise, Cherry looked hurt. "Wait, what? I thought..." She let her words trail off, not telling anyone what she thought in the end.

I wasn't sure what to say to their mixed response. I was still scared, but for some reason, I felt bad about Cherry and Halo's reply. I shouldn't have; I was the one cuffed to the damn bed, after all. *Maybe they didn't want to do it like this? Maybe it was all Alpha's idea to treat me like an animal? She does seem to be the leader.* Pulling my wandering mind back on track, I said the only thing that came to mind, "I—I'm sorry. I'd rather die than be someone's slave."

Alpha spluttered—it was exactly what she didn't want to hear. "You can't just—I—pff—No! Just, no! I said you don't have a choice."

Halo and Cherry were both staring at me in disappointment, hurt, and disbelief. Cherry looked on the verge of tears, like I'd just betrayed her.

I was speechless at seeing Alpha's outburst. It seemed that she never considered what she'd do if I chose death. It was a risky move, but it was the only move I had.

"If this is how you want to play it, then fine! You can sit in here all alone while you starve and rot." Alpha stormed out and slammed the door behind her, not waiting for the others.

Halo quickly followed after her. She opened the door and threw me a sad wave on her way out. "It was nice to meet you, Logan. Have a good day," she whimpered before she gently closed the door behind her.

Cherry walked over and sat on the bed next to me. Her intoxicating scent caught my nose, and it reminded me of our night together. She didn't say a word as she cast the first spell I'd ever seen on her bedpost. The crack was gone, and the bedpost was whole again. "Logan, I thought we had a good time last night," Cherry said quietly.

A mix of emotions churned through me. If I were to ignore the fact that she kidnapped me, I could honestly say that I had really enjoyed my night with Cherry. I would even have gone as far as to say that I felt some kind of connection with her and felt there was real potential there for something more. "We did. I had a wonderful time with you. It's just..." I sighed and pointed at my arm. "This is crazy. Insane, even. You girls are saying that I'm nothing more than a pet, or a slave. How do you expect me to hear that and be okay with it?"

Cherry leaned down and lightly kissed me. "I don't know. Maybe it's unreasonable, but I still hope you say yes," she whispered. Then she got up and went to the door.

"Cherry—" I tried.

She cut me off and refused to look at me. "Logan..." she trailed off as if she wanted to say more. But, then her tone shifted to something on the verge of tears. "You already broke my bed," she said. "I really hope you don't break my heart, too." Then she closed the door behind her as she walked away.

CHAPTER 4

The Contract

At first, I lay there, absorbing the gravity of my situation. Though the circumstances seemed dire, I held onto the well-informed belief that they wouldn't leave me to die. Their group message made it clear how significant I was to them; losing me would ruin their aspirations for a new pet and limit their ability to...grow in power? I wasn't familiar enough with their hidden world to fully comprehend all the nuances just yet.

With each passing moment, worry gnawed at me and tried to take root in my gut. Hunger clawed at my insides, exacerbated by the unsettling realization that I hadn't used the restroom since they cuffed me to the bed. I was grateful for whatever enchantment they must have used to spare me that embarrassment. Still, I found it difficult to face the grim possibility that I might end up indefinitely held captive.

As time passed, hopelessness gradually grew and blended with an unreasonable fear of abandonment. What if they *don't* come back? What if some arcane manipulation of time left me here for an eternity cuffed to this bed? They were silly thoughts. However, terror has a way of warping logic—as did the sudden realization that magic was real and not exactly on my side at the moment.

I decided to take action, looking to exercise as a source of solace. I attempted a DIY workout. Despite being confined, I exerted as much physical effort as I could. I had a momentary sensation of tranquility and my breathing became more rhythmic. That was nice while it lasted.

My lucidity came back, and I faced the truth again, this time a bit more mentally fresh and much calmer. Running was useless, so there was no point in escaping unless I was prepared to try and kill them—I wasn't. I wasn't the guy to murder three chicks, especially when one was clearly crushing on me and another was actually very sweet by nature.

The only way I was going to get any kind of freedom back was via following my initial gut instinct and attempting a negotiation. After all, it was just a simple question of supply and demand—I was the supply, and whatever it was that I offered them, they appeared to be fairly desperate for it.

And that brought on the question of...well, my life. What did I really have to live for? I was an orphan with no attachments—just a few classmates that were almost friends who may or may not notice if I never showed up to another course ever again. The only person I could think of who would really miss me was my boss at the Spartan warehouse, and that's just because he'd have to replace me. It wasn't like I was unpopular or anything. I just had a way of keeping my head down and avoiding attachments. I was focused on my goal.

But...what was my goal for? To one day get a girlfriend and make her a wife while working a job I hopefully didn't hate. The job offer I'd just gotten was basically to be the sexual plaything and partner in crime to three gorgeous witches, who seemed like they might more or less be analogous to girlfriends when I got right down to it. Did I really need to deliver packages anymore? How badly did I want to keep going to school?

I came to a decision. I would be willing to work with the Hocus Pocus waifus if I were given some respect, consideration, and benefits. Instead of being a submissive pawn, I would be a willing partner in a mutually beneficial relationship. If they could sign off on that, I would sign on. They could call me a pet if they wanted, but at the end of the day, I wanted rights and some form of compensation.

A smirk bent my lips as I realized that I actually had most of the cards. It was just a matter of waiting for their return and persuading them that negotiating was their only course of action to get what they wanted. Still, it was obvious that they wouldn't be arriving anytime soon as the light faded and the shadows grew.

As I lay there hungry, mentally exhausted, and uncertain of what my future held, I gave in to the release of sleep, hoping to find relief from the fearful thoughts invading my mind.

I woke up with a sore wrist and the morning light shining through the window. My stomach growled angrily, and my mouth was as dry as a bone in the desert. It wasn't long before I heard muffled voices heading toward the room. A knock sounded at the door, followed by Alpha chiding someone.

"You don't have to knock. Just go in," Alpha asserted.

"Come on, be a little polite. He might be our pet, but that doesn't mean that we can't be nice," she gently argued as she opened the door. She offered me a bright smile as she walked in, and handed me a glass of water. "Good morning!"

"Good morning, Halo. Thank you," I managed before gulping it down. It was the most delicious water I'd ever tasted. Not that there was anything special about it, but it hit the spot like nothing else ever had.

She accepted the glass when I returned it to her. "You're welcome!" Then she turned and closed the door behind her as she walked out, giving me one last look before she left me alone with Alpha. I couldn't begin to guess what she was thinking, but it didn't seem unkind.

I didn't know Alpha, and I wasn't sure how ruthless she might be. She seemed to share some traits of a wolf, so that was one clue. It was a gamble, but I was willing to bet that she respected strength and confidence. I needed to take control of the conversation if I wanted to make any headway. I needed to show her that I was capable of going toe to toe with her, but also worth her time.

I sat up and favored her with a determined gaze, eyeing her up and down in a way that was less sexual and more appraising. "Well, we had our fun. Let's cut the shit and talk already."

Alpha folded her arms, her tone sharp as she spoke. "And, what exactly do we need to *talk* about?"

I took a deep breath to steady my nerves and pushed forward. "I know that you want me as your familiar, but I'm not going to be your subby puppet. I'm not some caged animal—I'm a human being, and one that clearly has value to you. It benefits you to treat me with care and respect."

"How so?" she asked, rolling her eyes but humoring me.

"Because you clearly need me more than you let on, or we wouldn't still be doing this—and respect is the only way I'll agree to give you what you want."

Her yellow eyes narrowed. "You're in no position to make demands, male. If you don't cooperate, then I'll just leave you here to starve to death."

It wasn't easy in front of this powerful woman, but I kept my composure. "Sure, you absolutely could. But, you won't. Think about it. Without me, your plans fall apart. I don't even know what your plans are, but even I can tell that I'm integral to them."

She waved her hand like she was swatting my comment away like it was an annoying fly. "Don't overestimate your worth. There are plenty more men out there who would happily replace you."

I shook my head. "Maybe, maybe not. But, there are none who can do for you what I can."

She laughed bitterly. "And, what makes you think you're so special?"

I kept my tone firm. "You girls said so."

Her brows furrowed. "What do you mean? Who said so?"

My eyes remained fixed on hers. "I read the group message on the computer. Before Cherry brought you and Halo back here, I mean. I broke the bedpost and escaped."

Her eyes flicked to the intact bedpost and back. She sighed and removed the cuff—a possible concession that I appreciated. "Okay. So you know. I don't see how that changes a goddamn thing." Her tail had gone taut, though, and her ears folded back like a nervous pup.

I rubbed my wrist. "It changes everything. I know what could happen to Cherry's powers if I refuse, for one thing.""

Alpha's eyes narrowed again. "I suppose it also means you know how good you'll have it," she muttered, her eyes trailing to my crotch for a moment before flicking back up to my eyes.

"Even so, I've got some ground to stand on here with negotiations, even beyond Cherry."

"Explain."

I met her gaze and didn't waver. "You can't force me into the contract. If I die then you gain nothing, and you lose your best prospect as a...Greater Familiar? I think that was the term I saw. I grew up mostly alone, you know. Starvation is nothing new to me. I'm broke because I work my ass off at a nothing job to pay for my night classes—and to be honest? I hate it. Being chained to a hot chick's bed post isn't half as bad as the life I was already living. Death isn't even the worst thing that can happen to me at this point. So bring it on. I'm officially calling your bluff. You need me to say yes more than I do."

She studied me for a time, but I held my stare, my face a mask of determination. Finally, she glanced away before putting her hands on her hips. "So, what exactly do you want?"

"I want us to negotiate terms. Wouldn't you rather have a familiar who's happy and eager to work with you, rather than one who resents you and works against you whenever he can?"

Her expression softened slightly. "And, what is it that you propose?"

I spoke honestly. "Only that I get treated with the same respect the rest of you share, and anytime one of you has a large task, or request for me involving any risk or serious labor, I want something in return. Let's say you cast a spell for me or do some other favor that I believe is equal in value to the task. We make it magically binding and in return, you get a guy who is a willing partner and wants to leave his old life behind to be with you."

She grunted. "That's asking a lot, Logan."

Again, my eyes refused to leave hers. "Those are my terms."

She didn't say anything as she eyed me. I held firm and showed as much strength as I could. Eventually, she huffed and left the room. Once she was gone, I let out a deep sigh of relief and let my head fall back against the headboard.

• ♥ • ♥ • ♥ • ♥ • ♥ •

I sat, patiently waiting. I played my cards, and now it was up to them. My stomach growled again. I could deal with the hunger, but it didn't make it any less unpleasant. Fortunately, I didn't have to wait very long. After only a few minutes, a knock came at the door.

"Come in," I said.

Halo walked in with a smile, her wings fluttering happily behind her. She handed me my clothes. "Come with me, please."

I offered her a tentative smile, but my nerves were on high alert. I watched cautiously as I dressed. So far, Halo had been nothing but nice to me, but that didn't mean that I trusted her yet. Even if she did have angelic wings and a gorgeous smile, she was one of the witches who kidnapped me.

I followed Halo to the dining table where Alpha and Cherry already sat. A large plate of pancakes sat in the middle of the table. There were multiple types from plain to chocolate chip and even banana. Around the plate were bowls with various freshly cut fruits, creams, and syrup.

Halo took her chair and I saw one more place set for me. I figured this was a good sign. I was sure that Alpha already discussed my terms with the others, and this felt like an olive branch. I remained cautious and my nerves kept me on high alert, but I tried not to let it show.

We sat in silence for a minute or two, and I prepared a plate for myself. I saw the girls all stealing glances at one another. I ate my first plate rather quickly since I was so hungry, though I tried not to seem desperate. The taste was almost orgasmic. As I forked seconds onto my plate, I finally broke the silence.

"So, Alpha, does this mean that you've accepted my terms?" I asked before taking another bite.

She looked at me, considering her words. "Not quite. Let's call this more of a trial run. It's a chance to see how well we can all get along."

I nodded as the knot of tension in my stomach loosened slightly.

Halo flashed me a pretty smile, and Cherry winked at me. The angelic blonde set down her glass. "What do you think of the pancakes?"

I was mid-chew, so I waited to answer until I swallowed. "They are incredible. Did you make them?"

She nodded happily while chewing. "Mhm!"

"You did a fantastic job," I said, and I meant it. The brief exchange seemed to help ease the mood of everyone at the table.

"So, what do you think is tastier? The pancakes, or me?" Cherry asked me with a wink, her fork pointing from the pancakes to her lips.

I almost spit out my food since that was the last question I expected. Halo and Alpha both laughed.

"Golly! Logan, you don't have to answer that. I don't want Cherry to feel bad," Halo said while covering a giggle.

I couldn't help but smile at their antics. "So, how did you girls get into—uh—witchcraft?"

Alpha shrugged. "It's a long story, but let's just say it was something we were born or otherwise thrust into. What about you? What's your story?"

I hesitated. I wasn't quite sure how much I wanted to reveal to the women who kidnapped me. But, I did set terms and it seemed like they were going to accept at this rate. If we were going to work together I'd have to extend a little trust at some point.

"Well, I grew up without any family, in the system. I got in my share of trouble and tight spots. As I grew older I worked odd jobs here and there just to get by. The last few years I've been trying to get my education so I might be able to make something out of my life," I said.

Alpha nodded with a look of respect in her eyes. She seemed to be warming up to me, and I figured that my gamble had paid off. "Well, rest assured, you're definitely going to make something of yourself if you end up with us."

Halo perked up. "How lucky that your life led you to us!"

Halo was so damn sweet and cheery that it was hard not to nod along with everything she said. I took a sip of milk. "So, how did you three meet?" God, this conversation was awkward.

Cherry put her fork down and pushed her plate away from her. "I met Alpha and Halo at Hot Topic."

"Gosh, I met Alpha at a bar for witches. We had a swell time and have been together ever since," Halo said as she offered both of her friends a beaming smile.

Cherry started playfully arguing with Halo over the former taste debate. Their argument soon shifted to who was going to get to take me to some sex toy boutique store called "Witch and Moan" first. Alpha watched the two with amusement. The longer I sat with my captors, the more comfortable everyone seemed to be. For the first time since I woke up in cuffs, I found myself thinking. *Maybe this Familiar thing won't be so bad after all.*

Eventually, Cherry and Halo excused themselves to their rooms. I finished up the last of my food when Alpha got my attention.

"Alright, Logan," Alpha said.

"Hmm?"

"We agree."

I smiled, feeling more comfortable with all this after our meal, but some of my nerves returned. "Oh. Okay. Good. I'm really happy that we could come to an understanding," I said with a genuine smile.

Alpha allowed a half smile and held out her hand. "Then we have a deal."

I took her hand in mine and instantly noted how soft her skin felt—and how strong her grip was. "Yes, we do."

She let go and stood. "Wait here. I'm going to check on the others. We'll come and get you when we're ready."

· ♥ · ♥ · ♥ · ♥ · ♥ ·

After about fifteen minutes or so all three girls walked in. Alpha wore a determined expression. Cherry threw me a wink to go along with her grin, and Halo waved cutely at me with her beautiful beaming smile.

"Alright, are you ready to begin?" Alpha asked me.

I nodded.

"Yay! I'm so excited!" Halo said while clapping. "Now we're going to get a big powerup!"

"This is going to be so much fun! Once we get into the room, you'll need to strip down to your boxers again," Cherry chimed in.

I smiled nervously. "Okay. So, how does this work?"

"Get over here. Your part is easy," Alpha said.

The trio led me to the living room, and my stomach twisted with nervous energy. Once we reached it, my eyes went wide. The thick curtains blocked out the light of day, leaving the room with only flickering candlelight. A large pentagram in the center of the room was illuminated by the soft glow.

Each girl stood silent, forming a triangle at the points of the star. They were all focused and serious as they pointed at the center while staring at me. I gulped as I fought to overcome a surge of apprehension.

I knew they had a contract ritual, but I thought it was going to be a piece of paper, and maybe I'd poke my finger and sign in blood or something. This was fucking crazy. But I knew there was no going back. I made the best deal I could, and that was that.

I squared my shoulders, stepped into the middle of the pentagram, and looked down. My demands were written into the pentagram's designs, along with other symbols. I found the girls' familiar contract details as well. The terms were simple—I got a vote in most matters, but they could compel me to serve them. In return, though, they would owe me an equal favor. There was some other stuff, guaranteeing I wouldn't betray them and vice versa. The language slightly favored the girls, but the deal I was getting was certainly a hundred times better than the initial offer.

Movement caught my attention, and I looked up.

Cherry was holding a knife. As I turned my head I saw all three girls had similar blades.

Internally, I panicked, wondering if I was wrong and was about to become a sacrifice after all. But before I could do anything, the girls all made cuts on their own palms. They all spoke in unison as they said, "Ij telecal te proom fan ouns affeit!"

My breathing quickened as they each took a step closer to me. I broke into a nervous sweat. One by one they stepped up to face me. Alpha approached first, and the reflective candlelight in her eyes mirrored the fire that was already there.

She took my hand and turned it palm up. I didn't react as she ran the knife across it, keeping my cool despite the beating of my heart. She held her bleeding fist over the contract writing on the ground and let her blood drip onto the words. She nodded for me to do the same, so I did. I squeezed my fist and let the blood drip where it was meant to go.

Alpha put her bloody palm against mine, almost like a disgusting high-five. Then she said, "Bloed bidt uns unot te inde fan liven. Ij meree taar te con. Ij wull eernor et rof soffer ouns proom." Finally, to my surprise, she kissed me. It wasn't much, just a quick, chaste kiss. But, her lips were soft and gentle, and I found myself wanting more.

After the kiss, I felt a warmth inside me. It was like an electrical ball of heat that crackled with power. Halo stepped up to me next and we repeated the process. She offered me a kiss that was a little more intimate than Alpha's but still wasn't laced with all that much lust or passion. She tasted like pancake syrup.

The strange ball of power grew in its intensity. I didn't know what to make of it. Then it was Cherry's turn. Again we repeated the same ritual, and she repeated the strange language. I had no idea what they meant.

Cherry leaned in and kissed me as well. Her kiss, however, was full of passion. It reminded me of the night before, when we arrived at the front door of this very apartment. However, she didn't let it last long, and her face remained serious. After a few more moments, she also returned to her place at the edge of the pentagram.

The ritual markings in the floor began to glow a bright yellow, then shifted to blue, and then red. The girls raised their hands to the sky and tilted their heads back. They all said, "Ij arjin ferond!" And, just like that, the glow faded. The ball of power that had felt like it would explode inside of me spread out throughout my entire body before settling into place. It felt almost like it was gone, but I somehow knew it wasn't.

I was shocked that it didn't hurt at all. In fact, I felt...incredible. I looked down and saw my hand had already healed. The symbols and words of our contract were gone, and the pentagram looked like nothing more than a sort of demonic part of the decor. Then the entire mystical mood was broken by a shout.

"Yay! Great job everyone! We did it!" Halo squealed with excitement. Then she bounced up and down, clapping giddily, and I struggled not to stare too long at the jiggling that ensued.

VIRGIL KNIGHTLEY, EDGAR RIGGS

Logan, buddy, what have you gotten yourself into?

CHAPTER 5

A Whole New Underworld

I stood there, blinking, feeling as if a weight had been lifted off my shoulders. Cherry's infectious smile softened the mood in the room, and even Alpha seemed more laid back than before.

Speaking of the redhead, Alpha waved her hand, extinguishing the candles as the overhead lights flickered back to life. Following in her footsteps, Cherry cast her spell, orchestrating the return of the candles to their designated spots on the shelves. Before long, things were back to normal. Well, as normal as this place was before, anyway.

I watched all this transpire with an uncanny sense of detachment. I had just been turned into the Greater Familiar of a coven of three beautiful witches. My old life was... irrelevant. From here on, I could simply never show up to work or class again, abandoning my old apartment, my schooling, and my career with a few well-timed text messages, and probably no one from my past would ever care or bother to check up on me. In a way, it was freeing. In another way, it was kind of depressing.

Once the binding ritual concluded, an inexplicable shift occurred within me. It took me a minute to notice it, but it settled in gradually, without a doubt. My anxiety around the girls dissipated, replaced by a sense of connection, and I felt assured that they were experiencing the same feeling toward me, too. It made them feel familiar to me, as though we had always known each other somehow. I assumed it came from the completion of the ritual. What else could it be?

Halo brought me my clothes, and I began to dress. She watched with big, blue eyes as I donned my outfit before turning over to face her leader. The clothes seemed cleaner somehow than I'd left it.

"Wow, that was... intense," I remarked, breaking some of the awkward silence.

Alpha, who was now receiving a healing spell from Halo, reddened slightly as she met my gaze, her eyes flitting down to my crotch just as I tucked my bulge into my shorts. "It was necessary for the bond. You agreed to this."

Cherry grinned mischievously. "That's nothing, Logan. You should see some of our other rituals. Sometimes we get naked in the woods for them. It's a hoot." She punctuated her statement with a wink.

Considering Cherry's love for bad puns, I couldn't help but wonder if their other rituals involved owls. Alpha approached me as Halo blushed and retreated into the kitchen.

"I appreciate that you agreed to my terms," I said.

Alpha shrugged off my compliment, but her eyes wandered over my figure just before I put my shirt on. Suddenly, I felt very pleased at the fact I made regular use of the gym on campus. "Yeah, no worries. Tonight, we'll discover your true potential."

I nodded. "Hey, I've been meaning to ask. Are your names nicknames or...what's the deal with them? They're all kind of quirky."

Halo came back from the kitchen with a plate of cookies, chiming in. "Yup! Witches don't reveal their true names with each other, at least outside their covens. Names have power in our trade. Want some cookies?"

I arched my eyebrow. "Not right now—What's the risk? Not with the cookies, but names, I mean."

Alpha brushed a lock of hair from her eyes. "It's a security measure. Invoking someone's real name in a spell is much more powerful than using a pseudonym. It makes us more or less immune to each other's curses. All witches at our level have been scrubbed from national databases, too, so it's next to impossible to find out someone's real name against their will. Soon you will be scrubbed from those databases too."

"I see. That makes sense. In any case, I like the names you've chosen. They suit you," I said, nodding at Alpha.

"Good for you," Alpha replied dismissively, though I thought she might have seemed a bit more flustered by me than she let on.

"Will I need a nickname?" I wondered.

Alpha shook her head. "No. You're a familiar. First of all, you're under the protection of our magic, so spells are much less likely to harm you, including spells to divine your true name. And as long as we don't call you by your middle and last name in front of other witches, you'll be fine."

I internally fist pumped and thanked God that few people would ever have to know my middle name was Reginald.

As I finished dressing, I asked, "So, what's next?"

Cherry tapped her chin thoughtfully. "You should make peace with dropping out of school and quitting your job. You're ours now, big boy, so you won't need those silly things."

Kneeling to tie my shoes, I pondered aloud, "Am I to assume that includes abandoning my apartment?"

"Ha! Oh, yeah! Speaking of which, you should end your lease right away. Don't worry about money or rent," Cherry advised.

"But where will I live if I end my lease?" I inquired. Of course I already sensed the answer, but I didn't want to be caught being presumptuous.

Cherry licked her lips, placing a hand on my arm and caressing my bicep with her fingers. "If you're a good boy, maybe I'll let you sleep at the foot of my bed like my own little puppy."

"What? You're not afraid that I'll develop a foot fetish?" I teased.

"Hey! Okay, look. I just have very small feet and I'm self-conscious about them," Cherry said with a pout. "If it's you... I guess I don't mind you worshiping my little piggies every now and then."

I chuckled. "I saw your feet in the shower. They are lovely. You have nothing to be self-conscious about."

Alpha rolled her eyes and groaned, but her tail swayed happily. "Great, he's got a foot fetish."

"What?! I don't have a foot fetish!" I protested good-naturedly, holding up both hands to defend myself, getting laughs out of the three of them.

Laughing, Cherry quipped, "That's it. I'm throwing away all my toe socks." I almost scoffed, but she shut me up with an unexpected kiss on my cheek before joining Halo on the sofa.

Halo's wings fluttered happily as Cherry sat beside her, both of them eating from her plate of cookies. "Logan, don't worry. We don't judge.

You can like our feet all you want. It doesn't bother me. We're beyond stuff like that now!"

"It's true," Cherry giggled. "Soon you'll be extremely familiar with every part of our bodies. Our feet are the last things for us to be self-conscious over."

I shook my head in disbelief. Surrounded by gorgeous witches I was destined to have frequent sex with, and I was being teased about a non-existent foot fetish. I sighed with a placid smile. "Okay, so, quit my job, end my lease, and drop out of school," I concluded. It sounded like a whiplash of a Honey Do list, but in the end, what did I really have to lose? "You said don't worry about money, but why?" I asked.

Alpha shrugged and joined the other three, leaving me standing before them as they munched on Halo's celebratory cookies. "We robbed a bank in Canada last year. We'll be set for a while. And if we run out, we'll just do it again."

My jaw dropped. "Okay... So, it looks like I have some tasks ahead of me," I said, attempting to ignore the fact that my new roommates were probably the hottest bank robbers the world had ever known. "Will I have a room here?"

"It's right across the hall from mine, big boy," Cherry said with a wink.

"Feel free to spend the day as you wish. Settle your affairs as needed. But, you should consider getting some rest early. We'll be heading out late tonight," Alpha advised me, tossing me a smirk before dismissing me with a wave of her hand.

♥ ♥ ♥ ♥ ♥

As I stepped out of the house, the warmth of the sun greeted me, yet anxiety coiled in my gut. My cell phone lay lifeless in my pocket, prompting me to walk to my apartment to recharge it—or to just get the charger, anyway. Knowing I'd be home, it seemed like a good time to pack that and everything else I had. Conveniently, I didn't have all that much. I made a mental note to inquire about my phone bill from the girls later, but I figured they'd handle it.

Honestly? With no bills to pay, I kind of felt like a trophy husband for a harem of supernatural hotties. I didn't hate it. It could be worse. And with the contract I'd negotiated, I knew that I was going to be enjoying my new life more often than not. It was a hell of a lot better than delivering packages.

Inside my apartment, a surreal aura of normalcy enveloped me, almost erasing the tumult of recent days. If not for my fresh connection with the girls, I might have questioned my sanity. Plugging in my phone, I began stuffing clothes and my laptop into duffel bags and even some plastic bags from the grocery store.

My phone's battery was over half full when I checked, which was plenty to start severing ties with my mundane life. My first call, quitting my job, lacked all emotion on both sides. They kindly reminded me of the two-week notice protocol, lest I risk placement on their 'do not hire' list. I apologized and cited an emergency, and to their credit, they didn't press any further and wished me the best.

Still, a creeping dread was forming in my gut. This was a big change. I fought off the nerves and continued. I dialed the school next, informing them of my withdrawal. They promised to refund my recent tuition payment, which was a nice silver lining.

With professional and educational matters addressed, one call remained. But, with each dial, my anxiety mounted. The site of my rundown apartment stirred up old memories—nights spent with friends and hook-ups, days spent poring over textbooks… There were some memories worth recalling, even in my old life. Nevertheless, I terminated my lease, and they gave me thirty days to vacate. That version of Logan Morrison was gone now. Things had changed.

Part of me was still terrified of making a huge mistake because I had worked so hard to get this life—to pay for my own college, to get a job and be on track for a career, even if it was boring... It wasn't much, but it was everything I worked for.

Before panic consumed me, I took deep breaths, unexpectedly reflecting on my night with Cherry. She was my kidnapper—or, former kidnapper. But, since the binding ritual, that didn't seem to matter anymore. It wasn't the best way to kick off a new relationship, but for some reason I trusted her now—trusted all of them. I focused on our connection in my mind. I replayed the image of her winking at me in my thoughts, making me smile. Thoughts of her dissipated my fears. With my worry lifting, I focused on my packing, feeling my accelerated heart rate subside.

As I opened my closet, I instinctively reached for the light switch, only to be met with utter darkness. With a shrug, I contemplated fetching my flashlight before realizing it wasn't necessary. Despite the lack of illumination, I had no trouble navigating the dim space. This unusual vividness with which I could see in the dark wasn't something I remembered encountering before. A boon of the bond, perhaps? Alpha did mention it benefiting me.

After I finished packing, I couldn't ignore how tight my shirt felt, too. Removing it, I caught sight of myself in the mirror. "Holy shit! I'm jacked!" I exclaimed, momentarily struck by my enhanced physique. I was already in solid shape before any of this happened. But now? I looked like an action hero! Though my muscles weren't massive, the newfound definition in my build was undeniable.

Glancing down, I pulled my pants and boxer open and gazed into my waistband. I half-expected to see some kind of change there, too. When I found nothing was different, I decided that was probably for the best. Cherry already struggled to take me on as I was the last time we boned. So, with a newfound good mood, I grabbed my bags and bedding, suddenly eager to return to my new home.

I was almost at my destination when I encountered a pizza girl holding a large pizza box. She was pretty, the kind of chick most guys would feel lucky to land, and definitely the type I normally went for. But after my night with Cherry, I found myself uninterested in this girl. Frankly, she wasn't in my witches' league at all.

"Hey there!" she called out cheerfully as she eyed me up and down.

"Oh, hi. What's up?"

"Well, I got this pizza, and they already paid for it," she thumbed at the door behind her, "but no one's home. I can't just leave it here, so I thought, maybe a big strong guy like you might have a use for it?"

Feeling my hunger return, I was more than happy to accept free pizza. "I mean, I'll take it if you're sure."

"Awesome! Let me just," she said, producing a marker and writing her phone number and name—Jessica—on the lid. "There. Perfect. Now, here you go! Hope it fills you up," she said, handing it to me. "And if you're looking to fill up someone yourself, just call my number."

Feeling flattered and confused, I thanked her and went on my way. Reaching the door my hands were full, so I knocked on the door with my foot. I couldn't help but feel—lucky. It wasn't just about the free pizza or newfound strength; there was a sense of inexplicable blessing. For a second, I entertained thoughts of ideas about buying a lottery ticket, though I thought better of it a moment later.

The door swung open, revealing Halo's radiant smile and fluttering wings. "Logan! You're back, and you brought pizza!" I returned her smile and followed her inside. While she took the pizza, I stored my bags in my room before joining the girls at the table. "Best familiar ever!" They were on the verge of opening the box when Cherry caught sight of the lid.

"So, who's Jessica?" she inquired, one brow raised.

I sheepishly rubbed the back of my neck. "That was the pizza girl who gave it to me."

"What? Did you ask for her number because she was wearing flip-flops?" Cherry teased, her grin devious.

I shook my head, suppressing a chuckle, and decided to ignore her comment as I lifted the lid.

Alpha wasted no time reacting to the pizza before her ears flattened. "Aww! Who ruins pizza by putting pineapple on it?!"

While it wasn't my usual choice, I didn't mind it. "Have you ever tried it before?"

"Why would I need to try it? It's pineapple, and that's pizza. It doesn't belong," the redhead retorted with a huff.

"Gosh, Alpha! You should keep an open mind. You never know how much you might like something, even if it's not the way you expected it to be," Halo chimed in with a giggle, her wings folding behind her as she, too, eyed the pizza before eying me. "Thank you for bringing it in! We're pretty stuffed on my cookies, but I think we can handle this!"

Alpha glanced at me skeptically before grabbing a slice and taking a bite. Her eyes lit up in surprise and her tail started swaying furiously behind her. I almost laughed, but she quickly regained her composure. "It's okay, I guess," she remarked, already reaching for another slice.

"I'm glad everyone's here because I wanted to ask you all about something. So, I'm stronger than I was this morning. Like, a lot stronger. I'm also really fast, I can see great in the dark, and I feel really...lucky, I guess, for lack of a better word. Is that normal?" I queried, observing their reactions.

Yellow eyes were staring at my chest and arms. "You *are* looking," Alpha cleared her throat, "stronger. Your shirt is a lot tighter than it was when you left."

She was right. My shirt and pants had both gotten tighter. Instead of my casual fit, it felt like I was a jock who intentionally wore small clothing to show off. "Yeah. I didn't notice just how tight it was until I left my place."

"It's normal, but it shouldn't have happened this fast. You're adopting some of our lesser gifts. The night vision from me, the strength and speed from Alpha, and the fortune blessing from Halo," Cherry said with wide eyes. "So quick! Badass!" She made a fist and shook it.

"You must be way more powerful of a Greater Familiar than we thought you'd be," Halo muttered, her eyes shining as she, too, took note of my elevated physique.

A feral smile grew on Alpha's face. "Get some rest if you need it, because tonight is going to be fun."

· ♥ · ♥ · ♥ · ♥ · ♥ ·

After taking Alpha's suggested nap, I woke to her shaking me awake. I yawned, only having snagged a few hours of sleep. Swiftly dressing, I joined the girls and we hopped in their car. We set out for an abandoned park on the outskirts of town. Upon arriving we spread out, scouring the area to ensure it was totally deserted. Surprisingly, the girls swiftly confirmed our solitude with a few practiced spells.

"So, how does this all work?" I inquired eagerly, rubbing my hands together.

"Before the binding ritual, we didn't know your full extent of abilities. But now that we're connected, they're more easily discerned," Alpha explained.

I nodded, nerves and anticipation bubbling within me. It was akin to the excitement I felt while ascending a roller coaster's peak before the exhilarating descent. This felt like a big moment somehow.

Alpha's grin reflected my own. "You possess the ability to shift into a form aligned with our affinities. It's something all Greater Familiars can do, but your changes will be more extensive than theirs, based on the lore for your type. A simple spell will trigger it. Plus, being near you enhances our magic. You've likely noticed your heightened senses when near us as well. Lastly, you hold the power of a portable dimension for storage."

"Like a bag of holding?!" I exclaimed, taken aback.

"Of all those impressive abilities, dimensional storage excites you the most? You truly are a nerd," Cherry teased, a playful smirk adorning her kissable red lips.

I shrugged. "What can I say? It's always been a fantasy of mine. How do I use it?"

Halo jumped in—literally. It pulled my attention to her bouncing bosom. I quickly averted my gaze, though her faint blush said I was caught. "Well, it's quite simple," she explained, summoning her cell phone. "Focus on your storage space, then visualize what you desire and where you want it when retrieving it. To stow an item, touch it and concentrate on putting it inside."

Suppressing inappropriate thoughts, I mimicked her instructions with my phone. It vanished before my eyes, leaving me dumbfounded. I frantically searched my pockets, then pulled up my shirt to see if I'd randomly find it bulging beneath my skin before a cough redirected my focus. Halo and Cherry were fixated on my abs, with red creeping up their necks.

Alpha couldn't help but palm her face and shake her head, suppressing laughter. I chuckled nervously, meeting Cherry's wink with a sheepish grin. Then, following Halo's instructions, I extended my hand and attempted to conjure my phone. Just like magic—since it *was* magic, probably—it materialized in my grip exactly where I had envisioned it. "That's so freaking cool!" In my excitement, I quickly pulled it in and out of my storage a few times before ultimately leaving it inside.

"If you think that's cool, wait until you see this..." Cherry's voice cooed at me. All three girls took a few steps back as Cherry raised her hand, pointing at me. A soft glow surrounded her finger as she uttered, "Borden eh nubel!"

Okay, first, being told you're going to shift into a new form, and actually shifting into said form, are vastly different experiences. I was wholly unprepared for what transpired next. It wasn't painful, but I felt every part of the transformation occurring within me in extreme detail.

My clothes tore away, falling to the ground. A tail sprouted from the base of my spine, and my toes elongated into formidable claws. Fur erupted across my body as I continued to grow larger. My forearms stretched, fingers extending, leathery wings unfolding that connected my wrists to the base of my rib cage. My ears elongated and covered with hair. Then, my lower jaw split, teeth protruding into menacing fangs. Overwhelmed, I toppled forward, emitting a scream that echoed through the park, not at all similar to my usual voice—a horrifying shriek.

Though the new body felt oddly natural, an avalanche of sensory input assaulted my mind as sound waves reverberated around me. I discerned the presence of hundreds of bugs, and the flights of twenty birds and bats taking off from a nearby tree, with another fifteen already soaring above. Even the subtle movement of the old swing set, moved by a passing gust of wind, didn't escape my attention. I struggled to process the deluge of information, falling to the ground in a futile attempt to clear my head.

"Logan! Logan, you're okay! Calm down!" A familiar voice cut through the chaos, sounding different to my altered ears. I forced my eyes open to confirm—it was Cherry. She cupped my face in her hands, and smiled at me. "Focus on me, baby."

I complied, fixing my attention on her. Since the binding happened, I had always felt a subtle compulsion to do as the girls' said, though it could be resisted, I was sure. However, in this monstrous form, Cherry's command to focus on her felt a bit more like an imperative I couldn't refuse, even if I wanted to. It unsettled me, and I hoped she would never compel me to do anything I truly found horrifying. But then, seeing her gazing affectionately into my eyes as she held my bestial face in her hands, there was nothing between us but trust.

I tried to speak, but it emerged as a deep, growling groan. Yet she still seemed to comprehend somehow. "No, silly. We didn't shrink, you grew bigger," Cherry explained before kissing me on the snout.

Growl-chirp? I attempted to articulate.

"That was your echolocation. You'll get used to it. You just weren't expecting it. Try a smaller scream this time," she instructed me.

I raised my head and emitted a small, short shriek. Information still flooded back from all around me, but it was significantly reduced and much easier to manage. She was right. All it took was focus and preparedness.

Roar-chirp?

She laughed. "No, you won't stay like this. You'll transform back after I end the spell. But, let's see what you can do first," Cherry stated.

The next thing I knew, a bright flash hit my eyes, and I blinked. "Gosh! Sorry! I had to get a picture of this so you can see how cool and scary you look later," Halo apologized.

I emitted a horrifying sound that apparently passed for laughter.

"I don't know if that was a good response or a bad one," Halo said, frowning.

"It was a good one. He laughed," said Cherry, patting me on the head. "He's sooo cute!"

"We have different definitions of cute, apparently," Alpha said.

"Yeah! He's such a good boy!" Cherry remarked before peppering my monstrous face with kisses. "Mua mua mua!" I didn't want to admit how good it felt. It brought me an unexpected amount of happiness to be doted upon by her in this form, and I doubted I'd feel the same about the action in my normal body—not that I'd dislike it. But, carpe diem, right? So, I allowed myself to have fun with her praise and affection.

"Now, go see what you can do to that dumpster," Cherry commanded.

I got off my belly and rose on all fours, towering over the girls by a few feet. I walked towards the dumpster, the movements feeling natural to me now. Each step resonated like a giant's footstep, leaving imprints where my feet and hands had once been.

I discovered that grabbing things with my bat-like hands was more awkward than I was accustomed to. However, using a finger and thumb, I grasped each side of the dumpster and pulled. The sound of steel tearing filled the park as I exerted more of my strength. Once I had ripped it entirely in half, I discarded both parts, sending them soaring through the park and crashing into trees.

I turned and walked back to them, analyzing their responses. Six eyes full of stars stared at me, and they all jumped up and down, embracing one another. "He's going to kick so much ass for us!" exclaimed Alpha. "He's way stronger than I thought!"

"He's *so* strong! It's amazing! I can't wait to see him using my bonded form for him," expressed Halo. "Gosh, Logan! You sure know how to make a girl's night!"

"I can't wait to take him on a mission! He's such a good boy. My big boy!" Cherry chimed in. "I'm gonna fuck the fucking shit out of that good boy soon, too," she muttered under her breath.

After a moment, they calmed down. I chirp-barked back at them. Best I could tell, I was a monstrous vampire bat thingy, inspired by the vampiric quirk of Cherry's nature. That led me to wonder what exactly I'd be when I tried out my magical forms inspired by Alpha and Halo's bonds with me.

"Oh! Sure. You can turn back now," Cherry said. She pointed at me and said, "Borden eh humensel."

Changing back into my own body was like putting on an old pair of shoes—it felt comfy and right. My head tilted to the sky, and I stood still and relaxed, taking it all in. My body felt better than it ever had before. After a few moments of basking in the cool night air, I heard Alpha let out a breathy, "Holy shit."

I lowered my head and opened my eyes with a big grin. Until I saw three bright red faces looking at my crotch. Halo was biting her lip hard. Cherry was licking her chops, and Alpha?

She was totally slack-jawed. Only then did I look down and realize that I was completely naked. "What the hell?!" I shouted as I rushed to cover myself.

Alpha looked up quickly before looking away, her face as red as her hair. Halo was covering a giggle, and Cherry was openly leering with a grin.

"So, we forgot to tell him to put his clothes into his dimensional storage right as his shift begins, didn't we?" Alpha asked.

"Yeah, we definitely forgot," sighed Halo. "I'm not too sorry about it, though."

"Speak for yourselves. I didn't forget. I just didn't tell him," said Cherry.

Alpha conjured an illusionary outfit for me. It left me feeling just as exposed as before, as I knew they could see right through it, but at least no one else could tell if we ran into other people. Or, at least I was *pretty sure* no one else could tell. My witches definitely could, though. Halo especially was glancing at me a lot with a soft glow to her eyes and a blush on her cheeks.

Not that Cherry and Alpha weren't staring, but Halo more or less couldn't peel her eyes off my dick.

My self-consciousness was banished when a wicked smile spread across Alpha's face while we were walking back to our car. "Hey, Cherry. You said you can't wait to take our boy here on a mission right?"

Cherry grinned. "Yeah, what do you have in mind, babe?"

Alpha smirked and crossed her arms. "Trial by fire."

CHAPTER 6

Trial By Fire

I lifted a finger in curiosity. "When you say fire...?"

Alpha chuckled. "Not *literal* fire."

I let out a sigh of relief. "Thank goodness."

"What I mean is a heist to steal a magical amulet protected by two deadly Sentinel Familiars," she said, her excitement a tad too animated for my liking.

Halo gasped. "The Lunar Amulet!?"

My eyes widened—a heist sounded like a big deal. Maybe more than I was up to on my first night as a familiar. "On second thought, are you sure we couldn't just go with literal fire?" I asked nervously. It's not like I was afraid of breaking into places and stealing stuff. I'd done plenty of that in my youth. But the notion of facing off against not one, but two giant, monstrous beasts? Not exactly my idea of a good time.

Cherry rushed to me, giggling excitedly, her fingers roving my chest. "Oh, yes! I want it! Logan, baby! My good boy, my bestest boy in the whole world, you'll help me with this mission, won't you? Won't you, baby?!" Cherry asked, her nails trailing my chest down to my belt, where she gave my illusionary waistband a playful and suggestive tug.

I would've preferred to wait a bit longer and practice my new abilities, but I knew that wasn't an option. It wasn't just that I felt the pull to help a gorgeous woman I was attracted to, but at least some degree of magical compulsion had its hold on me too—what they wanted, I wanted, at least to some extent. The contract sealed the deal, nudging my decision in one direction over the other.

Her flirty touch calmed my nerves, and I took a deep breath. "Alright. I guess I'm in," I said with a reluctant smile.

Alpha smirked. "For a second I thought he was going to disappoint me. I dare say this new pet just might be working out after all."

"Pet?" I asked, arching a brow at Alpha while Cherry mashed her face into my chest and nuzzled me happily. "I thought I was your equal?"

"It's a term of endearment. And you aren't our equal, per se—we still control you, but the deal is much more in your favor than it should have been. So don't complain."

"You're our puppy, but that doesn't mean I won't be your horny bitch," Cherry cooed as though she thought her words were sweet and romantic. I almost flinched at them, personally.

"Noted," I said.

The Vampire Witch grinned, then hopped on her tiptoes and planted one on me. Though it seemed like a thank-you smooch for agreeing to her deal at first, I quickly realized it was the magical seal that finalized our agreement. When our lips touched, a cozy glow enveloped us. It split in two, gradually condensing until it settled on the back of our right hands. The warmth got stronger, nearly crossing into painful territory before It disappeared, leaving behind a tattoo-like mark on each of our right hands. As the mark took shape, I sensed it locking into our connection.

Cherry let go of me and stepped back, bouncing with excitement. "Yay! This is gonna be a blast!"

"How do we plan on getting away with it? The other covens are always watching," Halo said as a slight frown creased her otherwise flawless face. It sounded like a fair question to me.

Alpha waved her hand, conjuring a miniature version of the museum without its roof. My jaw dropped as I took in the incredible display. "Whoa. Can you do that for any place?" I asked.

She blushed and didn't look away from her illusion. "No, not without prep. I've been putting this together for a while, actually. But, I'm not sure of the best way to pull it off."

She waved her hand, and several places lit up, along with a blue transparent dome that covered a smaller artifact exhibit. "Every exterior door has an enchantment on the lock. If we try to use magic to open them, it'll set off a silent alarm, and the covens will come running. There's also mundane security, but that's easy to bypass. However," she pinched two fingers and then spread them out as if she were working with a tablet to enhance the view. The illusion zoomed in on the amulet's exhibition. "Here are the other big obstacles. The dome, the hellhound, and the arctic fox—two Sentinel Familiars owned by the other covens."

"I don't know about this. Are you sure he's ready for it?" Halo asked.

Cherry's expression turned serious as she stared at her, even as she continued to hug me like a needy girlfriend. "*We* can handle it," she said with conviction. "He'll learn best on the job—we all will."

I wasn't nearly as confident as Cherry was, but I had just ripped a dumpster in half, so maybe I should have been. "Maybe tell us about these familiars and the dome?" I suggested.

Alpha nodded. "The dome blocks magic and physical objects alike. If you attempt to break it in any way, it will send signals out just like the locks will, and the two covens will rush to the museum. They have an ancient truce that neither of them will try to take the amulet because it would upset the fragile balance between them. The hellhound is a familiar of the Salem Coven, and the arctic fox is a familiar of the New Moon Coven. They are equal in power, meant to hold each other in check as much as defend against other thieves. The primary difference, other than looks, is that the hellhound can breathe fire and the fox can breathe ice. They don't get along, but they have orders to work together to protect the amulet."

My brows rose at a sudden realization. "Cherry said she could understand me when I was transformed. What about these Sentinel Familiars? Will they be able to expose us or will we need to kill them or wipe their minds or something?"

Shaking her head, Alpha said, "No. You won't need to kill or mind wipe them. Sentinel Familiars are smart, sure, but not as smart as Greater Familiars. Their communication is very basic."

I took in all the information and examined the illusion further. After a few moments, I had a solid plan—assuming it was possible. I pointed to the back door near the loading docks. "This might not be the closest ingress, but it's our best point of entry. I can pick the lock without using any magic, so the enchantments are no problem. Cherry and I will enter there. She'll use her spells to disable the surveillance or hide us from it. Alpha, can I assume that once the dome is down it won't be able to send magical signals anymore?"

Alpha was looking at me curiously, but she nodded. "That's right. If its power drains or it's broken, it'll reset itself after about a minute. If no one touches it after that, it won't send them again. But, while it's down, it's down."

"Good. There are probably still at least one or two regular guards in the museum. Either they can't see the familiars, or they are working for the covens. Either way, we don't want them to see what's happening. Halo, Alpha, can the two of you create a second dome on the inside? One that will prevent the signals, sound, or sight from getting out?" I asked.

"Hmm... Well, I can block the signals, but only for a few minutes. So once you start taking the dome down, you need to finish before the timer runs out. From that far away, it'll take a lot of energy," Halo explained, tapping her cheek in thought.

"And I can modify the dome to prevent the sound and visuals from getting out. It's going to take us a lot of concentration, so that's all we can do to help," Alpha said. Her expression shifted from focus to something closer to respect. I felt pretty glad to detect that change on her face. "Since you're bonded with us, we can probably watch your progress with our crystal ball. So, you can give us the signal when you're ready for it."

I grinned. "That's perfect. Okay, Cherry and I will head back to the house and change into some dark clothes. It'll help hide us just in case. While we do that, Alpha, you and Halo find us a van or something so we can get out of there as soon as possible once we get out. Also, if you can come up with a fake amulet to replace the original, it'll take them longer to realize it's missing and make it harder to track us down. Meet us in the alley a block away from the museum," I checked the time on my phone, suddenly grateful that it was in my dimensional storage. "In about an hour and a half."

With a start, I realized that I had just given them all orders. Cherry was grinning at me, though, and Halo covered a giggle. Alpha looked at me with one questioning brow raised and a smirk. "If that's alright with you, Alpha?" I coughed.

"It's a good plan, so I'll allow it—*this* time," she said with narrowed eyes. I thought I could sense a hint of playfulness in her tone.

I rubbed the back of my neck. "Thanks. We'll see you girls soon."

We split up to go our separate ways. Cherry bumped me with her shoulder to get my attention. "Huh?" I asked.

"I mean, I already knew you had some big balls," she winked and let the sentence hang.

I shrugged. "I don't know. It just felt right. I didn't mean to step on anyone's toes."

"Yeah, don't step on my toes. My little piggies are too cute and itty bitty, remember?" Cherry said with a silly grin.

· ♥ · ♥ · ♥ · ♥ · ♥ ·

Cherry and I had a blast, laughing and joking as I drove the car back home. The moment I entered my room, the illusionary clothes disappeared. Whether it was intentional or just luck,

I couldn't tell. Hastily, I threw on some black jeans and a long-sleeved shirt, trusting Cherry to keep my identity under wraps. I stashed my old lockpicking set and some spare clothes in my dimensional storage before heading to the living room to wait for Cherry.

Finally, she emerged from her room and sauntered in, clad in a full-body black latex suit that left little to the imagination. After a quick twirl to flaunt her assets, she playfully slapped her own butt and winked at me. "Like what you see, big boy?" she teased, looking like a vampiric version of a certain sexy superhero.

I managed to compose myself and replied with a nod, feeling like a kid being offered a cookie. Cherry giggled, and we headed out together. Using an illusion spell, Cherry disguised our clothes until we reached the van parked in the alley. Halo and Alpha waited for us, dressed just like Cherry. I fought the urge to stare and focused on the task at hand, ignoring how underdressed I felt.

"Alright, we're good to go. Cherry, give us the signal when you're ready for the shields. Just remember, we can only hold them for a few minutes. If things go south, get out fast. You'll have maybe a minute to make it back to the van before the covens arrive," Alpha explained as she handed Cherry what looked like a flawless copy of the Lunar Amulet.

"Understood," I replied, feeling the nerves twist in my gut.

Cherry nodded with an uncharacteristically serious look on her face.

"Good luck, you two!" Halo chimed in with a beaming smile and two thumbs up. "You've got this!"

Her encouragement made me grin for a moment, but it did little to calm the butterflies in my stomach. Nevertheless, I put on a confident front, squared my shoulders, and followed Cherry to the rear loading docks. As I looked up at the cupolas crowning the old museum, I couldn't help but be impressed by the grand architecture of the structure.

We slipped into the back lot, staying hidden as Cherry worked her magic. A shimmering aura enveloped each of us, rendering us invisible to the security cameras, just as we planned. Luck was on our side with ongoing renovations in the old building. While the front half boasted new magnetic locks, the back door by the loading dock remained secured by an old deadbolt. My skills were a bit rusty, causing a slight delay in unlocking it, but I managed all the same, relying on tricks I'd learned on the street as a kid.

Feeling exposed without a mask, I had no choice but to rely on Cherry's enchantment to keep us concealed. We moved cautiously, stepping heel to toe to muffle any noise, following our planned route. Finally, we spotted the dome—and the intimidating figures of the hellhound and the arctic fox.

The fox was a majestic sight, standing four feet tall and six feet long, with three fluffy tails. Despite its soft-looking white fur and cute black eyes, it definitely seemed dangerous. I watched for a while, witnessing it exchange a disdainful glance with the hellhound. That one looked kind of like a massive black pit bull with red spikes running down its spine. Drool dripped from its jaws as it growled at its partner.

"Damn it!" Cherry muttered under her breath.

I turned to look at her, confused. "What's the problem?"

"I didn't expect the shield to be this strong. I—I don't think I can break through it," she said with a defeated tone.

We had come too far, with the amulet just fifty feet away. This was our maiden voyage, and failure was not an option—not to me. I clenched my jaw and balled my hands into fists. "You're stronger than you think. You have to make this work, or we're fucked. Remember, you're even more powerful now that I'm around, right?"

She nodded, a pensive expression crossing her features. "I guess so."

"Come on, babe, you're a total badass. I'll distract those beasts, and you focus on breaking the shield—the plan is perfect. Together, it'll be easy-peasy," I said, a final reassurance coming to mind. Something about the first time we met came back to me...the moment I told her I didn't want her to fail her exam. Even though the exam itself didn't exist, and that was all a front for her true intentions, the mere mention of failure made her indignant and focused. I cleared my throat and reached out, caressing her cheek. "You're not a failure. I believe that to my core."

As if my words ignited a fire within her, Cherry's eyes lit up with determination. "Damn right I'm not, chubby cock," she declared with a wink.

I nodded, not in love with that new nickname, but if it got her confidence back, then fine. "Alright, give them the signal, and I'll make my move."

Cherry looked in the air and gave a thumbs up to the ceiling. "Go go go!"

A second, larger magical dome enveloped us and the smaller exhibit, exactly to plan. With a surge of magical compulsion, I swallowed my nerves and dashed out into the open, grabbing both familiars' attention. They wasted no time, charging at me simultaneously. To my surprise, they seemed slower than expected, giving me a slight edge in anticipating their moves. As one maw snapped, I spun, narrowly evading its attack and causing the fox to collide with the hound. The hound retaliated, but the fox disregarded it, focusing its speed on me.

Huge claws slashed towards me, one after the other. I dodged left, then right, narrowly avoiding the razor-sharp claws by mere inches. Glancing at Cherry, I saw her already searching for a weak spot in the shield. My momentary distraction almost cost me dearly, as I barely managed to leap backward, narrowly escaping the hound's lunging attack aimed at my throat.

The hound's reckless charge sent it crashing into the fox once more. This time, the fox reacted by biting the hound's leg, igniting a brief skirmish between them. Realizing I couldn't defeat them in my current state, I wasted no time.

"Cherry! Shift me!" I yelled.

Without hesitation, Cherry turned and pointed at me, shouting, "Borden eh nubel!"

Just in time, as the two familiars cleared the air. I refocused on them as a massive paw slashed at me... But, my body had already begun to transform. Before I could stow away my clothing, three claws sliced into my chest.

Still, I managed to bear the pain and store my clothes as my transformation took hold. My skin thickened, reducing the would be gashes to minor scratches. Fur sprouted over me, my hands morphed into massive claws, and my arms extended into winged appendages. Resisting the urge to scream, I loomed over the two challengers. How *dare* they oppose their superior?

The arctic fox and hellhound exchanged glances before turning their attention back on me, as if silently agreeing to put aside old grudges and unite against their common foe. I was proud to be the Doomsday in this Batman V Superman moment. A second later, a black maw opened, emanating the depths of hell, hellfire blasting forth. Another maw followed suit, echoing the depths of Jotunheim, as a piercing arctic wind came at me.

Raw power surged through my body as I bounded back against a massive pillar, then launched myself into the expansive gallery, spreading my wings. With a single beat, I angled myself toward the two useless pups as twin blasts—one fire, one ice—shot straight at me. A surge of impending doom rippled through my body, and instinctively, I let out a powerful shriek. Waves of sound clashed with the flames and frost, pushing them back until they faded and I continued my dive.

In the final moment, I tucked in my legs and shifted my position, leading with my feet. My talons slammed into both the fox and the hound's heads, gripping onto them tightly. Flapping my wings, I ascended into the sky, then flipped both familiars, letting their dazed bodies plummet to the floor below. My goal was merely to incapacitate them; killing them would alert the covens that something was amiss, despite our shield. I could deduce as much from the fact that Alpha was able to track me with her crystal ball even with the shields in place.

It was then that I noticed Cherry casting a massive spell that enveloped the entire dome protecting the amulet. The dome vanished, and Cherry dashed in while I descended to the ground. Without warning, Cherry shouted, "Borden eh humensel!" and I began to shift back to my human form. Almost fully shifted, I summoned my clothes, envisioning them on me as before, dressing just as the fur retracted, preserving my dignity. Though, there was a slash in my shirt exposing three bleeding scratches.

As our shield dropped, both beasts lay dazed and bleeding. A casual observer would assume they had harmed each other, but I figured it wouldn't take long for the other covens to figure out what really happened, assuming they had a way of communicating with their familiars. I glanced over at my partner. Cherry was finalizing the position of the fake amulet before rushing out to meet me.

"C'mon, we gotta go!" She shout-whispered. The covens must have enchanted the area around the exhibit, as there was no visible damage from my battle with the familiars. Cherry and I stuck close as we retraced our steps out of the museum. Once beyond the lot, she dispelled her spells concealing us from surveillance and cast another illusion on our outfits.

When we reached the van, Alpha was already in the driver's seat, and Halo had the door open. Cherry and I hopped into the cargo area, collapsing next to each other, both panting from the run and adrenaline. I turned to Cherry and grinned, unable to contain my relief and pride. She smiled back, then enveloped me in a tight hug. "WE DID IT!" she exclaimed.

"We did it," I echoed. "You were incredible. You dismantled that shield flawlessly," I praised.

"Me? Did you see yourself? You were such a freaking badass! You took those mutts down and made them your bitches!" Cherry exclaimed. "Mua mua mua mua!" She covered my cheeks with kisses, and I had to imagine that red lipstick now covered my face.

But then our lips collided. It held a deeper passion than our first kiss—less about lust and more about intimacy and a bond that felt more earned than it had even an hour before. Our connection sparked, igniting something far more intense. But then, Cherry seemed to snap back to reality and realized what we were doing. She quickly pulled away as her cheeks flushed crimson. "Uh. Good familiar," she said, awkwardly patting me on the head.

I coughed as Cherry avoided eye contact. Glancing over, I saw Halo grinning ear to ear, sitting cross-legged with her chin resting in her hands, leaning in to watch us. "Golly. Don't mind me. You two are so adorable!" she exclaimed.

Alpha steered the van into an abandoned parking lot and cut the engine. Turning to face us, she said, "Nice job, both of you. You were outstanding. But we'll discuss it more when we get back. We'll leave the van here, disguise our appearance, and walk home. The fake amulet we left will only throw them off for a short time, and things might get heated as they try to piece together what happened, so we're laying low for a bit. Clear?"

"Yes, Alpha," both Halo and Cherry chimed in.

I nodded in agreement. We exited the van, and Alpha cast a spell that removed any evidence of our presence. As we walked together, animatedly sharing our stories from our own perspectives, my mind wandered. I wasn't sure whether I felt more excitement or fear about where my life was headed. But as I glanced at the three gorgeous witches beside me, a sense of optimism washed over me.

CHAPTER 7

Balancing The Scales

We arrived back home together—mission done and dusted. I felt a little buzz in my hand, like when your phone goes off. Not uncomfortable, just a reminder. Time to sort out my reward, I figured. *What kinda spell would she sling my way? What do I even need?*

Behind me, Cherry let out a gasp. "Cherry, everything cool?" I asked.

"My power..." she mumbled, staring at her hand.

"Oh, right! You two haven't figured out Logan's compensation," Halo squeaked, clapping her hands excitedly. "This is new!"

"Your power's on pause till you sort out what Logan gets. This is why I wanted him as just a pet," Alpha groaned. "This will be a pain to navigate."

"I'll—uh—I'll make him breakfast tomorrow morning. Done," Cherry said, eying her hand. She fist-pumped the air triumphantly, making me snicker. "Listen, you dumb tattoo-thingy! I figured out my end, so give me my power back!"

Her offer seemed way off the mark for fairness. And our deal was pretty clear—I had to agree in my heart that the reward evens the score between us. But that didn't stop me from laughing at her antics. "Cherry, pretty sure breakfast was in the cards anyway."

"Nothing's certain!" Cherry jabbed a finger at me.

"Oh, shush, you," Halo giggled. "We both know I was already planning his waffles and french toast for tomorrow." She strutted to the living room, beckoning us to follow. "We've got just the magical artifact for balancing minor contracts—or have you forgotten?"

We trailed after her. Alpha lounged on the couch, checking out the Lunar Amulet, while Halo grabbed a set of scales off the shelf. They looked ordinary—a classic set with two plates on a pivot. She pressed her hand against it and chanted, "Bin trar end honlik. Evenlance te dens fan te hert." A golden glow engulfed the scales, then settled inside. Glimmering runes lit up the surface.

I was mesmerized. The ladies didn't seem as impressed, but that made sense. To them, this kind of thing was a normal part of their world, but to me, it was amazing. I wasn't used to magic yet, even after realizing my own powers as a shapeshifter and having my physique enhanced by a mystical bond to these witchy cuties. Honestly, seeing these scales light up like that made me a bit sad that I lacked traditional magic myself.

Halo smiled warmly at me. "This enchanted scale is now activated. It can't lie and will always be honest about the heart's desires," she put up one finger—now going full instructor mode. "But how do we use it to measure the heart's desires? With these," she said as she turned and grabbed two small, nondescript figurines from another shelf.

My eyebrows scrunched up. "How are those gonna measure our heart's desires?"

"Like this," said Halo, holding both figurines. With one in each hand, she pressed them against Cherry's and my chests. "Refectern te dens fan te hert."

I felt this weird sensation in my chest, like paper tearing, but the sound was the feeling. It was kinda freaky, to be honest. And then, poof, it was gone.

As Halo pulled back, my brows knitted together. "What was that?"

"That spell just swiped a piece of your soul and stuck it in the figure. But don't worry, it's just a tiny chunk, your soul's gonna patch itself up in no time. The bits in the figurines? They'll be linked to you until we dispel them. See, look." Halo showed off both mini statues.

They used to be just plain metal dudes. But now, one looked exactly like a mini Cherry Cola, all sassy with a hand on one hip, blowing a kiss with the other. She was confident and alluring, true to form. It made me grin—until I saw mine. It was like looking at my old self. Clenched fists, staring off into nowhere with this lonely vibe. Brows all furrowed, jaw set. It hit me, you know? I did look pretty good in a brooding sort of way, though.

The girls were eyeballing my figure, not saying a word about it, to their credit. But when I peeked at Cherry, she had this small smirk. I didn't have time to ponder over what that meant because Halo was apparently raring to go with the next step of this process.

"The next part is easy. Place your figures on the scales, Cherry makes her pitch about what she wants to do for you. Logan, if your gut says it's fair, the scales even out. If not, it's a no-go, and the scales will show that, too. Cherry's powers stay gone until it's sorted. If she doesn't come up with anything, she'll be unable to use magic until she delivers," Halo explained.

Cherry and I nodded. It was simple enough to understand. I honestly kind of hoped that it wouldn't be too hard on her. I could see how this was irritating and stressful. "Got it."

Halo placed each figurine on the scale. Mine sank low, but Cherry's soared high. "Alright, Cherry, give us your best pitch!" Halo chirped.

Cherry looked tense but nodded. "For Logan's help last night, I'll whip up breakfast tomorrow." No movement on the scale. "Okay, fine. I'll cover breakfast *and* lunch." Still nothing, and I definitely wasn't surprised. I busted my ass and fought off monsters for that amulet. I was already going to be eating breakfast and lunch, so what exactly did that offer do for me? She squinted at me. "Alright... I'll—uh—ugh." She threw her hands up. "I dunno! Why's this fucking thing stuck? What's your deal? What do you want?"

I shrugged. I had no clue about the extent of her powers or what they could do. I wanted to ask her for a spell, but I didn't want to get too fixated on one idea now if it turned out she couldn't pull it off, and I didn't know a damn thing about the girls' magic or actual capabilities just yet. I was just as unprepared for this as she was. "I'm not sure," I muttered with a sigh.

With a stomp of her foot, Cherry grumbled, "I should've set terms before the mission."

Halo giggled. "Gosh...You're thinking about this all wrong, honey."

Cherry crossed her arms and gave Halo a squinty look. "What do you mean?"

"If he doesn't know what spell to request, keep it simple. Men aren't that complicated. They all want the same thing. Just offer to suck his cock every morning for a week," Halo said, bouncing her shoulders with a simple shrug. "You already told me you like the taste, right? So it's not that bad of a deal."

My eyebrows shot up, and Cherry's cheeks went red. She gave me a skeptical glance but caved in with a saucy grin. "For Logan's help with my mission, I'll wake him up with a blowjob every morning for a week."

My heart raced as the scales tipped drastically. My side was still lower than Cherry's, and the fulcrum was a bit off, but that was major progress.

"What?! How is *that* not good enough?" Cherry pouted, shoving me lightly.

I cleared my throat. "This honestly seems like a silly and totally unnecessary idea, but if it balances the scales and gets Cherry's powers back, then I won't complain but... I risked my life for you out there, didn't I? We're onto something for sure, though, so maybe if you added that you'll do it while completely naked, and let me freely touch you, that would balance everything out?"

Cherry scoffed, glaring at me as her blush spread. Then she added, "And I'll do it naked, with my little piggies exposed and all, and Logan can touch me as much as he wants while I suck him off."

Instantly, the scales balanced, making Halo jump up and down, cheering excitedly. "Yay! See, easy-peasy."

Alpha chuckled, crossing her arms over her chest as she leaned back into the couch. "Wow, that was easier than I thought. That's all it's going to take?"

"It's a small price, sucking a cock that I've already fucked. That amulet is worth a hell of a lot more. Especially when I planned on blowing that chubby thing often enough anyway..." Cherry mumbled.

I tried not to let my glee at her comment show and acted as if I didn't hear her. *You need to play it cool, Logan.* I advised myself silently.

Alpha's amused smile was evident in her voice before I even looked at her. "So, let me get this straight. Logan will do anything we ask him to do for sex?"

"Yuppers! Because he's a man! Goodness gracious—it's so great because we were already planning to have sex with him eventually," said Halo's excited voice. "All we really have to do to balance the scales is offer him an occasional magical blessing that benefits us all anyway, then promise some sex that leans a bit more into his tastes and pleasure than usual…and we should be all set!"

"Unlimited requests for sex?" Cherry asked with a grin. "Talk about a win-win!"

Alpha's face suddenly turned as red as her hair, and she shrugged. "I mean—it's definitely a good deal that's hard to pass up."

I shuffled my feet. "Hey now, I'm not that easy," I weakly protested. Actually, I was totally that easy.

Alpha's eyes lit up with amusement, and she was quick to call me out. "You followed Cherry home after just meeting her and banged her so hard that she had to use Halo's healing magic to walk straight the next day."

I lifted a finger and opened my mouth to argue, but then closed it again. I tucked that little tid bit away as a self-esteem raiser for a rainy day.

Halo patted me on the back. Her smile and sugary tone eased my mortification. "Aww, it's okay, big fella! You belong to us now. So as long as you're only easy with us, then we're square."

I lowered my hand and shook my head, unable to wipe off the small smile on my face. "I feel like such a slut," I muttered, earning laughs from all of them. I might have been miffed about being called 'easy', but that didn't mean that I didn't fucking love this arrangement. Still, I wanted something more with them—a meaningful relationship, unlike anything I had before. I felt a hint of it when Cherry kissed me in the back of the van earlier. That...was everything. That kiss was full of passion, love, and mutual respect—camaraderie, even, but hotter than that.

Still, I felt like I had to point something out. "Well, sex won't always be good enough. It's not like I'm a caveman or something," I tried to explain. "If you serve pancakes every day, eventually people get tired of pancakes."

Halo gasped. "That's not true!"

"It is," Alpha muttered.

"It definitely is," Cherry confirmed with a groan.

"Not saying I'll get tired of sex with you, to be clear," I grunted, holding up my hands before they misinterpreted my careless words. "I'm just pointing out that if you only offer one kind of reward, it'll lose value."

"Very true," Alpha said, nodding. "Halo mentioned offering occasional blessings to you—that could benefit us all. I think that's a great idea, and something I'll look into."

"Also," Halo said, raising a single finger in the air, "I'd like to point out the opposite effect is also true. You might find that what you considered a heavy mission full of danger doesn't feel like such a big deal after a while when you get stronger. So it goes both ways."

I nodded, acknowledging the good point. "Huh. I didn't consider that."

"Smile, hot stuff," Cherry said, jabbing me in the arm, "You're not the one who's gonna have a cock in their mouth every morning this week."

"Hey, Cherry! It looks like Logan's going to be the one feeding you breakfast tomorrow!" Halo said with a giggle.

"I still want pancakes, though," Cherry murmured, making the rest of us laugh.

Alpha raised her hand to get everyone's attention as the noise died down. "Alright, now that that's settled, listen up. Like I said, we'll take time off to plan our next steps and wait for things to calm down. Tomorrow, everyone is free to do what they want, but stay indoors as much as possible. Now, it's been a long day, so let's get cleaned up and get some rest."

Halo poked me in the chest. "You should probably make sure you wash your dick extra clean tonight so Cherry can really enjoy herself in the morning," she said. I couldn't tell if she was joking or not, but I nodded in agreement anyway.

• ♥ • ♥ • ♥ • ♥ • ♥ •

We relaxed on the sofa for a while, watching TV and engaging in idle conversation. Cherry sat on my lap and even fell asleep with her head on my chest, but woke up when Alpha nudged her.

"Girls, you two should go. I need to talk to Logan about something. Logan, stay where you are," Alpha commanded.

Halo stretched, yawned, and waved goodbye as she rose from the sofa and headed to her room. "Good night."

Cherry gestured towards her narrowed eyes with two fingers, and then towards me before silently leaving. I furrowed my brows, not knowing what that was about, before taking a seat near Alpha. "Hey, what's up?"

She studied me for a few moments. "You're not what I expected."

"Really? What did you expect?"

"Honestly, a little bitch who would be too scared to do what we needed him to do. One that couldn't really contribute unless I forced him to. The magical world doesn't sit well with ordinary people. They always panic," she said.

I chuckled. "Well, I'm glad to know that I'm not a little bitch."

She grinned, her tail wagging behind her, which made her a bit harder to take seriously as it was so cute. "Me too. I wanted to let you know that I think you were right about fighting for this arrangement. I realized something when I watched you with Cherry—what you will be able to do for us out of genuine care and connection is going to be so much more powerful than what you'd be able to manage as our slave."

I nodded, smiling at her. "I agree." I wasn't sure what else to say.

She drew back a little and looked at the TV, which was muted. "You proved me wrong. I thought I was going to regret it, but you bring more to the table than I thought a Greater Familiar ever could. More than a normal Mating Familiar, a Lesser Familiar, and a Sentinel Familiar put together. In the future, you might rival the Greater Familiars of the other covens. Keep up the good work, and I'm certain your future rewards will be much better than Cherry's."

I ignored the revelation that Mating Familiar was a thing...for now. "Thanks. That means a lot coming from you. I thought my life had gone from shit to shittier when you first abducted me. But, now..." I let the sentence hang, contemplating my next words. "But now I feel like my life has kind of started over again. It's like I'm right where I'm supposed to be. Does that sound dumb?"

"No," she chuckled. "I'm feeling the same about your place here. I couldn't have asked for a better pet." She punctuated that statement as she patted me on the head.

I watched as Alpha's tail wagged back and forth happily behind her. I realized it was more like an animal's tail than I initially thought and might help me read her genuine emotions better. While I was lost in thought, Alpha noticed me staring at her wagging tail.

"Does it bother you?" she asked.

I looked up at her. "Hmm? The tail? No. Not at all. I like it. Your ears too. I think they are cute as hell."

Red crept up her neck as her ears lay flat and her tail lowered. "You really think so?"

It was rare to see Alpha acting shy, and she was too damn adorable when she looked so vulnerable. I gave her a wicked smile, slipping into a lower tone of voice. "Sure. Everything about you looks incredible. I'm a big fan of the abs, too. Your ears and tail only add to how fucking hot you are."

In an instant, her confident smirk reappeared. "You're damn right I'm fucking hot."

I chuckled. How do you conceal them while you're out? Is it just a spell?"

"Nah. Any of us can hide our affinities from normal mortals. To non-magic people, they're hidden by default. I can even hide them from you. It just takes a small amount of concentration and... Poof!" As she said it, her tail and ears disappeared, making her look totally human.

I grinned like a child seeing their grandpa pull a quarter out of their ear for the first time. "That's so cool!" My expression fell, and my eyes went distant after a moment. "Wait, so when I saw Cherry's eyes flash red, and her fangs showed up another time, she was just losing her concentration?" I asked.

"Yup. She had to focus on you more than a normal person because of the witch blood running through your veins."

"Wow. I was sure I was hallucinating at the time. But, what do I know?" I shrugged.

She grinned. "Nothing."

I put on a mask of mock offense and put a hand on my heart. "Ouch!"

Alpha laughed. "Do me a favor?"

I wasn't sure if she meant a formal request or not, but I went with it regardless. "Sure. What do you need?"

She smiled. "Remember my name. It's Alice Farrow. I don't want you to use it or anything—but I feel like you should know."

I nodded, honestly kind of flattered by the show of trust. "I will. Thank you for telling me."

Alpha's smile broadened and she put her hand on my thigh, making me gulp as she leaned in closer. "You're a good familiar. We got lucky with you. The world is really going to open up for our coven now. Take a shower and rest. I'll see you in the morning." She closed the distance and planted a small kiss on my cheek. Her hand grazed along my thigh as she stood, and she walked away.

"Night," I said with a grin before heading to the shower.

• ♥ • ♥ • ♥ • ♥ • ♥ •

I let the hot water in the shower soak and rinse away the day's dirt and stress from my muscles. I stood with my face tilted up, letting the warmth flow over me. I thought about all that had happened and how my life changed rapidly. Lost in my thoughts, I barely noticed the shower door sliding open.

Two smooth arms wrapped around me from behind and pulled against my chest. It startled me at first, until two soft mounds pressed against my back. I made to turn, but the intruder stopped me with a squeeze.

"Relax, baby. I'm only here to make sure you wash up properly before my meal in the morning," Cherry purred. "Hold still."

I did as she requested, my breathing quickening as the steam billowed around us. She released me, and I heard her opening the soap bottle, preparing the loofah. Then the coarse feeling began brushing against my shoulders and neck, then down along my back and arms. After she scrubbed my backside and legs, she ran her body up and down against me, letting our skin caress each other as the suds covered her as well.

"I hope you like it, baby," she whispered as her soapy breasts pressed into me. "I'm sorry if you feel like I lowballed you with the first offer out there."

I chuckled at that as I luxuriated in her touch. "It's fine," I said. "It worked out in the end."

"Truth is, big guy...I'm such a slut for you that it never occurred to me to offer something like that because I'd gladly suck your cock anytime I got a chance."

I felt my heartbeat elevating at her words. "Ah. That makes sense then."

Cherry must have used a spell because the shower nozzle shifted, aiming away from us and freeing my face and chest from the hot water. I stayed motionless, still following her lead, and listened to another bottle being opened and closed. Soon, two hands were running through my wet hair, lathering it thoroughly. Her fingernails gently scratched my scalp in small circles, sending little shivers down my spine. It was all so relaxing that, despite our closeness, I wasn't even hard.

"That being said—I hope I'm not shooting myself in the foot by letting you know you can have me any way you want, any day you want," she muttered.

"How do you mean?" I asked.

She paused. "Like—I'm kind of worried that you won't value my offers on our contracts since I can't help but want you all the time. Why accept an offer for a week full of wake-up sloppy toppy when you know I'd do it for free, right?"

I smiled at her words. "I'll try and be fair about it," I said.

Her hand pulled on my shoulder, showing that I should turn around. As I did, I noticed Cherry turning around as well. The shower nozzle shifted again, the hot water going over my shoulder in an unnatural arc and landing on her head and back, rinsing her pale skin. Once the water shifted again to hit its original position and rinse my back, I took the hint.

I took my time as I gently washed her slender back, tight ass, and glorious legs. Then I washed her hair in return, taking just as much care with her as she had with me. Even though I wasn't making any assumptions during this surprisingly intimate shower, it didn't stop my length from becoming partially erect.

Cherry finally turned back around to face me, the water again changing its direction and flowing overhead and running down her back. My face split in a smile as I followed its trail until my eyes fell on Cherry's incredible body. "Wash only, cutie. No funny business," she said with playfully narrowed eyes.

I nodded at her, straining not to grin too broadly. I washed her body and maybe spent a little extra time making sure certain parts were cleaner than others, but I didn't cross any lines, doing exactly as she requested. I even made sure to clean her 'little piggies'. Again, Cherry flicked a finger, and the water shifted when I finished. It rinsed Cherry until no suds remained before returning to its original position, her spell ending.

She smiled as she took the loofah back and cleaned my front. Her hand roamed freely, and Cherry dropped to her knees, skipping my groin and washing my legs. She gradually guided the loofah to my balls, lathering them thoroughly, and smirked as my manhood stood fully erect.

"Now, let's make sure this big fella is ready to go in the morning," Cherry cooed. As soapy bubbles covered my shaft, Cherry took hold and stroked it. She studied my manhood as she worked it over, her other hand massaging my balls. Her breasts jiggled as she picked up her pace.

My cock throbbed in her hand, and I knew that in only a few minutes I'd lose myself to orgasmic bliss. Cherry grinned up at me and her tempo increased again. "Wow, baby, you're so dirty. This is going to take a bit more scrubbing to get you all squeaky clean."

I reached down, running my hand through Cherry's wet hair and across her cheek. She took my thumb between her lips and sucked on it, giving me a preview of what was to come, before she made me—well, you know. Every twisting stroke of her soft hand brought me closer to the inevitable.

After only a few minutes, my balls were tightening and I knew I was about to explode. But to my utter dismay, her hand slowed down rather than sped up. Cherry's eyes glowed brightly as she grinned mischievously up at me, with my thumb between her fangs. Then she stopped. "What's wrong? I told you I was here to make sure you were cleaned and ready for me in the morning, cutie. You don't think you're clean enough yet?"

I wanted to protest and file a complaint, hell maybe even lawyer up, but then, mercifully, she cackled maniacally as she suddenly resumed a frantic pace with her hand. A jolt of pleasure shot through me like lightning, causing my girth to thicken in her grasp. Every pump of her fist released more of my load all over her chest and stomach until I had no more to give.

Cherry leaned forward and gave my tip a quick kiss. "Much better." Giggling, she stood and rinsed herself off before climbing out of the shower. "Go straight to bed now! I'll be making sure you're *up* bright and early, baby." Then she shot me a wink before snapping her fingers, causing steam to rise from her body as she sauntered out the door.

CHAPTER 8

A Heavenly Day Off

Slipping into a deep sleep, I found myself back in the shower with Cherry in my dreams. Her hands roamed my body, igniting every nerve, while mine traced the curves that drove me wild. Attempting a kiss, she playfully halted me with a finger on my lips, her fangs gleaming as she winked.

Halo and Alpha cheered us on from the sidelines, holding a bowl of popcorn as if it were the Super Bowl. It struck me as odd, especially seeing Halo waving a foam finger proclaiming

"Number 1 Witch." I diverted my gaze, only to find Cherry dropping to her knees, transforming the shower into a museum. Adorned with the Lunar Amulet, we became the spectacle, our observers admiring its beauty as if it were fine art.

Locking eyes with Cherry, I surrendered to her touch, oblivious to the spectators, the cheers, and the foam finger as her tongue slid up my shaft and she took me into her mouth. Her lips around me overwhelmed my senses as the realization of my dream slowly dawned on me. The scene blurred with that epiphany, leaving only the sensation of her tongue on my skin.

Awakening, I discovered that the waking world did not disappoint me. There was a nude beauty before me on hands and knees. Cherry Cola was already between my legs, ass up, face down in my groin, my cock already deep in her throat. Her red eyes met mine as she pleasured me. "Mmm!"

"Fffuck," I groaned, her hand teasing my body as she throated me. Her fingers ran up and down, from my thighs to my sternum, tickling me in a pleasant way as she sucked me off like the slut she last night claimed to be for me. She bobbed, taking me to the base before releasing me.

"Good morning," she greeted, her tongue teasing as she stroked me. She planted a few soft kisses on my tip and hummed happily as she rubbed it against her blushing cheek.

"Uh, yep. It sure is a good morning. There's something I need to discuss once you're done," I managed.

Spitting on me for added lubrication, she quickened her pace. "You can talk while I work," she suggested, engulfing me once more.

"Holy shit. Okay. I realized—oh fuck, that's good—" I started before her eyes sparkled mischievously. Now it made sense why she preferred conversation during. She enjoyed the challenge, but I could play along.

Cherry's red lips let me go. "You just figuring out how good I am at sucking dick?" she teased before diving back in.

"Mmmm—nah. I knew that already."

"Yhuheher," she giggled with me still in her mouth.

I chuckled. "Don't talk with your mouth full. It's rude."

Her eyes narrowed, and she picked up the pace.

"No, what I meant was, I don't wanna be just a sidekick. After last night, I want a real spot on the team, you know? I want a say in things. It'd be nice to have—*Jesus*—a vote," I managed, but just barely.

My cock popped out of her mouth, and she held it against her lips, lost in thought. "It'll be nice to have Jesus?" She smirked impishly before pressing the tip of her tongue into my glans.

"You know what I meant," I muttered.

She kissed my cock. "Fuck, you're tasty. Umm...I'll bring it up with the crew. We'll see what they say. Now, if you've got nothing else to say, zip those lips and let me do my thing."

I did as told, staying quiet as Cherry went back to work, licking, sucking, and stroking. "Mmm—fuck I love your chubby cock so much," she groaned. "My new best friend." After her teasing the night before and that steamy dream, I knew she wouldn't take long to make me finish.

Cherry slipped a hand between her legs, her moans growing louder. "Guh–hah! Shit, I hope you don't mind if I strum my pussy while I do this, baby. Aww FUCK!"

"Why the fuck would I mind?" I grunted.

It didn't take her long to climax while pleasuring me—she even beat me to the punch. She brought her hand back up, using both to work my shaft, spreading her own girlcum across my cock as added lubrication. With my tip in her mouth and her tongue swirling, she egged me on with her moans. "Mhm! Mhm! Yeah, baby, cum for me! I fucking need it in my mouth, baby!"

I obeyed promptly, groaning as I throbbed, releasing into her mouth.

As my load filled her, her eyes widened, and she let out an excited, muffled squeal. "Mmmmm!" She savored every drop, swallowing it down like she was the submissive pet. Only when my body stopped trembling did she pull away with a loud pop, swallowing one last time before kissing my tip and winking. "So, how'd I do for day one?"

"Damn. You're unreal," I panted.

She let out a happy sigh. "Cool. That's sorted for today. Halo whipped up some breakfast. Catch you later," she said, winking as she hopped off and left the room.

· ♥ · ♥ · ♥ · ♥ · ♥ ·

After throwing on some clothes, I joined them in the dining room where Halo had laid out a feast of breakfast classics: eggs, bacon, sausage, and biscuits. Also, yes, pancakes too. The girls were deep in conversation, mostly done with their meals by the time I sat with them. They teased Cherry about her first daily duty to me, and laughter filled the room at her expense, but she joined right in.

I loaded up on a different kind of protein than Cherry just did and gulped down some orange juice, then pondered what to do with my day. I couldn't remember the last time I had a break from work or school. Now I just...didn't have either of those things in my life anymore.

"We're taking it easy before the full moon. So, chill out and have fun, but keep a low profile. We're laying low, got it?" Alpha declared as she stacked her dishes in the sink. Then she shot me a shy glance, her ears flattening before turning to Cherry. "Cherry, come with me. We need to talk."

Cherry's crimson eyes met mine briefly before she reluctantly agreed. "Fine. But you owe me ice cream later," she insisted.

Alpha didn't say anything, just nodded in agreement, and the two exited the room.

I got up, carried my plate to the sink, and turned on the faucet.

"What are you up to, silly?" Halo asked with a playful grin.

"Oh, I figured since you went to the trouble of making breakfast, I could at least clean up," I replied.

She chuckled and waved her hand dismissively.

I recoiled in surprise as the plate I'd just placed in the sink levitated, while a scrub brush swooped in to clean it. In no time, the dish sparkled, steaming dry before floating into the cupboard. The rest of the dishes followed suit, one by one.

Halo laughed and grabbed my hand, leading me towards the front door. "Come on. They can wash themselves. I'm declaring you my boyfriend for the day, so you're taking me shopping and showering me with affection!"

I followed, brows furrowed. "It's not that I don't want to, but why?"

She turned to face me, walking backward, her wings fluttering excitedly and with a radiant smile on her face. "Well, because it sounds like fun, darn it! Do we need any other reason?"

Nothing could wipe the smile off my face. "Do we need an agreement or anything for this?" I asked curiously.

"Nope. Unless you think spending the day as my boyfriend would be a chore," Halo said with a playful pout.

I laughed. "Of course not. It sounds like a great time."

Her smile returned. "Good, because I'll probably make out with you for fun, anyway. About time I got my first kiss, I'd say!"

"So...what are we shopping for?" I asked, brushing past that declaration.

She snapped her fingers, and her wings disappeared, even to me, causing my eyes to widen. She opened the door and led me outside. "Other than getting some new clothes, there's a Hot Topic in the mall that holds silent auctions for occult items and provides witchy services. I figured that would be a wonderful opportunity for you to see more of your new world."

My brows rose in surprise, and excitement built inside me. The two of us got in the car since the mall was a bit too far to walk, and drove there together, me behind the wheel despite the fact that it was probably Alpha's vehicle. All along the way, we talked about everything she liked and disliked. I asked her questions about her past, interests, and hobbies. In return, she asked me more about myself. I shared some of the better stories, avoiding the dark times to not ruin the mood.

The two of us casually explored the various stores, and laughter and smiles filled our time together as we grew more comfortable with each other. We got hungry and walked to the food court. Halo ordered some fried rice, and I ordered a slice of pizza. When we sat down, I took Halo's spoon before she could pick it up.

"Hey!" she shouted while laughing.

I smiled and scooped up a bit of her food and brought it to her mouth. "Go ahead."

She opened her mouth, never taking her blue eyes off mine as she leaned in and let me feed her. She covered her mouth with one hand as she giggled and chewed. Then she grabbed my pizza and held it up for me.

I opened my mouth and leaned in, but before I could take a bite, she pushed the pizza against my face, covering my nose and mouth in sauce. She began laughing and letting out a snort. "Ha-haha! You should see your face!" *SNORT*

The moment her snort came out, her eyes went wide, and she covered her mouth and nose with both hands. "You weren't supposed to hear that!" she said as she kept her flushed cheeks mostly covered.

I chuckled, a smile splitting my face as I wiped it with a napkin. "Why? It was the most adorable thing I think I've ever heard," I admitted.

She hesitated to uncover her mouth. "You mean it? You don't think it was stupid?"

"What?! No! It was the best! You have the best laugh. I want to hear more of it," I exclaimed.

"Okay, I'm glad you like it," she said, finally uncovering her face. "Wanna feed me again? I really enjoyed that."

I fed her and managed to make her snort at least two more times before we wrapped things up. When we finished, we tidied up our mess and headed to a clothing store. Halo linked her arm with mine, pulling me to the side before planting a kiss on my cheek. Warmth spread through me, and I couldn't help but wonder how the day could possibly get any cozier than this.

• ♥ • ♥ • ♥ • ♥ • ♥ •

We finally reached the clothing store. Being the manly man that I am, I wasn't a big fan of shopping for clothes. This stop was the one I was looking forward to the least on our trip. I tried not to let my disinterest show, but Halo caught me immediately.

Her mouth opened in feigned disbelief. "Don't be like that. I promise it won't be that bad."

I grimaced. "I was that obvious huh? Shops like this have never really been my thing. I'm only here because I like a certain someone enough to be willing to suffer such an injustice." I grinned.

"Oh, injustice is it?" she said with a devious grin that made me wonder what she was plotting.

"Yes. The great injustice that all my brethren must face. It is a trial, a tribulation, a burden that we bear for the women we like," I said with a fist in the air and mock conviction.

Halo laughed. "You poor, poor thing." She put the back of her hand against her forehead as she looked up with despair. "Whatever shall you do?!"

"My lady, I shall endure," I said with my jaw set and a fist to my chest.

We both burst into laughter. Her eyes turned to slits. "Gosh, I think you're going to have a far better time than you assume—my Mr. Poor Oppressed Dreamboat."

I grinned at her, shrugging my shoulders noncommittally. "Challenge accepted."

We spent some time looking through the clothes. I didn't pay much attention to the various girly garments, but I did pay attention to the lovely blonde next to me. Halo led us toward the changing rooms and I tried to break off to find a chair to wait in. But... Halo didn't let go of my hand.

"Where do you think you're going?" she asked with a mischievous smirk.

"I was just gonna—"

She let go of my hand and waved hers in the air. A soft glow emanated from her fingertips as she cut me off. "Nope. You're coming with me. How else will I know if these outfits look good enough to buy or not?"

Now, this was a fun development. I assumed her magic would hide us, and no one would see me follow her inside. So, like a kid walking into a candy store, I followed Halo into the changing room. I took a seat on the bench, getting comfortable with one leg crossed over the other.

She blushed and smiled while she pulled her top off, exposing her black bra beneath. Then Halo did a slow turn before flipping her skirt up and letting it fall, only giving me a quick view of her panties. Halo giggled and then straightened out her legs together, and unhurriedly bent over as she slowly pulled her skirt down until she was touching her toes. Then she straightened up gradually before wiggling her hips.

"See, clothes shopping isn't so bad," she purred.

"Mhm," I said distractedly. "Much better than I remember."

Halo's body was perfect. It differed from Cherry's, but was equally flawless. Where Cherry was more lithe, Halo was both petite and curvy. My eyes shamelessly traveled from her plump, perky breasts to the curve of her hips and juicy ass.

"You know, Logan. Cherry told me all about the night you two shared," she said while pulling on another shirt.

I quirked a brow. "Oh? Hopefully all good things."

Halo practically purred, her eyes crescenting as she looked at me with a hunger I hadn't seen in her until now. "They were very nice things. The truth is, we didn't tell you everything. You see, you're kind of a loophole for us."

My confusion only grew, along with a hint of anxiety. "What do you mean?"

Noticing my expression, Halo was quick to reassure me as she tried on another outfit. "It's nothing bad. As witches, we have to be virgins to keep our powers strong. But, by binding you to us, it means that sex with you won't count toward spoiling our purity, since you're basically like an extension of us now."

A look of realization appeared on my face. "I see... I heard Alpha mention Mating Familiars."

"Yes," she said. "Bigger covens can afford to take normal human men as sexual servants to keep them satisfied while not despoiling the witches. Most men join willingly. As a rare human Greater Familiar, you can do multiple jobs for us at once!"

My eyes opened as I remembered something I saw in the group chat between the girls when I was still their prisoner. This was sounding real familiar all of a sudden. "Wait—Cherry and I fucked before we made the contract. Does that mean she lost some of her power?"

"Fortunately, it didn't happen. She took a chance on you, though. If you died afterwards or waited over a month before completing the contract she would have been permanently weakened, maybe even lost everything. But, since you got smart real quick and joined the crew, the magical connection was made soon enough that it didn't count against her. She took a big risk by choosing to go all the way with you. Alpha suggested we just kidnap you from your delivery van or drug you," Halo cheerfully explained as she changed her outfit again.

I let out a sigh of relief. "Thank goodness, I would have felt terrible if I were the reason she spent the rest of her life as a magical cripple."

"Aww, golly, you're so sweet. But, yeah, having sex with you is, well, kind of like masturbating—from a magical perspective, anyway. We can get away with anything we want as long as it's *your* body having its way with us. So, if you see us all eying you like a juicy piece of meat sometimes, that's why," she said with a giggle.

"Well, you probably should have emphasized that point back when we were negotiating. You probably would have gotten a better deal," I joked.

Suddenly, Halo's grin and tone turned sultry. She held up a bra and panties. "Would you like to watch me try these on?"

My eyes widened. "Of fucking course I would."

She stripped off her top and bottom, standing in nothing but her underwear again. A blush crept up her neck, and she turned around, dragging off her panties and then unclasping her bra.

Halo faced me again with her arms covering her breasts and crotch. I looked on, an intensity burning in my eyes, and I wanted nothing more than to see every bit of this angelic woman. She bit her lip and uncovered herself slowly, looking away.

"Fuck. You're perfect," I said.

"Do I make you hard?" Halo asked nervously.

I uncrossed my legs and stood up so she could see the massive tent I was pitching. I eloquently replied, "Yep."

She giggled, seeming to gain more confidence. "Good. I'm really glad. You've been such an amazing pretend boyfriend today. I think—" She licked her lips, her nerves slipping through. "If you copped a feel, I wouldn't be offended." She shrugged one shoulder.

I stepped up to Halo and grabbed her lower back, pulling her close. My fingers slipped between her legs and spread her open as I explored her center. She fell into me, grabbing hold of my shoulders.

Halo's breath shuddered, and she instinctively pressed into my hand. "Wha–Oh! Gosh!"

I massaged her pearl before slipping a finger inside her tight little pussy. After a moment, I slipped a second finger in and she gasped.

"I—Mmm fuck—I meant my boobies," she said between moans.

I smirked. "You didn't exactly specify." I gripped her plump ass and squeezed while pulling my fingers out of her and using her fluids as lubrication to better massage her. Slowly, I circled her nub as she whimpered against me and thrust her hips.

"Ah! Logan, you're so—Mmm—so good." Her breasts pressed tightly against my chest and her body tensed. I kissed her along her neck and slightly increased my pace. "I—Mmooh-fuck—Logan! I—I—I!" She bit down hard on my shoulder and almost screamed, allowing my shoulder to muffle the sound. "AH!" Her body shook against me as I continued to pleasure her as she rode out the waves of bliss.

In the middle of her orgasm, a knock sounded at the door. "Is everything alright in there? Do you need help?" came an unfamiliar voice.

"N—no! AH! FUCK ME! Everything's f—fine! It's just—the food court lunch isn't agreeing with meeeAHH! GOD! I'll be out in a min—OH FUCK—Eeeaahh!" Halo unconvincingly lied. Finally, after another minute of that, she came down from her orgasmic high. Halo stared up at me, her body still twitching as she worked to catch her breath. She had a look of pure awe on her face. "Where did you learn to do that?"

I grinned. "Experience. One of my girlfriends a few years back was a cougar. She taught me a lot about how to please a woman."

"Holy shoot. Give me her address. I want to send that woman a box of chocolates," Halo said. She looked down at the new panties. "I don't think I'm gonna try those on. I'm pretty sure that my drooling pussy would ruin them, and then I'd have to buy them."

I laughed, and we gathered up her things after she got dressed. She picked out a few of the shirts she liked and we stopped at the register. As we were walking out of the store, I overheard the girl at the counter mumbling something about a lucky girl. I smiled, taking the bags in one hand and Halo's hand in the other.

"Hey, how would you like a little taste of my magic sometime?" Halo asked.

I glanced down at her ass and grinned.

She playfully slapped my arm and laughed. "I didn't mean that, nerd! Haha! *Snort*. I meant real magic. I know we didn't make a contract today or anything, but I've had such a great time that I think a little reward is in order."

My brows shot up at that. "I mean, if you're alright with it, then definitely."

"Good. I might have something in mind. But, for now, let's just say I'll owe you a small favor," she said.

As we stepped into Hot Topic, I wasn't sure what to expect. The store didn't look magical to me, but I'd been wrong before. However, it seemed Halo wasn't in a rush to explore the back room or wherever the magical items were.

Just like the rest of our date, I went with the flow.

We weren't very far into the store when I took a step and—*BRRRAAAAP*—I froze after the long, loud sound of a fart died down, and slowly turned to face Halo.

She was struggling to hide her snickering. "Logan! Gross! How could you do that in front of a lady like me?!"

I narrowed my eyes, trying hard not to laugh, but failing. "You little..." I bent down and picked up the whoopee cushion that somehow made its way beneath my foot without me noticing, and held it up in front of her with a playful accusatory glare.

Halo burst into laughter, her adorable snort joining in on the fun. "Little cutie? I'm pretty sure you were about to say little cutie."

I laughed with her and put the toy back on the shelf, before catching up to Halo, who ran ahead in excitement.

"Oh, my god! Look! Funyo Pops! Ooo, it's Vick and Emmy from Zombie Bride! I love that movie." She rushed to the shelf, gushing over the plastic toys.

"I liked it. He was just a normal man who found himself in a whole new world full of strange and unusual things. And in the end, he finds himself falling for a girl that he initially found to be terrifying. It sounds more and more familiar by the minute," I said with a cheeky grin.

Halo turned, slowly. Her lips curled up into a huge smile and she quirked a brow. "Oh? Just how familiar are we talking?"

Taking a step closer, I didn't let my gaze leave hers. I stared into the blue depths of her eyes. "I'd say at least three-quarters of the movie so far," I said, our bodies only a foot apart.

"I see," the blonde beauty said, her eyes glancing at my lips. "But, if I remember right, Vick was starting to fall for multiple girls by then."

I'm not too proud to admit that I blushed at that moment. But, I kept my cool. "He did, didn't he? Can you blame him when they were both incredible?" I asked, leaning in a little closer.

"Not one bit," she said, before she closed the distance and kissed me. "But I would be a little jealous if I were Emmy."

Her arms wrapped around my neck, and I grabbed her waist. Her lips were soft, and she tasted like maple syrup. Lips parted, and our tongues danced. I felt our connection flare between us, and my heart pounded so hard she could probably hear it. We allowed ourselves to bask in the moment of our first kiss. But, all good things must come to an end, and we eventually pulled apart, both of us catching our breath.

"Golly, your lips are just as talented as your fingers," she said.

"You're not so bad yourself," I replied.

She let go of me and grabbed my hand. "C'mon! Let me show you the *real* store."

Before she pulled me away I grabbed the Zombie Bride toys from the shelf and we walked to the counter. A pretty goth chick rested her chin in her hand, clearly bored. I paid for the toys and she bagged them up for me. Then Halo leaned in and quietly said, "Witches be crazy." I assumed it was some kind of password because instantly the store went black all around us, only to light back up a second later.

The room transformed in an instant. The shirts and playful memorabilia were all gone, replaced by grimoires, magic wands, candles, and animals of all kinds in cages. I scanned the room in awe. Halo put her arm in mine, and we started walking around the room.

"We're here so I can make a bid on a very important item," she said.

"Which one?" I asked.

"A rat's egg."

"Ahh. Wait, a *what*?"

CHAPTER 9

The Rat's Egg

"Yup!" Halo exclaimed cheerily as we sauntered hand in hand through the mystical half of Hot Topic.

We leisurely ambled along while Halo pointed out the various animals up for auction. Beyond the stereotypical cats, rats, and ravens, there was a plethora of less common options. We paused to witness one of the black eggs hatch, and to my astonishment, a guinea pig emerged. The cheeky little thing glanced at me, sniffed disdainfully, then arrogantly turned his back on me.

"That little shit," I muttered.

"Haha! Well, that's a solid rejection," Halo chuckled.

"What's he good for, anyway?"

"They make excellent scouts. They can convey basic messages through their squeaks and chirps, and they're very smart—most can understand human languages the moment they hatch. Plus, they're low-maintenance familiars, and people adore their gentle nature. But this little fellow seems to have taken a disliking to you," she said with a shrug.

Together, we moved on from the haughty guinea pig, encountering even more creatures. Eventually, we stumbled upon a recently hatched piglet alongside a rather sizable egg. "Halo, no offense to this adorable little guy, but who would choose a pig as a familiar?"

She crouched down, extending her hand through the cage to scratch the piglet under its chin. Its tiny tail wiggled furiously. "Pigs are versatile creatures. They grow to be incredibly strong, and their keen noses can detect various mystical plants that potion specialists use."

"And what about this enormous egg?"

"That's probably a horse. They've fallen out of favor since cars became a thing, but they still have their uses for some witches in rural settings," she explained before leading us forward.

It seemed intriguing to me that a pig could be more useful than a horse in the modern magical world, but when I thought about it, it made perfect sense. Even so, this was all quite a lot to take in. "What are the grimoires for? Do they just contain spells? Is there an encyclopedia for witchcraft?"

Halo plucked a grimoire off a shelf but didn't open it. She merely examined the cover. "Grimoires contain spells, rituals, and various other tips and tricks for witches. They're FWBW."

"F—? Huh?"

She giggled at my confusion. "FWBW. For witches, by witches, you know? Like any other community, us witches like to leave our stamp on things. Many write up a grimoire to share their wisdom—often for sale like this one. Sometimes, they stash their deepest secrets in private ones, only passing them on to a chosen apprentice."

"Why not crack open that one?"

"Never a good idea to dive right into a grimoire. The juice inside can mess you up if you aren't skilled in casting those spells, or if they're way too potent for you. And you should definitely steer clear of them. You never know what havoc they might wreak on a non-witch like you. Plenty of non-witches have kicked the bucket with an open grimoire by their side," she said, dead serious.

I gulped. "Understood. Would've been nice to know earlier, to be honest. Just in case I got nosy about one sitting in the living room," I blurted out, feeling a tad irritated about that.

She chuckled. "Aw, you're so cute. We seal ours with magic so only members of our coven can open them. You may be one of us in a sense, but you don't quite fit that requirement. You think we'd keep something like that from you and risk our cute pet's life?" she teased, arching an eyebrow.

I grinned sheepishly. "Fair point." Then I sidled up to a shelf stocked with wands, letting my curiosity overpower my embarrassment. "How about these wands? Haven't seen you wield one before."

Halo snagged a smaller wand, its surface white with a vine pattern etched all along it. "Wands are mostly for initiates or weaker witches. We started Cherry on one when she joined us. Once we've got some experience under our belt, we tend to ditch them. They're handy for casting more potent spells than usual, but not essential. Honestly, they're kind of a crutch. I've still got mine, but you probably won't catch me with it anytime soon."

I nodded with interest at that. "I'd be down to check out your wand sometime."

She smirked, glancing at my crotch. "Goodness... Maybe I'll show you mine when you show me yours," Halo said, her voice taking on a sultry tone that mixed in an interesting way with her very sweet voice.

I coughed awkwardly, trying not to make a scene in the mystical Hot Topic. "So, what's the deal with that rat egg?"

Halo giggled. "This egg's been on my radar for over a month. I've been saving up for it."

"I thought you robbed that bank? Is it really that pricey?" I asked, furrowing my brow.

"Not money, silly," she said, pulling out a golden coin from her pocket. It emitted a slight aureate glow, making me think of a sort of holy light. "I've been saving these up."

"What are those?" I asked, feeling a bit awestruck.

"It's a Spell Token. During a witch's downtime, she can channel her leftover spell power each day to create Spell Tokens that other witches can use for extra power. It's a witch's main form of currency."

My frown returned. "But doesn't that mean the big covens hold all the power and wealth?"

Halo shrugged off my concern. "Yup, but here's the kicker: people usually want specific *types* of Spell Tokens. The New Moon and Salem covens are big with like, nearly a hundred members each, but they're full of your more run-of-the-mill witch archetypes, so their tokens aren't that valuable. In the end, they still come to us for the good stuff."

I nodded, getting the gist.

"My tokens are celestial since I'm an Angelic Witch. Celestial Tokens allow witches with no connection to heavenly magic to use my tokens and cast celestial spells."

"So, you're saying you three have unique affinities not found in the big covens?" I asked.

"Exactly! The three of us have distinct and potent affinities. That doesn't mean there aren't other witches with similar affinities out there, but it means we're not at a major disadvantage, even if they've got more people than us."

Eventually, we stumbled upon the only white egg in the store. To me, it looked like a regular egg, just larger. If I had found it in the mundane world, I wouldn't have assumed anything special about it other than its size.

"Here it is!" Halo said excitedly. "I spotted it here last week. It's an albino rat egg, and the seller wants Celestial Tokens. Since no one's bid yet, I'm going to make the buyout offer—fifteen full Celestial Tokens. Then I'll finally have a familiar!"

Confusion clouded my expression. "I thought I was your familiar."

She hushed me and quickly glanced around to make sure no one was close. "Shh. You're my familiar, but you're what we call a Greater Familiar—shared among our whole coven, and with unique powers connected to the coven's core members," she whispered before changing the subject a bit and talking louder. "This here's a personal, or Lesser Familiar. Not quite the same thing."

I nodded, still super curious about how it all worked. Mating Familiars, Lesser Familiars, Sentinel Familiars, and Greater Familiars... I wondered how many types there were. I watched as the sale happened, realizing it was just like any other silent auction. She wrote down her witch name and her offer—*Halo Kitty, 15 Celestial Tokens*—then left the paper and gave her fifteen tokens to the cute goth chick behind the counter.

I grinned at her excitement. I assumed that there were other witches with Celestial Tokens out there. Since none had bid yet after a month, I couldn't help but think this egg wasn't all that special. Another possibility was that Celestial Tokens were hard to come by. In any case, it clearly meant a lot to her, so I was happy for her.

The clerk took the items and said, "A broomstick courier will probably deliver the rat to you later tonight, assuming the seller takes the buyout. But, between you and me, she will."

My eyebrows shot up. *They can fly on broomsticks?!* Halo grabbed my arm and snuggled up to me as we left the store. "You can fly on broomsticks?" I said, all excited, not able to keep my wonder at the fact to myself.

"Yep. We can," she said.

"What about me? Can I fly on broomsticks too? Since I'm your familiar?" I asked, hope shining in my eyes.

She frowned at me and bit her lip. "No, sorry, Logan. You can't fly one on your own, and you're too big to join us on ours. It would take up way too much magic to get around quickly with you that way. When we're with you, we're walking or taking a car—in rare circumstances we may be able to use a ritual to teleport. But—I don't mind. I'm really enjoying the extra time we get to spend together," she said, squeezing my arm a bit tighter.

You could hear the disappointment in my voice, but I didn't let it get me down. "Oh, gotcha. But hey, I like hanging out with you too."

She must have seen I was bummed and tried to cheer me up. "Well, maybe in the future we can cast a spell so you can fly by yourself. That could be worth a shot, right?"

I grinned and slipped my arm out from hers, then slung it around her shoulder, bringing her in closer. Her hand rested on my waist as we strolled along. We fell into a comfortable silence until we hopped into the car.

• ♥ • ♥ • ♥ • ♥ • ♥ •

"Logan, today has been gosh-darn amazing. You've been the ultimate pretend boyfriend," she said, her lashes fluttering and hearts practically in her eyes. I could tell she had a lot of fun, and honestly, I did too. Plus, I learned a lot in the back half of the trip.

"I mean, I am pretty awesome, right?" I shot back with a cheeky grin.

She playfully swatted my arm with an exaggerated eye roll. "You're so cringe."

I cracked up. "I'm just kidding. Today was fantastic."

Halo suddenly struggled to maintain eye contact with me, and she spoke quietly as she asked, "Logan—Alpha told me she told you her real name. Is it true?"

I nodded, my face going a bit more serious. "Yeah. She did. Alice Farrow."

"Then...I wanna tell you too, okay? Because I think you're worth it, and I want you to feel the pressure."

I laughed. "What pressure?"

"The pressure that a pretty girl likes you a lot and is putting her trust in you. Got it?" she asked as she licked her lips and stared up into my eyes.

"Got it."

She paused for a minute. "It's...Serena." Her gaze dropped slightly, pink coloring her cheeks.

I lifted her chin until her blue eyes met mine. "Serena? That's a very pretty name."

"Yup," she said nervously while pointing at herself with both thumbs, attempting a playful tone. "Serena Goulding, aka Halo Kitty."

I beamed. "Sure thing, *Serena*. Your name is just as wonderful as the rest of you."

The moment her name slipped from my lips, the vulnerability was gone, replaced by a hunger that burned in her eyes. "Say it again..."

"What? How gorgeous you are—*Serena*?"

Halo dove at me with insane passion, her lips crashing into mine like a violent wave against the shore. She bit down on my lower lip, almost drawing blood, as she climbed into my lap and straddled me. Her hips ground into mine like she couldn't wait any longer, and before I knew it, my seat fell back, leaving me lying flat.

"Holy goodness, I need you. I need you inside me so darn bad." Her hands pawed at the hem of my shirt, pulling it up and over my head. As I helped get it off, I felt her nails digging into my skin, leaving ten hot scratches down my chest and abs.

Halo didn't seem like the type to lose her cool all that much, so hearing her get so passionate got me all worked up. "Fuck. I want you too."

She wasted no time in undoing my jeans and freeing my manhood. Her hand wrapped around it, and she stared down, her eyes going wide, and mouth dropping open. "Holy shoot! Cherry wasn't fudging kidding! I mean, I saw it before, and it was big, but it wasn't *this* huge!" Her gaze shifted to me, a look of total disbelief.

I smirked. "It gets a bit bigger when it's hard. Brace yourself. We'll just take it slow at first," I suggested.

The hunger never left her eyes, and she set her jaw. "Nope. I need you inside me now—all the way in. I've been a virgin my whole life and I never felt tired of it until I met you...now, all I can think about is having you make love to me." She flipped up her skirt, tucking a part of it into the waistband. Next, she pulled her panties to the side and positioned my tip against her tight, dripping entrance. Her palm pressed against her pelvis before she lowered herself, hilting me inside of her. "OH! cheese n' rice! Nyah!"

I groaned as her tight walls gripped my shaft, a hell of a welcome into her pussy. My jaw dropped at the immense pleasure that bordered on pain as her muscles tightened even more. I watched her hand glow a golden hue before her grimace of pain instantly turned into a sigh of relief. "Healing spell?" I asked.

Her eyes were closed, and she bit her lip but nodded. "Holy heck. It feels so...full. Y—you're so deep inside—where no other man has ever been or will ever be!" Halo gently circled her hips, testing the waters. While her healing spell helped her adjust to my size, it was still the tightest fit I'd ever experienced before. "I've been thinking about this since the moment I first laid eyes on you."

I couldn't wait for her to do more than her teasing circles. I felt our connection flaring, only making me feel even closer to this absolute beauty, and I grabbed her hips and lifted her before dropping her back down. She squealed in surprise before the pleasure took over. "EEK! Logan-nyaah! Your cock feels so—God, yes!" It only took a few times before Halo took over and started bouncing. The sounds of her ass slapping against my thighs joined our chorus of moans. She leaned forward, one hand on the car door, the other on the center console, and rode me like her life depended on it.

"Shhoot! Ah! Your dick feels so ffffucking–" Halo said before her eyes widened and she slapped one hand over her mouth. Despite the look of shock on her face, she never stopped riding me and moaning through her hand. After a moment, she pulled it away and closed her eyes as she picked up her pace. "Gosh! Ah! Pardon my–mmm yes! LanguaAh! Yes, baby!"

I would have chuckled at that if I wasn't busy lifting her top and bra, freeing her from their constraints and letting her bouncing breasts sway. I massaged them, and took turns pulling and playing with her pretty pink nipples. As I pinched them, I felt her wetness increase, her muscles tense, and I knew she was reaching her first orgasm. "Logan! I'm about to—Oh my GOD! I'm cumming! Ah! I'm—it's gonna get *all over*!"

Her juices forced their way out between us, making a mess of my jeans, but I didn't care. While her ability to move on her own was diminishing because of the spasms that rocked her body, I took hold of her slender waist once again and lifted, dropped, and thrust, fucking her harder. It sent her immediately into another round of bliss.

"I—Oh, yes! Harder, baby! Harder! Mmm—yeah just like that! Ah! Yeah!"

Sweat droplets formed on my brow as I grunted and found another gear, meeting her request.

"Ye—ye—ye—YES! Ooh, Log—ahn! Ahh!" I wasn't sure how much longer I could last. Halo's pussy felt too good, and with our magical connection flaring, it was becoming too much. But her begging was the final straw for me. "Logan! P-Please! I need it inside me! Fill my little pussy until I'm overflowing! I—Ah!" she cried out as she reached yet another apex of pleasure—or maybe the first one never ended. I was overwhelmed by the intensity of her pleas and the forceful contractions of her walls, which made it hard for me to hold back.

"It's about to happen," I warned her. My cock thickened and pulsed inside of her, but I kept thrusting. Every motion caused more and more of my hot seed to fill her womb.

"Mmm. Gosh, yes! Keep cumming! I want it all, honey. Aghh!" Halo threw her head back, leaning against the steering wheel, accidentally sounding the horn. Lost in her blissful spasms, she didn't move from the horn right away. Only after they settled did she fall forward onto me, letting her lips lock with mine. "Logan..." she whined, catching her breath. "You came so much, I'm gonna make a mess of my seat when I move."

"My jeans are already ruined," I commented.

She pulled back from my lips and grinned a drunken grin. "I wanna frame those jeans. Your cum is all mixed up with my cum," she sighed contentedly.

I couldn't help it. I laughed. She laughed along with me, both of us breathing hard—until I heard a tapping on the windshield. Halo shot up, and we both looked at the female security guard who stood at the driver's side window with flushed cheeks.

She didn't bother waiting for us to roll down the window, instead raising her voice loud enough for us to hear. "You two—uh—you can't do that here. I'm gonna have to ask you to leave," the guard said.

Halo's face turned into a cherry, and she quickly pulled off of me and into her seat, fixing her clothes. I was still in shock, staring at the other woman who, I realized, wasn't staring at me. She licked her lips, and I followed her gaze to see my cum-covered cock still standing fully erect, and in a rush, I pulled up my pants to cover it up. I felt as if a spell had been broken when the guard shook her head as if clearing out the cobwebs, and her blush deepened when she met my eyes.

I offered a wry smile. "Sorry about that, ma'am."

"Uh—yeah," she replied with heavy breaths. She seemed reluctant as she said, "Just—uh—don't let it happen again, alright?"

As I pulled my shirt back on, I suspected she had been there long before Halo accidentally sounded the horn, and only then stopped us. "We'll make sure we go somewhere more private next time. I apologize."

"Y-yeah. You do that. Have a good day, sir." Then the guard quickly walked away.

In response to her leaving, I fired up the car, shooting Halo a glance. She was nibbling her finger with a huge grin and rosy cheeks. "Guess that's my bad, hehe!" she giggled.

I just chuckled and shook my head. "Twice in one outing? It's almost like you enjoy getting caught."

She strapped in and leaned into my shoulder with her hand on my lap. It was intimate, but not in a sexy way. It was...vulnerable, I guess. Close. "Logan? Was it—did I do a good job? It was my first time and all..." she asked nervously.

I turned and planted a kiss on her forehead, eliciting a smile. "Certainly got my seal of approval."

She let out a soft giggle before a big yawn escaped her. Her voice got quieter as she spoke.

"Good, glad to hear. Thanks for today, Logan. I had a—*yawn*—blast."

Before I could say anything back, she was out like a light. I froze, making sure not to jostle her. As she continued to snooze, I sat there in silence, not daring to turn on the radio and risk waking the sleeping beauty next to me. I chuckled as her wings popped back out while she was resting.

When we left the house, I thought today would just be a goofy adventure, exploring more of the magical world I stumbled into while doing some light clothes shopping. It was that, but also a lot more. I'd been with a few girls before and shared some intimate moments, but this was different. It was hard to tell if it was the magical bond between us or just us clicking. *Probably both.*

Love was never really my thing, especially growing up without a family or real friends. I didn't really believe in the concept all that much. Why would I? But damn, whenever I looked at any of the witches I was bound to, my heart did a little flip—even Alpha, but especially Cherry and now Halo. I couldn't help but wonder, *Is this what it's like when you're falling for someone?*

I guessed that time would tell if that were the case. But glancing down at the pigtailed blonde as she slept, I knew I wanted to find out. No matter what lay ahead, one thing was certain. *I'm ready to see where this flying broomstick takes me.*

Wincing at the thought, I put the car in drive, starting our trip home. My cheesy metaphor was a disappointing reminder that I couldn't fly on broomsticks. But before I could come up with a better metaphor that didn't involve brooms, my thoughts were swept away by the soft snores coming from the beauty next to me.

CHAPTER 10

Ms. Cola

Only one day had passed, and there was still zilch about the Lunar Amulet as far as news circulating in the witch community. No one came pounding on our door either, so that was promising.

Still, after the security guard incident in the mall parking lot, Alpha didn't want us going anywhere if we didn't have to—at least not until we warded the Lunar Amulet with obfuscation magic. So, we kept ourselves occupied indoors, deciding to play it safe and lie low as much as we could.

Waking up with Cherry's lips wrapped around my cock felt like a goddamn blessing every morning. I tried not to dwell on how miserably sad I would feel after her week was up because the thought always brought a tear to my eye. I was getting spoiled by her attention and got too used to starting my day with a sweet release. Screw Folgers—at this point, they needed a new slogan.

This morning I woke up barely pre-climax with Cherry fingering herself to completion just as I was about to finish in her throat. I'd been up late the night before, having some quality alone time with Halo in her room. I must have been dead tired to almost sleep through Cherry's blowjob, I realized. Lucky for me, after she gulped down the first load, she said it didn't count if I slept through most of it and demanded a do-over. Being the gentleman I am, I obliged.

After several long minutes full of licks and kisses among other things, Cherry was swallowing for a second time. When she was done, she crawled up to cuddle with me, resting her head on my shoulder.

Cherry's finger traced patterns on my chest. "We're going to spend the day together. Just you and me, baby."

I turned my head to look at her and she adjusted hers so I could see her face rather than the top of her head. Grinning, I asked, "You don't think the others will try to steal me away from you?"

She shook her head with a fanged smile. "Nope. Halo has to create more Spell Tokens today since she spent most of her spare celestial ones on the rat egg, and Alpha's busy planning for the ritual. So that means I've got you all to myself."

Leaning in, I kissed her forehead. "So, what'd you have in mind? I don't think Alpha wants us to go out and about yet."

"You can call me Ms. Cola, because this time, I'm your teacher, baby," Cherry said while bopping my nose with one finger.

I cocked a questioning eyebrow. "Oh, really? Well, Ms. Cola, what's the subject today?"

She patted me twice on the chest. "You'll find that out once you're dressed and ready for class." Then she hopped out of the bed, swaying her hips on the way to the door.

What can I say? I took the bait and stared the entire time, grinning like a fool. Cherry looked back as she opened the door, catching me in my obvious leer. She winked. "Don't be late. Meet me in my room ASAFP. I'll be there soon." Cherry sauntered off, gently closing the door behind her.

I dressed quickly and went to Cherry's room. An oddly familiar table and chairs sat in the middle of it. They hadn't been there the last time I was here, I noted. "Is that the—"

"The table from the Student Union? Yup!" Cherry said as she walked into the room holding a large brown paper sack with a receipt stapled to it. "I consider it a holy relic now, so I'm going to keep it."

I chuckled, running my hand across the smooth surface. "You stole it? Is it really the same one?" My hand brushed a rough spot and I looked down. Someone had recently carved a heart into the wood with 'C + L' written inside. Cherry's trademark bat wings crossing the plus sign clued me in on who the artist in question was. "Did *you* carve this?" I smirked as I asked the obvious question.

Her eyes shot to the table and her cheeks flushed a red. She tried to act confused, setting the bag on the table and scratching her chin as she examined the carving. She failed miserably. "N—no. It wasn't me. Huh? That's quite the coincidence." Then, she promptly changed the subject. "Sit. I'm teaching you about spells today." Cherry pulled a grimoire and a folder of papers off the shelf, placing them on the table.

My brows shot up and I could swear there were stars in my eyes. "I'm going to learn spells?! Are there, like, reagents or something I need in the bag?"

Cherry snickered, clearly laughing at my eagerness in a rather deflating way. Her small laugh crushed my hopes. "No, you still can't cast spells, silly." She pointed at the bag. "The bag is your breakfast."

I frowned. "Then why am I learning about spells?"

"Alpha said something about you learning to recognize some of them. It'll help you in battle or something like that." She shrugged. "I don't even care why. I just need to get through this stuff, and then we can have some fun together." Then she tossed me a wink while opening the grimoire.

Opening the bag I found a sausage breakfast sandwich, a hash brown, and a bottled orange juice. I quietly started eating as Cherry finished her preparations. Sinking my teeth into the scrumptious-looking sandwich, my eyes went wide. "Where did you get this from? This is incredible. Is it some magical restaurant or something?"

Without looking up from a few pages she was shuffling in her hands, she said, "Nah. Ordered that on Door Dart. It's from *This Hole In The Wall That Serves Great Breakfast Food*."

"What's the name of the place?" I asked, still enraptured by the flavors on my tongue.

She shrugged. "That's its name. *This Hole In The Wall That Serves Great Breakfast Food*."

"That's a really long and oddly specific name, but I kind of appreciate it," I muttered. But soon enough I moved on from that and enjoyed the rest of my meal, making sure to eat over the wrappers so I didn't leave any crumbs behind. "Okay! So, let's get this crackin'. I've actually been meaning to ask some questions about your spells for a while."

Cherry had papers spread out in a chaotic mess all over the table, but she seemed to know what she was doing, so I didn't question it. She looked up at me, a slightly annoyed expression on her face. Then she grinned. "Fine, ask whatever you want. You only get three questions," she said with a wink.

I chuckled at the reference to our first encounter. "Okay, deal. What language are you using when you cast spells?"

She flipped to a specific page in her grimoire. "Who cares what it's called? It's some ancient language passed down by witches over the centuries. People say that most witches used to speak it fluently, but not anymore. We only use it for spells and rituals now."

It was hard to argue with her logic. Did it really matter if I knew the language's name or not? I guess not. "Alright, but why use that specific language instead of English?"

A pen appeared in Cherry's hand with a puff of smoke and she set it on the table. Her eyes glowed red as she pointed at the pen and said, "Jump." The pen did a small flip on the table. Now I was really confused. If the spell worked with English, it made no sense for them to learn this ancient forgotten language.

Before I could voice that opinion, Cherry's eyes glowed again, still pointing at the pen she said, "Jingen." The pen launched from the table until it hit the ceiling and fell back down. She smirked. "That's why. For whatever reason, it channels the magic better. Don't ask me how because you'd have to be someone like Morgan le Fay to understand how that shit actually works."

Promptly, I closed my mouth, which I'd only just realized was hanging open. The difference in the spell's strength was enormous, so that settled that question in my mind well enough. I furrowed my brow. With only one question left I needed to get a little creative. "Morgan le Fay was just some fictional evil witch from the King Arthur tales."

Her eyes slit with suspicion but she took the bait. "That's where you're wrong. She was as real as you or me. It's rumored that she was one of the witches who helped revive the ancient language. And, she wasn't evil. Well, not all of the time. She was pretty complicated—a lot of back-and-forth stuff. It's not like King Arthur was a saint or anything. He's just a classic case of the winners writing history and declaring themselves the good guys."

Scratching my chin in thought, I said, "Man, stinks she lost to him. Sounds like she didn't deserve to go out like that."

Cherry blew a raspberry. "Sppt. Wrong again, Mr. Morrison. Don't you worry, 'cause Ms. Cola will instruct you properly. No one knows if she's dead or not. She was so powerful, who knows what kind of spells or magic she had at her disposal? For all we know, she created a pocket dimension somewhere with her own little world inside it, and still lives there to this day. It wouldn't be the first case like that."

I blinked. It took several moments for me to process that information. "That doesn't seem possible."

She shrugged. "Well, it is. Now, ask your last question so we can move on and get the boring stuff over with already."

Shaking my head, I set those thoughts aside. Then I grinned. "You know what, I think I'll save the last one for later."

Cherry playfully rolled her eyes and picked up one of the pages she had lying about. "Fine. We'll start with the basics and cover some of the spells we use to help you transform."

• ♥ • ♥ • ♥ • ♥ • ♥ •

We spent the next few hours reviewing various spells and what they meant. After that, Cherry gave me a list of the common spells the girls used in battle and told me I could memorize those on my own.

As the lesson went on and I looked over some from the list, I could see why Alpha wanted me to know them. Depending on what type of attack spell I heard them calling out, I could react accordingly even if I didn't have a line of sight on what they were doing. Still, memorizing this much would take a while, and even longer to apply it.

She led me to the kitchen where we made some chicken nuggets, or 'chicky nug-nugs' as

Cherry liked to call them, for lunch. I asked what we were doing next, and she triumphantly declared that to be my third question. It seemed that just because our study time was over, it didn't mean Cherry was done teaching me yet.

After lunch, Cherry wanted to school me in video games. We parked ourselves on the floor in front of the old rabbit ear TV. Cherry opened the cabinet of the TV stand below it, revealing a classic Super Nintendo with none other than Street Fighter II locked in. She passed me a controller and started it all up. As I navigated the character select screen, I asked, "Are you like a pro gamer?"

She tapped around on the D-pad a few times, trying to decide who to choose. "Not really. It's not like I'm on some competitive esports team or trying to be a famous streamer or anything like that. We just have some downtime here and there and it's a fun way to pass the time."

"Fair enough. Are you ready to get your butt kicked?" I asked with a smile as I selected Ryu.

Cherry landed on Chun-Li and slowly turned her head to face me. Her eyes were glowing. "You want a piece of this? Who am I kidding?" she lowered a hand down to her side as if she were displaying herself as a prize on a game show and winked. "Of course, you want a piece of this. Bring it on, big boy."

With a 'Round 1. Fight!' it was go time. It was at this moment that Cherry learned I had very little experience playing video games. She caught me off guard, jumping with a flip to dodge my punch, and followed it up with a roundhouse kick to the back of my character's head. As the match went on she proceeded to prove her timing and skill far surpassed my own. Round 2 came and went much the same. When she hit me with a jumping kick, the announcer shouted 'KO', and Cherry threw her arms in the air with a radiant smile.

She shouted, "All bow down to the glorious Cherry Cola!"

"She's lucky I wasn't the one holding the controller, or things would've gone real different," Alpha announced as she strolled into the room.

Cherry turned, squinting at her furry-eared leader. "That's only 'cause you cheat!"

Alpha let out an exasperated sigh. "I don't know how many times I have to tell you. Uppercutting you every time you stupidly jump isn't cheating."

"Sounds like something a cheater would say," Cherry muttered with a huff and a puff.

I shook my head, amused, then turned my attention to Alpha. "Anything up with you this morning?"

"I heard Cherry's battle cries and wanted to make sure that she went over the spells with you," the redhead explained.

"Yes! You know I always do my job. If that's all, you're cutting into my Logan time. Shoo! Shoo!" Cherry said, waving Alpha away.

Alpha rolled her eyes. "Fine, but my money's on Logan next match," she said, exiting the room with a happily swaying tail.

The Vampire Witch wasted no time, turning back to the screen. "Alright, you ready?"

Cherry's excitement was infectious. At that moment, seeing the bright fanged smile on her face, I forgot all about magic, witchcraft, and familiars. I just... kind of stared for a minute.

Her brow furrowed. "What?" She reached up, touching her cheek. "Is there something on my face?"

Shaking my head, I chuckled. "No. I was just wondering, does this count as a date?"

Crimson eyes flashed, but then she looked around shyly. "No way. This can't count as a date. We're in the living room playing video games. This is just hanging out."

"I don't know, I mean, people have staycations right? Isn't this kinda like that but with a date?" I prodded.

Her eyes narrowed playfully as she fought off a smile. "You really want this to be a date, huh? Too bad." She stuck her tongue out at me before looking back to the screen with a smile while selecting her character. Then, without looking back at me, she scooted over until our legs were touching.

"Hmmm...What do you say we play for it? If I win, it's a date, and if you win, it's not." I held out my hand.

Cherry gave me a raspberry and a wink, which was a really odd combination, but she kinda made it work. "Sppt! Easiest bet I ever won!" Then she shook my hand.

This time, I selected E. Honda, the sumo guy. The fight announcement popped up on the screen and I went full button mash on her. Cherry tried to hit me with combos and grabs, but my flurry of random strikes proved to be too much for her as I took her down in round one.

She narrowed her eyes at me. "You little—"

"Better pay attention! Round two is starting!" I interrupted.

This time, I came at her and my luck wasn't so good. I ended up jumping and she caught me on my descent with a high kick, sending my character flying back. And as I tried to stand, she pelted me with a barrage of combos. Cherry's relentless assault ended round two.

"You're going down!" she shouted.

At first, I thought she was right, and all was lost as round three was in full swing, and things had heated up. But with a quarter of my health left I managed to back away from her assault before coming back at her with an endless stream of random button presses resulting in kicks, punches, and leg sweeps. Before we knew it, we were both down to an eighth of our health bar. Cherry came in for a punch and I blocked. I was practically licking my chops as I furiously tried to land the finishing blow.

Then it happened. The leg sweep felt around the world. It seemed like slow motion as the character squatted, narrowly avoiding a punch, and spun, its heel connecting. My health bar dropped to zero. "KO!" shouted the game's announcer.

Cherry dropped the controller and wriggled in joy. "Take that, button masher! How dare you challenge the mighty Cherry Cola! Victory is mine! It's not a date! We're just two people hanging out who just so happen to be madly in love and who have a lot of sexual interactions with each other! Muahahaha!" she shouted with an evil laugh.

Unable to help myself, I snickered at her outburst.

"I'll teach you to laugh at Cherry Cola!" she shouted playfully. She turned and practically tackled me to the ground. We fell back in a heap of laughter.

"Oh yeah!" I said, then I reached down and tickled her sides.

Cherry started laughing hysterically as she rolled over and I followed, coming up to my knees as she squirmed to try and free herself from my wrath. "Logan! Logan! Stop! Hahaha! No more! You win!"

I stopped tickling her as we both caught our breath, our laughter slowly fading. Reaching for her, I brushed the hair from Cherry's face, letting it join the rest that was fanned out on the floor under her. Crimson eyes met mine, and they glowed brightly. I glanced at her lips, and she did the same to mine. Still smiling, I lowered myself until we kissed.

Before the kiss went very far, Cherry started giggling. I pulled back just enough to let her speak. "It's still not a date. But I think I'll let you take me on one if you want," she declared before pushing her mouth back into mine.

CHAPTER 11

Harpy and the Beast

Our last day of isolation had finally come. Tonight was the night of the full moon. Alpha chose this night because this was when the amulet boosted the girls' power the most, and she wanted the strongest ward they could create to protect and hide it from prying eyes.

The four of us piled into the girls' car, and Alpha drove us out to the forest. Traveling with the amulet in our possession was risky, so we kept chatter to a minimum on the way. Everyone remained vigilant and kept their eyes peeled. Even though the odds of trouble seemed low at this point, we had to be careful.

Halo and Alpha cast spells to grant themselves the same night vision that Cherry and I enjoyed. Blue and yellow eyes glowed brightly in the dark. Their mystical displays still fascinated me. I wondered if the bit of jealousy I felt, knowing I couldn't use magic on my own, would ever go away.

It was unreasonable to fixate on it in any case—I could shapeshift and had the physique of an olympian thanks to them. It's not like I wasn't doing well for myself in these witches' care.

As we entered a large clearing, the moon shone down on us in a silvery glow. I watched as all three beauties undressed in front of me. Seeing Alpha nude for the first time, I couldn't help but take special note of her muscular, yet very feminine body. I did my best to ignore my growing excitement and focus on the task at hand, though. We weren't here to fool around.

Alpha walked up to me, and I failed miserably as I tried not to watch her breasts jiggling with each step. She smirked as I pried my eyes up to meet hers.

"Here's a quick recap on your duties tonight. We need you to protect us while we complete our ritual. This forest is a powerful place, and the perfect location to ward the amulet, but Dark Fey creatures live in these woods. The ritual's power will probably attract them, and if it does, they will attack. They are very territorial beings, and they hate witches. If the Dark Fey come, you kill as many as you have to. Can you do this for us?"

I firmed my resolve and nodded. "Yes. I'll keep you safe, don't worry."

She stepped closer, grabbed the back of my neck, and kissed me. My hands rested on her hips as we shared a more passionate kiss than our first. The glow of our contract lit up around us before condensing and forming a tattoo on the back of our right hands. Alpha ended the kiss, her face all business despite the flush creeping up her neck. I stared at her expectantly as she took several steps back.

She pointed a finger at me and said, "Borden eh eas!" Her hand flashed a vibrant yellow, and I felt my body change.

I chucked my clothes into my dimensional storage as thick black fur sprouted all over my body, and my skin thickened, the color changing into a deep gray. My hands and feet morphed into massive paws with huge, deadly, razor-sharp claws jutting out. I dropped to all fours, feeling my chest, legs, and muscles bulging to monstrous proportions, while a massive tail unfurled behind me. My face stretched and contorted into a vicious maw, my teeth extending into deadly fangs the size of kitchen knives.

I thrust my colossal head to the sky and let out a deafening roar. Sleeping birds scattered in terror at the monstrous sound. My enhanced hearing easily picked up the sound of a camera. Glancing down at the three small and gorgeous witches, I spotted a smiling Halo shrugging and stashing her phone away.

The girls switched to business mode now that their protector was primed. They clasped hands with the amulet resting on the ground at the center of their small circle. The trio began chanting in an unfamiliar tongue—unfamiliar to me, anyway. At first I thought it might be latin, but this time it seemed...like something else. Their voices took on an almost ghostly quality that carried through the air, bouncing off the trees. The trio's chorus of three voices soon seemed to multiply to six, then twelve. The Lunar Amulet was engulfed in a bright blue glow. As soon as they commenced their bizarre dance around the amulet, a scent hit me. Some instinct told me that the aforementioned Dark Fey were en route already.

I bellowed with rage, thinking the beast's own thoughts like they were mine. *How dare these puny little insects attempt to harm my mates! What absurd delusions they harbor, thinking they owned any territory where my majestic paws tread.*

The first Fey came into view, stopping at the edge of the treeline with a look of murder in its beady black eye. "Witches!" it screeched. "Kill the witches!"

Without hesitation, I rushed forward and lashed out, slashing across its feeble chest, nearly tearing it apart. Too easy. Almost boring.

They truly were pathetic creatures. They resembled what I imagined fairies might look like, only they were a deep gray, almost black, with bat-like wings, pitch-black eyes, tiny sharp teeth, and sharp claws on their hands and feet. But compared to the grandeur of my form, they were nothing.

Three more to the south—I darted around the circle, sparing only a moment to ensure the girls' safety, slashing the first fey while grabbing the second in my jaws. The first one dropped dead instantly, and I savored the taste of magical blood as I chewed on the second fey's corpse.

A searing pain scorched my back as the third raked a claw just deep enough to penetrate my skin. Roaring in fury I spun, batting it from the air and slamming it to the ground, crushing it beneath my paw.

I spat out the dead fey in my mouth, knowing this wasn't the time for feasting. A group of ten approached from the north, much too close for me to dispatch them all at my current speed before they reached my girls in the circle. And after seeing how deep they managed to get into my skin, I knew all too well how fatal that could be for one of my girls if they were caught unaware.

Adrenaline surged through my veins, and the world slowed. I was upon them in a flash, leaping into the air, soaring over the ritual circle and covering more than fifty feet in a single bound. Each paw left nothing but fey goo splattered on the ground as I landed. The little assholes were still trying to ignore me. What a useless tactic against my mystical might.

Their wings were way too slow in my adrenaline-fueled heightened state. Three more dropped into a pool of black blood with a single swipe. One turned back and went for my face. I barely moved my head an inch, narrowly avoiding the loss of an eye. But the little bastard cut a gouge just above it. Blood trickled down, slightly obscuring part of my vision.

Like a lightning strike my maw shot up, snatching it from the air and biting it in half. The last two went for Alpha, but there was no way I'd let them harm my pack. I was there just in time, shredding one with a claw and the other with my teeth.

I snarled as I scanned for more enemies, but none came. With a shout, I let out a mighty roar of triumph. This was *my* territory, *my* pack, and *my* mates to breed—and no scrawny little fairy would take any of it from me.

Panting, I listened. The singing had stopped, and I looked down at my beautiful mates, all smiling up at me. Their ritual was complete, and I'd succeeded in my task.

I strode over, letting my paws leave huge tracks, and settled down in front of them. Alpha leaned in, hugging my massive head, heedless of the blood as she scratched behind my ear. "Good pet," she cooed, nuzzling me sweetly. My enormous tail wagged in time with hers, creating a soft breeze, and I let out a low, happy growl. "Such a good boy, Logan. Mommy's talented boy," Alpha praised me. "Yes you are! Yes you are!"

I emitted a soft bark—well, soft for a monstrous behemoth of a beast, anyway.

"Sure. Anything for Mommy's good boy. Halo, heal him," Alpha commanded.

"Of course! It'd be my pleasure." Halo placed one hand on my forehead and another on my back. Golden light emanated from her hands, healing my wounds.

Alpha pointed a finger at me. "Borden eh humensel!"

The yellow flash of her hand triggered my transformation. I waited for the right moment, then summoned my clothing from my dimensional storage and stood. Back in my human form, I realized there was an awful taste in my mouth.

"Uh, Logan?" Halo said, pointing to her kissable lips. "You've got a little something..."

And then I remembered feasting on the Dark Fey bodies and relishing the taste of their blood. "Ew, gross!" The girls all laughed as I frantically spat out black blood. *I really need to get a grip on my personality when I shift.* The activation of my powers had turned me into such a monster, not just physically, but changing the way I thought and experienced the world, too. I decided I'd bring it up another time if it became a problem, but for now, my only issue was the horrifying taste in my mouth.

"Hold on. Let me," Halo said, pressing a finger to my lips. "Cloon end revernie. And now, just to make sure it worked..." She leaned in and started kissing me. Her tongue explored my mouth, and the awful flavor vanished, replaced with the Angelic Witch's refreshing maple syrup flavor.

"Enough," Alpha growled. "I already miss the other version of him."

"I just had to check and see if my spell worked," Halo innocently chirped as she pulled away from my lips, a bead of spit connecting us.

"AH—HEM!" Cherry exclaimed loudly. "You damn well knew the spell worked."

Halo let me go, and I caught her smirking at Cherry as she walked away. Cherry never stopped glaring at her as she went. All three girls got dressed again, and we walked out of the woods together. We had no issues on our way back to the car, and I assumed that might have had something to do with the display of power we showed in the clearing. *Probably scared off any threats,* I noted.

Alpha took the driver's seat again. I got in the back, only to be surprised by Cherry climbing in on the other side while Halo followed me in, leaving me stuck in the middle with a girl on my left and right. "No one wants to sit up front?" I sheepishly asked. "It's a bit of a tight fit back here."

"Gosh, that's not the only thing in here that's a tight fit," Halo said, grinning impishly at me.

Cherry ignored Halo and looked at me with an exaggerated look of surprise. It wasn't convincing. "You know what, baby?" she asked as she looked far too thoughtful while tapping her lips with a finger. "I think you're right! We are pretty crammed back here. Oh! I have an idea!" Then she pulled my arm over her shoulder and laid her head against my chest. She threw her legs over mine and pressed her body into me as much as she could. "Ahh," she said, as if she just took a refreshing sip of capri sun. "This is much better."

I smirked. "Works for me."

Halo narrowed her eyes as she glared at Cherry. Then she did the same. "Yes... much better."

Alpha snorted when she looked through the rearview mirror at us and quirked a brow. "Pathetic sluts."

I smiled wryly and shrugged.

"Let's focus on more interesting topics. Did you all see how badass Logan looked using my affinity?" Alpha asked.

Halo perked up and pulled out her phone. "Heavens, yes! He was so scary!" She unlocked her phone, and I noticed the background was a picture of me, but one taken at least days before we met, when they were still scouting me. She caught me looking and blushed.

"We'll talk about that later," I said with mock sternness.

She opened the gallery and showed me the pictures she had taken of both forms I'd used so far. My jaw dropped. I could only see a few parts of my body when I shifted, so seeing in full just what I looked like from another person's perspective blew my mind. "See how cool you look!" Halo squealed.

My attention turned to Cherry as she held up her phone. "I've got way better pictures of you on my phone. Videos too."

My eyebrows shot up as I looked at a selfie of Cherry with a fanged smile and her tongue sticking out. The tip of my cock rested against her tongue, and she was winking at the camera. She flipped to the next, and it was a video of her crimson eyes staring into the camera as she deep-throated me. Even though I'd grown accustomed to the sight, it still aroused me to no end.

A breathy whisper came from beside me as Halo watched. "Flipping hot."

I noticed Cherry smirking, no doubt having heard the blonde's words.

I mentally waddled out of their horny conversational detour. "Wait a minute, you filmed that while I was sleeping, didn't you?!"

Cherry blushed. "I mean—you can't prove that it's you—unless..." she stared at my crotch.

I chuckled. "I'm not pulling my dick out in the car again."

"You weren't the one that pulled it out last time," Halo said with a naughty grin.

"See! You can't prove it was you, so I did nothing wrong," she said, sticking her tongue out at me.

Alpha chimed in, "Hey, Cherry, how many dicks have you sucked before?"

"One. This mouth is exclusively for Logan's cock!" Cherry proudly declared.

"So, if you've never sucked anyone else's cock but Logan's, who's that in your video?" Halo asked with a smug grin.

"This proves nothing!" Cherry pouted and put her phone away.

Halo and I laughed, and I leaned my head back to relax, letting the girls chat for a bit until Alpha mentioned something about breakfast and wanting bacon and eggs. The mention of eggs made me realize something. "Halo, do you think us being away from home for the ritual could have affected the store's ability to deliver your rat egg?"

Halo's eyes bulged. "Darn! Hold on." She picked up her phone and called the Hot Topic in a hurry. Being around the girls enhanced my senses, so I could make out the voice of the same friendly goth chick from the other day.

"Halo! I'm so glad you called. The courier couldn't find you. We have your egg here at the store," the girl said.

"Awesome! Can I swing by and pick it up within an hour or two?"

"Yeah, that's fine. We'll see you soon!" the clerk said before hanging up.

• ♥ • ♥ • ♥ • ♥ • ♥ •

After swinging by the mall so Halo could run in and pick up her egg, we made the much shorter drive home. We entered the house, and Halo squealed in excitement, carrying her white egg as if it were a child and going to her room. The other girls weren't nearly as excited about it, understandably so.

"I don't know why she's so pumped about an albino rat. There are way better familiars out there than a rat," Alpha said.

"I know, right? I don't see what makes it so special," Cherry said.

I shrugged. "I guess it doesn't really matter, does it? It's Halo's familiar, and she's stoked about it. Let's just be happy for her."

They reluctantly agreed.

I took a seat on the couch and settled in. "Do either of you have familiars?"

Cherry shook her head.

Alpha sat taller with a look of pride. "I do. He's a reddish-colored box turtle. I named him Akimbo."

I perked up at that. "How come I haven't seen him?"

"He mostly lives in the terrarium in my room. He's slow to trust newcomers. You should have seen when I introduced him to Cherry," Alpha said, laughing.

"Fucking Akimbo," Cherry grumbled at the memory.

I leaned forward in my seat. "I've got to hear this."

Cherry squinted her eyes at me, but I just smiled.

Alpha struggled to contain her laughter as she told the tale. "So, Cherry came looking for me. She saw Akimbo on my floor and ignored my warning that he wasn't exactly a people pleaser. He refused to come out of his shell. So you know what Cherry does?"

Cherry rolled her eyes. "Does it matter what I did? Your turtle is crazy."

I took the bait with a smile, ignoring Cherry's protests. "What did she do?"

"She pokes his shell over and over, saying 'Hey! Turtle! Get your ass out here and say hello!' and shit like that, and I warned her again. Then she lay down to get a better look at his face, and said, 'Hey you! What are you doing in there?' Ha! Akimbo snapped out of his shell and bit her right on the nose. She honestly had it coming." Alpha's ears twitched as she fell back on the couch, holding her stomach as she fought to contain her laughter.

I chuckled, finding more entertainment in the look of pure joy on the redhead's face than in the story itself.

"C'mon! It's not even that funny," Cherry whined.

I put my arm around Cherry and pulled her close, hoping to cheer her up. "Sounds like Akimo is a real scamp. He's probably just jealous of how cute you are, so don't worry about it."

"I mean—I am *really* cute." She shrugged.

"If you don't have a familiar, is there one you're keeping an eye out for?" I asked the Vampire Witch with genuine curiosity.

Her eyes lit up. "Yes! I'm only interested in finding a black snake. But one that's not a total dick is hard to find."

Alpha, finally having calmed down, sat back up, her tail wagging excitedly. "Logan, my mark is flaring up, which makes me realize we still need to square away my debt. Do you want your reward now, or a bit later?"

My breath hitched as my mind instantly went to inappropriate thoughts after my last reward, but I kept my cool, not wanting to make any assumptions. "I'll take it now." I stood and eagerly walked to the scale.

Alpha joined me. She had her figurine made by Halo earlier, so we were ready to go. Her figure stood tall and proud, with hands on hips and a determined look toward the future. She placed it on the scale, and I took mine off the shelf.

I examined it briefly. To my surprise it was a little different than before. It seemed like a bit of the emptiness in its eyes was gone, and it had a small smile on its face. Then again, I could have just been imagining it. Refocusing on my reward, I dropped it on the other side of the scale.

As before, my side went low while Alpha's rose. Alpha's eyes met mine, and she smiled. "I know you want a more involved role in the coven, and to be more than just the team's cute mascot. You'll never be a witch, and there's nothing I can do about that. I'm sorry. But your role as a Greater Familiar is far more important than you know.

"You're poised to become an equal part of the team in time. As a token of my thanks, I crafted a ring for you. It can hold one blessing at a time, and with practice, you'll be able to swap out blessings that were previously given to you as rewards. For now, it has only one blessing—a strength blessing based on the aspect of the bear. Do you accept this ring in payment for your efforts tonight?"

Before I could even say a word, the scales balanced, and I scooped my jaw off the floor. "Yes. I accept."

She slipped the ring on my finger, and my muscles instantly swelled. If previously I looked like Ryan Reynolds, now I looked halfway to He-Man. I flexed my arms and wondered if I needed to get a new wardrobe. I noticed that both Cherry and Alpha were eyeing me hungrily, and I grinned. Feeling like an 80s action movie star, I thanked Alpha and left to take a shower, ensuring I was washed up and ready for Cherry's ministrations in the morning.

CHAPTER 12

The Witching Hour

My eyes fluttered open as the sensation of a warm, wet tongue took its time, gradually making its way from my balls to my tip. Soft lips pressed lovingly against my shaft as Cherry proved just how much she adored my cock. Looking down, I found her staring up at me with slitted eyes and lips that were far redder than usual. The reason became obvious when I saw the lipstick prints all over my shaft. "Mua, mua, mua. Good morning, baby. Mmm-mua!" she said, animatedly peppering my dick with kisses.

Cherry's head dropped lower while she took one of my balls into her mouth and gently sucked on it. She stretched a hand and massaged my abs while the other caressed my manhood. I groaned with desire at the sight of her worshiping my cock like it was her religion. She swapped to my other ball as she moaned and continued her work. "Mmm. Tasty-Wasty."

"Fuck, you really know me so well already," I muttered as I reached down and ran a hand through her raven hair.

She slipped my balls out of her mouth and affectionately slapped my shaft against her cheek, grinning. Her mouth displayed her fangs as it hung open, her face a mask of adoration and need in equal measure. "Mmm, baby. I heard from Halo and Alpha that they told you their real names."

I nodded, not really in the frame of mind to respond with words as she started pressing kisses into my cock while stroking me at the base.

"Just so you know—because I like you a lot, I'll tell you mine. But don't call me it, okay?"

I shot her a thumbs up.

"Cheryl," she said. "Cheryl Coleman." And then she throated me aggressively, making me rapidly blink as I tried to commit the name to memory.

"Okay. Got it." I tightened my grip on her hair, and she moaned while devotedly giving me head.

Cherry straddled my leg, and I could feel her wetness dripping on me before she pressed her pussy into it, slowly pleasuring herself against me. "Oh, baby. My poor pussy can't take it anymore. Sucking your majestic cock every morning—Mmm." She groped my muscles and kept kissing, licking, and adoring my length. Each action drove my need for more.

"Why not just fuck me then?"

"Because, this stupid fucking deal—ah, mmm." She started grinding herself against me faster before finally taking me into her drooling mouth. Crimson eyes stared up at me with an almost painful look of desire. She didn't stop going until she left a ring of lipstick at the base of my shaft, letting out a long moan as she took her time coming back up and off my cock, smearing several of the fresher kiss stains. "Mmmmm. I have to make you cum with my mouth first," she said as she turned her head sideways and planted more loving kisses up my cock.

I nodded, being the gentleman I am, and assisted the fine lady. I tightened my grip on her hair and guided her mouth to my tip. Her lips parted eagerly, allowing me to push my cock deep into her throat. My leg got drenched from her juices as she quickened her pace, her muffled moans vibrating against my manhood.

Pulling her head up partially, I thrust into her throat. Her moans and wetness urged me on, signaling her desire for more. "Mhmmm!" I gripped both sides of her head and began using her mouth like a sex toy. I felt my release building as her eyes rolled back, and she started to spasm, her cunt-honey gushed and soaked my leg and the bed. Her muffled squeals of delight were music to my ears. "AHHMMM!"

My body tensed, and I grunted as I exploded into her throat. Mid-release, she started patting my leg and gagged. I let her go, and she immediately released my length, replacing her mouth with her hand, stroking my thoroughly coated member. Her hips continued grinding against me as she rode out her orgasm. "Fuck yeah! Ah! Keep cumming, baby! Cum all over my fucking face! Ah!" Who was I to deny such a request? I continued sending burst after burst of my seed onto her pretty lips, nose, and cheeks.

After finishing, she wrapped her lips around my tip and deep-throated me once more. "Holy shit, big boy. I didn't think you'd make such a mess after I swallowed half of it. So fucking rude," she said with a naughty grin. Using my cock instead of her fingers, she wiped my cum from her face, licking and sucking it clean each time.

I chuckled. "Hey now, I feel like you can't blame me too harshly for that."

"Fine. That's fair. But I can blame you for this," she said as she climbed onto her knees and straddled me. Her hand began stroking me back to firmness, and she positioned my tip at her entrance. "I'm gonna fu—"

"You two need to come out here now!" Alpha shouted as the door flung open. She blushed upon seeing us, but her stern look remained.

Halo stood behind her, worry and desire in her eyes as she peeked past Alpha while biting her lip. "It's really important. You have to see this."

Cherry gritted her teeth. "This better be good! My poor pussy has suffered Logan's cruel neglect for too long, and if it doesn't get what it wants, it will riot! You both will feel its wrath!" She climbed off me and stormed out of the room, leaving a trail of wetness behind her.

I quietly wondered what her pussy's wrath entailed.

I quickly got dressed and followed them to the living room, dealing with that awkward feeling of disappointment when you have to wrangle your erection back into your pants after being so ready for another happy ending. Soon, the sound of an old-fashioned broadcast reached my ears. As I entered the living room, I saw their old, boxy TV with the classic metal rabbit ears was on.

"That old thing actually picks up shows? I thought it was just for games," I said.

Halo nodded. "Yup. Since the mundane world stopped broadcasting on VHF spectrums, the witches started using it."

Alpha pointed at the couch. "Sit. I was watching No Charm, No Foul, and a commercial mentioned the story they'd be covering on *The Witching Hour* this morning. It's about to start."

The show kicked off with generic music that sounded like it came from the early '90s. I expected to see a man and a woman sitting at the news desk or something—a common sight. However, it was two women. One, a very attractive blonde, and the other, a heavy-set brunette, were sitting together on comfortable chairs—the third chair left empty. A small smoking cauldron sat on a coffee table in front of them, and the wall behind was full of shelves with vials, candles, grimoires, and more. I felt silly as I remembered all witches were women.

Broadcaster 1: *Good morning, witches! Welcome to the Witching Hour. I'm Sarah Sanderson.*

Broadcaster 2: *And I'm Mary Sanderson.*

Sarah: *We have important news for you this morning, and it could spell trouble for us all.*

Mary: *That's right, Sarah. There has been a robbery at the Fresco City Museum. But, they didn't take just any old artifact.*

Sarah: *No, they didn't, Mary. Someone has stolen the famous and powerful Lunar Amulet!*

Mary: *The balance in Fresco City has already been in turmoil for some time, and with the* *number of skirmishes rising between two main covens, many believe that war is imminent.*

Sarah: *Before we dive into all that, we did something a little different today. You'll notice we have one empty seat this morning. That's no accident.*

Mary: *We have a special treat for you today. Our sister Winifred is at the scene of the crime.*

Sarah: *And, we are going to let her explain why the theft of this specific artifact is causing such a storm. Winifred, are you there?*

The scene changed to one that was far too familiar. A slightly older witch with red hair was standing in front of an empty display where our fake copy of the Lunar Amulet used to be. As she explained, the other hosts' voices came on, but the screen remained on the new witch.

Winifred: *I'm here, Sarah. You can see behind me that the display case is empty. During daily inspections by both the Salem and New Moon covens, they noticed the amulet no longer held a magical glow. After further inspections,* *they concluded that the amulet on display was a fake.*

Mary: *Do they know when someone replaced the real amulet?*

Winifred: *No one is admitting that they know when the real amulet was taken.*

Sarah: *Can you tell us more about the history of the Lunar Amulet and why it's so important?*

Winifred: *According to legend, the Lunar Amulet, an ancient artifact, was created by Hecate, the fabled Moon Witch of Ancient Greece. It's said that she drew down the moon with her magic and created an amulet from one of its stones. Witches have always highly desired the Lunar Amulet for its ability to boost the power of an entire coven.*

Mary: *How exactly does the Lunar Amulet work?*

Winifred: *That's a fantastic question, Mary. Activating the Amulet can boost a coven's power based on the Moon's cycle. The lunar phase determines how much of a boost the coven gets. A new moon will give almost no boost at all,* *but a full moon will give the coven's power a sizable upgrade, making spells more potent and Spell Tokens quicker and easier to generate. The amulet even makes advanced rituals that were previously out of reach into genuine possibilities—of course, this is all relative to the starting size and power of the coven in question.*

Sarah: *If the amulet is so powerful, weren't there powerful defenses in place to prevent its theft?*

Winifred: *There were indeed. Not only was it protected by two Sentinel Familiars, a hellhound from the Salem Coven, and an arctic fox from the New Moon Coven, but it had an extremely strong magical dome that allowed nothing physical, nor any spells to pass through it. As soon as someone touched the dome, it should have notified both covens immediately. I learned both animals were wounded only a few days ago. However, it seems they occasionally fight since they don't get along, so this didn't alarm anyone. Now, they suspect that someone may have taken the amulet that night.*

Mary: *Wow, that's quite the security. Do they have any clues how someone could get past such extreme measures with no one finding out?*

Winifred: *No, Mary. No one has any idea how this could have happened. But it would take an extremely powerful coven to get past security like this. Unless a powerful new coven is on the rise that no one knows about, then the suspects are limited.*

Sarah: *A third coven on the rise seems a bit farfetched. I'm sure we would have heard about a group with that kind of power. Thank you so much, Winifred. We'll have a hot coffee waiting for you when you get back.*

Winifred: *I'll need it after this morning. See you soon.*

The scene shifted back to the two original witches. Neither myself nor the girls said anything as we focused and took in all the information we could get.

Mary: *See you soon, Winifred. It sounds like it would take an extraordinarily strong coven to break through those defenses.*

Sarah: *Mary, how do you think the two big covens are going to react?*

Mary: *It's difficult to say. Over two decades ago, both covens agreed to keep the peace and balance between them, and neither coven would use the amulet's power.*

Sarah: *Well—hang on for a moment. Winifred?*

Sarah looked confused, and the scene didn't change, but the sound of arguing and shouting appeared in the background as Winifred's voice returned.

Winifred: *Holy shi–yeah! I'm at the museum, which is still closed after the theft. Representatives from both the New Moon Coven and Salem Coven returned, both hoping to speak with me. However, as you can hear, they've broken out into a fierce argument. Both covens blame one another. *Crash. Boom* Oh no! Screw this! I need to get the hell out of here! They've already started fighting! This shit's cra–"*

The sound cut off, and Winifred's voice was gone. Sarah and Mary looked at one another, concern written all over their faces.

Sarah: *I'm sure that Winifred will be— *gulp* fine. Mary, why don't you move on and tell our viewers today's forecast?*

Mary: *Today's forecast? Apparently blood in the streets.*

The two hosts fell into a worried silence before the program suddenly went to commercial. The four of us all looked at one another. I was unsure of what to say.

Alpha's mouth curled up into a feral grin. "Good, let them fight."

Cherry's nostrils flared. "Yeah, to hell with those witches."

Halo's eyes curved. "Holy gosh! This is great news for us. They really have no idea we did it."

"Exactly," Alpha said. "While they are off fighting and weakening one another, we can keep building up our power."

Cherry grinned. "Those fuckers are so stupid. They spread their Greater Familiar between too many people. Unlike us, who get evenly spread by our Greater Familiar," she said with a wink.

I only acknowledged her comment with a smirk, knowing the topic was too important to get off track. "Speaking of their familiars, are they humans, like me?"

Alpha scoffed. "Hell no. Those dumbasses wouldn't know how to handle a real man like you as their pet. One is a flame drake. Think of it like a type of dragon, but smaller. The other is a fenrir. It's like a giant wolf with a snake for a tail."

I frowned. "A dragon? How am I better than a dragon?"

Cherry licked her lips with a naughty glint in her eye. "I used Halo's bad dragon once. You're *so* much better."

My eyebrows scrunched. I was even more confused now. "I thought Halo didn't have a familiar before me and the egg? And why is her dragon bad?"

Cherry opened her mouth to speak, but a hand quickly covered it.

Halo's eyes were bulging, and her face was redder than Alpha's hair while she refused to let Cherry finish that thought. She gave me a nervous smile and tried her best to recover and act as if nothing was wrong. "Ha—haha—ha. Don't worry about it. It's—uh—not a familiar. Just forget about it and never look it up on the Internet. Okay?"

I opened my mouth, then closed it. "Okay…" I drawled.

Alpha chuckled and shook her head. "You saw how big you are when you transform, right? You're a match for a proper dragon, let alone a drake. Not to mention, you can take more than one form, and you make us more powerful just by being near us. Your blood is more magical than that of most magical creatures. I don't know what bloodline you're from, but it's a powerful one."

"But you said that other Greater Familiars can also take on traits of their witches too," I protested.

Nodding, Alpha said, "That's true, but their ability to take on the forms is vastly limited by both their natures and intelligence. They don't transform nearly as much as you do."

Cherry, having finally gotten her mouth free from Halo, smiled. "Plus, you offer us other benefits that they could never get from their familiars," she said while waggling her brows.

I sighed in relief. "I see. The idea that I'm more powerful than a flame drake or a fenrir is crazy."

Halo was pulling herself together and fixing her pigtails. "You'd better start believing it. We've known this war was coming for a long time, and we're going to need you to be confident in yourself."

I sat up. "About this war. You girls have mentioned it here and there, and you even went out of your way to find and recruit me, but you never explained why a war between two other covens matters so much."

Alpha leaned forward in her seat. "Those covens aren't going to let all the other witches in the city just sit by and watch. When one starts losing, or realizes they don't have the strength to win, they'll start forcing other witches to join them. Think of it like a draft."

Cherry clenched her fists in her lap. "And there's no way we'd ever join them. Their leaders are all assholes who lie and only care about power."

Halo smiled. "It's true. And you'll probably have to fight their familiars at some point. When they come for us, and eventually someone will, we'll need you to help keep us safe. But don't worry, because I know you can kick their booties!"

Alpha grinned. "If they come, we'll deal with it. We're a bunch of bad bitch witches with an equally badass pet, after all."

Her confidence was infectious, and I grinned. "So, what's next?"

Alpha nodded, acknowledging the question. She took a moment to breathe in and offer a reply. "Right now, I'm thrilled that we came so far this fast—and it's thanks to you. For now, we're gonna lie low a while longer and let people start to forget about the amulet. We'll see if the covens officially go to war. If we think of more ways to build up our power before it starts, we might go for it. For now? Take some rest. Get cozy with each other. Strengthen those bonds."

I nodded. "Sounds like a solid plan." My stomach let out a loud growl.

"Oh, I forgot all about breakfast!" Halo said.

I stood. "Don't worry about it. I'll go pick us up something to eat. It'll free you up to check on your egg this morning."

"Are you sure? I could always—" Halo started to say.

"No. It's alright, really. I got this," I said.

Halo tilted her head to the side with a bright smile. She quickly stood and jumped at me, wrapping her arms around my neck and giving me a big hug. I had to grab hold of her back to help support her as her feet lifted off the ground. "Thank you. You're the best!"

I enjoyed the embrace and the gift of her scent that filled my nose before she gave me a quick kiss, dropped, and ran to her room. Amused by Cherry's narrowed eyes, I chuckled while watching Halo go. I set off toward the door. Before I reached it, Cherry caught up to me, grabbing my arm. I turned around. "What's up?"

Her cheeks were rosy, and she was looking down at her feet. The toes of her boots were pointing at one another. "I just—I want you to be careful out there."

I frowned, noting how vulnerable and nervous she was acting all of a sudden. "Is everything alright?

Slowly, she looked up. Her crimson eyes met mine and her lips stuck out in a pout. "It's just—You shouldn't be going out without one of us." She looked at her feet again. "You shouldn't be going out there without... *me*. If something happened to you I'd—I don't even *know*."

I realized she was genuinely worried about me. The sexy, flirty, chaotic, quirky Cherry Cola was growing genuinely attached to me in a way that seemed to transcend mere sexual attraction. The way she was acting was... so fucking cute. Honestly, I had already known I was growing attached to her as well, and not just because I fed her a rather unique breakfast smoothie every morning.

I lifted her chin with a finger until her eyes met mine again, and I gave her a reassuring smile. "I'll be fine. It's eight in the morning. That's not exactly the most dangerous time to be out and about, right?"

She paused for a moment, studying me. Then she reluctantly nodded. "Okay, you're right. Sorry—I'm being stupid."

"No, you're just being careful. I appreciate it. But I'll be back soon," I said, and then I leaned in and placed a tender kiss on her lips.

I walked out the front door, shaking my head and chuckling at her adorable, unnecessary worry. *What could possibly go wrong?* Oh, how naive I proved to be.

CHAPTER 13

Mistakes Were Made

I stepped out into the crisp morning air, soaking in the warmth of the rising sun despite the slight chill. As I strolled, I took a moment to reflect, realizing how damn lonely I'd been all my life until now. I hustled day in and day out, grinding away at work with few actual prospects for a bright future, throwing myself into part-time classes, never stopping long enough to acknowledge the void that was eating me up inside. What did I have to look forward to? Managerial gigs at warehouses? It's a good career, but did that really compare to a world of magic and my potential in it?

How much longer would I have kept fooling myself, thinking my grind was leading to happiness, when all it did was lead me to shallow, dead-end relationships? Thank fuck for Cherry, with her twisted tricks and the quasi-Stockholm Syndrome affection I'd developed for her and the others. If it weren't for them, I'd still be stuck waking up each day ignoring the growing void in my heart, rather than waking up each morning filling the void in Cherry's stomach.

But now? Now, life had some goddamn meaning. Saying my purpose was just to serve my coven would be selling it short. The bonds were getting deeper, and I genuinely wanted to be there for my witches. That lonely feeling I used to carry around like a ball and chain? It was entirely gone, wiped clean along with my old life. And I sure as hell wasn't looking back.

Thinking of Cherry, Halo, and Alpha brought a real smile to my face. Who'd have thought I'd fall for a bunch of kidnappers? Especially ones that were actual witches. Yet here I was, headed to grab those same babes some breakfast, and smiling while doing it. I glanced across the street at the Pump N' Go, looked both ways like the responsible adult I was, and strolled over with a big grin plastered on my face.

The ding of the door welcomed me as I stepped inside, but instead of feeling the warmth I expected, I was hit with an even deeper chill. I could see my breath, for crying out loud. Rubbing my arms, I scanned the store.

Seems like the damn heater is on the fritz, I guessed. I made my way to the roller grill and found a few breakfast burritos under a heat lamp, but they were colder than a witch's titty. It was at that moment that I realized just how wrong that old saying was, having plenty of experience with witch tits by this point. I chuckled to myself. *Guess I'll have to nuke the burritos when I get home.*

The store was dim as hell. I hadn't noticed because of the combination of my night vision, and the fact that my eyes were still adjusting from coming in from the sunlight. Most of the light in here came from outside, shining through the windows. Walking under a vent, I felt a blast of cool air. *Wait, is the AC busted? Why the hell wouldn't they just shut it off if the heater was broken? It's not gonna be that hot today.*

Grabbing some fruit and yogurt parfaits, I sauntered over to the coffee station. "Let's see. Black for Alpha and me, Vanilla creamer for Cherry, and a latte with two packs of sugar for Halo," I muttered to myself.

Having collected everything I came for, I hurried toward the counter, ready to get the hell out of this icy store. For the first time, I looked at the store clerk. She was a hot but flat-chested goth chick through and through. Her short black hair, pale skin, and piercings in her nose, ears, and lips caught my attention first. My eyebrows rose as I realized that her beauty actually nearly rivaled my ladies.

Despite her goth appearance, she was surprisingly sweet when she spoke. "Hey! Mind if I check you out?" she asked, her eyes already doing just that as they scanned me up and down.

"Hi. Yeah, sure," I said, placing all my stuff on the counter.

She smirked at me teasingly. "That's a lot of food for one man, even if you are a big one. You got roommates or something like that?" she asked, flashing a flirty smile.

I chuckled politely. "Yeah. A few."

She finally rang up my first item, her gaze never leaving me for more than a second. She pointed at her name tag, which was right atop the subtle slopes of her breasts. "The name's Sue Ellen. What's yours?"

I was getting some strange vibes from this chick, and as I thought about the condition of the store, I felt my instincts telling me something was wrong. The last time I ignored my instincts for a pretty girl, I got myself kidnapped. Even though that didn't turn out too bad in the end, I didn't think it was worth taking the risk. "My name's John. It's nice to meet you."

She frowned, and I couldn't help but feel like she sensed my lie somehow. "So... *John*." She eyed me sternly but tried to keep up the friendly facade. "What do you do for a living?"

Yeah, she definitely knows I lied. "I'm a part-time student and I work full-time as a delivery driver," I lied. This time, I said something closer to the truth to throw her off.

Sue Ellen narrowed her eyes. Then she finally scanned my second item. "Are you happy?"

At last, a question I could answer honestly. I smiled. "Yeah, I'm very happy. How about you?"

Her eyes widened a little. "Y-Yeah. I'm happy," she said unconvincingly. "Are you sure? You don't feel like something's missing in your life?"

My instincts once again told me that something was up. Then again, she seemed kind of like a sweet, misunderstood girl who was more than a bit lonely. "I used to. But these days I'm feeling pretty fulfilled." She took a deep breath as I answered, and I couldn't help but glance back down at her chest as it filled with air, making her small breasts strain against her shirt. As I looked down, I spotted something on the floor behind her, and I leaned in a bit more. My eyes went wide when I noticed a person was lying on the ground behind the counter. "Who's that?"

She looked down, completely unconcerned. "Oh, that's just my boss. She called me to come in early today because she didn't feel well. She wanted a few hours to rest."

"Isn't there a break room or something for that?" I asked, my brows furrowed, trying not to look suspicious.

She smiled at me, leaned forward, and rested her chin on her hand as she continued to scan my items slowly. "So, like, are you new to the neighborhood or something? How come I haven't seen you around before?"

My instincts screamed that this was all wrong, and I needed to get out. "I've been around. Must just be a difference in schedule. During this time of day, I'm usually occupied with either class or work." I made sure she scanned all of my things and readied my payment.

I threw the cash on the counter the second the total came up. "Keep the change," I said before I turned and hurried to the door. But when I put my hand against it, it wouldn't open. I pushed harder, and still nothing. Suddenly desperate, I rammed my shoulder into the door with all my strength—and bounced right off. Setting the bag of food and the coffee on the ground, I drew back my fist and punched the glass. But rather than break, it wiggled and pushed back as if I were punching rubber.

I slowly turned around. My eyebrows shot up as Sue Ellen was standing only fifteen feet away and didn't look so innocent anymore. Eight black eyes replaced her former two human ones. Four huge, hairy tarantula legs with clawed tarsi extended from her back. Her mouth opened too wide, and webbing shot out, hitting my chest and sticking me to the door.

Her mouth curved into a wicked smile. "I'm going to make you mine. You'll be *my* pet, and we're going to have a great time together."

I didn't reply with words just yet. Instead, I easily pulled myself forward, breaking through the webbing as if it were nothing more than a weak Halloween decoration.

The spider witch shrieked at how easily I shrugged her webbing off. "You've already been bound?! You've completed a Greater Familiar contract, haven't you?!"

I nodded. "I'm afraid you're too late. But, it doesn't have to—"

"NO! If I can't have you, then no one can!" Then she rushed me.

Now that I was ready for it, I batted away her next ball of webbing. Then I quickly dodged a spiked leg aimed for my head and dove into a forward roll over another that swiped for my legs. My roll got me more distance than I thought, and I took two more steps before turning around. She spun, with all ten fingers lit up, and small, glowing magical balls flew in my direction, one after another.

I dodged the first, feeling a searing cold slip past my cheek, then dodged the second before the third hit my thigh. My movement felt slightly hampered, and three more of the ten slammed into my torso. They were cold as hell, but ended up feeling like nothing more than decently powerful punches. "We don't have to fight!" I shouted.

She snarled. "AAH!" she screamed and then spat a ball of the web that expanded, blocking my view. I swiped an arm through it, breaking it to pieces, but before I could gather myself, she was on me again. I blocked, parried, and dodged before leaping away.

"C'mon Sue! We can talk this out. I don't want to hurt you." I tried to reason with her, but I remained in a ready stance.

With a flick of her wrist, the spider witch conjured a bolt of crackling energy and hurled it toward me. My eyes widened, but somehow I knew it wasn't strong enough to actually harm me. So with a swing of my arm, I backhanded it—all my hair stood on end as a jolt of power shot through my body, but I sent it crashing into the counter, causing lottery tickets to fly through the air.

While I was distracted by the flying tickets I saw her pull out a golden token. She held it up and shouted, "Elenst thun lifen!" The token flared a deep red and projected a perfect copy of itself that expanded into the air, displaying a large crimson circle around fangs with a droplet of blood hanging from one. I felt a pull on my chest, and as I looked down, a wavy, red, glowing line left my chest, heading directly for the spider witch. But, I felt my connection with Cherry flare and suddenly the line sucked itself back into my body.

She narrowed all eight eyes at the display, and with a guttural growl, she unleashed a barrage of spells, each one more potent than the last. I dodged those I could and was forced to eat those I couldn't. Powerful bursts of heat seared my shirt before ice shattered against me. Jolts of electricity randomly coursed through my veins. But, no matter how fierce her attacks,

I remained unscathed, shrugging off each blow as if it were nothing more than a love tap.

"Please, can we just talk now? My shirt is ruined." I didn't mean to sound like an asshole, but she must have taken it that way.

Frustration streaked across Sue Ellen's face. She abandoned her spells and leaped forward, her spider legs extending, razor-sharp claws all aimed directly at my throat. Diving into an aisle, I barely avoided her attack while she left a small crater on the concrete floor where I previously stood. Sue Ellen gave up all pretense of strategy and ran at me, her deadly claws attacking with a vengeance.

Backing down the aisle, I moved left and right, dodging her first two attempts to skewer me. Avoiding the legs forever wasn't going to happen. So, I started deflecting them with my fists and forearm. She screamed as she found another level of speed, forcing me to match her new frenzied pace. I leaned away from a swipe and grabbed a fuzzy spider leg, using its momentum to slam it through a metal shelf, causing the leg to get jammed.

I didn't want to hurt her, but I had to get her off of me. I quickly scanned my surroundings, searching for a way to end this without any bloodshed. It turned out Halo's luck really was on my side.

As I looked past the oil, I found it—and just in time. Sue Ellen roared in rage as her leg ripped free and she rushed me again. I held up the can of bug spray and pressed down on the nozzle, spraying a single squirt on her face.

She froze in shock, and we stood there for a moment, just staring at one another. I held the can, ready to spray again if needed. She stood in silence, confused, tilting her head. Until her jaw dropped and she covered her mouth. I heard her gut make an awful gurgling sound, and then she ran off, rushing through the door to the restroom.

I scanned the room, making sure it wasn't some kind of trick. There was silence. A loud noise caught my attention as a shelf crashed to the floor, but nothing else moved. I walked cautiously until I got to the bathroom door. The sound of a woman violently throwing up met my ears. Grimacing, I put the bug spray down and carefully pushed open the bathroom door.

'Sue Ellen' was crying and puking into the toilet. All of her eyes were closed tight, and she looked like she was in a lot of pain. Just like that, all my caution was gone, replaced by guilt. Since she knew she couldn't hurt me anymore, all that was left was a sad, vomiting girl. I felt genuinely bad for her. "Hey, are you alright?"

"Just go away!"

I stepped inside anyway. I grabbed some paper towels and ran them under the warm water. Coming up behind her, I held her hair and pulled it out of the way as she threw up again. When she finished, I let go of her hair and handed her the wet towels. "Here, for your eyes." She accepted the cloth and wiped her face with it. "Look, I'm sorry. I didn't mean to hurt you."

She sobbed and sat on the floor with her hands on her knees. Preparing another wet paper towel, I handed it to her so she could clean up her mouth as well. "Just leave. I failed," she murmured.

I brushed her off again. "Hold on." I swung open the bathroom door, grabbed a water bottle from the stack beside it, and handed it to her. "Here, take it," I said, plopping down on the floor across from her, next to the door. "So, who are you really?"

She sniffled. "I'm a witch. Name's Arachna."

"Nice to meet you, Arachna. I'm Logan," I replied, hoping my politeness would loosen her tongue. "Why did you want me as your familiar so badly?"

Arachna grabbed some toilet paper and dabbed at her eyes. "I'm a rogue witch. I used to be in a big coven in Minnesota. I left them to come here a few years ago—wanted to start my own coven. About a week ago, I used a spell to track you down, but I had some shit to deal with first. This morning was my shot. But... I'm too late."

"Why me?"

Her demeanor shifted, and she sat cross-legged, blowing her nose. "Wasn't only you at first. I was scouting for any potential Greater Familiar."

"What, any candidate? I thought Greater Familiars like me were rare."

"You're rare alright. Only one of your type I could sniff out. But, there's a load of others that can be Greater Familiars. Some are mythical beasts, magic-blooded humans like you, or folks cursed with vampirism, lycanthropy, or changeling's with lots of magic," she explained.

"Damn. Why go hunting for a Greater Familiar to start your own coven? Couldn't you just, I don't know, wing it?"

"Having a top-notch familiar makes a coven more powerful. Figured if I had the strongest around, I'd have witches lining up to join."

"Did your spell throw up any other options?" I inquired.

"Hell yeah, plenty. But you, you're the best of the best." Her sniffles were easing up, and she seemed less likely to hurl again. That was a relief.

"So, who's the chick behind the counter?" I asked cautiously.

"That's the real Sue Ellen. I—I didn't hurt her. I just used a sleep spell," she said.

"How did you know how to scan my stuff and use the register, then?"

"I used to work at the Pump N' Go on Main and Carver."

I considered telling her I used to fill up there in my work van a few times in the last few years but thought better of it. That seemed like it would only be salt in the wound.

"So, if I'm desired that much, why do you think it took witches so long to find me? It seems like someone would have picked me up years ago, but suddenly I'm in demand."

Arachna shrugged. "You probably had some kind of warding spell protecting you that only recently broke. Most likely was a female family member of yours that kept it going for so long and died. Did you lose anyone recently?"

I shook my head. "No. I've been an orphan all my life. Never had any family that I know of."

Arachna's head dropped. "I should go."

I frowned. "Wait, you don't have to be alone. You could come with me and meet my roommates. I can't guarantee that they'll want to recruit you, but I can put in a good word."

She looked up, eyeing me cautiously. "Are your roommates with one of the big covens?"

I shook my head. "No. Not at all. They're a small coven, but they are great. You'd really like them."

She sighed. "Hmm...No."

"Are you sure? We can exchange numbers in case you change your mind."

She seemed to consider it until she shook her head. "No. I need to move on. If I have to keep looking at you, then all I'll see is a reflection of my failure. This is goodbye." She waved her hands in a complex pattern and then she vanished in a cloud of smoke before I could say another word.

I scoped out the empty bathroom and mulled over my next move. Pulling out a spare shirt from my pocket dimension, I swapped it with the ruined one and stuffed the old shirt back in. Heading towards the front door, I snagged our breakfast and coffee before stashing them away in my dimensional storage. My thoughts drifted to the store clerk and how fucking cold it was in the store.

Glancing around, I saw the place was trashed, and with Arachna out of the picture, I had no clue if her surveillance-disrupting spells were still in effect. But, as I glanced up at one of the cameras, I saw it was still blocked with webbing. A quick inspection showed all the others were covered the same way.

Slinking behind the counter, I tried to rouse the woman on the floor, but she wasn't budging. She was still breathing, but if she stuck around in this cold, she might not be for long. I scooped her up and laid her down on the sidewalk under some shade before dialing the cops.

I hovered nearby where the clerk lay, waiting it out for the cops to roll in. I pondered Arachna for a few minutes, the poor girl. *Did she have any clue about the impending war? Was she pulling an Alpha, scouting for her own badass crew to dodge being some big coven lackey? Should I even have any sympathy for her after she tried to off me?* Too many questions, not enough answers.

The cops showed up with an ambulance in tow. I explained the lie I'd concocted, how I stumbled upon the store turned icebox with the clerk knocked out. I even flashed my empty pockets and my wallet sporting only a measly twenty to prove I hadn't taken anything. My life was crazy enough without having to worry about being a suspect in some bizarre crime. They grabbed my number and congratulated me for being a stand-up citizen before sending me on my merry way.

I started my trek back home, reflecting on how fast I brushed off Cherry's warnings. *Could others still track me now that I'm under con-*

tract? Or was it only the ones who scoped me out before I became a familiar who could find me? Only my ladies at home could answer those concerns.

But that was a problem for future me. For now, I soaked up the sun's warmth on my skin. Looks like I'd be eating my words when I got back, and I hoped Cherry wouldn't be too upset when I admitted she was right to worry.

CHAPTER 14

Rage of the Tortoise

I took a deep breath and swung open the front door. Cherry wasn't there, fuming and tapping her foot like I expected. Relief flooded over me. But that relief was short-lived when I stepped into the living room and found all three of them waiting.

"Logan, you're back," Halo beamed, her eyes sparkling.

Cherry shot up from her chair, almost sprinting towards me before she stopped, eyes narrowed. "Logan..." she drawled.

I gulped. "Yeah?"

"Why the hell are you wearing a white shirt? It was black when you left. And don't give me that sun-bleached crap! Halo tried pulling that on me once, but I ain't that gullible. I googled it," she said with a hint of pride.

I wasn't sure how to respond to that. "Sun-bleached?"

"I told you I'm not falling for that!" Cherry snapped, pointing a finger at me.

I shook my head. "I wasn't going to say that. I was just confused."

She eyed me suspiciously and rolled her eyes. "Sure you were. Spill it, what happened? Why were you gone so long? Cheating on me? Trying to make me die of worry?"

I chuckled before getting serious. "I wasn't—never mind. Okay, I went to the Pump N' Go and bumped into another witch."

"You *what*?!" Alpha stood, arms crossed, nostrils flaring.

Halo also jumped up. "Holy heavens, are you okay?!" She rushed over, pulling up my shirt and giving me a quick once-over for injuries.

"I'm f—hey!" I had to pull away when Halo's hand started wandering south. Not that I wasn't up for it, 'cause damn, that sounded fun, but I knew the others wouldn't let that slide until I explained.

Halo pouted and pointed a finger at me. "Fine, but I'm doing a full check later, mister. Better safe than sorry."

"I'm good," I laughed. "Everything's intact. And no, she didn't see or touch it."

Cherry let out a dramatic sigh of relief. "Thank fuck! I thought I was gonna have to choke a witch."

Alpha growled impatiently. "That's not the point. We can tell you're unharmed. Good. Now, spill it."

I raised my hands in surrender. "Alright, give me a sec, and I'll explain everything. But first, let's head to the kitchen. I'll heat up breakfast. Killing two birds with one stone and all that."

The redhead nodded, her tail and ears perked up. "Everybody, dining table, now."

I pulled everything I bought for them from my dimensional storage. While passing out the coffee, Cherry clapped her hands and wiggled her fingers over the burritos. I felt a sharp heat emanating from her hands. Within seconds, the burritos were steaming hot.

"Enough delaying. Tell us," Alpha demanded, taking a sip of her black coffee.

I set down my burrito, one finger signaling for patience as I finished chewing. "So, I walked into the store, and it was cold as hell. Figured the heater was busted and shrugged it off. Grabbed the food and coffee and took it to the register. This goth chick was there waiting to check me out."

Cherry crossed her arms. "Check you out, huh? Where's this slut? I'll choke her."

Halo squinted at me too.

I rolled my eyes. "Not like that. Ring up my stuff at the register." *Even though she did totally check me out*, I thought to myself, but no way was I admitting that right now.

Cherry uncrossed her arms, only to cross them again, and then uncross them. She seemed torn between being mad at me or not.

I pressed on. "While she was scanning my items, she kept asking me some weirdly personal shit." Holding up a hand, I tried to pre-emptively stop their likely questions. "I lied my ass off, don't worry, but she seemed to sniff out my lies. I spotted someone unconscious on the floor behind the counter, paid up quick, and tried to bolt out of there as fast as I could."

Alpha scanned me up and down. "But if you had to change your shirt, you didn't really escape, did you? Where is it?"

I sighed and summoned the tattered remains of my old shirt, tossing it onto the table. Alpha's nostrils flared. Halo and Cherry both gasped. "She asked if I was already bound. I told her she was too late, and she attacked me. It turns out she was a spider witch. Obviously, a few of her spells hit me, but they weren't anything I couldn't handle. She was really strong and fast, but she couldn't do anything to me."

Halo laid her hand on my thigh. "You poor thing." Then she gradually slid her hand up to my crotch and squeezed.

I cleared my throat and smiled. "I was trying not to hurt her. When she was asking me stuff at the counter, she seemed like a sad, lonely girl."

Cherry placed her hand on my other thigh. "Baby, you're too nice. You should have ripped her head off," she said in a sugary sweet tone. Then she slowly slid her hand up to my crotch as well, only to find Halo's hand had beaten her to it. The two women glared at one another, and the next thing I knew, they were in a small slap fight just above my groin.

Alpha noticed the commotion and rolled her eyes. "Enough!"

Halo and Cherry immediately stopped fighting, and each rested one hand against my bulge without touching one another. They batted their lashes, trying to act innocent, Cherry inspecting her nails, and Halo examining her parfait.

Alpha motioned for me to continue. "How did you get away? Spider witches are talented at restraint."

I took a sip of coffee. "The webbing didn't do much to me. Then I grabbed a can of bug spray and doused her." I shrugged.

Two red wolf ears fell flat, and Alpha stared at me. "That worked?"

I nodded. "Yeah. She bolted to the bathroom and started puking and crying. Honestly, I felt terrible about it. So I helped her out a little and tried to get some answers."

"So who was she?" Halo asked before spooning some yogurt into her mouth.

"Her name is Arachna. She said she's a rogue witch, and she found me with a spell a little over a week ago before the four of us agreed to a contract. It wasn't until today that she had the time to track me down. Said she wanted to start her own coven and figured that with the strongest familiar, she'd have witches flocking to her wanting to join." I took a bite of my burrito. Damn, for gas station breakfast burritos, they were actually great.

"I see," said Alpha as she looked out the window.

"But if she could track me down, can other witches find me the same way?" I asked.

Alpha shook her head, but then stopped. "They can if they found you before we contracted you, just like Arachna did. But we were searching daily when you suddenly showed up on our radar. And we didn't wait to come for you. There was only a two-day window that other witches could have found you."

Cherry squeezed my thigh so tight I thought she'd break something. "No more!"

My eyebrows scrunched. "No more what?"

"No more leaving the apartment without one of us!" Halo said with fire in her eyes.

"Are you serious? But I handled her easily." I protested.

"I'm glad that you managed it. But she's right. You don't leave here again without one of us with you. And we are all staying inside the rest of the week," Alpha said with a snarl.

I didn't feel that she directed her anger toward any of us. It seemed to be more of a protective anger. The look in her eye made me fear more for anyone's life who tried to hurt our coven than anything else. Hoping to change the subject, I looked at Halo. "So, how's the egg doing?"

Her beaming smile returned. "It's started wiggling, and it glows in the dark. Both are great signs that it's healthy. I think it's gonna hatch sometime today!"

"That's awesome!" I said. The other girls said nothing, and it seemed they were still digesting everything I told them. So, I dropped the chatter and focused on my food, and we all finished our breakfast in peaceful silence.

A couple of hours passed, and I was lounging on the couch, watching *When You Witch Upon A Star*, a historical documentary about astrological witchcraft. Cherry had her head nestled in my lap, and I rested my hand on her stomach. We'd been engrossed in the show for about half an hour when Halo sauntered in, taking a break from keeping an eye on her egg.

"Cherry, can you move?" Halo whined slightly, her wings folded against her back.

"Why should I move?" Cherry countered, raising a brow.

"Because I want to sit on Logan's lap."

Cherry growled a little. "Fuck you. As if."

Halo stomped her foot, her wings extending slightly. "You've had him for the last thirty minutes. It's my turn!"

Cherry stuck out her tongue. "Finders keepers, losers get no dick. I recruited him, so he's mine first and foremost, and you get my leftovers at best."

"That's not even how you—Urgh! That isn't how it works! He's a community good—and he has a say, too! Logan's not a slave, remember!" Halo snapped.

Cherry rolled her eyes. "Yeah, I know. Of course I know. No one cares about him like I do."

At this point I was torn between watching the drama play out and finding an opening to try and calm things down. Halo placed her hands on her hips and squinted at Cherry. "You know, Logan would prefer to snuggle with me instead of you, anyway. My boobies are softer."

The Vampire Witch's fists clenched and she bared her fangs. "What the fuck did you just say, you fuckhead? Obviously, he'd rather cuddle with me when I'm the one lovingly waking him up with this mouth every morning!"

White wings flared out as Halo pointed at Cherry. "Logan and I shared meaningful bonding time at the mall. The only thing you've given him is sex and blowjobs! There's no emotional depth to your relationship, so he'd clearly prefer to snuggle with someone he shares a real emotional connection with! Right, Logan?"

Cherry's eyes widened with fury, and she snarled, sitting up and pointing back at Halo, "Witch, please! If you didn't have your head so far up your butt, then you'd be able to see that Logan is hopelessly in love with me, and I with him! That's the way it is, right, baby?!"

My jaw practically hit the damn floor at the shitshow unfolding before my eyes. *I mean, what the hell?* I looked from one woman to the other, trying to process the drama like some messed-up witchy soap opera.

Struggling to figure out what the hell to say, I just blurted out the first thing that popped into my head, "Ladies, I am not playing favorites. You're both amazing." I instantly regretted it. Saying anything at all was like tossing gasoline onto a fire.

Both of them shot daggers at me with their glares, then turned their gazes on each other. The tension was so thick you could cut it with a rusty, crusty butterknife. I was half expecting punches or spells to start flying any moment—until the boss barged in.

Alpha sauntered into the room, sporting an oversized shirt that barely covered her crotch. She also had her turtle, Akimbo, in tow, who seemed just as pissed as the rest of them. "What the hell is happening in here?!" Alpha growled.

Cherry jabbed her finger at Halo with a sneer. "This greedy slut thinks she can snatch Logan away from me when I was the one who recruited him and who loves him the most!"

Halo shot back, feathers all ruffled. "She's the one trying to hog Logan all to herself! Just listen to what she's saying!"

Alpha glanced at me, eyebrow raised, while Akimbo narrowed his turtly eyes at me suspiciously. I just sheepishly shrugged. "I'm as lost as you are," I grunted.

The boss-lady shifted her attention back to the feuding women. "Alright, enough of this bullshit. I'm in charge, and you're going to do what I say," she declared, shutting down any argument.

Halo and Cherry reluctantly nodded.

First, Alpha laid into Cherry. "Cherry, you're oversexed and way too needy."

Halo smirked at Cherry, who looked like she'd been slapped.

Then Alpha turned to Halo. "And you are just as pathetically head-over-heels as her."

Cherry smirked at Halo wickedly.

"So here's the deal. I've barely spent any time with Logan alone, so I'll babysit his ass for a while so you two can cool down. Meanwhile, you're gonna watch over Halo's egg and be ready when it hatches," Alpha ordered.

Both Halo and Cherry looked like they'd been sucker-punched, mouths gaping open in disbelief. "This is absolute crap!" Cherry yelled.

"Not fair!" Halo shouted.

I held up my hands, though. "I think it's a fair compromise."

Alpha didn't bother trying to argue and started toward her room. I quickly followed behind, finally seeing a way out of that madness. As I looked up, I saw Akimbo, who had climbed even higher on Alpha's shoulder, peering at me with his squinted, suspicious eyes. Lifting a foot, he pointed to his eye, and then at me. Briefly, I considered if I'd gone insane.

Before I could give it much thought, I found myself in Alpha's room. She had an all-in-one gym machine in the corner, and exercise mats on the floor. I had a feeling that she didn't actually need them because of her affinity, but we all have our hobbies. The other corner had a full gaming setup. I almost laughed when I noticed her headset had animal ears on them. It seemed redundant to me.

Alpha set Akimbo on the floor and glanced at me. "Sit."

Since people normally didn't tell turtles to sit, I figured that was for me. I took a seat on the edge of her bed.

"No. Sit on the floor," she said.

I frowned but sat on the floor like she wanted, figuring she had a reason for it.

The redhead walked in front of me and took off her baggy shirt, leaving nothing else on but a small pair of simple panties and her sports bra.

Alpha had a body that was fit in the best way. Toned calves and thighs led to a slim, narrow waist. My eyes continued their trip up to her belly button and toned abs as she showed off an impressive six-pack. The only thing soft about Alpha was her ample rack.

I shrugged. *Well, if she wants to get right down to business...* I undid my belt.

She snorted. "What are you doing?"

I looked up with a frown. "Fucking your brains out?" I drawled.

The gorgeous redhead laughed at me, only making my frown deepen. "I'm not some subby brat like Cherry, and I'm sure as hell not a cuddle-drunk pushover like Halo."

I nodded, feeling my cheeks burn while I buckled my belt.

Alpha sat on the edge of the bed and leaned back on her hands, looking down at me. "I only took my shirt off because I'm not a total bitch and want my handsome pet to have something nice to look at." She suggestively ghosted her fingers along her abs.

"Well, I appreciate that. You're definitely eye candy," I said, accepting her concession.

She extended her foot and started tapping against my bulge with her toes. "I figured I'd let you indulge in your fetish. You're going to give me a foot rub. And if you do a good enough job, maybe I'll take off a little more."

"I don't have a—" I started to say, but was interrupted by her snicker and foot tapping against my groin. Well, I may not have a fetish, but I certainly didn't hate cute feet, I realized. In the end, the offer was too good to pass up. So, I took her foot in my hands, resting it on my legs. Using both thumbs, I started kneading the ball of her foot, before gradually guiding them down to the heel several times. Fortunately for Alpha, the same cougar that taught me a thing or two about pleasing a lady also taught me a thing or two about massaging a lady.

"Mmm—damn, that's nice," Alpha said with a small moan. "Color me surprised. Good boy."

I felt a thumping against my leg. When I directed my gaze downwards, I noticed Akimbo head-butting me. I smirked at him. He backed up, looked up at me, and then ran one foot across his throat and pointed at me. My brows scrunched, and then he did his best to run at me. But he was a turtle, so it was pretty damn slow. I watched until he finally reached me and head-butted me again. I shrugged and refocused on my task.

"So, these rogue witches? How much do you think we need to worry about them and the other smaller covens?" I asked as I focused more on her heel.

"Oh—mmm—it's like this. Rogues, or solo witches, make up around 30% of the witch population—nnnn—fuck, you're good at this. The difference between a rogue and a solo witch is that rogue witches used to be in one of the big covens, but either got kicked out or left. Solo witches are usually just ones that choose not to join a coven. The rest—mmm yeah, right there—the rest of the city is in one of the two main covens. But, ahh—a little—yup, that's the spot, mmm. But, there is a small percentage, maybe 5-10% who formed their own mini covens, like us," Alpha said.

I shifted my focus from her feet and worked my way to her calf. "I see."

"God, yes. I need this after this morning's workout. Rogue witches and solo witches can be unpredictable. Like you—mm—found out this morning. They have no rules except their own. They also tend to be pretty—fuuuuck—tough, or they wouldn't be able to last on their own. I'm actually really impressed that you—*ah yeah*—stood up to one in your human form."

Continuing my work, I noticed her moaning and groaning had only increased, and she became even more distracted, not even answering when I asked her how I was doing the first time. I smirked up at her and asked again. "So, am I doing a good job?"

"Hmm? Oh, yeah, you're doing a great job," she said distractedly.

"Well, a deal's a deal, right? Does that mean you're going to take off the rest of your clothes?" I asked with hope in my eyes.

She lifted her head, quirked a brow at me, and smirked. "I said I might take off more, not necessarily all."

"Do I get to choose?"

She tilted her head, considering. "Well, since you've been such a good boy, I'll allow you to pick which one."

Without hesitation, I reached up and pulled down her panties. She lifted her ass to help me but blushed a deep scarlet. I looked between her legs at her shaved, glistening pussy and stared.

Alpha tried not to show her surprise, but her ears standing straight up, her blush, and her slightly flustered expression gave her away. "You—I can't believe—why am I surprised that you picked those?"

I grinned and went back to my task. Slowly, my hand crept up her thighs as I massaged her firm muscles. Gradually bringing my fingers closer to her center.

She let out the girliest, cutest giggle I'd ever heard from the strong woman. "I know what you're doing. Just go ahead. Touch it."

Often I thought of myself as a kind man. The type of man who would go out of his way to help others in their time of need. And, when a lady just so happened to have a wet pussy in front of me and instructed me to touch it, how could I deny her? Impossible.

I slipped my hand between her strong thighs, first rubbing her mound and massaging the lips. Then I separated them and allowed my fingers to explore gradually between her folds, moving up and caressing her shy clit.

"Fffuck. That's my good boy." I looked on as her tail swayed left and right, and she let her head fall back.

While I continued slowly massaging her pearl, I reached behind her to grab her ass, but with too much of it on the bed, I couldn't get a good grip. So, I grabbed her tail instead. I gently pulled it as I stroked it. *That seemed to get her going.*

"Logan! Holy—Mmm—shit!"

I grinned and stopped petting her tail. Leaning forward I spread her lips and licked her from her opening, all the way up past her clit and onto her shaved pelvis. She shuddered in response. So I did it again, enjoying how damn good she tasted.

Raising her head, she growled at me, her yellow eyes full of hunger. "Fffuck! Ah! Stop fucking teasing me!" She put all of her weight on one hand and grabbed the back of my head with the other, forcing my face against her dripping slit, and started grinding it aggressively against my mouth. "Mmm—Ah! That's right! Right fucking there! Lick my fucking pussy, Loga—Ah! That's a good pet. See? It's not so bad being Mommy's plaything, is it?"

It indeed was not. I indulged her and lathered her folds with my tongue while slipping a finger inside. Muscular legs wrapped around my neck and she locked her ankles, keeping my head in place while she rotated her hips against me. I looked up to see her face staring back at me. "Oh, yeah. You fucking—mmm—like the taste of that pussy, don't you? Ah!"

"Correct, madam," I said. Puckering my lips, I sucked on her pearl while I beckoned her hither with my fingers inside her. She stopped holding herself up with her arms and dropped to her back, freeing up her hands that she used to grab both sides of my head. Alpha used my face like a toy while I pleasured her. I gripped her tight ass and squeezed as her juices started dripping down my chin. "Yeah! Yeah! Don't stop! That's Mommy's good bo-OY! OH FUCK!"

I redoubled my efforts as she sped up her pace. Her nails clawed at my scalp as she pulled my hair. A part of me worried I might need some Rogaine after this session. Alpha started screaming in bliss as she reached her peak. "Fuck! Don't stop until I'm don—AH! YES! LO—OH—GAN—NYAH!"

Remaining diligent and opting to acquiesce to the lady's polite request, I kept going as orgasmic spasms rocked her body. Her back arched, and her thighs were squeezing me so tightly that I thought my head would explode like a watermelon with one too many rubber bands around it. Once she'd finished riding her orgasm, she released my head and pulled me by the hair off of her drenched mound. "Mmm—such a good familiar," she said as she ran her fingers through my hair. "Now get into this fucking bed."

"Yes, ma'am." I climbed up between her legs.

After pulling her top off and exposing her perfect breasts, she undid my belt, button, and zipper. When I reached to pull my pants down, she slapped my hands away and wagged her finger. I tried to kiss her, but Alpha put said finger over my mouth and smirked. "We aren't there yet."

Sliding higher and pushing my head down, she positioned her breasts under my mouth. When a perfect pink nipple touched my lips, I immediately took the hint. I licked, nibbled, and then sucked on it. My eyes widened when a delicious burst of something like sweet milk leaked into my mouth. I coughed, as I wasn't expecting it, but it wasn't an unwelcome development.

Alpha laughed at my reaction. "It's a beast affinity spell witches use to feed familiars of all kinds. Drinking from my breast will make you stronger over time, and you'll feel fuller longer than you would with normal food. Plus, it'll make you more in tune with magic."

Fuck it. Can't really say this is any stranger than being a familiar for a group of hot witches in the first place. I latched back on, sucking down her milk eagerly. If it was going to make me stronger, then I was more than eager. Meanwhile, Alpha reached between her legs and fished out my cock. She let it go and must have gone diving into her own depths because it soon returned slick and the scent of her sweet juices flooded my nostrils.

Giggles came from above my head. "I wonder what my pet likes more? The taste of my juicy pussy, or my milk?"

I gripped a breast in each hand, swapping from one to the other as I drank down every drop I could. Alpha stroked my shaft with a firm grip, twisting her wrist as she went up and down, but she was going so agonizingly slow. It felt so good, but I needed more from her, so I bucked into her hand.

"Such a greedy boy. You want to cum, huh? Yeah? Fuck Mommy's hand then," she squeezed my cock tighter. "Fuck it like you would my tight, hot pussy. Imagine puncturing my virginity—you're gonna, you know. Any minute now with how good you've been lately. That's it, my good boy, thrust your big cock. Mmm. It's going to be so, so good, won't it?" She licked my ear as I continued to follow her commands while lapping at her nipples. Her urging was driving me insane and sending jolts of desire through my body. I went faster, and Alpha picked up the pace of her stroking as well as a little reward.

"There you go. Mmm. You need to cum so bad, don't you, handsome? You can't wait to explode for me. Of course you can't. You know your role." She started jerking me off even faster, so I stopped thrusting and let her do as she pleased. "That's right. I can feel how hard you are. Your cock is so fucking huge for me. I love it. Mmmm," she moaned, her breaths coming in harder and heavier. "You're about to cum, aren't you? Do it. Cum for Mommy. Cum for me, now!"

Not only were her words extremely fucking hot, but to my surprise, our bond also seemingly compelled me because of the urgency in her demand. My mouth released her nipple, and I lifted my head as I grunted. My body tensed and orgasmic bliss exploded out of me.

"C'mon, be a good boy for Mommy and cum! Ah! Yes! There it is! Mm-hmm. Keep coming for me, get it all out, baby," Alpha cooed. I emptied completely, covering her stomach, hand, breasts, and neck. She continued pumping my length until every drop of seed spilled from my tip.

When I was done, Alpha cast a spell, instantly cleaning the mess I'd made of her. Smirking, she patted me on the head and purred, "You're Mommy's good boy. Those bitches in the New Moon coven would wish you were theirs. Now, don't you feel better?" she asked, kissing the top of my head.

I looked down across her incredible body, and I noticed her tail was sticking out to the side, wiggling a little. "You know, before this, I wasn't even feeling particularly bad. But I feel fantastic now."

She grinned.

I decided that now was a good time to test a theory I had. Reaching down, I started rubbing her stomach. Sure enough, her tail started wagging like crazy and she moaned.

"Mmm—fuck," she said before she caught on to what I was doing. Her cheeks turned scarlet, and she quickly rolled over, laying on her stomach. Her tail still wagged furiously though.

I smirked.

Her stern tone came back as she instructed, "Get back to massaging my body. No one said you were finished yet."

I chuckled. "I don't know. Now that you're naked, I don't know if I'll be able to resist fucking you," I said as I threw my shirt on the floor.

She grinned deviously. "What will be, will be."

As I prepared to get back to work, I had a strange feeling that I was being watched. I looked down to see Akimbo glaring at me. I smirked at him and flipped him the bird before grabbing two firm cheeks, one in each hand. He shook his little head, turned his back on me... and pissed on my shirt. I sighed. *Fucking Akimbo...*

CHAPTER 15

Logan Jr.

After a few hours, and going a few rounds with Alpha, we lay on the bed as she enjoyed letting me spoil her with belly rubs, while I slurped up every last drop of her breast milk that I could claim. We were gearing up for another round when a knock came at the door, distracting us from our fun.

Alpha groaned. "What is it?"

Halo shouted through the door, "The egg! It's hatching! We're in the living room!"

"We're coming!" Alpha shouted back, suddenly excited. I found it charming how much she cared about being there in this moment for Halo, so I got caught up in the spirit of it as well. "Hang on! We're coming!"

However, an annoyed Halo replied, "I know... I heard you cumming—a lot."

Alpha rolled her eyes at the door and then turned to me. "Get up. Fun time's over for now."

I scrambled for my clothes, almost putting my shirt back on when the smell hit me. I cringed and could swear I heard that damn turtle snickering. Slipping on my third shirt of the day, I ran to catch up. Alpha hadn't bothered and strutted into the living room in her birthday suit. I caught up in time to hear Cherry growling under her breath, something about "stealing my goddamn man."

Alpha stared blankly back at her. "I'm not stealing anything and you know it."

Cherry's glare could melt steel. "First you cheated in Street Fighter II, and now you're a man-thief."

Alpha growled and rolled her eyes.

"Really?" Halo complained, glaring at Alpha's nude form. "*Really?*" Then she turned to me, giving me a bright smile as the familiar twinkle returned to her blue eyes. "Hey, Logan. Milk mustache? I thought Alpha didn't allow drinks in her room?"

I frowned, touched my upper lip, then frantically wiped my mouth on my sleeve. I chuckled nervously. "Oh, I was just—uh—bonding with Akimbo. Yeah, that's it. I thought sharing some milk with him might be good. Familiars have to stick together right? Ha, aha..."

"Aww. You got to give the little guy time. He'll come around. But you, Alpha—you should've stopped him. Milk is bad for turtles," Halo lectured, glaring as she looked the naked woman up and down again.

Alpha blushed and changed the subject. "Enough chit-chat. The egg's hatching."

All eyes turned to the egg. This little rat was earning major points with me right from the get-go for bailing me out. I already preferred him over Akimbo. Still, it was pretty damn weird seeing a rat's paw bust through an eggshell. A tiny pink nose poked out next, sniffing the air, before the familiar chewed its way free.

Halo gushed. "My baby!" she cooed as she held out her hand palm up, letting the little white rat crawl up her arm. She scooped him up, placed him against her soft chest, and gave him a tight hug. The little guy squeaked with joy, and I couldn't blame him. Prime real estate.

Alpha smiled warmly. "Congrats. He's cute."

Cherry looked on with a hint of jealousy, but her smile was genuine. "Yeah, he's cuter than I thought. Congrats."

"I'm glad you got the familiar you wanted." Seeing how happy she was sent a warmth through me. I smiled at her.

She giggled in reply to us. "Thanks, everyone!" Her blue eyes glanced at me. "I already have the perfect familiar. But, I love this little cutie too!"

After their first bonding session, the girls got ready for the quick ritual to bond the two as witch and familiar. They chanted a bit and then used a needle to prick a small hole in Halo's finger and then one in the rat's paw, making him squeal in pain. Halo pressed her finger to his paw, then pulled away and kissed his tiny wound. A soft glow surrounded them both, and Halo used a healing spell to fix his paw. A tiny golden light beamed from her finger onto his little paw, which I thought was adorable.

As the ritual wrapped up, I figured it was a great time to ask a couple more of the questions swirling in my head. "So, what's the big difference between all the familiars? And what's the backstory?"

Alpha turned to me first. "You know there are Lesser Familiars and Greater Familiars. Lesser Familiars are like super-smart pets who help their witch out however they can. Greater Familiars can take on the affinities of their coven members and often have their own unexpected powers. The third type is Sentinel Familiars. Those are a witch's second familiar. They're more powerful and bound to a single location to act as a guard—like the ones at the museum. Only the most powerful witches have both a Lesser and a Sentinel Familiar."

"But witches don't have to be super-strong to have a Greater Familiar since they're shared within a coven, right?" I asked.

"Exactly. And we've already discussed Mating Familiars before, so...let's not retread that."

My eyes widened as I thought about old folklore I'd heard. "Wait a sec. I remember hearing about witches' familiars being demons in animal form. Am I...?" I gulped, letting the question hang, suddenly unsure if I wanted an answer.

Cherry and Alpha burst into laughter, pointing at me for my adorably ignorant question.

Chuckling, Cherry quipped, "A semen demon, maybe. Unless you spent your childhood living in Hell—" Cherry froze suddenly as she heard what she said and apparently connected it to what she knew about my past. Cherry looked down in shame. "Baby, I'm sorry, I didn't mean—"

I chuckled and cut her off quickly. "Don't sweat it."

Immediately she perked back up as if nothing was wrong. "Okay! If you don't care, and I'm not in trouble, then good."

"Actually," Alpha smirked, "legends say that once, a few thousand years ago, a massive group of demons escaped the Hells. Apparently, they went on a fucking spree. By that, I mean a spree of massive orgies with humans, animals, monsters—whatever they could. It took the Angels years to send them all back to the pits. Many believe that all modern monsters and magical bloodlines are descendants of those hybrids."

Halo finally stopped cuddling her new familiar and hoisted him into the air. "I officially name you Logan Jr.!"

"What the hell?! You can't name him Logan Jr .," Cherry protested, her jaw dropping and arms crossing. "That's so messed up!"

Halo placed Logan Jr. in his new enclosure. "Why not?" she asked, her tone snippy.

"Because I was gonna name my future familiar Logan Jr.!"

Halo smirked. "I know you were. You mentioned it earlier. That's where I got the name."

"You fucking asshole!" Cherry yelled a magic word and flicked her wrist, a gray glow forming around her hand. The next instant, a zipper replaced Halo's lips, silencing her. "Try calling that rat by that name now!"

Two hands waved, glowing a faint gold, and Halo cast a spell of her own at Cherry. Suddenly all of Cherry's clothing phased through her body and fell to the floor, leaving her naked. Cherry gasped and tried to grab her clothes, but they kept slipping through her fingers.

All this fighting over me was getting frustrating. "Hey! Enough of this," I said. "What the hell? Pretty sure you were all down with the whole 'sharing me sexually and magically' stuff before. Wasn't that the arrangement?"

"These two are just being childish," Alpha said, rolling her eyes.

In a shocking turn of events, Halo started stripping off her clothes as well. My eyes widened, and my eyebrows shot up.

Cherry looked at her with incredulity. "What the fuck are you doing?"

With a flick of her wrist, Halo's mouth returned to normal. "Because! You're naked, and Alpha's naked, and now Logan isn't looking at me hardly at all anymore! It's grinding my gears!"

Alpha looked like she was about to have a stroke. "For fuck's sake! You two need to get a grip! Logan is OUR familiar. He's supposed to be our secret weapon. Get your shit together, or he'll be our undoing. If you two don't learn to share, then we'll all be fucked—and not in a good way," Alpha said, firmly asserting herself and glaring at the girls.

Cherry and Halo both pouted and crossed their arms, looking away from one another.

"Looks like I have to fix everything myself." Alpha turned to me. Her hands glowed yellow, and she threw one up and the other down. My arms went in the air, and my shirt flew off, followed by my pants and boxers falling to the floor. "Lie down on your back."

My eyes widened as I looked down at my instantly naked body, and I opened my mouth to ask a question. But she didn't wait. Instead, she pointed at me and used our bond to compel me. "Lie on your back, now!" she commanded. "Don't speak unless spoken to for now. I need to teach these two a lesson, and sorry to say it, but you're going to be an accessory to that lesson."

I nodded and obeyed, lying on my back. "Trust the process," I muttered.

Halo pouted, but the fury never left her blue eyes. "What are we supposed to do?"

"You're going to learn how to share," Alpha pointed at both girls. Then she pointed down at me. "First, the two of you are going to watch me ride our pet—"

Halo cut off Alpha with an angry whine, "But, Alpha—"

"No buts. You're not only going to watch me ride Logan, but you're going to masturbate while you watch."

Internally, my mind was reeling. *What the fuck is this porn logic?* I thought, though I didn't hate it.

Cherry's nostrils flared. "Alpha! Look, I can pretend it doesn't happen behind closed doors. I just put on my headphones and—doo do doo—listen to my music. But you want me to watch my precious cinnamon roll get ruined by someone else's pussy?!"

Halo agreed. "Yeah, this is messed up! He's mostly mine! I can't accept this bull-shrimp!"

Alpha refused to back down. "This isn't up for debate! Sit down and start stroking those pussies, witches. That's an order from your coven leader."

Halo and Cherry grumbled but complied. Despite their protests, they positioned themselves on either side of me so they could get the best possible view of the action, while treating me to a perfect view of their dripping slits whenever I turned my head.

The toned redhead dropped to her knees, straddling me. She gripped my cock at the base. "Take a good look, ladies. You see this massive cock?"

Halo and Cherry barely grazed their labia and sat in silent protest.

"It wasn't rhetorical!" Alpha emphasized each word of her question. "Do you see this massive cock, yes or no?"

"Yes, Alpha," both Cherry and Halo reluctantly said in unison.

"Good. This is *our* cock. This cock belongs to us all." She stroked me slowly. "Spread those legs more, girls. If Logan can't see your gaping pussy while you rub those clits, then you're doing it wrong."

This was the hottest experience I'd ever had in my life. My cock was already throbbing as her smooth hand kept gliding up and down. I looked to my right and saw Halo spreading her legs even wider, her juices spilling onto the floor below as she massaged her pearl. Glancing to my left, I saw the same scene, but from the fanged Vampire Witch, who already had a puddle forming below her while she played with her pussy.

Alpha smirked. "Good girls." She pressed my length against her body. "Look, ladies. Look just how fucking deep inside me this enormous cock is going to be. Take it all in... before *I* take it all in."

Halo and Cherry both pouted with a furious hunger in their eyes.

The fiery redhead hoisted herself up, guiding my tip towards her dripping pussy, eager for action. Her juices were already flowing, coating my cock before it even entered her. With a sinful, maybe exaggerated moan, she lowered herself onto me, taking me inch by inch, her pleasure echoing in the room. "Oh, fuck..."

Even though I'd already been balls deep in her three times today, the sensation was mind-blowing every damn time. It was like she had some magic spell keeping her tight, as tight as when she gave me her virginity earlier. Her muscles clenched around me, amplifying the pleasure, while her velvety walls worked their magic. I couldn't help but groan as she took me all the way in.

"Gosh, baby, I need you to do me so hard," Halo whimpered, fingers teasing her own wetness.

"I need that cock so fucking bad," Cherry moaned, picking up the pace.

I glanced between the two girls, then back at Alpha. "Hey, eyes up here, pet. You don't wanna miss the show," the Beast Witch chimed in, her tail wagging eagerly behind her. With toned muscles on display, she rode me slow and steady, giving everyone a front-row seat to the action. "Hell yes. Halo, you wish you were on this cock right now, don't you?"

"Yes, Alpha!" Halo exclaimed, chest rising and falling with excitement.

"And you, Cherry? Don't you wanna taste *our* handsome pet?" Alpha teased. To be honest, at this point I was starting to feel like we were the Soviet Coven.

"F—fuck. I love him so damn much," Cherry admitted, her hand playing with her nipple ring. "Him and his chubby fucking cock."

Alpha leaned back, stretching out her body while massaging my balls. With a slower rhythm, she kept grinding and working my shaft. "Damn, your cock feels so fucking good. Think I'm falling in love with it. Oh!"

I couldn't tear my eyes away. Cherry's flawless body was a sight to behold, her crimson eyes locked on mine one moment and then watching as Alpha's pussy devoured me the next. With her mouth slightly open, her fangs peeking out, and her tongue teasing her lips, she was pure temptation. And those tits... they were practically begging for attention as she played with herself. "Logan! I want you, baby!" Cherry cried out, desire dripping from her voice. "Please, let me have you, too! I'm yours forever!"

Halo's wings extended and fluttered, their movement flicking her pigtails. She caught me watching and locked her blue, slitted eyes on mine, biting her lip. Her arms reached down, squeezing her supple breasts together as she focused on penetrating herself with one hand and caressing her clit with the other. "Please! Ah–nyah! I need you inside of me!"

I shifted my focus back to the furry-eared domme riding me. Her body was as flawless as the others, but different. Reaching forward, I rubbed her tight abs, sending her tail into a frenzy. "God yes! I'm going to make you cum inside me. You're going to fill my fucking womb while these two needy sluts of yours watch and finger themselves like good girls."

"Yeah," I grunted, not sure what else to say from all the sensory overload. Her words were driving me as crazy as her wet slit was.

"You hear that, ladies? I think Logan likes it when we get along." Alpha leaned forward, pressing her plump bosom against my chest. "Come here, my pet. I think I'm ready for a kiss."

Our lips met, tongues caressing each other as we made out. Louder whines sounded on either side of me. Alpha continued to not only ride me in front of them but properly make love to me while they watched.

Suddenly, the sound of loud moaning came from the sidelines. Alpha and I both turned to see Cherry shuddering. "Mmm—oh fuck! AH!" As she rode out her orgasm, Cherry never took her eyes off of us.

"Did you like that? Did you enjoy watching her share like a good girl and cum for us?" Alpha asked as she sat up.

I nodded with a righteous conviction.

"Mmm—Tell them. I know it will—oh yeah—turn you on more if they watch. Tell them—ah—tell them you want them to watch as you cum inside me," Alpha said as she groped her breasts.

Despite the whining I heard coming from the sides, what she said was true. That might make me a shitty person, but I wanted them to watch.

"Fuck yeah, I do. I want both Cherry and Halo to watch me fill your tight pussy."

Alpha's grin widened as her pussy stroked me faster. "Get over here, Cherry. You've been such a—mmm fuck—good girl. You get the front-row seat on his face while I get my fill. Ahhh YES!"

Cherry wasted no time, hurling herself towards us, her dripping pussy descending onto my eager mouth. The taste of her sweetness flooded my senses, and I devoured her like a starving man on a desert island. "Mmm, you're fucking tongue is so good!"

Halo growled, feeling left out. "This isn't fair! Why does she get to ride him while I just watch?!"

The sound of Alpha's ass smacking against me picked up its tempo, creating even more delightful moans. "Oh fuck yeah! Finish up, and—oh my god this fucking dick is so—mmm—and maybe I'll let you ride this—mmm-monster!"

I knew I was close to blowing. Alpha rode me like a wild animal, which seemed fitting, and I grabbed Cherry's tits, playing with her nipple rings like a pro. She proved the rings weren't just for show as she cried out, "Ah! You drive me fucking crazy, baby!"

Halo was losing herself, whimpering and working her clit like a frantic DJ on a turntable. "Frick, frick, frick. Come on, come on!"

Meanwhile, Alpha's walls tightened around me. "Cum with me! Be my good boy and fill me up while they watch!"

I couldn't hold back any longer. My balls tightened, and I sucked on Cherry's clit as if my life depended on it.

Cherry screamed, "You're—Ah!—you're a fucking god, baby! FFUuuuuUUcK!"

Alpha was losing it too. "Let go! Give me your fucking cum, pet! Give it to me!" she demanded as her pussy gripped me like a goddamn vice. "Fuck, Logan, I beat you to the finish I'm—cumming! Ahhhhhh!"

At the same time, Halo was reaching her peak. "Fffflipping finally! OH—yes!"

The chorus of moans pushed me over the edge. I exploded into Alpha, my body trembling with ecstasy. Cherry continued grinding on my face, relentless in her pursuit of pleasure.

"Holy shit!" Alpha cried out, still riding me. "Look at that! He's—oh fuck—filled me up so much, it's pouring out. And he's still going! Don't you wish this was your pussy, Halo?"

Damn, she was really laying it on thick, reveling in it, punishing the girls for their spat. But it was fucking hot. I rode out my climax before diving back into my duty, slurping on Cherry's sweet pussy.

"See that, girls? Look how much Logan loves this cunt. This is a pussy that knows how to share a worthy male. Get over here, Halo," Alpha commanded. She dismounted, leaving my poor cock a sticky mess covered in our combined juices. "Get on, but no magic. Give him a pussyjob until you get him hard again. Then you can fuck him."

Halo straddled me as I delved deeper into Cherry's depths. "Finally! I need your cock so bad," Halo said.

"No, turn around," Alpha ordered.

"But I don't wanna see her! It'll kill the mood," Halo protested.

"If you don't turn around, you won't ride *our* pet's magnificent cock," Alpha warned.

"Fine..." Halo turned around obediently, her lower lips instantly grinding against my shaft, coaxing it back to life.

But even with my face buried under Cherry's tight ass and pussy, I could sense the tension in the air. I knew both women were shooting daggers at each other, especially as Cherry's hips started grinding harder on me.

"You two better kiss and make up," Alpha demanded.

"Forget that. It's bad enough I have to see her on his cock while I'm riding his beautiful face," Cherry protested.

"What?! No way! How can I enjoy his majestic penis if I have to ruin my experience by smooching with *her*?" Halo argued.

"No debating this! And it'll turn Logan on to know you two are making out while you use him like your personal sex toy," Alpha said.

By now, Halo's pussy job almost had me fully erect again, and I was savoring Cherry's taste too much to stop sucking her clit.

"I won't do it unless Logan tells me to!" Cherry said defiantly.

"Yeah, sorry, but Logan decides what I do with these lips," Halo agreed, her voice dripping with irritation.

I threw up both thumbs, struggling to talk with my mouth full. "Hewwyagoforit!"

Alpha was probably smirking at that. "See, I know what *our* pet likes."

Halo's tight little pussy slid onto my already sensitive shaft, and I couldn't help but groan. Pressing my tongue into Cherry's center, I felt her lean forward, the sound of kissing mixing with Halo's intense fucking.

Then came the *SLAP*, just above my head. Followed by another, from slightly farther away. Halo and Cherry began moaning into each other's mouths as they got heated, spanking each other and pleasuring themselves on me.

Tongues explored, hands roamed, and bodies writhed as the women rode my face and cock. Halo and Cherry's anger dissolved into passionate kisses and groping. Alpha guided my hand to her dripping pussy, and I eagerly obliged, plunging fingers inside as I rubbed her pearl, providing relief to all three of them at once.

As the end approached, I met Halo's bounces with my own thrusts. Bodies shook and spasmed, orgasms hitting us hard. I grunted, releasing into her hot depths, painting her inner walls white as she coated my shaft in return.

"Gosh, yes! AH!" Halo screamed, her ecstasy filling the air.

"Oh, God! I'm gonna fill his mouth with my cum! AHhhh!" Cherry shouted, exploding into me.

"Yes! Yes! I'm fucking cum—Oh fuuuck!" Alpha screamed as she coated my hand.

Noisy squeals of womanly pleasure filled the room. After the orgasmic bliss subsided, Alpha relaxed with her back against the couch, and Cherry and Halo cuddled up to either side of me. With a sore jaw, cramped hand, and spent cock, I lay there, grinning like a fool. *This is the peak, the pinnacle of existence. My life is complete, and from here, it's all downhill.*

I furrowed my brow, staring at Cherry as she tried to catch her breath. "Enjoy yourself?"

She giggled, a mischievous glint in her eyes. "More than I should have."

I nodded, a smirk tugging at my lips. "Good," I said before we lapsed into a comfortable silence.

Suddenly, a squeak shattered the tranquility, and Halo gasped. "Oh shoot! I totally forgot about Logan Jr.! He's probably starving." She bolted up, dashing over to tend to her pet. I couldn't help but admire Cherry's handprint on her firm jiggling ass as she ran, already anticipating the delight that came with spanking it, thinking back to the sweet sounds it made when Cherry did it.

Cherry growled at the mention of the pet's name, rising to argue with Halo once again. I exchanged an amused glance with Alpha, both of us rolling our eyes before bursting into laughter. I shot a grin at the fiery-haired witch. "Guess you can't win 'em all..."

CHAPTER 16

Experimentation

Things were calm, so I was lounging on the couch with Cherry's head on my lap as she delved into a grimoire. Ever since our outrageously hot four-way, Alpha had been glued to the TV, looking for any morsel of news on the coven war or the amulet that she could find. Halo was sprawled on the floor, softly snoring while Logan Jr. nestled between her boobs—*Clever little bastard.* I idly ran my fingers through Cherry's dark locks, enjoying the silky smooth strands between my digits as I watched the news with Alpha. My mind kept drifting to recently minted memories, a smile tugging at the corner of my lips. Glancing down at the Vampire Witch, I admired her flawless features and found her already staring up at me.

She grinned, flicking one of her fangs with her tongue. "Hey, do you think it would be improper if I sucked your cock while I read my book? It comforts me," she said sweetly, winking, but definitely not joking.

Just like that, my rapidly growing bulge pressed against the back of her head. Before I could respond with just how proper I thought that suggestion was, Alpha cut in with a growl. "Not now."

Cherry arched her back, peering upside down at Alpha with a pout, her head pressing into my crotch and making things even harder for me. "Why not?"

Alpha rose from the couch, stretching out her limbs. "Because I need you to keep an eye on the TV for news while I whip up some Bestial Spell Tokens for us to sell. You can't do that with your nose buried in a book—or in his pelvis for that matter."

The talk of Spell Tokens roused another growing curiosity in me. I tilted my head, focusing on Alpha. "About Spell Tokens, Halo gave me a rundown at the mall—how it's your primary currency and how the different affinities help witches to cast spells that are outside of their affinity. But I want to know more."

Feeling Cherry's movement in my lap, I noticed her holding a mirror that she'd grabbed from somewhere. She held it up in front of my stomach, bobbed her head a few times, then shook her head and adjusted the mirror. I ignored her, turning my attention back to Alpha.

Alpha settled onto the floor cross-legged. "Like you said, they're basically our money. That's one reason the three of us formed a coven. With our rare and strong affinities, we stand a good chance of becoming a top-tier coven despite our size—thanks to you and the Lunar Amulet, specifically."

Cherry stole my attention as she unzipped my pants and wrapped her hand around my shaft. "I can make this work…" Just as she was about to pull it out, she was interrupted.

"Cherry," Alpha said, "run to my room and get my purse."

Cherry's eyes remained glued to the mirror as she snapped back, "Can't you see I'm busy here? I'm trying to watch the news for you." She continued trying to fish my cock out.

"*Now*, Cherry," Alpha growled, cutting through Cherry's horny haze.

"Ugh. Fine!" she huffed before scurrying off.

I zipped my pants back up with a guilty shrug.

Alpha rolled her eyes and smirked. "She was about to use a mirror to watch the news while she sucked your cock, wasn't she?"

I cleared my throat. "Yup."

It was less than a minute before Cherry returned, dropping the small coin purse on Alpha's lap. "Cheating thief ruining my goddamn snack time," Cherry muttered under her breath.

With a shake of her head, Alpha laid out several types of Spell Tokens on the floor in front of her.

I leaned forward on the edge of the couch to inspect the tokens. Cherry noticed my new position, pouted, and sat next to me with her elbows on her knees and her chin in her hands. Her lips kept their pout while she pressed her cheeks up, forcing her eyes to squint. I noted how adorable she looked, but focused on the lesson.

There were a variety of tokens on the ground, each offering a hint of the affinity they contained. Alpha quickly identified our coven's tokens. She pointed to each, one after another. "This one with the wolf's head is a Beast Token, this one with the fangs and drop of blood is a Vampiric Token, and this one with the angelic wings is a Celestial Token."

I glanced over at the others, seeing a sword, cloud, fire, and one with a thumbs up, among others. I was just about to ask about the thumbs-up token when I spotted a spider, and my eyes slightly widened. "Hang the fuck on a minute. The spider token, how common are those?"

"The Arachnid Token? Not very common. Why?" Alpha furrowed her brow.

"So, Spider Witches aren't exactly a dime a dozen, huh?"

"No. They are as rare as our affinities."

"Do you know who made that token?"

"Nope. We buy ours at Hot Topic."

I scratched my chin in thought. "Pump N' Go."

Cherry waggled her brows and nodded sagely. "Sure. You could pump in me and go, absolutely."

I shot Cherry a grin. "I did pump in you, but you sure as hell didn't let me go," I teased.

She smiled with a mischievous look in her crimson eyes. "That's true. I might need to break out those cuffs again soon."

A cough from Alpha snapped me back on topic. I cleared my throat, giving Alpha my full attention again.

"You're thinking that the token's from the same witch you fought, aren't you?" Alpha asked.

I nodded. "Yup. You ever met her?"

Shaking her head, Alpha replied, "No. It's like the other silent auctions. I've never met a Spider Witch before."

"Same here. But someone spends a lot of Arachnid Tokens on my tokens. We trade with each other a ton, but I've never met them," Cherry added.

I let out a bitter chuckle. "Small world isn't it? The Arachnid Witch at the Pump N' Go tried to use a Vampiric Token on me. I felt my connection with you protect me. I thought maybe our bond shielded me from Vampiric spells. But what if it was actually protecting me from *your* magic specifically?" I mused.

Alpha nodded. "It makes sense. Our coven charter and contract with you prevents us from intentionally harming each other. If they were using the token infused with another witch's magic besides Cherry's, then it should have worked. Well, as well as any other spells she threw at you," she noted, her red tail flicking behind her.

"Speaking of witches, what are the different types of witches? Sorry, I know that's a big question." I said that as I dropped to the floor, picking up various tokens and inspecting them.

Cherry slid over on the couch behind me, wrapping her legs around my torso as she rubbed my shoulders. "Not as big as *something*," she purred in my ear.

Two furry ears twitched, but otherwise Alpha ignored Cherry's innuendo. "There are hundreds of types of witches. Too many to cover all at once. Each has their own grimoires and traditions."

"Halo warned me about the grimoires and their danger," I said.

Alpha nodded. "Cherry here started from zero. She had to create her own grimoire and learn spells through trial and error. Now she's got a few more that she picked up along the way."

The topic of Magic always left me with so many questions. Some spells the girls did were completely invisible, just a flick of the wrist or a few whispered words. Others needed rituals, glowed, changed the temperature of the room, or gave off calming or creepy vibes when cast. "I see you girls casting similar spells all the time. Is there, like, a basic magic that every witch can perform? And when do they specialize?"

Patiently, Alpha nodded at me as I finished. "Yeah, there is a basic magic. Some grimoires teach all kinds of general magic that all affinities can use. However, even though they're the same basic spells, we still have to connect to the magic through our affinities."

I nodded, trying to keep up. "So, it's like the magic faucet, but you need a specific glass to drink?"

"You're so fucking obsessed with filling glasses," Cherry muttered behind me.

Looking over my shoulder I said, "Right, you'd rather have a '*nice thick sausage*' instead." It was a reference to our first meeting in the Student

Union, and it took me back for a moment, making me grin.

Cherry waggled her brows.

Alpha brushed her off. "Yeah, kinda like that. But each affinity has its own spells, with strengths and weaknesses. Take healing spells, for example. All witches can patch up a minor cut and stuff. But some affinities heal way more serious things. Nothing can beat Celestial Magic and angelic healing. They can heal pretty much anything short of true death—body, mind, and soul."

Barely containing my shock at how powerful Halo's healing apparently was, I tried to absorb everything Alpha said. "Can you tell me about your attuned magic—maybe show me something cool?" I shifted my position to get a better view of Cherry too.

Cherry giggled like a mischievous imp. "Hell yeah, watch this." Aiming a finger at the sleeping blonde beauty, a red ball of power shot from Cherry's fingertip and into Halo's neck without leaving so much as a blemish on her skin. Tiny red sparks drifted behind it like a miniature comet. At first, nothing happened. But then, only a few seconds later, a small crimson mist wafted out of Halo's mouth and zoomed across the room, diving back into Cherry's finger.

Logan Jr. caught on to what was happening and hissed. Halo's eyes popped open after that. Her nostrils flared as she sat up so fast that she almost launched poor Logan Jr. across the room. She caught herself, quickly putting the rat down, but fury burned in her fierce blue eyes. "Cherry! Don't steal my libido! I need it for Logan!"

Cherry snickered like a maniac but otherwise ignored the angry witch. "My vampiric affinities are great for robbing people of certain energies and essences, but that's not all I've got up my sleeve. I can morph into a few animals too."

My eyebrows shot up at that. "Really? Turning into animals? That sounds awesome. What can you shift into?"

Cherry tilted her head and tapped her lip as she mulled it over. "Well, let's see. I can be a wolf, a bat, and a rat. Plus," she flashed a wicked grin. "I can patch myself up if I suck the blood of a human." She winked with suspicious timing. "But don't sweat it, you're too magical for it to work with you."

I wasn't sure I was sold on the whole blood-sucking thing, but there was something about the animals Cherry could morph into that gave me pause. Unfortunately, before I could give it any consideration, Halo started taunting Cherry.

"Oh, so you're saying that you don't want to suck Logan?" Halo quipped with hands on hips.

"What?! Of course, I do! Watch, I'll do it right now!" Cherry shouted.

"Are you sure you won't be too busy sneaking out to suck—Ah!" Halo shouted in surprise.

Cherry launched herself at Halo, cutting her off and sending them both crashing to the floor. "You fucking witch!"

Alpha rolled her eyes but continued with my lesson. "Anyway, bestial spells include shapeshifting similar to what Cherry can do, but they aren't just for that"

"Dirty twat waffle!" Halo bellowed as she and Cherry tumbled past us, grappling for dominance.

To her credit, Alpha carried on as if nothing was amiss. "I can use it to communicate with wild beasts and tap into their auras."

"I'll shut that mouth with my twat waffle! Serves you right, fucking waffle loving angel-slut!" Cherry grunted as they rolled past us again, heading back the way they came.

"That's why Beast Tokens are so popular. They make it easier for witches to train their familiars and find animals for help," Alpha concluded.

Halo and Cherry finally came to a halt, grappling right in front of us. Halo was straddling Cherry's face, pinning her down between her thighs. "I win! And for your punishment, since you're so keen to make threats, I'm going to sit on your face just like this while Logan fucks me from behind later."

"This is bullshit. You cheated," came Cherry's muffled protest.

Ignoring Cherry's complaints, Halo tightened her grip. She joined in Alpha and my conversation as if everything was perfectly normal, despite Cherry's tapping in an attempt to surrender. "My powers are all related to healing, purification, retribution, protection—stuff like that."

The more Cherry tapped and shouted into Halo's center, the deeper Halo's blush became. I adjusted my pants at the sight. The current topic was too exciting to get sidetracked. "Alright ladies, how about you show off some of your badass magic? Show me one of your favorite spells."

Cherry, still confined to her 'waffle prison' shouted, "I'll go first!" Despite Cherry technically already having gone first, I wasn't going to turn down the chance to see more magic.

A red mist expanded from her body, quickly forming a cloud, obscuring her from view before condensing and slipping back into her new form. The mist quickly shrank into a large black rat with red eyes. She squeaked as she ran, freeing herself from the enviable prison Halo's thighs had created. Mid run, another puff of red smoke burst from her tiny body. It quickly condensed into the form of a black wolf with the same red eyes as she finally reached my lap where she curled up contentedly.

Unable to resist, I began petting her soft fur as Halo handed me a red Solo cup. "Here, take a sip," she said.

I did, then frowned. "Beer?"

She nodded, smiling at me as she took the cup back. Her glorious white wings spread out on her back. She looked at the liquid in the cup as her blue eyes glowed and a golden light shone around the cup. As quickly as it began, it ended. She fluttered her wings happily before they folded behind her back again while she handed me the cup.

I sipped, then looked into the cup. "Water?"

Halo shrugged. "Not very flashy, but it's fun to prank people at the bar with it."

I nodded, acknowledging the point, then observed as Alpha strolled over to the window. She pushed it open and whistled. Seconds later, pigeons flooded the room, flying in circles and causing utter chaos. Before I could object, they were gone, all flying back out into the world. Alpha glanced at me with a questioning brow.

"Impressive," I said to all the girls with a smile while scratching Cherry under her chin. "You're all so powerful." A glimmer of hope entered my eyes. "What about Spell Tokens and me? Do you think I'll be able to use them for anything?"

Halo's expression softened. A pitying look replaced her smile. "No, I—"

A gasp escaped Alpha's lips, cutting off Halo's denial. "Hang on!" Alpha said before rushing off. Halo and I exchanged curious looks. Before we could ask what was going on, the redhead was back with a grimoire I'd recently seen in Halo's room. I stood up, cradling Cherry in my arms. Halo and I joined Alpha as she sat the grimoire on the desk, flipping through it until she found the page about binding contracts and essences to magical objects.

"What do you think would happen if we bound our essences and an open-ended contract through our connections with Logan to a token of our affinity? In theory, he could use the token to accept the contract attached to it and activate the transformation," Alpha said with wide eyes.

A red mist replaced Cherry in my arms. I felt nothing but a warm tingle and an increase of weight as she transformed back into her normal form. I looked down in surprise at the woman I now held in a princess carry. She grinned, gave me a quick peck on the lips, then looked at the other ladies. Her eyes twinkled with excitement at the prospect.

"I'll try it!" Halo shouted excitedly. "He hasn't used my form yet."

Cherry and Alpha nodded enthusiastically. I sat Cherry down and bounced on my toes in anticipation. Sure, if it worked, I'd still be taking the same forms I did before, but I'd technically be casting the spell myself. It was the first step in my dream of being able to wield magic on my own. If they were wrong in their assumption that I couldn't use Spell Tokens for anything, then maybe they were wrong about me wielding magic in other ways.

A golden token with angelic wings popped into Halo's palm. Her mouth tightened into a thin line as she squinted at the token. Then, her eyes shifted from blue to gold, and she kissed the token. The familiar golden glow of our binding magic formed around her before condensing. But, instead of going into her hand and forming the tattoo like usual, the power slid down her arm and all went into the token. A smaller version of the tattoo joined the angelic wings.

I looked on hopefully. "So, you put some of your power into the token, and what? You put what you wanted in exchange for using it? Like, the opposite of how we do things when you request my help?"

Halo nodded. "Yup. Try it," she said as she tossed the token to me.

I held up the token, inspecting it. I felt a tendril of power from it enter me, and suddenly I knew exactly what to do. It was as if the token imprinted instructions into my mind. I understood how long it would last and the cost of using it. Using it was up to me and if I felt the cost was worth it or not.

If they wanted me to be more powerful, they'd have to put more magic into the token, increasing the strength and duration of the form. In this case, I thought it was more than worth the cost it asked of me. Taking a few steps back, I looked the girls over, watching as they looked on with excitement, and even though I knew I didn't need to, I kissed the token.

This time, the transformation wasn't as drastic as I was used to. I watched the girls shrink as I grew to at least eight feet in height, feeling grateful that the living room had a vaulted ceiling. I stashed my clothing quickly as shiny metal armor replaced the skin on my arms and legs, like scales that flared out from my body in V-shaped patterns. Larger, decorative plating covered my groin, stomach, and chest. The chest plate contained a sizable glowing golden diamond in its center.

A pair of shining metal angel wings caught my attention as my back suddenly felt heavier. My offhand was abruptly holding a massive shield with two spikes on the bottom and a huge golden diamond in the upper center. My dominant hand was holding a large, shimmering silver blade. The metal plating covered my head, and my vision changed. I had a perfect 180-degree field of view. All of my peripheral vision was incorporated, seeing everything within my sight with perfect clarity.

I didn't even need to shift my focus when a flash came from a squealing Halo. "This is going to be my new desktop background! Eeeee!" She jumped up and down with excitement, and for a moment, I was amazed by my capability to focus completely on all three breathtaking women at the same time. With a thought, the shield and sword were gone.

"Holy shit, that's so cool," Cherry said.

Alpha beamed. "Very impressive. You look badass. Halo, what did you charge him to use the token?"

Halo grinned. "Oh, not much. He just has to snuggle with me all night long."

Cherry and Alpha both rolled their eyes while I grinned. *Talk about a win win. Totally worth it.*

CHAPTER 17

Date Night

After a few more days of lazing around, catching up on the news, engaging in another foursome, and squabbling over who gets what, we were all feeling stir-crazy. The constant bickering between Halo and Cherry was getting unbearable, and I wasn't sure whether to intervene or let it play out. Eventually, I retreated to my room, squeezed in a workout, took a shower, and lay on my bed with a towel around my waist, staring at the ceiling as I wished for some clarity.

The click of my door opening grabbed my attention. I wasn't disappointed when Cherry walked in, dressed in nothing but a merlot-red bra and thong with tiny black bows front and center. She sauntered over to the bed and crawled up between my legs, licking her crimson lips, fangs out on full display. Despite her being half of the problem I was stressed over, her dangerous yet seductive aura still got my blood pumping.

Cherry's hand slipped under my towel, gripping my growing manhood. "Mmm. Mind if I join you? Never mind. I don't care if you mind or not, 'cause I'm doing it anyway."

A mix of emotions hit me as the door opened again, revealing Halo's beaming smile. Unlike Cherry, Halo sported a lacy blue bra with white trim and matching panties. Her smile faded into a frown when she spotted Cherry beside me.

Strutting over, Halo focused her attention back on me and crawled next to Cherry on the bed. "Scoot over. Alpha says we gotta share."

With that, she yanked my towel open, making Cherry shift over.

Cherry resisted, but Halo's physical strength won out. "Fine. But you can only play with his balls. This cock's mine since I got here first."

Halo, already fondling my balls, scowled at Cherry, who was busy stroking my shaft. "That's not sharing."

With a smirk, Cherry licked my tip, eyes locked on Halo. "Tough luck, babe. You snooze, you lose."

Squinting blue eyes met a crimson gaze, and Halo lunged forward, claiming her lick with a smirk. "Think again, witch."

Rolling my eyes, my reaction went unnoticed by the squabbling duo at first, but I'd had enough. In a fit of frustration or inspiration, I grabbed a fistful of Cherry's hair and one of Halo's pigtails, pulling them down until both women's lips were pressed against the sides of my length.

Two pairs of eyes widened as they peered up at me. "Look, I'm getting tired of all this fighting. A little bickering and a few catty remarks are fine, but you two have been getting out of control. From now on, if you push it too far, I'm ditching you and going to screw Alpha instead. Got it?"

"Mhmm!" two muffled voices chorused, their lips wrapped around either side of my shaft.

"Good. This is how this is gonna go. You're both going to turn those asses toward me. If you're behaving and playing nice, then I'll use my fingers. If you misbehave, I'll take them away. Do you understand?"

Again, both muffled voices agreed, "Mhmm!"

I eased my grip as they enthusiastically obeyed my instructions. Keeping them at a 45 degree angle to my body gave me the perfect blend of access and visibility. Finally, all those logistics classes were paying off. With the preparations complete, I reasserted my grip on their hair and took charge once again.

I guided them up and down as they both eagerly kissed and licked my shaft. And since they were behaving, I released their hair to free up my hands for other recreational activities. Reaching forward, I slowly caressed and massaged their firm asses as I watched.

Occasionally their tongues would accidentally touch, and I'd squeeze their asses to let them know how much I liked it. They were smart girls, and I wasn't surprised when they caught on quickly and started making out around the head of my cock.

They were playing so well together that it only seemed fitting to start rewarding them. I slapped both their asses, eliciting moans of pleasure and a shout from Halo: "Gosh, yes! Harder, baby!" I obliged, giving them a harder slap. Then just for good measure, I gave them one more.

Halo's head dipped, disappearing as she worshiped my balls, while Cherry's lips parted and she began sucking on the tip, all while they both stroked my shaft. After a few moments, Halo slipped me out of her mouth. "Mmm, golly, baby, your balls taste so good—ah!"

She was interrupted when I slid both girls' panties to the side and slipped a finger into each of their tight, wet, slits.

"Mmm!" Cherry moaned before releasing my tip. "Not as good as this thick fucking cockhead tastes," she prodded.

As a slight punishment for Cherry's minor attempt to antagonize, I removed my finger. Her response was swift and expected as she began to pout and beg, "I–I'm sorry! I won't do it again! Please put it back in, baby!"

Halo giggled. "That's what you get."

Without wasting any time, I started fingering Cherry again, and pulled my digit out of Halo.

Cherry stroked my shaft like a seasoned pro. "Ffuck! You're so good with your fingers, baby. I need more!" Then her eyes glowed and I could swear that I saw a lightbulb turn on above her head.

In contrast, Halo's head shot up, and her giggling was swiftly replaced by her own set of apologetic cries, but her hand still dutifully massaged my balls. "Logan! No, I'm sorry! I didn't mean it, it was a silly joke. I promise I won't—glug."

Her words were swiftly cut off as Cherry pushed her head down and forced my dick into Halo's throat. "See! I can share! I'm a good little slut for you, baby! Reward me more?" Cherry cooed like she'd just performed the most romantic gesture the world had ever seen.

If I weren't busy gasping from the instant sensation of Halo's tight warm throat engulfing my cock, I would have happily agreed. Instead, I reached over with my only free hand and slapped Cherry on the ass before inserting a second finger inside of her. As far as I was concerned, that kind of innovative thinking deserved a little extra reward. "Nyah! Ahh... Wow, baby! Don't fucking stop!" she cried out as she continued to guide Halo's head up and down my length.

For Halo's part, she took this new development like a champ, desperately bobbing along with Cherry's direction for all she was worth—earning her own pair of slightly used

Logan phalanges in the process. She moaned around my length as I fucked her with my digits. "MMMmmm!"

Eventually, Halo was forced to come up for air, and Cherry greedily took her place. Halo's hips pushed into my hand as she begged for more, "Holy moly! You know just what my pussy needs, baby! I want more! Please give me more!"

I couldn't deny such a polite request, so I picked up my pace and did my best to wreck those pussies with my fingers. All the while the girls swapped back and forth between my cock and my balls in an impressive display of coordination. I only wish I had a free hand to wipe the tear from my eye as I looked on and learned that teamwork really did make the dream work.

I knew my end was growing near, so I pulled out of them and started furiously rubbing their firm pearls. Their cries of pleasure brought me even closer to reaching my limit.

"Oh fuck! You treat my pussy so—ah—good. Ahhh!" Cherry moaned.

"Don't stop, baby! Ah! Please! I'm so—mmm—gosh-darn close!" Halo begged.

Cherry was slurping on my cock like there's no tomorrow, and I felt it getting thicker by the second. Her eyes lit up as I stiffened even more in her mouth, and she knew I was about to blow. "Mhmm! Mhmm!" Cherry encouraged before the first spurt of cum shot into her throat.

She pulled off my tip and Halo joined her as the two continued stroking my shaft. The sight of the two witches as they tilted their heads and started making out around the tip of my cock as I came was magical–pun intended.

Rope after rope of my warm seed shot in the air before landing on their faces and hair, painting them in white. Just as my orgasm ended, both girls reached their peak.

Cherry's body trembled and she cried out, "Yah–Mmm. Fuck, baby! Ah!"

Halo's body spasmed at the same time while she moaned. "Oh gosh, Logan, baby! I'm–Ah!"

Suddenly, my feeling of arousal was joined by confusion and sheer amazement all at once.

Halo started licking Cherry's face frantically, trying to take the mess for herself. "Give me that! It's mine!"

Rather than simply back away, Cherry was on the same mission, trying to swipe all my cum from Halo's face. "No! You give it back! I was here first! The cum is mine!"

Shaking my head in disbelief, I watched as they rolled off the bed and onto the floor, grappling for dominance once again. I decided to look on the bright side. At least they were working together for a little while. *One step at a time, Logan. Take the wins where you can get them,* I reminded myself, before getting dressed and slipping quietly out of the room.

Eventually, things settled down, and we were back to chilling in the living room. With tensions over the amulet easing in the city but tensions over cuddle time with me heating up in the house, we decided it was time for us to get out for a bit. Alpha declared we were all going out for dinner.

There was a round of cheers and applause at the decision. Well, I cheered and applauded, anyway. Halo and Cherry were back to wrestling again.

· ♥ · ♥ · ♥ · ♥ · ♥ ·

With a "Woohoo!" I ran out the front door, only for two girls to come sprinting behind me.

"Shotgun!" Cherry shouted when she noticed me getting behind the wheel.

"Aww! Not cool!" Halo whined.

"Enough!" Alpha snapped, apparently finally having had enough. "I won't tolerate this fighting tonight. We all need this, and if you two don't cut it out, then Logan will just take me out alone."

Immediately both girls beamed at her sweetly and held each other's hands as if there was never a problem to begin with.

"Here, please allow me to get the door for you," Halo said through her fake smile.

"Thank you. You are the—the best, I guess," Cherry also said through gritted teeth with a mischievous smile.

With everyone in, I started the car and headed in the direction opposite the museum.

"Good girls, keep it up and maybe I won't keep Logan all to myself when we get home," Alpha said.

Cherry ignored her as she placed her hand instantly on my lap.

I didn't want to start trouble by admitting how wonderful and peaceful that sounded, so instead I asked, "Where do we want to eat?"

Cherry's tongued a fang as she thought. Then she gave me an impish grin. "Depends, are we talking blood? Because if so I could go for some Italian."

I frowned at her and checked the rearview mirror. "C'mon, really? I'm gonna lose my appetite."

Her lips puffed out into a pout. "I was only teasing! My answer is the same, though. Pasta sounds really good right now." She was too cute to be mad at, so I just smiled and shook my head.

"How about some sushi?" Halo interjected.

"I'm not opposed to putting something thick, round, and raw into my mouth," Cherry smirked with a wink. I chuckled and shifted her hand back closer to my knee after it mysteriously drifted closer to my inner thigh. She started pouting again. "I don't want sushi, though," Cherry complained.

Alpha sighed in exasperation. "Let's stop flirting and pick a place. I'm starving."

To no one's surprise, Halo was firmly on Alpha's side on this one. "She's right. You shouldn't be wasting time flirting, and we can't keep driving with nowhere to go."

Cherry sulked and crossed her arms. "Fine. But after we pick a place, I'm going to flirt as much as I want."

"How about Chinese food? There's that one place, Wok On The Wild Side, we've been hoping to check it out for a while, right?" I suggested, hoping to salvage the mood.

"Yeah, I like that idea. We're getting Chinese food. That's final," Alpha declared, sinking in her seat and crossing her arms. "See how easy that was? Fuck."

"So... Logan..." Cherry leaned in closer to me, her hand finding its way back up my thigh. She grinned mischievously. "Maybe after dinner we can talk more about what to do with your eggroll and my fortune cookie."

With an eye roll, Alpha let out a sigh, and I spent the rest of the drive deflecting Cherry's playful touches. No matter how much I would have enjoyed Cherry's attention on the road, keeping the peace for at least a few hours was worth it.

• ♥ • ♥ • ♥ • ♥ • ♥ •

The Chinese place turned out to be a buffet. We stopped by the line, grabbed some plates, and started filling them up. An old man on the opposite side of the buffet line saw both Halo and Cherry as they took turns kissing my cheek and groping my crotch. He threw me a thumbs up and his wife slapped him on the arm.

Alpha sat across from me, leaving Halo and Cherry free to take the seats on either side. Two feet slipped out of shoes, and next thing I knew, toes were creeping up and down my legs.

Alpha wasn't playing around, though. She finished chewing a bite from an egg roll, then jumped right into her agenda. "Listen up, ladies and pet. We need to figure out what our next steps are going to be. The way I see it, we're having a classic Icarus moment—we flew too close to the sun because we could, and now things are a bit dangerous. We have the Lunar Amulet *and* the best Greater Familiar in the city, maybe the state, so we have a hell of an advantage despite our small size, but now we have to figure out what we'll do next to gain more power."

At the mention of this serious business, both Halo and Cherry sobered up. While their feet didn't leave my legs, they did halt their creeping climb to my thighs.

"The only thing I can think of is expanding our coven," Cherry said, taking a swig of her drink.

Alpha scrunched her brow after slurping down some lo mien. "That would make us more powerful, and it feels inevitable, but I don't want to do that until I'm sure we have to. It would get us extremely noticed."

Halo cocked her head. One of her trademark pigtails nearly landed on the table as she rested her chin in her hand. "We should just ditch Fresco City. We could go to a town with no big covens and hide out there, y'know?"

Red hair swayed as Alpha shook her head. "Maybe one day, but not yet. We aren't ready for that."

Being the uncivilized brute I am, I let my curiosity bulldoze my manners, and I blurted out my question right before I finished chewing. "Why not? I mean, what are we even doing here in Fresco City in the first place? Why here? I don't see what our endgame is."

Cherry shook her head. "Hell, at this point, neither do I. A few weeks back, ruling the city sounded badass. But now that we've got Logan, all I wanna do is kick back, enjoy life, and enjoy my happiness while improving my magic. I'm thinking we just rob another bank and set up at a beach bungalow somewhere. We could lounge around all day, rocking nothing but bikinis while we spoil our pet rotten."

"Can't say I'm not down for that," I chimed in.

With a shake of her head, Halo piped up, "Cherry's forgetting something major."

I frowned as I noticed the Vampire Witch's face grow tense in confirmation. "What's that?" I asked.

"We have to amp up our power if you're going to ever impregnate us," she said like we were discussing the damn weather over dinner.

I almost choked on my drink as I did a spit take. "Say what now?" It wasn't a total surprise. In the group text I read when I first was kidnapped by them, I did notice that they mentioned letting me breed them, but it wasn't something that had come up since then, so I thought it was something to discuss in the distant future.

Halo giggled. "That's the endgame, dude. We're aiming to build the ultimate coven so we can live by our own rules without fear and start our own families. We all wanna pop out some kids someday, too. By having you breed us, we can tap into the full potential of your bloodline and fuse our potential with yours."

"But none of you are—" I started to ask as my brows raised in concern.

"Nope. None of us are preggo," Alpha cut in. "Witches can't just get knocked up like regular people. Well, it *can* happen naturally, but it's rarer than a unicorn. What, did you think we were all on birth control when we let you creampie us again and again or something?" she asked, smirking.

I spluttered. "I—I—I... wait, are there real unicorns?"

Alpha just shook her head and chuckled.

After taking a deep breath, I gathered my thoughts and calmed down. It was on me for jumping to conclusions and never asking these questions before now, but I'd just been so caught up with my beautiful lifestyle that I hadn't considered it much. "So, you're saying you don't have enough magic to get pregnant?"

"It's not about lacking strength, it's about not having the right attunements and being ready enough to withstand the spell. For a witch to get knocked up, she normally needs a Fertility Witch," Alpha explained.

Halo chimed in. "They're about the rarest type of witch, too. If they weren't, the world would probably be full of witches by now."

"And the biggest covens always have them on lockdown," Cherry added. "That means they control who gets to breed and who doesn't."

"So, for us to make sure you'll give us all the daughters we want, we need a Fertility Witch of our own, which means we need to be strong enough to snag one. Lucky for us, there's a famous witch of that kind right here in Fresco City who hasn't been recruited into any coven. That's why we're here," Alpha explained.

I was left speechless, trying to wrap my head around the bombshell they just dropped. Shit went from casual to life-altering real quick. This was the first time they'd mentioned how badly they all wanted kids, and to be fair, I wanted a family too—someday.

I glanced up from my food at Cherry, who gave me a reassuring smile and nod. Seeing Halo's worried expression, I locked eyes with her next. "Logan, how do you feel about—"

Alpha cut her off with a scoff. "It's not his job to have opinions on our endgame. This is why we have him. Like it or not, he's gonna pump out as many daughters as we want."

"What about sons?" I asked.

Alpha stared back at me blankly, like I'd just said Happy Hanukkah to Santa Claus. "With a Fertility Witch, we can guarantee we only have daughters. Sons can't be witches. It'd be a waste. Sorry, you don't get an opinion on this one."

"No. I wanna hear what he thinks, whether he's got a say or not," Cherry said in a rare moment of defiance. I felt her grip my hand under the table, giving it a reassuring squeeze as she turned to me, waiting with a gentle smile.

I let out a deep breath, trying to calm myself before I said something to Alpha that I'd later regret. "I grew up without a family. You all know this. People had two opinions of me. Either they pitied me or saw me as a waste of resources." I noticed the shame on Alpha's face, though she quickly schooled her expression. "Becoming a dad is not something I'm in a hurry to achieve, but I do like the idea—one day. I don't like taking the possibility of having a son entirely off the table.

"Sometimes I wake up in the middle of the night confused about everything, assuming it was all a dream until my surroundings sink in. I feel like I have class or work in the morning and that all of this has just been a starvation-induced hallucination. Those nights a part of me panics and I feel like I've made a huge mistake. I ask myself how all of this madness happened to me. But then I think about the three of you, and those fears slip away.

"It's those thoughts of you girls that help me realize how special what we have is. And, I admit, I don't hate the idea of spending the rest of my life with all of you. You're all hot, fun, and total badasses. But having kids is another thing altogether. I do want to be a dad one day. If I don't have a choice about when that happens, I'll do whatever I can to be a good father, even if I have no examples of my own to look to."

"It's not your job to be a father to our daughters," Alpha pointed at me matter-of-factly. "Your job is to protect the three of us, keep us sexually satisfied, keep our magic thrumming with power, and eventually give us our daughters to raise. The only fatherly duty you'll have will be to protect the children just as you'd protect us. We'll teach witches how to be witches. What could you possibly offer them?"

I was stunned by what she said, but not surprised. She didn't say the words to hurt me, but they still felt cruel. Cherry leaned against me and squeezed my hand—not ready to speak up, but offering some kind of reassurance, at least. I appreciated that.

Halo frowned at Alpha, though, and had something to say. "We can figure out his role as a father when the time comes. When I have a baby, I definitely want Logan to love her with me." She cradled her egg roll like a child. "I can imagine him holding our little girl, playing with her little toesies, tickling her tiny belly, and teaching her to talk and—drive a van, I guess. I think he'll be a great dad."

I noticed Cherry's eyes were a little wet as she took in Halo's words.

Alpha seemed unimpressed, however, causing my frustration to bubble inside me again. "Great, we let our food get cold because of all this talking," she growled. "It's all useless to discuss anyway. Logan—you know your job. It hasn't been that bad of a fit for you, I dare say, so be grateful for what you have. That is all."

With that, no one said a word throughout the rest of the meal. Halo and Cherry constantly tried to hold my hands under the table as I ate, forcing me to rotate which hand I used. I could have just let them feed me, but I didn't like the thought of looking like a child who needed to be fed at the table. Especially when I learned Halo liked to tease me when she fed me, saying things like 'Here comes the aiwpwane'.

Eventually, we finished eating and paid at the register. I quietly prayed for anything that could break the tension between Alpha and me, or it would be a long drive home. We walked out of the restaurant and headed to the car—or we tried to. When we stepped through the exit, we didn't find ourselves in a parking lot. We were in an open field, the lights of the city far in the distance, and we weren't alone.

CHAPTER 18

The Standoff

It took us a moment to orient ourselves as we realized we weren't where we expected to be. We stood smack dab in the middle of a massive open prairie, far outside of the city, but we could make out buildings miles and miles away. The moon was half lit, but still shone like a spotlight down upon us in the dark field, giving plenty of light for all to see by, even those without night vision. A soft breeze blew on the wind, but that wasn't what gave me the chills.

Across from us, about fifty feet away, stood seven other witches. I scanned them, trying to determine their motives and use the knowledge the girls taught me on one of our many days in seclusion to discern what kind of witch they might be.

On the left was a brunette with long wavy hair. Symbols and runes covered her skin, each one giving me bad vibes like she was walking around covered in curses—she had to be a Hex Witch. Next to her was another brunette who had her hair tied up in a bun. Her skin shimmered with various colors and her belt was riddled with vials and pouches—she was definitely a Potion Witch.

Then I noticed an incredible blonde with her hair in a long ponytail. She was the first witch I saw wearing glasses, and they looked damn good on her. She dressed like a sexy librarian and held a book in her hands. She was easily on par with the beauty my girls shared. Her green eyes met mine and she gave me a slight smile. From what the gals told me, the only type of witch that would carry a grimoire with them to a potential fight was a Grimoire Witch.

I didn't think flirting with potential enemies in front of my girls was a good idea, so I quickly averted my gaze far to the right. There stood a pretty redhead in a black dress. The only thing that gave me a hint of her affinity was the belt she wore with several different wands sheathed on it—no doubt a Wand Witch.

Next in line was another blonde with short curly hair. She was lithe and wore a scarf around her neck and held a broom in her hand. That was a Broom Witch if I'd ever seen one. Number six of the seven's black hair peeked out from beneath her chef's hat. She wore white robes and held a frying pan. I could guess the affinity but I'd have to ask the girls about her later. *Is she a Kitchen Witch? A Cooking Witch?* I wasn't sure, so for now I just decided to dub her, Chef Witch.

The last, but certainly not least, stood in the middle of them all, and I assumed she was the leader. She was maybe five feet tall with light green skin, long dark green hair that looked more like vines, and large black eyes. She smirked, running a hand down the pink flower petal atop her head. This witch was a solid ten. She wore a black corset that barely contained her bust, and hanging off her hips was a matching miniskirt that exposed a tempting amount of leg, all the way down to her bare feet.

Cherry was standing to the far left of our lineup, with Alpha, Halo, and finally me at the other end. My suspicions were confirmed when the short, plant-like witch sauntered closer. Her higher-pitched voice wasn't a surprise, and even if she was an enemy, I had to admit it was adorable.

The green witch stopped after only a few feet and put a hand on her hip. "Well, well, well, if it isn't Alpha and her freakin' ragtag group of misfits. You've found yourself in quite the predicament, haven't you?"

Alpha's ears perked up, her tail stiff as a board. "Hello, Rose."

"Oh, Alphypoo, you're just as tough-looking as ever," Rose said with a wicked grin. "What a waste of a perfectly good witch that you started your own coven of rejects."

Crossing her arms, Alpha scowled at her. "Cut the crap. What the hell do you want? Why are we here?"

Rose sighed. "Fine. You know what I want? What I really, really want?"

"What? Tell me what you want, what you really, really want," Alpha said.

Rose's lips suddenly sank into an angry pout. "You shouldn't have to freakin' ask. You know damn well that we're here for the Lunar Amulet."

Cherry scoffed. "What?! You think *we* snatched it? Just us three? You have to be kidding. You think we're that badass to pull off such a cool-ass heist right under the big covens' noses?"

The librarian-looking witch gave a polite cough. "Apologies, Ms. Cola, but I'm confident we are not mistaken. Like you, we also found

Logan and have been tracking him for weeks now. We had planned to make our move, but when we caught up to him, you had already lured him into your home."

Man, I had to admit, one way or another I was apparently always going to end up the Greater Familiar of some fucking coven. First Arachna and now them?

"I fail to see how you being a peeping Tom and spying on me fucking Logan has anything to do with the Lunar Amulet!" Cherry protested, resting her hands on her hips.

Rose's cheeks turned a dark shade of greenish brown, which I figured was her version of blushing. "Hey! We ain't peeping Toms! It ain't our fault you left the freakin' curtains wide open when we were already spying on your horny ass! And it's not like I—flicked my bean to the two of you banging or something!"

The librarian maintained her calm facade, but her cheeks were flushed. "Ahem, let's get our facts straight. He was the one fucking you and doing it quite a wonderful job at it if I remember correctly."

"It was sooo hot," Rose gushed, biting her lip and squirming. "Okay, maybe we did touch ourselves a bit, but that's beside the point! Stop trying to make me confess!"

Cherry smirked with bratty pride. "You have no idea. He pounded this pussy so hard, I broke our damn couch. You should see some of the shit we've done. I got tons of vids on my phone—"

"Wait, tons?" I muttered.

"Cherry, Rose... Honestly, you two," Alpha interjected, cutting the chaotic exchange off. "Let's circle back around to the topic at hand."

My raven-haired lover crossed her arms. "Yeah, my bad. Sorry."

"Ahem!" Rose interrupted, clearing her throat. She crossed her arms under her ample chest and lifted her chin. "As I was saying, we're here for two things! The Lunar Amulet and Cherry's cell phone—or a link to her iCloud video folder."

"We already told you, we don't have it," Halo chimed in. "The amulet, I mean. The video folder is—I'll text you later."

Rose rolled her eyes. "Oh, come on, honey bunches of oats! We ain't dumb. Connect the dots! See!" She held up two fingers on each hand, then touched her finger tips together, as if that explained it all. "Told ya! We ain't freakin' stupid. You snatch our Greater Familiar candidate one night, and the next, the Lunar Amulet disappears. While the rest of the city is engaging in a—forgive the term—Witch Hunt—"

Gasps rang out.

"—You have all been conspicuously quiet. In lockdown, basically."

"Alright," I muttered, holding up my hands, "look. You've got us all—"

Rose looked at me with surprise and interrupted me. "Excuse me, but the babes are talking. You can speak when spoken to. What the fuck? Can't keep your pet on a leash?"

Halo gritted her teeth. "You'll speak to him with the respect he deserves or live to regret it!"

Rose shook her head. "Tsk tsk. You poor things. Look girls, he's got them wrapped around his cock."

The bookish witch coughed and glanced at me with a blush. "Well, I can't blame them, it is a damn beautiful cock."

Rose rolled her eyes. "Well, obviously! But what was I supposed to say? Around his finger?"

"Honestly, that sounds like a hell of a time too," the librarian replied.

Rose faked clearing her throat again. "AHEM! So, as I was saying, we're here for three things! Give us the Lunar Amulet, Cherry's iCloud, and let us borrow Logan for, like, a week. Hand them over, and we'll let you leave in peace!"

The blonde with glasses tapped Rose on the shoulder to ask, "Do we still need the iCloud if we take their pet? I mean, we could make as many videos as we want."

Rose scratched her chin as she mulled it over. "True, but Cherry is hot too. I still wanna watch it. So, yeah. We still want the iCloud."

Alpha shook her head. "Am I to understand that you think you're about to steal the amulet from us? You'd have to prove we have it, first."

"We don't need to prove shit," Rose said. "We freakin' know."

A predatory smirk spread across Alpha's lips. "How about I give you a counteroffer?"

Rose perked up. "Better be good, but we'll hear you out."

Alpha cracked her knuckles. "You either leave now, accepting Cherry's iCloud video folder as a peace offering and a token of goodwill—or we shove your brooms so far up your asses, you'll be shitting splinters in the morning."

Rose growled, and the other witches tensed visibly, taking threatening-looking stances. Pitch black eyes squinted with a dangerous glint. "If that's how you wanna play it..."

Before anyone could utter another word, Rose's hands began to glow an ominous green as she lifted her palms toward the sky. Vines sprouted from the ground all around us, attempting to bind us in place. Before they could tighten their grip, lines of red shot out from Cherry's body, connecting to the vines. The life force of the plants was quickly drained, leaving nothing but withered death in their wake.

"Logan," Halo said, grabbing my arm. "Fight with us, and I'll offer my own blessing for the ring Alpha gave you!"

Knowing how incredible the strength buff was, I knew I was getting a sweet deal for something I would have done for free. So, without hesitation, I nodded and pulled her close. Her left arm shot out, a golden transparent shield forming in front of us. Just in time too, as a burst of light crashed into it. Halo grunted into our kiss, but she stood firm. The golden light of our contract glowed brightly as tattoos formed on each of our right hands. She pulled back and pointed a finger at me, her hand glowing a bright gold. "Go kick some ass, baby! Borden ean engal!"

I nodded, worry lines creasing my brow, and took a few steps back as metal armor climbed up my skin. My body grew and shifted into the full powered version of my angelic form for the first time. Suddenly, I was the biggest target on the field, standing at least ten feet tall. As I launched myself into the air, chaos erupted all around us.

Glancing down, I checked on my girls, only to realize that my worry was unwarranted. This was the first time I saw the girls fighting as a team, and their experience working together was obvious. Halo's wings were out, and she wielded a smaller transparent version of my sword and shield. She covered Alpha's flank as the redhead flexed, arched her back, and let out a deafening howl at the moon. In the distance, several wolf packs howled in reply, signaling backup was on the way. Cherry had a glowing red beam shooting from two of her fingers, one already embedded in the Potion Witch's chest, the other being blocked by the book in the librarian's hand.

The Hex Witch's hand glowed with an ominous symbol, and I watched the same symbol form on Cherry's hand, causing her to scream in pain. Despite the agony, she held firm, not releasing her spell. My girls were all badass, easily stronger than these seven witches, but I could see how the numbers could overwhelm them in time.

Alpha began her transformation, but it suddenly halted when another symbol flew from the Hex Witch's other hand. I caught the Broom Witch about to take flight from the corner of my vision, and the Wand Witch was assaulting Halo's shield. The Chef Witch had shifted positions and was attempting to aid the Potion Witch against Cherry's assault. Rose pouted about her vines and started drawing a small summoning circle.

Looking down at the fighting below filled my heart with sorrow. These poor mortals, all fighting pointlessly over a petty thing like power.

My heart went out to Cherry as she screamed in pain, and a ray of golden light shone from my shield onto both her and Alpha as I shouted, "Purify!" The light crashed into the hexes on their bodies, causing them to disperse into motes of heavenly light. Alpha, freed from the hex, shifted into a massive wolf and growled menacingly at our foes.

I flew across the battlefield at breakneck speed, dodging and blocking spells that came my way. I landed directly in front of the Hex Witch and placed one hand on her shoulder. She tried to pull away, but my grip was too strong. The witch snarled and slammed both hands into my chest. They glowed blindingly bright with a sickening green light, but when she pulled them back, her face turned from anger into horror.

Just as I was about to speak, the Chef Witch swung her red glowing frying pan toward my face. Before it could connect I bellowed, "Come, mortal. It is time for you to seek penance." My one long, visor-shaped golden eye glowed, stopping both witches dead in their tracks. The Hex Witch screamed. "Tell me your sins," I calmly demanded in my deep, amplified, divine voice.

Tears streamed down both witches' faces as their feelings of guilt and shame were amplified while they confessed their most recent sins.

"I stole Rose's cookies and blamed it on Novella! I'm so sorry!" the Hex Witch shouted.

"And I lied about this week's soup! It wasn't homemade! It came from a can!" the Chef Witch shouted.

I let go of the Hex Witch's shoulder as she collapsed to the ground, shattered and sobbing as more of her transgressions played out in her mind. The Chef Witch joined her there as an equally blubbering mess.

Another shout rang out from somewhere to my right. "Are you freakin' kidding me, Jinx? Novella, I'm sorry I put my big toe in your soup. I only did it 'cause I thought you ate my cookies."

The librarian, now identified as Novella, shot back, "Wait? You put your toe in my soup?! And it wasn't even homemade?!"

"Hehe, maybe?" came a nervous reply from Rose.

I took pleasure in hearing one of the mortals apologize unprompted. Truly, the world needed more beautiful souls like hers. Then a bear stepped out of the summoning circle and charged at Alpha, preventing her from attacking Rose, but I could tell she wouldn't have any trouble handling it. Still, I raised my hand to her and shouted, "Blessed be the pure of heart!" My voice echoing across the battlefield as a white light enveloped Alpha before settling onto her fur, adding a layer of magical protection.

A glass vial smashed against the side of my face, releasing vapors everywhere. The liquid stung but otherwise didn't seem to cause any harm. I lifted my shield, blocking another vial. "Lay down your arms, witch. Seek forgiveness, and you shall find it," I said, extending my hand to her.

She sneered, "How dare a pet speak down to me!"

After reaching into her pouch and retrieving two vials filled with blood-red liquid, she drew back her arms and threw them at me. An extreme feeling of danger emanated from the vials, and I knew that letting them hit me would be a terrible mistake.

I caught one on my shield, but the other curved, bypassing it and smashing into the armor covering my torso. The blood began to bubble and expand as it grew tendrils that writhed over my armored flesh as it spread. I could feel the foreign substance trying to seep into my body through the tiny gaps in my armor, as if it had a mind of its own. The searing pain struck me as I felt something trying to invade my mind. Terror gripped me, and I dropped to one knee.

I screamed in agony, hearing Cherry's voice calling out to me from far away. "Logan! No!"

But suddenly, I felt a peace wash over me as I fought through the pain. How could I possibly be in danger? These mortals couldn't truly harm me. I was heaven's messenger, sent from above to guide them into the grace of the Light. I stood, trembling from the agony as the strange tendrils persisted in trying to force their way deeper into my being. "DIVINE PURIFICATION!" I roared into the sky, and a massive burst of golden light shot out from my body, sending a wave of purifying celestial magic in every direction. The bloody concoction changed color, transforming into a healing salve. I felt it cleanse the wounds it had previously caused, healing not only my body but my mind as well.

I opened my eye to see the Potion Witch staring at me in disbelief. I somehow knew that not only did every potion on her belt, now glowing brilliant white, become purified, but any dangerous concoction in her dimensional storage was also cleansed. It was the first time I realized that the storage space must have been linked to our souls. I set the idle thought aside for later.

I approached the bewildered witch and reached out my hand. "I forgive you." Rather than take my hand and accept my forgiveness, she turned and rushed father away from me, screaming in terror.

Howls echoed from all around as Alpha's wolves finally arrived. Rose had to redirect her vines from assisting her bear familiar and spread them out, attempting to hold back the oncoming tide of beasts.

I surveyed the battlefield. Cherry and Novella were exchanging spells, and Halo was fighting with the Wand Witch while defending Cherry's flank, healing and purifying as needed. One other witch remained unaccounted for.

I looked to the sky, attempting to find the Broom Witch. Sure enough, the lithe woman soared through the air, circling back around before diving toward Halo from behind. I bent my knees and launched myself into the air, my steel wings flapping and offering me a burst of speed. The Broom Witch wore a wicked smile as her scarf fluttered in the wind, her gaze fixed on my blonde beauty's back as she released her spell. I swooped in, blocking it with my shield, and watched her eyes widen as she found herself on a collision course with me.

With a thought, I dismissed my shield and sword, opening my arms. "Come into my heavenly embrace." She tried to turn, but she was moving too fast, and she came at me sideways. I caught her in my arms, her broom falling away. I lowered to the ground in front of Halo and shielded us with my wings. The Broom Witch's eyes were dazed and full of fear from her hard landing against my armor. My arms glowed gold as waves of healing light passed through her. Clarity returned to her, and I set her down. "Child, you must repent for your sin. Apologize to Halo, the righteous witch, Blessed Celestial Grace."

Halo's brows furrowed, and she cast another heal past me on Alpha. "Logan, seriously? Now?"

"Your grace, as Heavenly mandate says, forgiveness is always on offer for those who seek it," I said.

The girl nervously glanced between Halo and me. "I—I'm s-sorry, your—uh—Celestial Grace. Please forgive me." She offered a shaky bow.

Halo beamed at me, then gave the girl a gentle smile. "It's okay. Just go back to your side and don't mess with us anymore. Otherwise, I'll shove your broom somewhere it shouldn't go." Despite her words, her tone sounded far too cheerful to my ears. Halo patted me on the stomach. "Go finish this, big fella."

I dropped to one knee with my fist on my chest and bowed my head. "Of course, Heavenly Lady." Then I launched myself into the air, summoning my sword and shield once again. I wasted no time as I flew straight at the wand-wielding witch. She saw me coming, and realizing that none of her spells could pierce through my wings, she understood that fighting was futile. Tossing her wand to the ground, she threw up her hands in surrender. I nodded and redirected my flight.

Descending to the ground, I leveled my sword down at Rose's throat. "Come, little one—"

She cut me off with a gulp. "Fuck," she shivered. "You don't need to tell me twice, Daddy."

"N—no. That's not what I meant," I said, shaking my head. "Come here, kneel and—"

"But, baby, you're so tall that if I kneel I won't be able to—"

"Would you cut that out? Just ask for forgiveness and give up this fight, and we'll let you leave. By the seven layers of heaven, woman."

"Oh!" she said as realization struck her like a magic missile to the face. Rose's cheeks flushed a deep greenish brown. She laughed nervously. "That's my bad. I'm really freakin' sorry that we tried to steal you and your stuff."

I dismissed my weapons and patted her head. "You are forgiven, little one."

She bit her lip. "So would you maybe call me a good girl?"

"Uh—I suppose in the eyes of heaven's grace that you are—sort of—a good girl," I said, suddenly feeling confused about how I knew heavenly law and why I was talking so fucking weird.

She shuddered. "Nice. Okay, we'll go. C'mon girls! Back to the drawing board!"

I raised my palm sending waves of warm, golden healing light into each of them, and then a bit more at my women for good measure, even though I knew Halo already had them covered. In less than a minute all seven witches were mounted and flying off into the night.

I turned back to my ladies. "Blessing of the heavens be upon you," I said, putting my hands together in a sign of prayer. A white light glowed all around them. It was only a minor blessing that would help relieve the stress from the recent battle, but every little bit would help.

"Borden eh humensel!" Halo shouted with a glowing finger pointed at me.

I watched as my field of vision decreased and I came closer to the ground. My body was returning to its normal state. I summoned my clothes in time to remain decent and let out a sigh as relief flooded through me—along with a hint of regret. Losing my immense strength and the feeling of raw power coursing through my veins was always jarring, but slipping back into my regular form did feel like coming home after a day at work.

I anticipated cheers, but all I got were quizzical smirks.

Alpha raised an eyebrow. "Blessed be the pure of heart?"

Cherry chuckled. "Seek forgiveness, and you shall find it?"

Halo's brows furrowed as though in disgust. "Blessed Celestial Grace?"

I shrugged, sheepishly scratching the back of my neck. "Let's talk about it when we get home, I kinda need to try and process it myself," I looked around. "How exactly are we getting back, by the way?"

The girls looked at one another before nodding.

Alpha sighed. "We're too drained to teleport that far, we can't take you on our brooms, and we sure as hell aren't leaving our beloved Greater Familiar behind. Which means, it's going to be a long walk home."

I nodded, resigned to our fate. "I guess we'd better get going, then." Alpha patted me on the head with a smile while Cherry and Halo both kissed me on the cheek and held my hands. We walked mostly in silence, enjoying the stars in the sky that were usually obscured by the bright city lights. It was a good reminder that sometimes we had to enjoy the little things.

CHAPTER 19

The Second Blessing

The walk dragged on for *hours*. We made a pit stop at a late-night pizza joint to rest and have a snack. No one spoke a word as we took it to go and ate on the way. Every step grew heavier than the last as we realized just how bad things had become.

Instead of going straight home, we picked up the car from the restaurant. Thankfully, it was on the way and helped ease the rest of the trip. The feeling of my ass hitting the car seat was about as good a feeling as anything ever had been, and I don't say that lightly.

Entering the house around one in the morning, I braced myself for the inevitable talk that awaited us. The long walk gave me the opportunity to mull over our situation and consider what the hell was going on when I transformed.

While morphing gave me newfound knowledge and instincts, it also came with a shift in my personality. It hadn't caused any issues for us just yet, but the realization that I wasted precious time during our brief battle to say out of character nonsense weighed heavy on me.

But if I could harness the power without sacrificing a part of myself, then I could unlock the full potential of each form. Not only that, but with the Spell Tokens in hand, I could elevate my power to new heights and be more in control of it than before. The only problem was understanding the root cause of the mental alterations and finding a solution.

We collapsed onto the living room furniture, physically unfazed thanks to Halo's spells to ease the physical strain from the walk. But mentally, we were drained from the ordeal. The tension hung thick in the air. I knew just how tired we all were when neither Halo nor Cherry vied for my attention as they drifted into their own thoughts.

A yellow penetrating gaze locked onto me. "Alright, you've had plenty of time," Alpha said. "Tell us what's up."

With a resigned nod, I knew it was time to come clean. "Something strange happens to me when I shift. It's like I gain all this knowledge and new instincts, but... it comes with something else."

"Something else?" Halo's brow furrowed.

I nodded solemnly. "Yeah, something else. Taking on your angelic form tonight, I not only knew exactly what my abilities were but kind of lost my own identity. For that stretch of time, I really was just your divine guardian and nothing else."

Halo's frown deepened. "But you seemed just fine when you tried it out here."

"I'm not so sure about that," I admitted. "I didn't transform for long, and I wasn't at full power since the token was weaker for our test. Even then, I felt a little of the pull of that personality." I sighed as I leaned forward, and ran my hand through my hair.

Cherry's curiosity shone in her red eyes, but she looked as concerned as anyone else. "What about my form? You seemed okay using it."

"Well, about that..." I shifted uncomfortably. "I felt, I don't know, majestic? Like royalty? And I couldn't believe the," I made air quotes with my fingers, "*pathetic weaklings* dared to challenge me."

The corner of Cherry's mouth quirked up at that but fell just as quickly. "I guess we couldn't tell. You didn't really speak. I only get impressions of what you're saying, or how you're feeling if you're not talking directly to me."

Alpha crossed her arms and scrunched her brow. "Tell me exactly how you felt when you took my form. Don't leave out any details."

I admit, after the conversation we had earlier in the evening, I didn't exactly want to describe what Alpha's form did to me. I was afraid it would cause fresh arguments to break out. "I—uh—felt extremely territorial. The puny snacks had the nerves to attack—" I paused, catching myself before saying the next two words slowly. "you girls." Alpha narrowed her eyes, and I knew I wasn't getting out of this. I sighed. "I wanted to feast on my foes, protect my mates, and then breed them as I roared, letting every creature in the forest know who the true pack leader was."

Alpha smirked and rolled her eyes, but didn't waste a moment deciding on a course of action. "Halo, go get the *Rare and Mythical Monster Manual*. Cherry, get your grimoire. I think what Logan is dealing with is a battle of wills. It's the same thing new witches face when gaining their affinities. There might be more to his forms than we realized." There were no arguments or bickering this time. Both girls scampered off to collect the books and returned as quickly as they left. "Good girls. Halo, find the beast labeled The Alpha. Cherry, open to the chapter on gaining affinities for new witches."

"You don't think—" Halo said.

"I don't know yet. If I'm right, we can fix this," Alpha interjected, cutting her off.

"Here, *The Alpha*. Whoa, it looks just like Logan! Except this guy was much bigger—the size of a building. It says here that *The Alpha was the greatest beast of his kind. As an Okatku, its body was best described as a mix of bear, lion, and wolf. Its dominant personality left no room for threats in its domain.*" Halo looked at me with a glint of awe in her eyes.

"Cherry, what's it say about taking on new affinities?" Alpha asked.

Cherry's eyes widened as she absorbed the contents in front of her. "So, basically, it's a mind game," she said. "You either control the beast or become the beast. Is Logan... in danger?" Her gaze darted to Alpha, looking suddenly fearful. I appreciated the concern, at least, but was I... afraid? I wasn't sure.

Alpha's touch grounded me as she settled beside me on the couch. "Take a breath. It's not as bad as it sounds. We can fix this, but we need to understand it first," she explained, then turned to Halo. "Did you find similar creatures to Cherry's and yours?"

Halo nodded vigorously. I smirked as her blonde pigtails bounced with enthusiasm. "Yes! I found both of them. Mine's called The Celestial Guardian," she chirped, flipping through the manual. "It's all about righteousness and retribution, like a celestial enforcer." She paused, taking a moment to scan the text. "And for Cherry, there's the Athol, also known as the Bat King, a giant vampire bat."

Cherry's face scrunched up as she processed the information. "So, Logan turns into slightly smaller versions of these legendary creatures, complete with their personalities?" she queried, tapping her foot impatiently. "But why exactly these monsters in particular?"

Alpha scratched her chin. "Some of those monsters still have living ancestors, though they are much weaker. But each one listed in the book died centuries ago. So, I'm not sure—they might be some kind of totem spirits of our affinities, if I were to guess. In any case, he inherits their power and persona to some extent. He'll have to assert dominance over their minds to retain control. Unlike us, he's not permanently bound to these affinities. As he grows stronger, so does the risk of losing himself. However, I think it's just like new witches—if he makes them submit once, he won't have to do it again."

"During our first breakfast together, didn't you say people were born as witches?" I asked.

Alpha nodded patiently. "I said it's something most of us are born into. Witches are born with either their mother's affinity or something similar that's better suited to them. But not all witches are born witches." She looked at Cherry.

Cherry frowned. "I know that I'm not normal, but you don't have to look at me like that."

With an exaggerated sigh, Alpha dragged her hand down her face. "I'm not looking at you like that because you weren't born a witch. I'm looking at you like that because I want you to explain what you remember."

"Oh," Cherry blushed. "Just say so next time. All I remember was some crazy fuck biting me. I had weird nightmares, and I woke up two days later. I only found out I was a witch by accident when I met Squeaks at Hot Topic." She shrugged.

"Those weren't nightmares. It was a battle of wills. If you lost, you'd have been a vampire instead of a Vampire Witch. "

Cherry squinted suspiciously. "How did you know all this and we didn't?"

Alpha scoffed. "Because I actually read."

Cherry's nostrils flared. "Fucking know-it-all."

Thanks to Alpha's diligent studies and thorough explanation, I felt like I had a good understanding of what was going on. "I get it. Every time I transform, I'm essentially battling for mental dominance. How do I fix it? How can I suppress their personality?"

"Practice," Alpha said simply, "so far you haven't even tried fighting back. And, if I'm right, once you've won, you won't have to fight over that form ever again. But, keep in mind, as we grow the coven and you get more powerful, so will your forms. That's going to make your battle of wills a hell of a lot harder."

I sighed in relief. "Alright, I can deal with that." Taking a few moments, I considered the problem. We all knew that the coven was going to grow eventually. In theory that meant it would become harder to win each new battle of wills since the forms and 'totem spirits' would be stronger. *Makes sense*, I thought tapping my chin. But if the spirits grew stronger because of me, then it had to mean that my will would also get stronger. And each time I forced one to submit, wouldn't it be practice for the next? *So as long as I don't put off dominating these spirits, it shouldn't be that bad.* I looked up as my thoughts were interrupted.

"Good, that's figured out. Now I need your ring. These compulsions are becoming too much," Halo said, fidgeting and scratching her hand like an addict.

Quickly, I removed my ring, passing it over. "Sure, take it." My muscles began rapidly shrinking back to my typical fit physique.

Cherry pouted watching my bodybuilder physique dwindle. "Aww..."

I would have said something, but the golden glow from Halo's eyes was too enthralling. The ring floated between her palms as she gripped an invisible ball of magic surrounding it. My instincts told me the mesmerizing rotation of the ring held some significance, though I couldn't say what. Regardless of what it was, her eyes flared, becoming almost blindingly bright, and Halo's voice distorted into a beautiful chorus as if thousands of angels were chanting with her. "Blenen dith ing wemth engaltig proom!" The light in her eyes shot out like a beam into the ring. As her eyes dimmed, the ring grew brighter and a new glowing rune formed on its surface.

Right as it looked like it was going to explode, the light faded with a peaceful conclusion.

Halo panted, and her face was pale as she passed the ring back to me. "There you go. It's done." And with that, our hands glowed, the contract was fulfilled, and the tattoos faded away.

"Wow, Halo," I said, taking the ring back. "That seemed like a big one!"

Halo's chest heaved as she tried to catch her breath, but she grinned with obvious excitement as her wings fluttered. "Thanks. It takes a lot of power to do permanent enchantments. Put it on, let's see it."

I stood and slipped the ring on my finger. With that, the angelic blessing took hold, and I felt it right away. I didn't bulk up like a bodybuilder as I did with Alpha's blessing, though. Instead, my muscles tightened, becoming more compact and athletic. I felt more like a gymnast or parkour athlete—flexible, resilient, and fast, with extreme agility and explosive energy rather than raw power. Repositioning myself,

I took a deep breath and then performed a flawless standing back flip. Then a forward flip. Finishing that, I struck a pose.

Halo and Cherry clapped for me, and Alpha grinned but shook her head and rolled her eyes at us. But there was something else. I noticed something when I flipped—my physical changes weren't the only additions from this blessing. I hopped up on the arm of the couch and jumped as high as I could, letting my body glide back to the floor.

"Hey, you can fly?" Halo asked with a beaming smile.

Cherry blew a raspberry. "Sppt! That's not flying, it's falling with style."

"Hey," Alpha chimed in with a disapproving glare, "I'm pretty sure you stole that line."

Cherry stuck her tongue out at Alpha. "Don't talk to me about stealing, you thief. I borrowed it."

Alpha just sighed.

Just as I was about to sit on the couch, though, I noticed Cherry staring at my stomach with her eyes wide. Her jaw dropped, and a look of fear washed over her—no, not just fear, but unmistakable, raw, oppressive terror.

I flinched as she darted out of her seat with a sudden desperation. Before I could say a word or stop her, she pulled up my shirt. Her hand groped my abs. "Thank God. It's still there," she said with genuine relief, letting out a heavy sigh. "The six pack is safe."

I cocked a brow at her.

Alpha brought up the next topic, getting us back on track. Her words caused the dour mood to return, unfortunately, but it was important. With a concerned expression, she sat forward in her seat. "Shit's worse than we thought, and we haven't decided our next step."

A frown returned to Halo's too-pale face as her wings folded behind her back. "Yeah, it's really bad. I can't believe they found out."

"Those fucking witchy-bitchies. I bet they'll rat us out to the big covens," Cherry grumbled.

"Can we not use the term 'rat us out'? Logan Jr. finds it racist," Halo said, Logan Jr. squeaking in agreement.

Cherry scoffed and slouched back in her seat. "Logan Jr. *Waah waah waah*," she said in a high-pitched sarcastic tone while mimicking speaking with her hand. "Maybe someone would give a shit what he thinks if he'd change his fucking name already."

Halo's eyes turned into slits. "You're lucky I'm too drained to kick your bottom right now."

This time, I stepped in before Alpha. "Girls, c'mon, this is important. We need to figure out what the hell we're planning to do. I don't think they would rat—er, expose us—to the big covens. With the war going on, do they really want to put themselves on the New Moon or Salem coven's radar? Regardless, we've already seen that they weren't the only ones who tracked me down. How many more might have figured it out? There could be some upstarts who think using the information can help them gain favor with the bigger covens."

Alpha nodded. "Those were my thoughts exactly. There are plenty of witches out there who want to ride the pompous coattails of the big covens. We can only assume that if they don't know yet, they'll find out soon. Lying low isn't enough anymore."

All of us looked around the room at one another, concern marring our faces. I lacked too much knowledge of the witching world to know what our next step should be. So I did what every wise man did when they don't know—I asked some women. "Then what do we do next?"

Standing, Alpha stretched, her arms extending over her head as she went up on her tiptoes. Letting out a soft grunt, she dropped to her heels. "We leave for a while. Pack up our shit and go. We need to take some time to figure out how we're going to move forward, and that's a hell of a lot harder to do when we can't even go out to dinner without fighting other witches."

"Bank robbing and beach bungalow? Should I pack my bikinis?" Cherry asked with a hopeful glint in her eyes.

Meekly, Halo agreed. "Yeah, that idea is starting to sound a lot better."

Alpha put her hands on her hips. "It's not a vacation, and we're not going for good. Only a few weeks at most. We need time, and Logan needs to train. I'd say we leave tonight, but we need rest. Tonight, just get showered and we'll sleep in Halo's bed since it's the biggest. We take no chances anymore. In the morning, we'll get our shit packed and head out."

"What about breakfast?" Halo asked with a hint of sadness in her voice.

"We'll stop at a drive-through on the way. We'll splurge and get some Witchy-D's, alright?" Alpha asked, giving the blonde a gentle smile.

Halo nodded.

We took turns showering, everyone doing some packing while we waited for our turn. I had little to worry about. I already kept a lot of my clothes in my dimensional storage, a precaution I started making ever since finding myself nude in public once, not to mention my shirt being destroyed on a second outing.

It wasn't long before I cleaned myself up and hopped into Halo's bed. Though I found myself surrounded by three beautiful women, there was no fooling around tonight. The mood was still too somber for that, and we were all exhausted. Still, we clung to each other and took comfort in the closeness. With my mind finally finding some peace, I drifted off to sleep with a twitching furry ear under my chin.

CHAPTER 20

The Mystic Realm

I stirred as I awoke in a tangle of limbs, already feeling fantastic. Never had I experienced such a restful sleep in my life. To my left lay a fiery-haired beauty with Amazonian proportions, to my right a golden-haired angel sweetheart, and nestled against my groin was a sultry chaotic raven-haired cutie. With the light of the dawn peeking through the curtains, I planted a kiss on Halo's forehead as it was nearest to my face. She stirred awake gently, her soft snores fading as her blue eyes fluttered open.

When her sleepy gaze met mine, she greeted me with a bright smile and returned my kiss.

With a gentle touch, I scratched behind Alpha's ears, making them twitch. Her tail wagged enthusiastically and accidentally started thumping against Cherry's head. Cherry groaned into my boxers. "Nooo. Just five more minutes."

I couldn't help but chuckle.

Alpha raised her head, her yellow eyes focusing on me, a small grin forming as she leaned in for a quick peck on the lips. Her tail wagged even faster.

"Damn it! Fine, I'm getting up!" Cherry grumbled as she pushed herself upright. Her hair fell in disarray around her face, some strands ending up in her mouth. After a few futile attempts to spit them out, she resigned herself to using her fingers. She glanced down, noticing it was Alpha's tail that had disturbed her. Muttering under her breath, she clambered out of bed. "Thief, stealing my spot and assaulting me in the morning? Fucking bullshit."

We gathered our belongings, ensuring we had everything we needed packed away, along with extra provisions. Then, we set off. Alpha took the wheel, driving us to Witchy-D's, a witch-only drive-through nestled in an alley.

Despite its unusual setting, I found myself thoroughly enjoying the biscuits and gravy. At first glance, they appeared mundane enough, but the shimmering silver particles rising with the steam hinted at something magical laced inside. With each bite, I felt a bit more energized.

I became confused as we arrived at the mall. I thought that maybe we were stocking up on camping gear for our off-the-grid adventure. It made sense to head for a secluded log cabin in the woods, but my bewilderment only deepened as we stepped into Hot Topic. I squeezed Halo's hand as we walked into the store. "Why are we here? Do we need to pick something up before we go?"

Her eyes widened slightly as she seemed to realize something. She replied quickly in a hushed whisper, "Oh, Gosh! That's right, you didn't know. It's our fall back plan that we reserve for only the worst situations. We're taking a portal here that'll take us far away to a mystical realm. And before you ask, we have a way home. Squeaks can open the portal for us to come back here when we're ready."

I wanted to ask more about that, but by then we reached the counter where Alpha whispered a password to the same cute, petite, goth clerk I always saw, and the world shifted around us. Just like the last time, I was suddenly standing in an entirely different store full of witchy world merchandise while Alpha spoke for the group. "Hey, Squeaks. We're here for the realm portal we talked about."

Squeaks smiled from across the counter. "Hey, Alphie! You sure you want to go there? That place is dangerous, and really expensive to portal into and out of."

Alpha ran her hand down her face and groaned, "C'mon, I told you not to call me that! And yes, I'm sure we want to go." Then, she leaned forward and in a hushed tone said,

"We're already lying low, but we need to get completely off the radar for a while. I'll fill you in on the details later."

Suddenly, I found myself wondering just who Squeaks was if Alpha was going to trust her with that kind of information. But I knew better than to ask that now.

Squeaks sighed. "Alright, if you're sure. Follow me." She walked from behind the counter after collecting a sizable bag of tokens from Alpha, and led us to the back door. Her hands glowed black as she tapped several runic symbols that surrounded the doorway, each one lighting up a different color, and eventually, the door changed.

Rather than being a door with an 'employees only' sign on it, a swirling rainbow portal took its place. I gulped, not knowing what to expect. Squeaks looked at Alpha, worry in her eyes, and she said, "Remember what we talked about on the phone. Be ready right out of the gate. Stay safe, Alphie."

Alpha nodded, not seeming nearly as upset about the odd nickname this time. Instead, her jaw was set and her eyes were lit up with determination. "We will. I'll contact you soon." Then we all joined hands as Alpha led us through the portal to the so-called mystical realm.

I felt a cool, soothing sensation envelop me as I walked through. I had expected to be in a long, swirling tunnel that pulled me along to an unknown destination. Instead, I walked through a cool, colorful corridor and stepped straight into an enormous clearing in an ancient forest. The air felt thick, but not in a bad way. It was like all the cells in my body were screaming with joy at the sheer amount of magic surrounding us.

I looked at the sky, which was turquoise rather than blue, and the sun wasn't quite right, either. *Toto, I have a feeling we're not on Earth anymore.* Before I could ask questions, Alpha and the girls had already sprung into action. Alpha pointed to her right and left. "Girls, warding ritual now!"

Neither girl said a word in response, but both bolted in the directions pointed out to them, their expressions filled with their determination.

"Logan!" Alpha shouted. My gaze locked on hers and yellow eyes met mine. I understood how serious this must be, even if I didn't know quite why. "Keep an eye out. Use the tokens if you have to. We'll be busy for a few minutes. Local monsters could sense us at any moment."

I nodded. "I'm on it."

As Alpha commenced her ritual, her words more or less proved prophetic. A thunderous, incomprehensible hiss emanated from the dense tree line. At first sight, dread consumed me as I spotted the approaching horror. A colossal black serpent, a creature destined to plague my nightmares for years to come, slithered into the clearing. "Fuck, I hate snakes," I muttered, shaking my head at the unwelcome sight. "Oh well."

Easily a hundred feet in length with a body no less than three feet in diameter, its head loomed large, nearly the size of a Volkswagen Beetle. With resignation, I summoned a token, fully aware of the price it would exact, and pressed it to my lips.

"Looks like someone's in for belly rubs tonight," I chuckled as the contract magic formed around me, imprinting itself as a tattoo on my right hand. Then, my body transformed into the massive form of the Okatku. Limbs extended, fingers sharpened into razor-sharp claws, and fur sprouted across my body. Muscles bulged, and a massive tail shot out from behind me. With jaws gaping, displaying enormous fangs, I roared at the loathsome snake that dared encroach upon my territory and threaten my mates.

No. NO! Not that! I screamed inwardly, gritting my teeth against the invading personality. I roared, charging towards the snake. *Focus, Logan! Focus! I didn't let the witches enslave me, and I'm sure as shit not going to let this thing take over my head either.* Resisting, I made its instincts my own and urged my ego to resist.

The bestial presence continued to claw at my consciousness, but I refused to give any ground. Whatever this thing was, it was long dead, and I was alive. Me, Logan Morrison.

Growling, I lunged at the massive snake, adrenaline coursing through my veins, washing away all fear. Alongside it surged a wave of power. The snake struck, but how could a mere serpent challenge the Okat—*NO!* The sudden distraction as the beast's personality roared in defiance inside me was enough for the snake to make its move. I narrowly dodged its venom-filled fangs, but the force of its head colliding with my body sent me sprawling, disrupting my momentum.

I screamed, both inside and out, as I crashed to the ground. *Get the hell out of my head, you cocky mutt!* This time, I heard the roar within me. The beast desired control, but there was no way in hell I was going to let that happen. I rose to my feet, rushing at the black snake once more. It darted forward, but I dodged, slashing a deep gouge across its face. The serpent hissed in agony, hastily retreating.

Deep down, I knew I could have inflicted a hell of a lot more pain onto this creature if the Alpha inside would just fucking relent. *Look, asshole, if you want our mates to survive and our territory to remain safe, then you know what you have to do*, I said to it in my mind. *Otherwise, we'll continue this battle until we both die and then the snake will consume the girls.* I didn't know if reasoning with a magical personality inherited from a deceased mythical beast would work, but screaming at it wasn't accomplishing anything.

To my surprise, the beast hesitated, as if it was assessing, just watching me. I leaped back as the snake lunged, its jaws crashed into the ground where I had stood. Seeing the opportunity for what it was, I pounced onto its head, digging my claws in without mercy. The creature thrashed and writhed, but I didn't care. I held on with all I had, slashing like a crazed serial killer in a horror film. Still, it wasn't just taking it. The snake bucked like a mountain-sized bull as it tried throwing me off, and eventually, it succeeded.

Twisting in the air, I landed on my feet. I felt a sense of approval from the beast inside me, which I was grateful to have. The serpent hissed with rage, redoubling its speed, striking over and over in a frenzied assault. I didn't know the potency of its venom, and it gave me no time to strike back, so I had to work with what I had. I resolved to tire it out, knowing all I needed was one good shot to retake the momentum.

However, the creature's sudden stop caught me off guard. The snake flicked out its tongue and then glanced at the distracted witches. The black serpent's eyes thinned, and I swear it snickered before rushing for Alpha's back as fast as possible. Roaring with fury, I quickened my pace, putting everything I had into cutting off the reptile.

Without warning, the serpent pulled a U-turn and snapped forward, its mouth open wider than should be possible. Being full speed and mid-leap, I couldn't change my trajectory. *Fuck me...* I thought as I flew right into the snake's open jaws that snapped closed behind me. Fortunately, it missed me with its fangs. I felt it pulling me in, swallowing, and for a moment, terror struck me and I almost panicked.

I couldn't exactly take a deep breath to calm down, but giving up wasn't in my blood. I stretched out my claws and turned into a whirlwind of fury, slashing out in all directions. Muscles clenched, constricting, and trying to crush me to death, but I pressed forward with my immense strength, ruthlessly tearing holes through muscle, bone, and then scales. Making short work of its insides, I burst out of the massive serpent's body, covered in blood and gore. I expected to find it lifeless. Instead, the big bastard was still alive. Its head flailed wildly in the sky while guttural sounds of agony escaped the mouth of the behemoth.

As the serpent turned towards me, its eyes wide with intent, I braced myself. A surge of power erupted within my chest, magic pulsing through my veins, converging towards my throat. With the black snake mere feet away, I unleashed a deafening roar infused with mystical energy. The creature halted in its tracks, stunned, its head dropping limply to the ground, eyes glazed over. Seizing the opportunity, I lunged to the side, slashing, clawing, and tearing at its neck before it could break free from the spell. Finding the spine, I clamped down, my jaws snapping bone and ripping through nerves.

The beast's tongue lolled out, its eyes clouded over by death. Its body still convulsed, but I knew it was already over. Glancing down at the serpent, I realized I had grown a bit bigger, and the strange personality that once inhabited me was gone. It seemed I had proven myself worthy, earning its trust to safeguard our companions. In silent gratitude, I thanked the creature for the gift of its strength.

Panting hard, I checked on the ladies. They were just finishing the warding ritual, their chanting culminating in a shimmering barrier of red, gold, and yellow runes encircling the clearing.

The girls approached, grinning wide. Cherry dashed towards me, but to my surprise, she bypassed me entirely, going for the massive serpent carcass instead. Tilting my head in confusion, I turned as Alpha's voice reached my ears.

"Cloon allting," she spoke calmly, waving her hand. A white glow enveloped me, cleansing away the gruesome gore, even from my panting mouth. It was a relief to know I wouldn't have to taste it upon reverting to my normal form.

Dipping my head, I felt Alpha press her forehead against mine as she scratched gently behind my ears. "Good boy. You kicked the shit out of that colossal snake."

A joyful bark escaped me as the ground trembled beneath my excitement.

Alpha chuckled, and I nudged the contract magic, reverting to my human form and donning my clothes. Still forehead to forehead with Alpha, her hands cradling my face, I leaned in to kiss her passionately, desire burning between us. However, I broke the kiss before it escalated, whispering in her ear, "I think I've worked up quite an appetite."

She grinned mischievously. "Maybe if you keep being my good boy, I'll feed you later." Then she patted me on the head and joined Cherry, who was using a blade of magic to cut open the snake.

Before I could ask what she was doing, I felt the warmth from a golden glow surrounding me as Halo cast a healing spell. We embraced one another. "I'm so glad you're okay. I thought we lost you when that snake swallowed you whole."

Squeezing her tight, I kissed her forehead. "No way. I'm only a goner when you and Cherry swallow."

She sniffled and giggled. "I know," she pulled back, eyes glistening but a smile on her face, "but, don't be that reckless again, okay?"

I nodded with a reassuring smile and took her by the hand. I wanted to know why Cherry was more excited about the snake than she was about my epic victory. As we arrived, Cherry had a sizable chunk of snake meat cut away. She cautiously sliced open a sack nestled within the dead snake's body, revealing a cache of eggs. Cherry squealed, "Eeee! Look, look, look! It's here!!!" Cherry reached into the repulsive pile and pulled out a single, large black egg.

Alpha cast the same cleaning spell she used on me and in a flash, both Cherry's hands and the egg were spotless. I was grateful for that, knowing that soon those hands would probably be all over me.

Cherry excitedly rushed over to me, holding the egg up high. "I knew it was preggers! Logan, baby, Logan! Look! A familiar egg among all the other ones!"

I chuckled. "I see it. Congratulations."

"You mean congratulations to *us*!" Cherry said, beaming at me. She wrapped one arm around me and then held the egg up between us. Her gaze filled with emotion. "It's our first baby!"

I choked. "I'm sorry, what?"

Alpha rolled her eyes, but couldn't hide her amusement. Halo couldn't contain her giggles either.

"We're gonna have a little snake baby together! Gah! I'm so fucking excited!" Cherry cheered, cradling the black egg.

Internally, I worried that seeing me get swallowed by a serpent caused something to snap in Cherry's brain, and I figured that bringing up my dislike for snakes might send her past a point of no return. But she was adorable, so I waited before passing judgment. "I'm so happy you finally got your familiar," I said a little cautiously.

She frowned. "Not just *my* familiar. He's *our* baby."

Hesitantly, I nodded. *Best to pick your battles, Logan.*

"Alright, daylight is burning. Let's get some of those trees down and start building," Alpha declared.

"Won't that take a lot of magic?" I asked.

"There's so much ambient magic in this realm, we'll basically never run out," Halo said.

"We can farm a lot of Spell Tokens while we're here, too."

Cherry passed me the egg. "Here, watch the baby. Momma has work to do."

I frowned, not wanting to feel like dead weight. "Are you sure? I'm happy to lend a hand."

Alpha was already walking away when she called back, "You'll just get in the way."

I watched the girls form an assembly line. Alpha's glowing hands uprooted a massive tree. She directed it to land safely in front of Halo. Halo's hands glowed gold, and the tree lifted, breaking apart and transforming into an enormous pile of logs. The logs drifted over and stacked themselves in the center of the clearing. Cherry's hands glowed red, and the pile of logs turned into the foundation and flooring of a rather large building.

They repeated this process five or six more times until they finished building the quaint log cabin. My eyes bulged as they accomplished in ten minutes something that normally took days or even weeks or months to complete. I could tell by the looks on their faces that, at least for now, the tension and somber mood that weighed so heavily on us had been lifted. With the wards up and a shelter constructed, we finally had a safe place to regroup and rest.

The girls waved me over, and I joined them inside. Cherry brought the couch with her, and Halo had packed her bed, so we at least had some comfort. Still, we had running water, a place to bathe, and a toilet. I was somewhat curious, but I decided not to inquire about the magical means of waste disposal.

"Wow, you girls are amazing," I said, as I searched for a place to put the egg. Cherry was way ahead of me, having already prepared a spot with a blanket.

"So, Logan..." Halo said a bit too casually, as she pulled her shirt up over her head, exposing her bra. She sat on the edge of the bed, leaning back on her hands.

I smirked, walking across the cabin. But her next words made me freeze in place. She casually inspected her nails. "I, uh, noticed you used a Beast Token out there," she smiled wickedly at me. "What exactly was the cost to use such a *powerful* token?"

I gulped, stealing a glance at Alpha, who suddenly became engrossed in turning into a strawberry and fiddling with the fireplace as if she didn't possess a spell to make it work instantly.

"Well, it just cost me spending a night with Alpha, that's all..." I said unconvincingly.

Cherry looked on with interest.

Halo squinted her eyes suspiciously. "Are you sure that's *all* it required?"

Alpha coughed, still avoiding our gazes. "Pretty much, yep."

"Interesting..." Halo said. "You know, I just got my new familiar, right, Cherry?"

Cherry nodded, her eyes also narrowed with suspicion.

Halo's legs slowly kicked back and forth on the edge of the bed. "And, like any good witch, I wanted to ensure the best possible nutrition for my little guy. Cherry, I bet you'd like to know all about that too, now that you've got your snake egg, right?"

"That's unnecessary. We need to finish getting our temporary home in order and create a training plan." Alpha said, far too quickly.

Red crept up my neck, and sweat beaded down the center of my back, but I kept my cool... kinda. Sure, my voice cracked a little, but otherwise, I thought I was holding up fine. "Yeah. What Alpha said." *Nailed it.*

"No... I think I want to hear this. After all, we just worked *so* hard. I think we deserve a quick break," Cherry said, her eyes locked on me before she gave Halo her full attention.

"As it turns out, there's a fantastic bestial spell that allows a witch to create a *delicious* and nutritious meal for their familiars. Would you like to know what that is?" Halo asked, sounding like a smug detective that just solved a long and difficult case.

"I'll go get some logs for the fire—" Alpha said, walking toward the door. A red shield suddenly blocked the only door in and out of the cabin.

Cherry's hand glowed brightly. "I think it can wait."

Alpha gulped.

By this point, I was shuffling my feet nervously. I thought to myself, *maybe if I play along, they'll think I'm innocent.* "What—uh—what exactly is that, Halo?" I tried my best to look casual and curious. The looks on their faces said I was failing miserably.

"Oh! I'm *sooo* glad you asked, *mister milk mustache*," she said with an impish grin and two squeezes of her breasts.

Cherry gasped. *"Noo.* Really?" It was like a light turned on in Cherry's mind and she connected the dots. She grinned. "Logan, tell us exactly what the requirements were for the Spell Token you used—now." Cherry pointed at me, using the contract to compel me.

They already knew, I could tell. There was no point in fighting it anymore. I hung my head, ears burning. "I have to lay with Alpha, fool around, drink her breast milk, and give her belly rubs until she falls asleep."

Alpha stiffened, then slowly turned around, her tail and ears drooping. "Did you have to mention the belly rubs too?" she muttered.

I didn't have time to respond as Halo giggled like a madwoman. "There's only one way to make things fair..." she held up a Beast Token. "I'm making good on the small favor I still owe you from our date, Logan."

Cherry held one up as well. "Well, I won't be left out."

Halo licked her lips. "You'll just have to drink from all three of us tonight."

Both Alpha and my jaws dropped. We looked at one another, then back at the other girls.

As the shock wore off, Alpha's fearful embarrassment transformed into a grin.

I sighed and chuckled, relief washing over me. "I guess I'm eating at another buffet tonight..."

CHAPTER 21

Everybody Needs A Montage

"AHHHHH!" I screamed as I face-planted naked in the grass. Attempting to swap forms mid-air proved far more challenging than anticipated. Managing the mental gymnastics of swapping items from dimensional storage, remembering to bring tokens into my mouth, when I didn't have hands, and attempting to clothe myself when I failed, proved to be a challenge. In hindsight, I probably should have swapped back to the angelic blessing in my ring. My ring's recent alterations were a massive boon, and it was all thanks to the girls.

After a chat and explanation of what I wanted, they added two new additions to my magical ring. The first was an enchantment enabling the ring to transform alongside me, ensuring I could utilize its blessings in altered forms. Cherry extracted a hefty price for this, leaving my jaw a bit sore and my tongue numb for a full thirty minutes. The second addition was a general enchantment facilitating swapping between blessings without removing the ring. Thankfully, Alpha saw the practicality of my request. The fact that she felt it was an oversight on her part when creating the ring also lowered the price. However, for two days following, I found myself at her beck and call, obliged to deliver high-quality belly rubs and ear scritches whenever she snapped her fingers.

The last week was dedicated to vigorous training. My initial focus was breaking free from the personalities of my alternate forms. I assumed the more primitive, regal personality of the bat would be the easier of the two to break. Turns out, I was wrong. That big bastard was so entitled that I had to get creative. After some stress-testing, I realized it didn't like when we felt pain, so, after a few hours of spell-dodging practice with all three girls, and a quality heal spell from Halo, I found myself bat king free. The Celestial Guardian, on the other hand, turned out to be incredibly easy. I was shocked when I asked it to stop trying to take over my mind, and the freaking thing apologized profusely before leaving. He spent more time saying sorry and asking forgiveness over the intrusion than anything else.

The guardian's reaction made me question how my transformations really worked. Was I inheriting the powers from a spirit? I tried to ask the guardian, but he was gone before I could. Any attempt to get his attention after that was fruitless. He really was gone for good. Mulling it over for a little while led to nothing useful, so I decided to move on. With too much to do, I threw that topic on the back burner and went with "because it's magic" as my go-to answer for now.

"Gosh! Are you alright?" Halo's voice carried concern as she ran toward me.

Prying my face out of the mud, I looked up to the Angelic Witch with a groan. "Yeah. I'm good. Ow..." Summoning my clothing I dressed as I got up, feeling the warmth of healing magic rush through me. "Thanks, sweety. You're amazing." With a quick dust-off of my knees and a stretch, I straightened up.

Despite healing me only a moment ago, Halo worriedly examined me, inspecting my arms, legs, and face. "Cheese n' rice, baby. You can't keep scaring me like that."

I chuckled. "You just healed me, I'm fine. I've got to figure this out one way or another, right?"

She sighed. "I suppose you're right. I'm being selfish. I just don't like seeing you get hurt."

Wrapping her up in a gentle hug, I kissed her forehead. "What could I possibly have to worry about with such an amazing witch like you watching out for me?"

Redness tinted her cheeks as she giggled. "Logan... For Pete's sake, you're making me blush." Halo playfully slapped my chest, breaking the hug. "Okay, fine. But practice your transitions on the ground more first. Enough of this silliness in the air until then. Alright?"

I nodded, and with a look of determination on my face, I took off in a full sprint, ready to hone my skills further.

Thankfully, the girls were considerate with their tokens, understanding the necessity of practice and its long-term benefits. Most tokens had shorter durations, strategically designed for frequent form swaps. Medium-strength tokens were our normal, go-to tokens. They were one-time-use and allowed me to morph for up to 15 minutes, give or take.

Alpha even devised extra-strength multi-use tokens, providing up to an hour's worth of magic, four times the duration of normal tokens. The price was split into quarters. Each quarter of the token I used came with its own cost, payable only once the entire token was used up. The catch? I had to finish using that token before I could activate another extra-strength token of the same type. It kept things fair, which wasn't a problem because I didn't mind paying the higher price. Especially when the girls were using them to set up solo date nights.

It was fortunate that the girls had unlimited magic in this realm, as I found myself utilizing Spell Tokens constantly. Yet, they didn't seem to mind, relishing the attention they received as payment when I wasn't busy training. Every spare moment was dedicated to showering them with hugs, kisses, snuggles, belly rubs, or engaging in heartfelt conversations beneath the ethereal glow of the quad-moon light. However, as the second week drew to a close, all my hard work proved to be worth it.

· ♥ · ♥ · ♥ · ♥ · ♥ ·

It was days later. The trees blurred past me as I streaked through the forest in my human form, the angelic blessing amplifying my speed. With an explosive burst of energy, I leaped twelve feet into the air, activating a Beast Token mid-flight. Landing on all fours with a resounding roar, I felt the surge of strength as my muscles bulged, effortlessly toppling an enormous tree with a single blow before reverting to my angelic blessing as a new token appeared in my mouth.

My clawed paws transformed as I ascended the falling tree, morphing into the faster, more agile bat king. Emitting a loud, spine-chilling chirp, I sent sound waves echoing in all directions, pinpointing my target's location. Just as the tree began its descent, I propelled it faster with a powerful push, launching myself into the air. Flapping my wings and chirping once more to track its trajectory, I locked onto my target, initiating a swift dive.

Another token popped into my mouth, summoning magically reinforced steel wings as my form shifted into that of a humanoid celestial guardian. Switching back to my bestial blessing, my angelic armor bulged. Without summoning my sword or shield, my eyes adjusted, enabling me to focus on everything before me simultaneously. Swooping in, I fluttered my wings at the last moment, cushioning my descent as I crashed to the ground before my target. "Tell me your sin," I commanded, my deep, resonant voice echoing with angelic authority.

Cherry's eyes widened and she threw up both palms, skidding to a halt. "Shit!" She squeezed her eyes shut and gritted her teeth, grunting as she tried to resist my spell. Eventually, she relented, the words rushed out of her like a hurricane. "Every day this week I've been shrinking Halo's underwear by about five percent!" Her eyes bulged as she slapped two both hands over her mouth.

I guffawed at that, releasing the token's magic and returning to human form, my clothing restored. "Dammit Cherry, don't ever change."

Cherry Cola, sore loser that she was, pouted, arms crossed, blowing a strand of hair out of her face. "That's not fair. You cheated."

I wrapped my arms around her, still laughing. "Oh, I totally cheated. I used both blessings and all three forms. How else was I supposed to catch you?"

Uncrossing her arms, she hugged me back, her angry pout barely softening. She seemed unsure of how to respond to someone actually agreeing with her claims. "Yeah—yeah, that's right. Fucking cheater," she muttered.

I cupped her cheeks in my hands, lifting her face to mine, my smile wide. "Aww, c'mon. Don't be like that. If I cheated that means you won, doesn't it?"

She shrugged, her mood improving a little. "I guess."

My eyes narrowed playfully, and I pulled out my secret weapon—peppering her face with kisses.

She half-heartedly tried to wriggle free, but soon she started giggling, her repeated slaps on my chest becoming more playful. "Logan!" she whined. "Okay! Okay! I give up, I win!" she said, the contradiction oddly making sense. Finally, she ended my oral assault with a long, hard kiss, before taking my hand.

As we walked together, enjoying the soft sound of birds chirping in the air, I found myself continuously admiring the beautiful woman next to me. She caught my stare, her brow furrowing. "What? Is there somethin' on my face?"

I shook my head, smiling warmly. "No."

Cherry grinned mischievously, brushing a strand of hair behind her ear. "There could be if you want," she teased. Her grin shifted to a gentle smile. "What are you thinking?"

"I was just remembering the first time we met. And," I shrugged. "I'm really happy you kidnapped me, Cherry."

Hearts danced in her eyes as her eyelids curved. "Does that mean I can do it again?" she asked with a wink.

I chuckled, shaking my head. "I'm serious."

She waggled her brows. "So am I..." Her playful behavior slowly grew more earnest. "I'm really glad I did what I did too, baby. I—" She glanced down nervously before meeting my eyes, and we stopped walking. "You mean a lot to me. Like, a lot a lot. And, not just in the bedroom, or on the battlefield..."

I took her hands in mine. "Right back at you. Honestly, it's hard to imagine what life would be like without you at this point. The world before you, Halo, and Alpha was like a weird dream. I'm not even sure my old life existed anymore."

"This is what's real now." She winked, the timing barely making sense. Her arms wrapped around my neck as mine gripped her waist. Crimson eyes glanced at my lips as she rose onto her tiptoes. Slowly, I leaned in and our lips met in a kiss. It was unlike any kiss that Cherry and I shared before. There was no lust or hot passion blazing between us. A different sort of fire burned. My heart swelled, overwhelmed by something it never really experienced before. The kiss lingered for several minutes, and even then it wasn't long enough.

Breathlessly, we parted, staring into each other's eyes. I draped my arm over her shoulder and she wrapped hers around my waist as we resumed walking. Moments passed in comfortable silence before Cherry broke it. "Your aim is shit."

My brow furrowed. "What do you mean?"

She grinned with a naughty look in her eyes. "Your kisses. You missed my pussy by miles."

I palmed my face and groaned.

After killing the Black Emperor Serpent, all other predators in the area kept their distance whenever they sensed me nearby, turning the forest into a peaceful and magical place for us to spend our time.

Maybe it was because I was a Greater Familiar, and I had heightened instincts, but I could tell when we walked if the magic emanating from a plant was dangerous or not. This paid off when I reached over and plucked a particularly vibrant and glowing flower. The pistil was blood red, and the petals were navy blue.

I stopped Cherry and slipped the flower stem through her hair, behind her ear. The large petals brought out the crimson of her eyes, and she blushed, kissing me on the cheek. Sunlight peeked through the trees far above, rays of light dotting the mystical forest as we strolled along.

I felt like our relationship hit a major milestone, and I considered where it was all going next. One of those future steps, hopefully far into the future, were children. As I considered that I'd one day be a parent, it reminded me of thoughts I had as a child—curiosity about my own parents. One thought led to another and I realized that none of my girls ever talked about their moms or dads. "Hey, Cherry?"

"Hmm?" she asked, turning her gaze away from a critter scampering through the woods.

"Do you think I should, I don't know, meet your family or something eventually?" I asked, deciding to get my thoughts out there.

Her grip on my hand tightened, her body becoming rigid for a moment. "No."

"Hey, is everything alright?" I asked, stopping us and putting my hand on her shoulder.

She faced me, her eyes glistening. "Yeah. It's just, I can't go home."

"Why not?"

Cherry wiped a tear from her eye with a finger. "You know that I wasn't born a witch."

I nodded.

"I never lied to my family before. I couldn't imagine starting now." She sniffled and wrapped her arms around my waist, resting her face against my chest. "What am I supposed to tell them? Parents struggle enough with accepting their kids for not being normal. So, how can they accept me? I'm a fucking witch, Logan, with vampire fangs and everything. I'm not their little girl anymore."

Soft sobs emanated from Cherry as I held her. Gently, I rubbed her back. "Shh. It's okay. I wish I had an answer for you. I don't have experience with parents. But if you ever decide that you want to brave it with me, I'll do it. You won't have to do it alone. I promise." She lifted the tail of my shirt and pretended to blow her nose on it, eliciting a grimace from me. "Really?" I asked, trying not to sound too upset as I quickly stored my shirt into my dimensional storage so I could pick a clean one.

Cherry snickered, lifting her head and wiping her eyes, which were now leering at my exposed upper body. She ran a finger down my chest. "I didn't really blow my nose. I just wanted to see your chest." She shrugged, a mischievous smile replacing her previous frown.

I sighed as I pulled my shirt from my inventory and inspected it. Sure enough, it was clean. Shaking my head, I grinned. "Fool me once..."

Cherry's tone softened as she brushed her hair behind her ear. "Logan, what's holding you back? When it comes to kids, I mean."

I didn't answer immediately. Instead, I gave it some serious thought. "First of all, I think we're all having a good time and enjoying ourselves. If we add kids to the mix, we'll have more responsibilities and less time for one another. Eventually, the coven is going to expand, and I know that's going to cause greater stress on my time. Will I still be happy if I'm stretched even farther by children?"

Cherry frowned. "Don't worry about that. If I can help it, none of those witches will touch you. And, in a coven, other members help with raising the daughters of the core leaders. So, it's not like we'll have trouble finding babysitters. Children are also typically off-limits for coven wars, which makes it harder for enemies to plan attacks on us if we keep them close—another thing to consider."

I chuckled. "Good points, but that's not my only hangup. I don't know what it's like to have a father. Sure, I had a few that almost qualified as father figures as I grew up, but that's different. How am I supposed to raise a child when I have no clue what being a good dad even looks like?"

"Well, Alpha did say—"

I didn't let her finish because I didn't want to hear that again. "No. I know what Alpha said. But there's no way that I would ever let my kids grow up without me being there for them every step of the way. When I have kids, none of them will ever feel the way I did as a child. They won't go to bed without a bedtime story, and they sure as hell won't have to ever wonder if they'll know what being loved is like." I hadn't realized when I stopped walking. Cherry was staring intently at me as I caught my breath. At some point during my rant, my voice had risen in volume so much that I was almost shouting at her.

Cherry's hands were on my cheeks, love in her eyes. "Logan, I don't know about the bedtime stories, but you'll never have to wonder if you'll know what being loved is like ever again." Pushing up on her tiptoes, she kissed me. I clung to her, lifting her in the air and letting her know just how much I appreciated hearing that.

CHAPTER 22

EEEEP!

Cherry and I stepped into the cabin, where a familiar face greeted us warmly. Squeaks, the cute goth chick from Hot Topic, sat at the table with Alpha and Halo, her affinity on full display for the first time. With two adorable mouse ears perched atop her wavy black hair and a slender, elongated tail trailing behind her, she exuded an uncommon charm—that's for sure.

The visit caught us off guard, but it was a pleasant surprise nonetheless. As the blonde with pigtails bounded over, pulling me away from Cherry's grasp, I braced myself for a potential argument. However, Cherry was too preoccupied with checking on her egg, or as she affectionately referred to it, our baby.

Cherry waved enthusiastically as she darted across the room. "What's up Squeaks!"

"Hey, Cherbear!" Squeaks replied with her own wave and a smile that could soften the hardest of hearts. I wouldn't have expected such a sweet demeanor from a chick I previously took for a brooding mall goth.

"Logan! Come join us! We have a guest," Halo exclaimed, her trademark radiant smile lighting up the room.

Acknowledging the new arrival with a brief wave, I allowed myself to be dragged to the table, with Halo linking her arm to mine. "Logan, you know Squeaks from Hot Topic."

I extended my hand, accompanied by a friendly smile. "We haven't officially been introduced yet. I'm Logan."

Squeaks placed her delicate hand in mine, and I couldn't help but notice how incredibly soft it felt. "Nice to formally meet you, Logan. I was wondering when one of these girls would spill the beans about you."

Suppressing the urge to give her the elevator stare—for now—I asked, "So, is the nickname 'Squeaks' because of your affinity?"

Before she could respond, Alpha interjected. "No, we call her Squeaks because of this." Alpha reached over and poked Squeaks in the side.

"EEEEEP!" Squeaks squeaked, clutching her side and shooting Alpha an admonishing glare. She lightly slapped the redhead on the shoulder and laughed. "You ass-butt!" She gripped the bottom of her chair since her feet barely touched the floor. She hopped it over twice, scooting away from Alpha with a smirk. I couldn't help but chuckle.

Clearing her throat, Squeaks continued, "To answer your question, yes, it's because of my affinity, not because of..." She trailed off, casting a suspicious glance at Alpha.

Alpha raised her palms in a sign of peace as an impish smile played across her face. I could tell they had a long history together, and it piqued my curiosity. I found myself wondering why she wasn't in the coven. "You two seem to be pretty close friends. I never really got that impression when I saw you interact at the store."

"Oh, Gosh! Where are my manners," Halo said, quickly releasing my arm and heading to our cooler. "I'll make lunch. Squeaks, would you like anything specific?"

"She'll have some cheese," Alpha declared.

I frowned. "Doesn't that seem a little... I don't know, offensive and stereotypical?" I questioned.

Squeaks sighed in resignation. "It totally is. But, she's right. God help me, I do love me some cheddar."

Alpha shot me a smug grin and crossed her arms. Halo dropped off a few snacks at the table before she hurriedly prepared lunch for everyone.

Finally addressing my question, Alpha said, "Anyway, yes, Squeaks and I go way back. We've been friends since we were little. But, with her job, no one should think she plays favorites. Hot Topic is sacred neutral ground."

Squeaks quirked a brow and smirked. "Just friends huh? More like best friends. You know how much she likes having her belly rubbed, right? Well, on stormy nights she used to run to my room with her teddy—"

Alpha's cheeks matched her hair as she clamped a hand over Squeaks' mouth. "Okay!" She glared at the Mouse Witch. "We've been *best* friends for a long time." She cautiously withdrew her hand.

Squeaks smiled warmly at her friend. "Better. I always wondered…" she trailed off while looking at her drink. "Well, we haven't seen much of each other since she found her new pet." Her curious gaze shifted to me with a hint of jealousy.

Suddenly, I felt a little awkward. "Oh, I see. If you two were so close—" only for Squeaks to finish the question for me.

"Why didn't I join her coven?" she asked before taking a nibble of cheese. "Mmm, this is so good."

Alpha crossed her arms and frowned, and it seemed I had touched on a sore topic.

Squeaks finished her bite and sighed. "We argued over that a few times. But, in the end, it's simple. Our relationship was always on even footing. As I'm sure you've noticed, when Alpha is in charge, there is no even footing. She insisted it wouldn't affect our friendship, but I disagree. However, ever since you showed up, things have changed in a different way." She shrugged.

I wasn't sure what to say. I felt a little bad about her situation, and even though it clearly wasn't my fault, I still kinda felt like I shared some of the blame. "I'm sorry," was all I could say.

She giggled. "Sorry for what? For being kidnapped and pulling one over on my friend? Yeah, I heard what happened. She got what she deserved for thinking she could treat another person like they were nothing more than an animal." She gave Alpha a pointed look.

To my surprise, Alpha dropped her head, real shame marring her expression for the first time. "It's been standard practice for centuries to treat Greater Familiars as servants. I was only doing what I was taught to do."

"This baby-crazy brat probably said you don't get a say about your own daughters one day too, huh?" Squeaks asked with a knowing smile.

Alpha's ears shot up along with her chin, her jaw set. "That's different and you know it! Now you're being ridiculous!"

My hands shot up, begging for peace. "Please, I'd rather not get into that subject today."

Halo's arrival with more food helped quell the tension. Her palm was facing the sky with her fingers all pointing up, fingertips glowing. Five plates floated above it. "Jeepers! You've all got your knickers in a bunch. I have just the thing that'll help." Using her other hand she pointed from one plate to another, each one landing on the table, leaving one open spot for Cherry when she finished tending to the egg.

We sat quietly, but a little tension still hung in the air as we began eating our lunch. Cherry came over with a grin stretching ear to ear, completely ignoring the awkward atmosphere. She cradled her black egg, which she'd swaddled in a baby blue blanket. "Speaking of kids, look, Squeaks! It's Logan and my first baby!" she said excitedly.

I sighed, and Squeaks gasped. "You have a baby already?!" Then she noticed the black shell where a baby's face would normally be exposed in the bundle. "O—Oh!" She laughed. "I see. Wait? Is that—"

Cherry nodded rapidly, her raven hair bouncing. "Yup! It's my black snake. Logan killed a Black Emperor Serpent when we got here, and—"

Squeaks spat out her drink, red juice splattering all over Cherry's face. Cherry blinked in reply, licking some of it off, before launching into a mini-tirade. "What the hell, Squeaks!"

A cloud of black smoke erupted from the Mouse Witch's hand, quickly surrounding Cherry and the egg before dissipating. I almost shot up from my chair, ready for a fight, but the lack of movement from any of the girls gave me pause. When the smoke cleared, all the juice was gone. "I'm so sorry, Cherbear. But did you just say he killed a Black Emperor Serpent? What spells did you use on him? Did the three of you have to go all out to help?"

Halo shook her head so excitedly that one of her pigtails slapped Cherry in the face, adding insult to injury. I couldn't help but feel bad for my vampiric lover as she continued to be unintentionally bullied. "Nope! We didn't help him one bit! Golly, Squeaks, you should have seen it. He was so cool!"

"That's not exactly true. You girls made the tokens, so you still helped," I said, doing my best to remain humble, despite feeling my chest swell with pride at her praise.

Squeaks paused, looking me up and down as if seeing me in a new light. A hunger settled into her green eyes, and I couldn't tell if it was for power or something more carnal.

Cherry cleared her throat as she returned from putting her egg in its bed. Her face was a mask of irritation. "Ahem."

Squeaks clearly heard the cough. Instead of acknowledging it, she licked her black lips, green eyes locked on mine. After another long moment, she finally turned to the brunette and addressed it. "Sorry, Cherbear," she said, showing no sign of being sorry at all. "I didn't realize how strong Logan is, that's all."

My cheeks felt a bit warm, but I kept my cool and didn't look away from her gaze. Squeaks had a lot of connections because of her job, so showing my strength and confidence in front of her could help us get her to trust in our capabilities as a coven. It had nothing to do with how breathtakingly beautiful she was—mostly.

"He's not the only one who's stronger," Alpha said with pride. "Inspect me."

I watched with fascinated curiosity as Squeaks hesitated, but upon seeing that Alpha was serious, she nodded. Her eyes glowed black, the white of her sclera disappearing as she focused on Alpha's stomach. Her jaw dropped in awe. While I had no clue what she was seeing, I assumed it was some kind of magic source. "Holy shit!" Squeaks exclaimed.

Leaning over, I whispered to Halo, "What just happened?"

Halo whispered back, "She inspected her magical core. It's the source of our power."

"How come I haven't heard anything about that before?"

"Because it's considered super rude to scan another witch without her permission. There's no way to hide a scan, either. That kind of gobbledegook will get you in a pickle," she explained.

I nodded in understanding.

The look of disbelief didn't leave Squeaks's face. "How much of those gains are from Logan? The last time you had me inspect you was before you started the coven."

Alpha looked up, tilting her head from side to side as she considered. "Hmm. I'd say at least 75%. And, as he gets even stronger and the coven grows, we'll get stronger."

"Seventy-five," Squeaks mouthed. "Holy fuck," she breathed out. "That's incredible. He's a total monster."

"Huh, what would happen if they inspected me?" I wondered aloud.

Alpha scoffed. "We never inspected you for a reason. You're not a witch. There's no point."

Squeaks raised a brow at her friend. "I don't know, Alpha. You've been wrong about him before. Logan, do you mind if I inspect you?"

My brows rose, and suddenly I felt nervous. I hadn't actually meant to invite this situation. I looked at the other girls. Both Cherry and Halo were looking at me curiously, taking a break from their meals. They both shrugged. I shrugged back. "Well, I don't see what harm it could do. Go ahead." I stood, taking a step back from the table.

What happened next was highly unexpected. Not only did Squeaks' eyes glow, but so did Halo and Cherry's. Three heads tilted in confusion. Alpha noticed and rolled her eyes, but then she began inspecting me too. A yellow glow filled her gaze, and she furrowed her brow. Concern filled me as moments passed and still they said nothing. They all stared at me, silently observing until they each slowly started speaking.

"Goodness gracious, it's everywhere," Halo muttered.

"This doesn't make sense," Cherry grunted.

"What the...hell are we looking at?" Alpha asked.

"What? What do you see?" I asked, a bit of worry setting in. I started to pat my body down to try and find whatever the hell it was that they were talking about.

Squeaks squinted, staring more intently. "If I really focus, it loses some of the brightness. It looks like... veins."

That comment did nothing to calm my slowly fraying nerves. Before I could freak out, Halo put up a finger, requesting patience. She squinted as well. "My gosh! I see it. Well, isn't that something?"

After they all squinted and examined me a little further, the light in their eyes dimmed. "Well, is anyone gonna fill in the science experiment or am I just going to remain totally clueless?"

Squeaks shrugged. "The best I can guess is we're seeing traces of the magical bloodline that gives you your power. When we inspect you, at first it's just a bright glow, almost like your whole body is a magical core. But, when we focus and dim the brightness, it looks like a system of veins and the magic is pumping through them, spreading through your whole body."

I looked at my hands in amazement—until Cherry crushed my infantile hopes. "Yeah, it's probably because your body has to be ready to shift at a moment's notice since you're a Greater Familiar. Kinda like how your body is always ready at a moment's notice for other," she winked, "more intimate things."

Sitting back down dejectedly, I stabbed a chunk of meat with my fork a little too hard. Halo spotted my childish action and giggled, placing a hand on my arm. "Oh, poor thing. You're still special, baby."

"I know," I chuckled, taking a bite. But, with a glance at Alpha, she didn't look like she was necessarily satisfied with the other theories being floated. I put it on the shelf for more consideration at a later date.

Squeaks took a long sip before placing her drink on the table and pushing her plate forward. "Unfortunately, I didn't come here for the social visit, and I'll have to get to work in a bit. So, time to get down to business."

Alpha stood and spun her chair around, straddling it and resting her forearms on the back. "Tell us what you got for us, Squeaks."

Squeaks nodded. "Things aren't looking good in the city. Even though the war is picking up, there are rumors of peace talks."

Halo and Cherry looked at one another with concern.

The Mouse Witch continued, "There's a rumor spreading that it wasn't the bigger covens that stole the Lunar Amulet, and I think since no coven has demonstrated a significant boost of power, both sides are willing to believe it. It's the most likely cause for the peace talks."

"Got any idea where that rumor came from?" Alpha asked.

Shaking her head, Squeaks said, "No. Not where it originally came from. A solo witch sold me the news."

"Any chance it came from Rose's coven?" I asked.

She shrugged. "Doubtful. Rose came to me looking to buy information a few days ago.

When I shared that particular rumor with her, she got pissed. I specifically remember her saying, 'someone's trying to freakin' steal my shit,'" she squeaked in her best impression of Rose.

I chuckled and nodded. It made sense. Surely they wouldn't have given up after only one attempt, and therefore wouldn't have given out their knowledge to others who might steal the opportunity out from under them.

"The other rumor going around," she said, looking pointedly at me. "Is that a human Greater Familiar with an extraordinarily rare bloodline showed up on a lot of radars for a couple of days before disappearing. Most think a new coven contracted them. Crazy timing there, since the Lunar Amulet disappeared shortly after." She smirked. "I didn't inform anyone about the handsome man I've seen with you ladies recently. But that doesn't mean others can't put two and two together, as you already know."

Halo frowned, chewing on a pigtail. "Dodge rammit. This is such a big pile of dookie."

"Do you think the big covens know it was us?" Cherry asked, resting her chin in her hands with her elbows propped up on the table.

Squeaks shook her head quickly. "No. As far as I can tell, they don't know just yet. They do have their ways of getting information. It's only a matter of time before they figure it out and come for you. The longer you sit here planning, the more time you give them to make their move. Only question is whether or not you'll be ready for it when they do."

Silence fell over the table as we absorbed the news.

A few moments later, Squeaks spoke up again. "If you want my advice, I suggest you go back home and start taking action before it's too late. I'm guessing you probably achieved what you set out to achieve here already." She rested a hand atop Alpha's, squeezing it slightly. "I'd hate to see any of you get hurt."

Alpha smiled softly. "We don't plan on getting hurt. If anything, you'll have to worry about those witches getting stitches."

Squeaks rolled her eyes but chuckled. "How many times have I told you? That phrase is so dumb."

"No, it's not," Alpha said, a bit too defensively.

"Magical healing doesn't require stitches!" Squeaks' reply came, and I realized this wasn't the first time the two had this argument before.

"Ladies," I said, holding up a hand. "Sorry to interrupt, but I think we have more important things to talk about."

Alpha nodded. "Logan's right. This is going to take a while. How long are you planning on staying, Squeaks?"

"Actually, I've got to go now. My shift starts soon. But, it was really good to see all of you," Squeaks said, standing and pushing in her chair.

"We're really glad you came by!" Halo said as she started picking up emptied plates.

"Yeah, thanks for the info, Squeaks. We have a lot to think about," Cherry added. She glanced over at her egg in the corner, making me smirk.

Standing, Alpha walked with Squeaks to the bathroom door. The two spoke in whispers for a moment before they embraced, and the Mouse Witch kissed Alpha on the cheek. The doorway was replaced by a familiar rainbow portal. Before she walked through, she turned back to us. Squeaks waved at the girls. "Later, Halo, later, Cherbear!" She turned to me and blew me a kiss. "I'll see you later too."

Alpha playfully narrowed her eyes and poked her in the side.

"EEEEP!" Squeaks jumped and giggled. "Okay, Okay, I'm going. Later!" With a step, she was gone.

Returning to the table, Alpha took her chair, still straddling it. "I'm not gonna lie, shit's flying at the fan and it's gonna hit soon."

I grimaced at the unfortunate picture that expression painted.

"So, let's get this straight. Rose knows but didn't talk, tons of witches know about Logan, and everyone is gonna know that we stole the amulet soon," Cherry said, ticking off fingers.

"Fiddlesticks! This is so flipping bad. We can't dilly-dally anymore." Halo's usual smile was nowhere to be found. Instead, she was tugging on her pigtails and frowning deeply. "What do we do?"

"What do we do? That's simple, we get powerful enough that we can shove their brooms up their asses and send them packing." While Alpha was talking tough, I noticed her ears flattened and her tail drooped.

"But how? It's a whole pile of poppycock."

"I say we pile up on Logan's—"

"Cherry!" Alpha snapped.

Cherry's head and shoulders dropped. "I'm sorry. I'm just—I'm scared. I don't know what to do. We're all badass witches, and Logan is more powerful than any other familiar in the city, almost definitely, but they have a flame drake *and* a fenrir. I believe Logan can beat them both, but if they all come at us at once, how can the three of us take on dozens of witches?"

I took Cherry's hand in mine and squeezed.

Alpha smirked, maintaining her confident appearance despite our seemingly dire circumstances. "We don't."

Halo pulled her pigtails out of her mouth, where she had been nervously chewing on them, then tilted her head. "What do you mean we don't? Are we... running?"

Alpha frowned. "What? Hell no. We aren't little bitches."

My eyes opened wide as I guessed her plan. "Expansion?"

The redhead nodded with a grin. "That's right, expansion. We're gonna pick up some fresh talent."

"I don't know about you, but it's gonna take a while to get that many witches on board. It's not easy to reach out to all the rogue and solo witches in the city," Cherry pointed out.

I took a sip of my water. "Then we don't go after solos or rogues. Sure, we put the word out for them, but—mergers. That's a different story."

Furry ears twitched as Alpha pointed at me. "Got it in one. We're gonna pick up some other small covens. We'll gain members faster that way. A few rogues and solos may join too, as a result. That'd be a nice bonus if it happens, but maybe not even necessary."

Halo glanced at me skeptically. "While that idea sounds as scrumptious as a stack of pancakes, who would we merge with?"

"And how do we convince them to join when we might have the big two up our asses?" Cherry placed her hand on my thigh. "Not that I'm opposed to having something big up my—" Cherry tried to say.

"Use me," I said.

Cherry's eyes widened, and her cheeks flushed. "That's what I was thinkin'..."

I shook my head, holding back a laugh. "Not like that."

A throat cleared, and we looked at the culprit. "He means we use him and the Lunar Amulet as bait to lure them in. When they join us, both will increase their power a lot. And that's something we know all witches want."

Nodding, I pointed at Alpha. "Yes, that."

Halo held her pigtails out to the side of her head dramatically and frowned. "Hold the phone! There's no way I'll share Logan with that many witches."

Cherry gasped. "Forget those witches. We don't need 'em."

Alpha smirked. "Obviously. We already agreed not to keep Logan chained to a bed again. We'll have to let a couple join the house as inner members, and they'll have access to Logan, but still at a level below us *and him*. But the rest will be secondary members only. The only benefit they'll get from Logan is the extra power that comes from a Greater Familiar and their connection to us."

I frowned, unsure of how to feel. "Do I get a say in this?"

Alpha raised a brow. "Certainly. Would you choose differently?"

I opened my mouth, then closed it. She had a point. "No. I suppose I wouldn't."

"That's what I thought," Alpha said with a chuckle.

"This is a bunch of flunking bull-stuff," Halo whined.

"Gonna have to choke a witch," Cherry muttered.

But, they didn't really complain. They understood the necessity of sharing. Alpha gripped the back of the chair. "Question is, who do we target first?"

I didn't hesitate. "Easy. Rose's coven."

I was met by a questioning brow from Alpha, a slack jaw from Halo, and narrowed eyes from Cherry. "You just wanna bang the flower slut," she accused.

I threw up my palms, my brows scrunched with indignation. "What? That's not at all what I was thinking. Just hear me out. We just kicked their coven's ass, so they know how powerful we are. Who better to make an offer to first? We both get what we want—they get more power, and they help us with our problem. Plus, aren't they well-known among the smaller covens? It could open the floodgates to start merging the smaller groups under us."

Cherry frowned. "You're right. I'm sorry." A small mischievous smile crept on her face. "But, you still want to bang her."

I grinned. "Well, I can't say that I don't not want to. Plus Novella was pretty hot. Something about those glasses." I teased.

Halo gasped, her amusement obvious. "Oh my gosh! Logan! Don't be such a buttmunch!"

A feral grin grew on Alpha's face. "There it is. With Logan as bait, we're gonna catch a whole lot of fish."

CHAPTER 23

Hostile Takeover

I wriggled my way out of the cozy pile of soft bodies with a happy sigh. Last night Alpha orchestrated another four-way to help relieve some of the stress and tension that grew throughout the previous day's planning—truly the mark of a good leader.

Looking at my reflection in the mirror, I couldn't help but laugh. My hair was a sticky mess after three different women used my face as an impromptu massage chair. My own head reminded me of a certain blonde from a film I saw once. What was that called? It was something about a girl named Mary. Unable to recall the movie's name, I shook my head and hopped in the shower.

Emerging refreshed and dressed, I was surprised to find my three enchanting witches gathered around the breakfast table. They weren't messing around this morning. Everything, except for a small pile of my stuff, was already packed up, and the ladies were dressed for the day. *Magic showers... so not fair.* Quickly, I put all my things into storage and joined them at the table.

"Good morning, handsome!" Halo beamed at me while patting the open chair between herself and Cherry. The others were engrossed in their meal, leaving Cherry to wink at me and Alpha to offer a nod of acknowledgment.

Seating myself, I marveled at the breakfast Halo conjured up from our dwindling rations. "Good morning, ladies." I helped myself to some bacon, quickly gobbling it down. As the salty deliciousness hit my mouth, I realized how hungry I was.

Alpha pushed her empty plate forward, wasting no time in getting straight to business. "Keep eating. I'll keep this brief," she declared, her tone commanding our attention. "I got some intel from Squeaks this morning." We all nodded, silently chewing.

"Rose's coven has at least one member watching Hot Topic for our return at all times. They've been in a rotation, which includes Rose herself." Alpha paused, taking a long gulp of milk before continuing. "If they keep to their schedule, Rose will be on duty in a few hours. If she's there, Squeaks is going to open the portal.

"Logan, you're gonna be the bait. We'll go out through the rear of the shop, then fly around to the side door saying something about you meeting us at home. Your job will be to act cautiously and leave through the side exit of the mall. That's where we'll use Rose's trick against her. No doubt she'll be following you out. But when you both walk through the exit, we'll have her right where we want her."

Cherry stabbed her sausage a little too hard as she voiced her concern. "I don't like this. We're talking about leaving Logan on his own—it's too risky. He couldn't even walk to the gas station without being attacked. I'm not signing off on this."

Halo bit her lower lip and looked down nervously. "Jeepers, Alpha, I don't like it either."

I was with Cherry and Halo on this one. Unfortunately, we discussed it the night before. Time wasn't on our side and we couldn't afford to wait and scout out better options. With reliable information in hand, we had to act fast. So, despite my reservations, I knew this was our best option. I placed a reassuring hand on both of the girls' shoulders. "I know. I feel the same, but we all know why it has to be this way."

Alpha nodded. "Exactly. I wouldn't risk sending Logan by himself if I thought there was another way."

Cherry slammed her palm onto the table in an unexpected outburst. "Bullshit! All you care about is power! He's nothing but a pet to you!"

Nostrils flared and fists clenched as Alpha abruptly stood. Cherry flinched but held her ground, rising as well. Her crimson eyes glowed as she glared at our leader. The tension seemed to heat the air in the room.

The redhead gritted her teeth and set her jaw. After a few moments, Alpha took a deep breath, sat back down, and spoke as calmly as she could, "That's not true, and you know it. Logan is important to me as well. Truth is we're all stressed right now, so I'm going to forget that outburst and just say I understand your feelings, but someone has to make the tough call here."

Cherry's shoulders sagged as shame washed over her, and she sat too. "You're right. I'm sorry. That was uncalled for. And...I get it, I guess."

I squeezed her hand gently, offering silent support. Alpha was right, we were all stressed and the night's previous fun only provided a brief respite. The more we grew the coven, the less pressure we'd be under, and hopefully the quicker we could get back to enjoying life without major threats looming over our heads.

Alpha stood again, pushed in her chair, and said, "If you're all almost finished, we'll go over the final details before we need to get moving."

Quickly, we finished our breakfast and Halo spelled the dishes, cleaning and storing them. Despite my reservations, I did feel confident that I could handle one or two from Rose's coven alone. Even if I wasn't, I didn't have much of a choice. On the bright side, Cherry generously offered another week's worth of morning blowjobs if I fulfilled this request. That offer seemed beyond generous, but I had a sneaking suspicion that she just missed doing it. Either way, I didn't complain.

• ♥ • ♥ • ♥ • ♥ • ♥ •

A few hours later, as the girls finished going over the finer details of the plan, I found myself daydreaming about how delightful tomorrow morning would be. Before we knew it, a spiraling rainbow portal opened up in the bathroom doorway. One by one we stepped through to the familiar sight of the Hot Topic.

The cool sensation washed over me as the surreal feeling of stepping into another realm felt more like a trick of the mind. It took me a moment to get my bearings straight.

Squeaks greeted us with a friendly smile, but maintained her professional demeanor. "Thank you for your business. Hot Topic appreciates you. Will you be exiting using the Broom Pad?" Squeaks asked. The broom pad was apparently a magically warded location that allowed witches a discreet spot to cast spells to hide their broom flights.

"Sure! That sounds swell," Halo said.

Alpha turned to me, giving me a strict order and speaking a bit louder than was necessary, "We need to prep the ritual as soon as possible. You're making your own way back. No screwing around. Come straight home."

I played the part of the dutiful servant. "Yes, Alpha. Of course, I'll see you soon."

Cherry put a finger beneath my chin, turning my gaze toward her and holding it there. "And keep an eye out. You never know who's around." Cherry winked as she gave me a light pat on the cheek before the three girls walked out through the back door.

Looking around the store I could make out the top of Rose's head, her pink flower poking just over the top of a shelf. Not the best attempt at stealth, for sure.

Anyway, it was time to put on a show. I sighed dramatically before telling Squeaks I was ready to leave from the main store's entrance. Walking at a normal pace, I intentionally stopped as I exited the store, looking this way and that, as if I needed to puzzle out where I was going. Really, I was giving Rose time to exit the magical portion of the store so she could follow me.

Turning a corner I briefly caught sight of the Flower Witch in my peripheral vision and fought off the urge to look at her. She was hiding her affinity in a much more human form but still had her flower in her dark hair, wearing it like an accessory. I was intentionally walking to the side exit that led out to the alley. This ensured that she wouldn't make a move in the store, since I was handing her a much better location on a silver platter. So far it was working perfectly.

The smaller hall was quiet, and I could hear the footsteps behind me as I pushed open the side door, only to find myself in the living room of my home. Only a second later vines wrapped around me as Rose made her move the second she stepped through the door.

"I've got you now..." she said before her words trailed off and the vines slowly released me. "Aww, frick on a stick."

I turned around, beaming at her as the door clicked shut behind her and the portal closed. "Oh, hi Rose. What a fun coincidence!"

Rose was surrounded by three witches with predatory smiles. Alpha's arms were crossed. "Hello, there, flowerhead."

Halo gave her a finger wave. "Golly, Rose! Fancy meeting you here," she said, her words more threatening than cheerful.

With a stomp of her feet, Rose crossed her arms, glaring at me. "Hey! You tricked me! I was supposed to kidnap and interrogate *you*!" She huffed. "There goes operation 'I'm gonna kidnap Logan and trade him for the Lunar Amulet"

I frowned. "Wait... That was the name of your plan? Isn't that a bit—I don't know—lacking creativity?"

She shrugged, refusing to meet my eyes. "I like to keep things simple."

Alpha stepped forward, rolling her eyes. "Listen, Rose, since you like things simple, that's the way we'll lay it out for you—nice and simple for you so you can understand—"

"Why don't you complicate it for me instead?" she snipped with a sneer as she also crossed her arms and began tapping her foot. As if she was one-upping Alpha's posture. I was pretty sure she was being confrontational just for the sake of it.

Alpha blinked. "Why the hell would I do that?"

Smirking, Rose raised a brow. "Oh? Not smart enough to freakin' complicate things, *Alpha*? What a simple little puppy you are. Arf! Arf arf!" She started panting to add to her mockery, then punctuated it with a, "Freakin' *bitch*."

We all just stared at Rose, not sure how to handle that fun little outburst. Alpha seemed to need a minute to overcome the sheer ridiculousness of that statement, and, amusingly enough, I thought it might have actually bothered her a bit. I began to wonder at the level of Rose's intelligence. Was she stupid or a secret genius? For all I knew her persona was a tactic to keep people off balance, but it was impossible to tell. If that was it, though, it was kind of working.

Being the smart woman that Alpha *definitely* was, she recollected her composure and continued, "Like I said, we'll keep this simple. Your coven is going to join ours. You want the power of the Lunar Amulet and Logan, and we have them both."

Narrowing her eyes, Rose sat on the couch, then lifted a leg far too high while crossing one leg over the other, glancing at me as she did. I kept my focus on her face, though I still got a bit of a show out of the corner of my eye. "What's in it for us?" Rose asked.

Alpha frowned, her ears sticking straight up. "I literally just told you what's in it for you. You don't need anything else. Hell, you're lucky we didn't end you last time."

Rose rolled her eyes. "Puh-leez, honey. I'm not freakin' stupid. New Moon and Salem are both gonna come after you and kick your asses into the dirt, so clearly you'll need our help or by this time next week, you'll be fertilizer for my vines. Like you said, if you were gonna hurt me you'd have done it already. So, as I was saying, what's in it for us?"

Gritting her teeth, Alpha glanced from Halo to Cherry. "We have to do it."

Halo's pigtails furiously flailed in the air as she shook her head. "Dodge rammit! This is a bunch of bull honky!"

Cherry stomped her foot in protest. "Don't you dare! He's spread too thin as it is when we're the only ones he's supposed to spread!"

To my surprise, Alpha looked at me as well, reading my face. I sighed and shrugged. "We need them."

At my words, Halo and Cherry both pouted. Their reactions weren't a surprise because they were somewhat planned. We all knew that there would be a chance that we'd have to allow at least one or two witches into the inner circle. Those witches would have their own room at the house and direct access to me, same as Cherry, Alpha, and Halo. That didn't mean I had to sleep with them, but it was a possibility if I wanted it. It was a basic tactic designed to, hopefully, make Rose think she got one over on us.

Alpha eventually groaned, letting her arms uncross and rest against her sides. "Alright,

Rose. You win. We'll let *you* join the inner circle. The rest will be secondary members, though."

Our tactic almost worked. But, again Rose proved to be more cunning than we took her for. She leaned forward, black eyes fixed on me as she licked her lips. "I'll take that, but the rest of my girls deserve something too. I want at least one of them to join the inner circle in the future."

After we decided to go for Rose's coven, we already had a potential role planned for one of the other members that would result in them joining the inner circle at some point anyway. So, I wasn't surprised when Alpha rolled her eyes and agreed. "Fine but that's—"

Rose cut her off in a rush, "And I want the freakin' videos on Cherry's phone! No one ever sent those!"

"That's ALL!" Alpha shouted, pointing at the Flower Witch. "If you try asking for even one more thing, I'll spray your ass with weed killer."

Black eyes widened as Rose threw both hands in the air. "Okay, Jesus Christ! I get it. Keep the weed killer out of this. That's too far."

"Then if you don't want to be doused in Roundup, call your girls over and let's make this official," Alpha demanded, taking a seat across from Rose.

"What's your email, Rose? I'm gonna have to share the drive files with you 'cause they're too big. Kinda like Logan," Cherry said, snickering and with far too much enthusiasm. She was always excited to share videos of her and me with anyone willing to watch. I attempted drawing the line one night when she projected her phone screen onto the wall, only to be shut down by all three of my girls. Halo even popped some popcorn on the stove.

The suddenly nervous Flower Witch pulled out her phone and started to dial before turning her attention to Cherry. "It's uh—pinkflussy69 @witchyworld.com."

It didn't take long for the Rose Coven witches to arrive. With the preparations already prepared, the ritual began at once. Nine witches surrounded the circle, while Alpha stood in the center. Fingers glowed various colors as palms sliced open and blood dripped onto the candlelit pentagram below. All the witches began to chant, except for Alpha. "Ouns tee coksen arjin een. Ij meree taar te con. Alpha leit uns. ij preloft." Their bodies glowed a bright red and Alpha raised her arms into the air and said, "Iacvaar jour loyeit!" The red glow flashed bright and rushed into Alpha. And, just when it seemed like something big was going to happen, it was over.

The intensity of the moment was gone and the girls all healed their hands as they began quietly chatting amongst one another. It was almost like actors stepping down from a stage after finishing a scene they performed many times before. Honestly, I expected more from the ritual. It was just so anticlimactic, or so I thought until Alpha directed all the new girls to complete the ceremony by kissing me.

Before I had the chance to question the necessity, vines shot out from Rose's body, pulling her through the air to me. Mid-flight she shouted, "Time for some freakin' kisses!" Green legs wrapped around my waist and her arms were around my neck as she slammed her lips against mine so hard I thought I'd taste copper. On instinct, I wrapped my arms around her, stumbling before catching myself. After a few moments of her tongue invading my mouth, Cherry and Alpha worked together to pry her off. "Not yet! I need to finish the ritual!"

I tried not to smile but failed miserably. The next witch to step up was Novella. Those glasses were hitting just right, and if I were being honest, I was a bit excited. But I quickly learned that I wasn't as excited as Novella. She pulled the hair tie from her hair, shaking it out before grabbing the back of my neck and pulling me down. Her other hand wrapped around my waist and she even went as far as to wrap one leg around mine. Novella kissed me passionately and went just long enough to leave me wanting more. She shot me a wink before walking away. Cherry scowled at her and Novella smirked. "What? You don't own him," she said as she joined her friends.

The next few were less exciting. The Hex, Potion, and Broom Witches all gave me quick, shy kisses. The Wand Witch lingered for just a moment, before scampering off with a giggle. The last one was the Chef Witch. When I'd asked the girls about her affinity's official title they'd just shrugged and said I was close enough.

She poked me in the chest. "I'm still pissed at you for the last battle. They all call me Chef Witchardee now. It's your fault that I have to make homemade soup every couple of days now. Do you know how boring it is to make soup all the time?" she complained.

I shrugged. "Sorry."

She rolled her eyes dramatically before grabbing the back of my neck and forcefully kissing me for a few seconds. "You're lucky you're a pretty boy," she said with a huff before walking away.

"And you're lucky...I like soup," I said in a vain attempt to retort.

CHAPTER 24

The Not So Itsy-Bitsy Spider

All the witches left after the ceremony was complete with instructions to reach out to other small covens to let them know Alpha wanted to talk. Well, all except for Rose, who instructed Novella to pack up her things and bring them to her. We took a few hours to show Rose her new room, which she promptly decorated with vines and flowers of all kinds that covered the walls and emitted a wonderful aroma.

After that, we explained how to make tokens for me, and I tried out her form for the first time. According to Chery, I looked like the lovechild of Swamp Thing and the Jolly Green Giant, and it turned out the personality had a desperate need to... pollinate. After a few minutes of wrestling vines away from furiously blushing witches, I finally got it under control by placating the spirit with the promise I would get all the witches pregnant one day.

Not all the women were happy that I reined it in, actually, and a couple asked me if they could help me 'practice' commanding the vines later. I ignored those requests and went to my room, where I worked on gaining better control over my abilities. But I had the feeling that a few of the newer tokens would come with some creative demands.

Eventually, the magic wore off, and I took a quick shower. When I made it back to the living room, I encountered an interesting sight. Alpha was watching the news, while Rose and Cherry were being pushed on vine swings by

Halo. The scene was oddly sweet, and I chose not to reveal myself yet and just watched for a while.

"Golly, Rose, these swings sure are spiffy. We should have installed some a while ago," Halo said as she stepped behind Cherry and pushed.

Rose stuck her feet straight out as she leaned back. "I know, right? They're the freakin' best!"

Cherry giggled. "I already bought a swing. But it's for a different kind of fun."

My brows rose as I noted that intriguing development. Halo gasped. "Are you talking about a swing for hanky panky?"

"Yup! Hey, Rose, how do you walk around in your bare feet all the time?" Cherry tapped her boots together. "I couldn't imagine having my little piggies exposed all day long."

Halo shifted back behind Rose, who was losing momentum. Rose wiggled her toes. "It's kind of a requirement of my affinity. It feels much better to be closer to the earth."

I went to sit next to Alpha and see what the news was saying before I brought up a topic that had been on my mind for a while. But, as I was midway through the living room, Rose's swing whipped her off of it, sending her flying right at me. She shouted in unconvincing surprise, "Oh no—I fell!" Then she slammed into me and sent us crashing to the ground. Vines wrapped around me until I landed on my back, with Rose straddling me.

I quirked a questioning brow, looking up at her.

She ran a finger down my chest. "Wow. That's so crazy isn't—AH! Let me go! This is freakin' bullshit!"

Halo and Cherry grabbed the Flower Witch by each arm, both slinging spells to sever vines she tried using to hold on to me. They sat her down on either side of them, squeezing onto the couch, causing Alpha to scowl.

I got off the ground and sat in the chair. Alpha got up from the couch and sat on my lap. "Sit there and be a comfy chair for me, pet."

"Sure, why not?" I said, reaching up and scratching behind her ears.

Alpha shuddered at my touch but glared at Rose. "Listen up, Rose. You don't get to be intimate with Logan unless he wants it from you. He might be our pet, but he's also a part of the team. Like I explained earlier, he's got a special contract for a Greater Familiar, and you have to respect that as much as we do. Don't forget it. That's an order."

That Alpha was saying this out loud to a new coven member showed me just how far our relationship had come. There was a much greater deal of mutual respect between us, and I felt like we could be even closer if we could resolve a certain issue involving our future.

Rose gasped and her jaw hung on its hinges. "Freakin' what?! If you're not careful a contract like that is going to make him a Coven King!"

"Coven King?" I muttered in confusion.

"For Pete's sake, that's a bunch of nonsense. Do you really believe that old story?" Halo asked, rolling her eyes.

Cherry bit her lip and eyed me. "I don't know. He's kinda like my king already. Maybe even my god. I certainly worship him on my knees often enough."

I stopped scratching the furry ears in front of me and rested my hands on Alpha's hips. I furrowed my brow. "Uh–what's a Coven King?"

Alpha rolled her eyes, clearly annoyed by Rose's earlier actions and now her attitude. But, as always, she answered my questions to the best of her ability. "It's an old urban legend about a human Greater Familiar like you that ends up seizing control of his coven because they left too much slack in his leash. But the only case anyone can make are some of the stories about Merlin, and no one even knows if they're true."

My brows shot up, before they fell right back down as I asked, "Merlin was real? Wait, why am I even surprised about that at this point?"

Rose scoffed. "You say legend, but I say it's a prophets see."

Alpha's brows scrunched. "Did you just say 'prophets see?' I think you meant prophecy."

"I know what I said, *Alpha*! I said freakin' prophets see. You know, because prophets *see* the future? Duh," Rose snipped.

Realizing that this was going nowhere, I cleared my throat and finally brought up a topic I'd been hoping to discuss with the girls for a while now. "Ahem. There's something I wanted to ask you all about."

Alpha turned in my lap until her ass was facing me, sitting directly on my crotch. I frowned, tapping her on the shoulder. As she looked back, her tight ass ground against me, and it felt very intentional. I tried to ignore it, but my body betrayed me as my bulge pressed into her. She smirked. "What do you want to talk about?"

I coughed. "Well, I can't really see anyone past you."

"Oh? Well, allow me to move out of your way," she said. Without taking her eyes off of me, she leaned forward far enough for me to see everyone, but also pressed her ass even harder against me.

"This—uh—makes things both easier and harder." I quipped.

I scratched the base of Alpha's tail and realized, based on previous similar actions and threats she'd made, that she was doing this on purpose as a punishment to the Flower Witch. As my confusion cleared up, I didn't mind assisting with said punishment as we had this discussion. "I'm sure that with the other girls out there spreading the word, our coven will grow fast. Unlike the major covens who have little to offer, Alpha doesn't impose ridiculous rules and requirements on our members. That being said, I think it's a good idea to add another unique affinity to our coven."

Alpha looked back at me over her shoulder and slowly ground her hips in circles. "That sounds well and good, but I'm guessing you wouldn't suggest this if you didn't have someone in mind?" She bit her lip and stared at Rose.

I saw Rose breathing heavier while she quietly muttered, "This is so not fair."

Then I noted that neither Halo, nor Cherry looked particularly thrilled about the current seating arrangement either. I wanted to laugh but needed to stay on topic, and despite the nature of my current predicament, this was an important discussion.

"Yeah. I have someone in mind. I think we should recruit Arachna. She's strong, and in the coven, she'll be even stronger. Plus, she's got a unique affinity that we can get a lot of use out of, and she showed a lot of drive by trying to form her own coven and having the guts to come after me alone."

Then, to add insult to injury and help further punish Rose for her tackling me to the ground, I ran my hand up Alpha's back before taking a fistful of hair and pulling her head back. Her tail started wagging furiously, as if it were trying to free its owner despite its joyful demeanor. In my head, I could picture the cocky smirk on Alpha's face as she stared at Rose.

Cherry seemed to have figured out what was really going on by now because she wasn't nearly as upset anymore. "How are we going to find her? It's not like we have any leads."

Rose tried to snake a hand between her legs, but Cherry and Halo took each of her arms in their own, causing the Flower Witch to pout. Halo, who was acting like nothing abnormal was happening, chimed in, "Oh my stars and garters! I know how we can find her. She buys from Hot Topic, so Squeaks probably has a way to reach her."

Alpha lightly moaned as she made her grinding more obvious, "Mmm. Okay. Here's the—ff-fucking—plan. You three are going to Hot Topic to meet up with Squeaks. Once you get there, put up some Vampiric Tokens for sale with the specific price of an equal number of arachnid tokens. Squeaks can't give us her contact info, but she won't—Mmm-mind calling the customer to let her know some of her favorite tokens are in stock. Once it's set up, call us and Logan and I will take the car and join you."

The green woman narrowed her inky black eyes. "And why can't we all go together?"

Alpha stood, taking me by the hand and leading me toward her room. "Because Logan owes me, and if he's a good boy, then after he gets his fill, I'll let him fill me."

Rose pouted with puffed out cheeks as she stomped her foot.

I ignored it and with a beaming smile, I said, "Welp, I'll never let anyone say I'm not a man who doesn't repay his debts." I waved goodbye to the girls as Alpha and I disappeared into her bedroom.

• ♥ • ♥ • ♥ • ♥ • ♥ •

A little over an hour or a couple of rounds later, Alpha and I got the call and met up with the girls at Hot Topic. We set up a perimeter around the mall, including the Broom Pad, and waited. There was a brief argument about why none of the girls could wait with me, but Alpha shut it down quickly, citing things about distractions and security breaches. Cherry passed out long-range walkie-talkies that she was entirely too excited about while ignoring the several comments about simple communication spells.

Alpha: *Since Cherry insists on using the walkies for communication, there will be no random chatter. I expect the line to be free for relevant comms only. Over.*

Halo: *Roger that Alpha. Keeping the gobbledygook to a minimum. Over.*

Rose: *I still don't see why we're using these.*

Me: *Rose, you forgot to say over. Over.*

Rose: *Over. Over.*

Snickering, I could swear I heard the eye roll in her words.

Cherry: *Kshhh. We're using them because it's fun! Don't spoil it! Over. Kshhh.*

Me: *Cherry, you know you don't have to make the kshh noise right? The walkies do that on their own. Over.*

Cherry: *Kshhh. My point remains, Logan. Don't spoil the fun, or you'll have less fun in the morning. Over. Kshh.*

Rose: *Speaking of fun in the morning, can I join you? Over.*

Cherry: *Ksssh. NO. Over. Kssh.*

Cherry: *...But you can watch if Logan wants. Over.*

Alpha: *What did I say about comms? Well and truly OVER.*

Before any more unauthorized communication could come over the line, Halo spotted our target.

Halo: *Jiminy Christmas, I found her! Arachna sighted on the North side of the main building. Gosh, she's a cautious one. She's keeping a close eye on her surroundings. When you head this way, don't make a ruckus or she'll skedaddle. Over.*

Alpha: *You heard her. We're in public, so she can't do anything fancy to get away. Halo, circle around and come at her from the North, Cherry from the East, I'll come up from the South, and Rose, you come in from the West. Logan, you head to the North entrance and meet our new friend there. Over and out.*

After several 'Rogers' and 'over and outs', we were on the move. I positioned myself in the food court near the entrance to Hot Topic because I couldn't travel as fast without being noticed, and I served as a backup in case she slipped past the girls. With a quick but casual pace, I hurried toward the North entry as everyone else got into position.

Looking through the glass door, I saw her. She was still rocking the goth look even harder than Squeaks. Her lip, nose, and ear piercings made identifying her a piece of cake. I looked all around her and saw the other girls closing in, but they wouldn't be there before Arachna entered the building. *Time to shine, Logan Morrison.* Opening the door, I greeted her with my most charming smile. "Hey there, Arachna. Long time no see."

The Spider Witch froze mid-step, causing her to stumble, catching herself before freezing again. She stammered, "Y—You—but—it's you! What? Why? How?"

I chuckled. "It's alright, relax. I'm here as a friend." The timing of my words couldn't have been worse, as the surrounding actions seemed to contradict them. All four girls created a ring surrounding her.

Arachna rolled her eyes and looked around. "Sure. How exactly is ambushing me friendly? Please do explain."

Shrugging, I scratched the back of my neck. "I know how it looks, but you've got to see it from our perspective. The last time we met, you attacked me. Despite that, I don't think we ended on bad terms. We were worried that you'd run before we all had time to talk. What do you say we go across the street to the park, grab some ice cream, and find a quiet place to have a chat?"

Her tense posture deflated, and her shoulders sagged. "It's not like I have much of a choice, do I?"

Alpha chuckled. "Nope, you sure don't. C'mon, let's go."

COVEN KING 1

Our group made its way across the parking lot and I stepped up to the ice cream stand. I asked the girls what they wanted. Alpha asked for Rocky Road, and Halo wanted strawberry. Both seemed fitting. Cherry wanted vanilla, despite her being anything but, and Rose requested 'two freakin' scoops of dirt in a cup'. That's the one with chocolate ice cream and gummy worms, apparently. Then I turned to Arachna. "Alright, you're up. What flavor do you want?"

Hesitantly, she stepped forward. "What's your deal?"

I waved the question away like a troublesome fly. "Flavor first, deal later."

Arachna's frown was more of a pout, which was undeniably adorable. She scanned the flavors before pointing to one. "That one. Salted caramel. I love that one."

Holding up two fingers, I said, "I'll take two salted caramels—two scoops each." I turned back to Arachna. "Small world, that's one of my favorites, too."

We found a secluded spot in the shade of a tall oak and the girls threw up some discreet wards, preventing anyone from eavesdropping. Normally, Alpha would take the lead on these conversations. However, since I already knew Arachna, I took on the responsibility. I ate a spoonful of ice cream as I collected my thoughts.

"Logan, while I appreciate the ice cream and all, why am I here? I remember telling you I never wanted to see you again," she said before taking a small bite.

Nodding, I acknowledged the truth. "You did. But things have changed, and I think you know that." I gave her a pointed look.

Arachna barked out a laugh. "Changed?! That's the fucking understatement of the year. The fighting is out of control and the major covens are locking shit down. More than a few witches I used to hang out with had no other choice but to join the major covens and fight."

I nodded. "I'm sorry you lost your friends to those people. How long do you think you'll last out there on your own, though?" I crossed my legs and turned to my entire body to face her.

She looked down, her frown returning as she stirred her slowly melting ice cream with her spoon. "I—" she shook her head. "How long do you think? I couldn't start my own coven, and I couldn't even beat a familiar. Is that why you're here? You need a lackey or something to run errands for you?" She sounded more sad than bitter.

To my surprise, Cherry spoke up, placing a hand on the Arachnid Witch's shoulder. "Don't beat yourself up. You know what Logan is, but what you don't know is how frickin' powerful he is. Especially his huge—"

"She's right!" I quickly shouted, not ready to allow Cherry's mind to drag the conversation to the gutter. "If it helps, I killed a Black Emperor Serpent by myself. Out of the witches I've fought, you were easily the most powerful, ferocious, and skilled."

"*She* was the most skilled and powerful?" Rose spat while cracking her knuckles.

Chuckling, I let my spoon fall into my ice cream cup. "Rose, you and I didn't exactly fight. By the time I made it to you, the battle was over. So, how could I possibly add you to the comparison? But I saw how much work your vines were putting in. There's a reason we were already prepared to add you to the inner circle."

This seemed to placate the Flower Witch. The corner of her mouth curved upward into a smirk and she tossed her viny hair behind her shoulder. "Right, right... That makes perfect sense. It makes more sense than—*than*—" she paused, eyes narrowing while looking for the words. Moments passed, and she still said nothing while looking into the distance and rubbing her chin with her finger and thumb.

Eventually, we moved on, wondering if we'd ever know just how much sense my remarks made. I sat my empty ice cream cup on the ground next to me. "We don't want a lackey, Arachna. Alpha will explain."

Alpha added her empty cup and spoon to mine, starting a small stack. "Here's the deal, Arachna. I don't know you, only what Logan says about you. We normally wouldn't all come out just to meet a rogue or solo witch. But, I know what Logan is capable of, and if he says you're worth it, then I trust his judgment, regardless of what you think about yourself."

The goth woman looked at me, and then back down at her ice cream, her spoon tapping the edge of her cardboard cup as her cheeks turned a light red. "You really think I'm that strong?" she asked.

Without an ounce of hesitation, I nodded. "I sure as hell do. And with us, you'll be even stronger."

Leaning back on her hands with her legs crossed, Alpha said, "You know we have Logan, and he's not just strong, but enhances our power as well. On top of that, we have the Lunar Amulet, and we are growing fast. You've got a rare opportunity here to not only join us, but be a part of the inner circle. Since you were planning to start your own coven, I'm sure you already know that being a part of the inner circle means you'll be more powerful, have some voice in decisions, more leadership responsibilities, and of course, direct access to Logan and all the *benefits* he provides–assuming he wants to provide them to you, that is. That's something we aren't planning to offer anyone else right now. But if you decline, we'll assume you're going to end up an enemy."

Arachna lightly scoffed and rolled her eyes. "Of course, butter me up and then threaten me. Seems like one hell of a choice I've got here."

Halo frowned and scooted closer to the goth girl. She placed a hand on her knee. "Golly, Arachna, it's not a threat, honey. It's just the unfortunate truth. You can refuse if you want, and we'll even let you walk away today. But ask yourself, with all the facts laid out, is that what you really think is best for us all?"

Alpha nodded. "Well said."

"But don't dillydally, sweetheart, because we need an answer. Unfortunately, we're on a bit of a clock," Halo added with a grimace while tapping the back of her wrist.

Arachna sighed and examined her now very melted ice cream. She stirred it slowly as she considered her options. After a few moments, she lifted the cup to her mouth and gulped down the melted treat before adding it to our stack. "I suppose it's better to choose who I'll join rather than wait to get pulled in against my will. And after fighting Logan, there's no way I want to do that again," she threw her head back and grunted. "Ugh. Fuck it. I'm in."

I smiled. "Welcome to the team, Arachna."

Rose suddenly snapped her fingers. "Oh! I got it! It makes more freakin' sense than Logan not bothering to wear clothes around Cherry!"

I opened my mouth to protest, then closed it, and nodded. "She's got a point."

Cherry nodded solemnly. "She's not wrong... She's not wrong."

CHAPTER 25

Resting Witch Face

A week had passed since we picked up Arachna. During that time, I crushed my personal best for girls kissed in a seven day period. Not that I was trying, but all the contract rituals required it. Throughout the week, we were swamped with meetings and rituals as we added solos, rogues, and a few other small covens to our numbers. We were up to twenty members in total, which was approaching the same size as both major covens' inner circles were before the war began.

We were still small compared to both the New Moon and Salem coven, but all our effort was worth it, as we'd become somewhere around the third-largest coven in the city. With the power of both the Lunar Amulet and me increasing the strength of every witch, we weren't afraid if we had to take on either of the big covens—just not both at the same time, yet.

I couldn't believe that we'd gone from three witches to twenty in such a short time. The best part was that we didn't have to strong-arm anyone into joining—mostly. Aside from Rose and Arachna, anyway, and even that was medium strength strong-arming at best.

Along with the power, witches were excited about lower tithe rates and less strict rules compared to the other major covens. Many were disappointed when they learned they wouldn't have access to me, however, I figured that most were holding out hope for when we started 'breeding'.

I still had complex feelings about all of that. There was no way I was going to be a breeding stud who helped birth daughters for every witch in the coven. How would I help raise that many kids? Our coven was likely to continue growing, too. The whole thing seemed ludicrous, and despite Alpha's feelings on the subject, I refused to be an absentee father, not after I'd grown up without parents. My kids' lives would be different.

Looking up from the grill, I couldn't help but notice how small our portion of the backyard was. We had a decent-sized apartment with three bedrooms and one additional room that we also used as a bedroom. It was so large that I usually just called it "the house". But when we added Arachna, I opted to give up my bed so she could have her own space. Now, whenever I wasn't pulled into one of the girls' rooms for the night, I slept on the couch. Admittedly, that meant I'd only slept on the couch one night so far, but that wasn't the point.

A privacy fence separated our backyard from the others. Four gorgeous witches lay on portable deck chairs in bikinis, soaking up the sun. Well, three were soaking up the sun—Cherry had a large patio umbrella shading herself and the fifth chair, which still sat empty. The sound of the back door closing caught my attention, and I turned to see Arachna with a purple towel covering her body. A faint red tinted her cheeks when she saw me looking her way. All eight eyes fluttered their lashes, and she quickly tiptoed over to the open chair. The sight brought a smile to my face.

You'd think that having eight eyes would look terrifying, but hers didn't. Her bangs hung so that it allowed the six smaller eyes on her forehead to peek through. With her pale skin, piercings, and goth style, she really made it work. As I flipped a burger, I tried not to let my interest show as she nervously bit her lip and looked around before finally dropping her towel and showing off her black two-piece bikini.

Four spider legs stretched out behind her before she banished them to lie comfortably supine. If I hadn't caught my jaw fast enough, I'd have been scraping it off the grill with my spatula. By the way her cheeks flushed and the small smile that played on her lips, I realized she'd gotten the reaction she'd hoped for, but hadn't quite expected.

I cleared my throat and instantly regretted speaking as my voice cracked from the lovely view in front of me. "Ladies, who wants what? We got burgers, brats, and hot dogs."

Cherry lifted her head and grinned. "You can put any meat you want in my mouth, baby." She followed it up with a wink, which I could only see from the way her eyebrow moved. She apparently forgot that she had large sunglasses on.

Chuckling, I started using the tongs to flip each cylindrical bit of greasy goodness one at a time. "I meant the type you can swallow."

Instantly, I regretted my choice of words when all the girls giggled and Cherry hit me with the obvious reply. "So was I." She followed it up with an additional wink, this time remembering to lift her sunglasses first.

Alpha kept her hands behind her head, not bothering to move. "You're making my burgers rare right? If it's not leaking its juices, then you did it wrong."

"That's what she said," Rose quipped, causing another round of giggles.

My palm and my face shared an intimate moment as I snorted. "Inappropriate!"

As we were enjoying our afternoon off to relax and recuperate, a hawk screeched as it dropped an envelope from the sky. Alpha shot to her feet, pulling the sunglasses from her face and catching it before it hit the ground. The mood was very much slain.

Wasting no time, she ripped it open and read the card inside. "Fuck!" she seethed. "It looks like we're out of time. I was hoping we'd have at least another week, but it is what it is." The girls all crowded around and read the letter before Halo handed it to me. Some looked worried—others seemed determined. I had a feeling I already knew what it was about. Flipping the card over, I read the note.

Alpha,

It has come to our attention that your coven has been meddling with things it should not. Things like the Lunar Amulet. As the esteemed leaders of the Salem and New Moon Covens, we simply cannot allow such impertinence to continue.

We demand that you and your motley crew appear in Sinner's Field at 10 PM sharp. We shall discuss the consequences of your actions and you will answer for the trouble you've caused within the framework set by the elder witches of Fresco City.

If you or any of your members attempt to evade this meeting, we assure you, the consequences will be dire.

-Illumina of the New Moon Coven
&
-Demonique of the Salem Coven

Alpha grabbed the letter from my hand before setting it on fire with the grill. After taking a moment to process the news, she appeared to be the embodiment of confidence—but I noticed the brief flash of fear in her eyes. "They think we're going to back down *now*? Pfft. Just wait until they get a load of us. We might only have twenty members, but we're no pushovers. Girls! Eat quickly and make your calls. It looks like we've got a date with some arrogant witches tonight."

• ♥ • ♥ • ♥ • ♥ • ♥ •

Arriving at the so-called Sinner's Field—known to me as Giamatti Field, an abandoned football stadium that never finished construction, we took our positions. I'd asked Alpha about the ominous name of the field and she told me that it was supposedly the location of a major battle centuries ago. One of the biggest covens at the time made their final stand there before eventually losing to a host of 'holy warriors'. Of course that brought on even more questions that we didn't have time for yet.

The moon hung high in the blackened sky, and the city lights glowed in the distance. A cool breeze ruffled my hair as I stood in the middle, next to Alpha. Halo, Cherry, Rose, and Arachna were on either side of us. The six of us formed a front line as the remaining members of our coven took positions behind us. We'd arrived a little early, but still expected to find our enemies already waiting.

We'd come prepared after a brief meeting where Alpha laid out our strategy. The goal wasn't to start a fight, but to prevent one without showing weakness or deferring to them. It was time that we showed them the balance of the city was changing, and they weren't the only top dogs anymore. In case a fight occurred, we strategically paired every witch with a partner whose magic could complement their own and maximize safety and damage output.

The moon was only in the first quarter tonight, so we wouldn't have the full power boost from the Lunar Amulet. No doubt it was one reason they didn't wait. If they'd waited for a full moon, we'd certainly cream them, but if they held out for a new moon? They'd look weak. Checking my watch, I noticed it was already ten past ten. "Wow, they're really gonna pull that BS power move, huh?" I asked.

"Buncha pompous bitches. They make you wait for no damn reason," Cherry said with a snarl.

Before anyone could comment further, two huge portals opened about a hundred feet away from us. One was red, the other was blue. Simultaneously stepping out first were who I assumed to be Illumina from the blue New Moon portal and Demonique from the red Salem Coven portal.

Illumina was pretty much what you'd expect given her name. She had long white hair, and she wore a white robe with gold trim that showed a tasteful amount of cleavage, and a soft white glow emanated from her entire body. Following just behind her was her massive fenrir Greater Familiar.

Demonique was the polar opposite in appearance. Her hair was black as the night and hung down to the small of her back, and her black robes had a crimson trim. She showed off a little more cleavage as if she wanted to one-up her counterpart and had two curved black horns on her head. At her side was an enormous flame drake Greater Familiar. It resembled a dragon, and even if it wasn't as majestic as one, it was still intimidating. The one thing I hadn't expected? The flame drake's second head.

Behind them, witches poured out of the portals and took crude formations. Each coven brough around thirty of their members by the looks of it—most likely their inner circles. It was obvious they were trying to scare us with this power play, but that wouldn't work.

My girls stayed focused, but that also didn't mean we were foolish enough to underestimate our opponents. Even as strong as we were, they vastly outnumbered us. If this came down to an all-out brawl, there was no way to know what the outcome would be. One way or another, the population of Fresco City's most powerful witches would be decimated.

Alpha held up a fist, signaling that all our members should remain where they were. She looked from side to side. "Everyone stays put except for Logan." She grinned at me. "I think it's time they see what a *real* Greater Familiar looks like."

"They'll see that size isn't everything," Cherry said with a wink. Despite her off-color remark, I could tell from her eyes and the way she smirked, her jaw tighter than usual, that she was taking this as seriously as everyone else. She could be fun and flirty all day, but to Cherry, failure was never an option.

Nodding, I gave the girls a confident smile and took my place at Alpha's side. We agreed beforehand that it was best if Alpha did all the talking. Well, I say we agreed, but it was more that she ordered me to let her handle this, and I just so happened to agree with her. Butterflies were tying my stomach in knots, and I held a token in each hand, keeping them in my pocket, just in case. Regardless, I refused to show any fear. I knew that, one way or another, when we left this meeting, they were going to respect our coven's power.

The two groups all remained about eighty feet away from our group. It was obvious there was no love between the two, but they were working toward a common goal tonight. Alpha and I halved the distance, patiently waiting for the other coven leaders to join us. Of course, they took their sweet time, casually strolling with their stiff gait as if they were regal monarchs on their way to greet lesser guests. I hated them already.

Both witches approached us with their Greater Familiars in tow. As they stopped, each familiar bowed to their mistress and laid down beside them, both eyeing me cautiously. *Smart bastards, aren't they?*

Demonique was the first to begin. The wind blew, and she delicately brushed one strand of hair from her face with a finger. "So you're Alpha?" Demonique looked the redhead up and down dismissively. "I guess I should have expected it to be an untrained mutt. What else would make such a mess?"

Illumina's chin sat high in the air as she let out the most arrogant chuckle I'd ever heard. "Yes, that's her. The brat who's broken *so* many rules."

Alpha stood her ground, arms crossed and feet shoulder-width apart in a power stance. Her confident smirk was on full display, but I could see her fists clenching from their words. "I broke *your* rules—the rules you keep for your followers and each other. But I'm not under your control and never have been. Now, please explain why I'm here again. I didn't agree to meet with you just so I could be insulted by inferiors."

That was not at all what I was expecting her to say, but that was Alpha for you. She didn't take shit on a good day and it seemed she wasn't going to start now. I did my best not to laugh at the constipated looks of shock that the other leaders fired back, and even though I succeeded, I didn't manage to stop the grin on my face from spreading a little.

Illumina's eyes flashed with rage, but she quickly schooled her expression. Demonique, on the other hand, sneered. "Did you just call me—"

Waving her question away like an unpleasant odor, Alpha interrupted, "Shut your fucking mouth unless you're about to start explaining yourselves. I don't care who does it. Take your pick. Just tell me what you want."

Before Demonique could shout in a furious rage, Illumina stepped in. "First, you did not *agree* to meet us. Your presence was required. Second, you have broken the rules of our covens by intentionally upsetting the balance in the city. Furthermore," she raised one finger in the air as if this last statement was the final nail in our proverbial coffin. "You broke the treaty and stole the Lunar Amulet!"

Upon the declaration, Demonique's anger seemed to subside, replaced by a cocky grin. "So? What do you have to say in your defense before we cast judgment upon you and render your punishment?"

Alpha scoffed, uncrossing her arms and placing her hands on her hips. "You're fucking kidding me, right?"

Illumina's chin rose even higher into the air as she puffed out her chest. "Does this look like a joke to you?"

Alpha held up four fingers, putting one down with each point she made. "Now that you mention it, you do look like a pair of bad jokes, yes. So, let's get a few things straight. I did agree to come here to help you save face with your own covens, knowing how embarrassing it'd be for you if we didn't show and you brought your posse here. You're welcome. It doesn't mean we respect you or fear you. As for your rules and laws, well, as I mentioned we aren't in your covens, nor do we have any of your former members in ours, so none of that applies to us. Your treaty regarding the Lunar Amulet had nothing to do with me or my coven. It was strictly between the two of you. So, again, I'll ask, what do you actually want?"

The two coven leaders looked at one another, neither able to come up with a good answer on the fly. It was obvious that we hadn't actually done anything they could indict us for. They had no leg to stand on with any of the accusations they threw at us, even if it made sense that they were pissed. Finally, Demonique crossed her arms and clenched her jaw. "Even so, do you really think we'd let you do whatever you want? Do you think we'd let a third major coven go unchecked and amass power at a rapid rate out of nowhere?"

Illumina clenched her fists so tightly that I expected to see blood dripping from them. She sneered at my redheaded leader. "Yes, as Demonique said, you will not leave here with the amulet, nor will you go unpunished for your arrogance. You allowed us to waste resources on a coven war, stole a powerful relic, and seized a superior Greater Familiar for yourself that, by all rights—"

"Hey thanks!" I said, waving.

She growled, but my interruption took some of the wind out of her sails, it seemed.

Even so, things were spiraling fast. I agreed to let Alpha handle this, but I couldn't let it devolve into a full-on war. At least not if I could prevent it. Leaning over, I tapped Alpha on the shoulder and whispered in her ear. "Use me. Challenge them to a bet and use me."

As I leaned back, her head shot toward me. Her frown lessened, and she pivoted back to the two coven leaders. "How about we make a bet? Greater Familiar versus Greater Familiar. My familiar Logan here will take on each of your Greater Familiars in a duel. One at a time. If he beats them both, then each of you agrees we get to keep the amulet and stay in the city as the third major coven—but from here on we agree to your treaties as a concession to stymie further power creep in our favor. If we lose, we'll give up the amulet, and leave the city for good within a month, taking our entire coven with us. How about it?"

The two coven leaders turned around and began whispering to one another. After a few moments, they appeared to have reached a consensus. Illumina smirked, and I'll be damned if it wasn't the cockiest smirk I'd ever seen in my life. "We'll accept on one condition."

Alpha quirked a brow. "Oh? And what's that?"

Demonique's shit-eating grin left a pit in my stomach as she said, "Your Greater Familiar fights both of ours at the same time, in a two on one."

Before I could even consider the implications of this challenge, Illumina added one more stipulation. "In a fight to the death."

A collective gasp came from our coven. Deaths happened in battles between witches. It was a fact of life, but in most battles, witches made it a point not to actually kill their opponents. So, an actual sanctioned fight to the death was rare. Still, I wasn't a witch, and neither were my opponents.

My eyes bulged and Alpha's smirk was long gone. My gaze met her yellow eyes that showed something I'd never seen in them before: genuine fear. I glanced at the witches across from us and then huddled up with Alpha.

To my shock, her eyes were wet, she was snarling, and her lip was quivering. It looked as if she was on the verge of breaking out into angry sobs. "I—I didn't expect them to go this far. You're incredibly strong, but a two-on-one? I—fuck—I think we messed up."

Thoughts turned in my head as I processed our predicament. Their goal wasn't just to drive our coven out of the city—it was to kill me and gut the coven of all its power in one fell swoop, claiming the power boost I granted as well as the Lunar Amulet.

On top of that, I'd never seen my strong red-headed leader this upset. I knew that if they prodded her at this moment, she'd lash out at them with everything she had in a tear-streaked rage. It was unreasonable to blame her. She was facing two impossible choices. War, where anything could happen and she had no guarantees her friends would walk away, or the possibility that I might die. The odds of a terrible outcome either way were high. "What do you think my chances are?" I asked.

Tears slid down her cheeks as she looked at the ground. "Fuck. one-on-one you'd win for sure, but two against one? The odds probably aren't good." She sniffled, wiping her nose with the back of her hand. "What do I do? I can't back down—we don't have any more cards to play here. We could walk away, I guess, but then it's all out war and—" She froze. I gave her a moment to process her thoughts and come up with what she wanted to say, but she said nothing.

"It's okay," I told her. "Just speak your mind."

"I—I can't lose you. I—ugh—I fucking love you, okay?" she growled the words as if it made her furious to admit it.

The revelation stunned me. To be completely honest, I didn't think that I meant that much to her. Sure, I knew if I died, it would crush her dreams of birthing the most powerful witches the world had ever seen, but the thought of actually losing me seemed to terrify her. Despite the possibility that I might die soon, a delightful warmth washed over my heart. The corners of my mouth slowly grew wider and wider into a Cheshire Cat smile. "I know."

"Oh, fuck you," she spat, but then grinned.

Suddenly, I realized I might kill two birds with one stone. There was a chance that I could keep Alpha's dreams alive while preventing war and removing the only obstacle holding me back from accepting my feelings for her. I wasn't nearly as sure as I looked, but I made my choice, and she needed to see confidence in me. My hands were steady, and if not for my rapidly pounding heart, I could have fooled myself into thinking I was calm, too. "You're not going to be able to make this call, so I'm taking the burden off your shoulders. I will fight them for you, and I guarantee I'll win. But I also want something in return, and it's not cheap."

She studied me for a moment before sighing. "Dammit. You want to cuff me to the bed or some shit, don't you?"

I shook my head and tried to wipe the tears from her eyes. She slapped my hands away, and I chuckled at myself for thinking I could get away with that. "No. Although, that sounds like a fantastic time."

She glared at me.

Ignoring it, I continued. "You remember when I told you girls that eventually, I wanted more than just sex?"

She nodded.

"Well, that time's come. When we try to have children, I want to be a real father to our kids, to every child I have with a member of the inner circle. Yours too. Not only that, I want a guarantee of more than one child with each of you and one of the first two has to be a boy." There it was. I laid my cards on the table, and now all I could do was wait.

Alpha scowled. "So I finally admit that I love you and you pose that fucking deal while my back's against the wall with no good way out?"

Shrugging, I nodded, unable to stop my grin. "I'm not making a deal. I'm saying how it's going to be. I'm winning this fight regardless of what you say here today, knowing that when the time comes, you won't disappoint me."

She shook her head, and for a moment, I felt my heart drop. "You're ruthless as any witch, you know that? Fucking ruthless. I still don't like it, but screw it—fine. Honestly, the last time you forced me to agree to a deal I didn't like, it didn't turn out so bad. So, who knows, maybe I'll change my mind about this one too."

Knowing that we resolved my biggest concern regarding the whole breeding thing, other than how soon they wanted it, my heart swelled. And, I won't lie. There was a piece of me that felt excited about being a father one day.

"Are you two quite finished yet? We haven't got all night, you know," came Demonique's shout.

"If you're going to refuse, then you might as well hand over the amulet now and accept your punishment," Illumina said, as if that was ever something we'd agree to.

Turning my attention to our coven, I blew a kiss at Halo and winked at Cherry. Then I gave Alpha my attention again. She grabbed my cheeks in her palms and pressed her lips to mine. We shared a long, passionate kiss as the glow of our deal surrounded us. Rather than settle onto our right hands, it formed matching tattoos on our shoulders. Somehow I innately understood that was because the deal we just forged was a long term agreement.

Finally, Alpha broke the kiss, and we faced the coven leaders together. Alpha's confidence was back for all to see as she stood with hands on hips. "Alright, cowards. You're on. We accept. We will not only accept your cheating terms, but we'll beat you anyway. Let's magically bind this dishonorable deal already. Logan here has a couple of chew toys to play with."

CHAPTER 26

Double Double Familiars and Trouble

The three coven leaders met in the middle of the field and began the contractual binding ritual. Meanwhile, I heard shouts coming from behind me. Cherry's voice came through loud and clear. "You got this, baby! Win and I'll ride you like a broom the entire way home!" My mind tumbled over the logistics of that. How literal was that offer? What would that...look like?

Halo's voice came next. "You show those squeegee licking butt munchers who's boss!" Rose shouted, "Freakin' murder their assholes!" Arachna's shout came right after. "Yeah, what they said!"

As more and more of my coven started shouting words of support and encouragement, the two opposing covens started shouting, too. Some were throwing jeers my way, others were cheering on their own Greater Familiar. I stood, waiting for the ritual to end and doing my best to wear a confident smile.

Finally, three bleeding palms met in the air and a light flashed between them before a beam shot into the sky. Eventually, it faded away, and the bet was official. I felt like I could hear the announcer in my head before a professional fight.

Ladies and gentlemen, boys and girls, children of all ages, are—you—ready?!

A strategy started forming in my mind as Alpha headed toward me. The sounds of the shouting witches fell into the background as I focused my thoughts. *Split them up. Restrain one and fight the other. Never let them work as a team.* Alpha placed a hand on my cheek, her eyes fixed on mine.

Then, for the thousands in attendance...

"You've got this. Whatever happens, I love you. And if you die on me, I'll bring your spirit back and kick your ass. You got that?"

I nodded and gave her a quick kiss. "I've got this."

She nodded back, then stepped past me on her way to join our coven. I studied my opponents, watching as each coven leader gave their familiar a small kiss on the head or snout. The flame drake's horns extended further on both heads and smoke billowed from all four nostrils.

Meanwhile, the fenrir's wolf and snake eyes both glowed white, and its muscles bulged. Just like I could, they were taking on a shape that seemed inspired by their masters, but retained a bit more of themselves than I usually did.

Demonique and Illumina both left their Greater Familiars behind to join their covens.

And the millions watching around the world...

My angel blessing was active on my ring and I activated a spider token. The enemy crowd gasped as confused shouts sounded all around while I shifted without the aid of my witches. My body morphed as I became a massive monster arachnid with razor-sharp claws as tarsi. As I finished my transformation, Illumina shot a flare into the sky from her palm. No one moved, and the crowd went silent.

Let's get ready to RUMBLE!

The flare exploded, the flash happening before the booming sound reached our ears, and then all hell broke loose. The crowd erupted into indiscernible shouts of excitement, and my opponents and I were on the move.

Crouching low, the flame drake's muscles contracted before it exploded into the sky with a flap of its wings. At the same time, the fenrir rushed me in a full sprint. I spat a quick burst of webbing at the wolf's front paw, sticking it to the ground. It stumbled, unable to take its next step, and face-planted with a yelp. Quickly, I shot out a larger web that extended, latching it onto the ground.

Unfortunately, I wasn't able to capitalize on it because the flame drake was swooping in, hoping to take a bite out of me—or two. As a chorus of boos came my way from the majority of the audience I skittered to the left and spit a glob of webbing on the drake's foot. Allowing the strand to gain some distance, I gripped it between my claws and let the familiar pull me into the air behind it.

As we gained height and the witches looked like nothing more than dots, the drake caught on to me and turned one of its heads. Its cheeks puffed out with an orange glow and I released the strand of webbing, barely dodging the roaring flames that came my way.

Letting myself glide, thanks to my angelic blessing, I summoned a Vampiric Token into my mouth and activated it. The more I practiced taking on a form, the faster my body could morph into it, so as I became the bat king, it happened almost instantly. The flame drake turned in the air, both cheeks glowing orange again, but I built up magic in my lungs and released it with a mighty breath. A monstrous screech exploded from my maw and magical sound waves crashed into both of the drake's heads. It lifted its maws to the sky, roaring in rage as its fire burst into the air far above me. Temporarily disoriented, its wings faltered, and it began falling to the ground below.

Again, before I could capitalize on my advantage, a beam of light shot through my wing, nearly hitting my arm. The resulting hole was bad enough to affect my ability to fly, so I turned and aimed a dive at the ground, heading straight at the fenrir who'd just freed itself from the web. *Okay, so that's what the glowing eyes do. Got it. Gonna have to keep an eye out for those.* At least it seemed the beast couldn't rapid-fire the beams of light, so that was good news.

Or so I thought.

Swerving and dodging, I twisted and turned, avoiding beam after beam until even more came. Several beams hit me, and while they stung when they did, they couldn't do actual damage. *Alright, so if he charges it up it'll be bad, but the faster he shoots it, the less damage he can do. I can work with this.*

I swapped to my bestial blessing in the air, and my muscles bulged as I used another token and took the form of the okatku. However, just as I was about to crush the fenrir beneath my paws, I noticed the snake tail coiled, its fangs dripping with toxic venom. *SHIT!*

At the last second, I altered the plan. I let out a mighty magical roar as I reached the fenrir, stunning the snake. I had the beast right where I wanted him. However, the moment my claws dug into the wolf fur, I fell victim to the same fate as the flame drake's claws dug into my back, lifting me off the creature before I could do much damage. Roaring in pain, the claws dug deep into my hide before they released me, sending me crashing and tumbling to the ground below. Cheers erupted from somewhere, and I knew they weren't from my admirers. The sounds coming from my side were... very different.

I was back on my feet in an instant, quickly trying to assess the situation. Still, I didn't have any time as I sidestepped another massive beam of light. I'd barely dodged the beam that was mere inches from my flesh, and the stench from my burned fur filled the surrounding air. Blood dripped down my sides from the wounds in my back, and I knew my strategy wasn't going to work. I was going to have to take a beating from one while I ended the other as quickly as possible—or so I thought.

I feigned darting forward at the fenrir again, and the drake took the bait, diving to intercept. Quickly, I halted my momentum while morphing into the celestial guardian. My massive sword appeared mid-swing and sliced through one of the drake's necks as if I were a heroic knight from fairy tales. A fresh burst of cheers erupted from somewhere else, but I ignored it—I had to stay focused.

Following through, I spun, unable to get even a second to catch my breath before catching a glob of acidic venom with my shield. The flame drake smashed into the ground, rolling away from us as fire spewed from one of its necks where its head had once been until the wound naturally cauterized itself. I knew that this was the big moment, and I had to throw my all at the fenrir while the drake was recovering.

Dashing forward, I thrust my blade, aiming for the wolf's neck. It dodged to the right, and the snake began rapidly striking blow after blow, giving me no other choice but to block with my shield. After a few moments it finally ceased its assault to recover some stamina.

Time was short, and I knew the drake was returning to its feet. I pulled my shield to the side, about to strike a devastating blow to the beast, when I saw the bright glow in its eyes flash. I barely got my shield up in time to catch the massive beam on its surface. But, for the first time, the angelic shield wasn't enough. It held back most of the blow, but a sizable beam still broke through, colliding with the left side of my stomach.

I screamed from the burning in my gut as it penetrated my armor, sending me flying back and tumbling end over end. A massive cheer erupted from somewhere. The pain was excruciating, and I heard someone familiar scream from the sidelines.

Instincts told me I needed to move, so I rolled to the side, just in time for a second massive blast to make a crater in the ground where I'd just been. Blood was pouring down my back and from my stomach. "Healing Light!" I shouted, casting a healing spell on myself. It sealed the wounds in my back, but it did little for the wound in my gut. Magic from the wolf's attack clung to my wound, resisting the healing magic.

If I survive this, I'm definitely asking Halo about the limitations of healing magic. I thought as the short timer on the quick token I used wore off. I felt my body shifting back to my human form, and on instinct, I clothed myself from my storage. The flame drake and the fenrir were slowly walking toward me from a distance, stalking their prey for one last strike.

Desperate shouts came from one side, and loud cheers and malicious laughter came from the other. *Is this it? Did I overestimate myself? After finally finding the life I never knew I wanted, this is the end, huh? I don't know how I'm supposed to beat them.* Doubt filled my thoughts as I questioned everything. Another scream erupted and this time I knew it wasn't me. I turned toward the shout to see that Halo had both hands cupped around her mouth to amplify her voice. "Quit lollygagging and fight!"

Alpha screamed, trying to use the bond to compel me to get up, her eyes glistening. "Get up and fight, NOW!" My heart hurt to hear the worry and pain in their cries. But then, another voice shouted louder than the others. Cherry cried out, "LOGAN! YOU'RE NOT A QUITTER!"

Cherry reminded me of who I am. *She's right. I'm not done yet. I didn't quit growing up on the streets alone. I didn't quit when I couldn't even afford to eat while working every day while going to classes. I didn't quit when I woke up handcuffed to a bed in a stranger's home. And I sure as FUCK am not going to quit now.*

I stood and gritted my bloody teeth as some seeped down my chin. The hole in my gut must have gone all the way through, since blood was still pouring down a part of my back. To this day, I still don't know why I did it, but I shouted at the two Greater Familiars, "You think I'm finished?! Then come get some, you—fucking douchebags!" Okay, I admit, it wasn't the most creative or badass thing I could have shouted, but it did the job of taunting them, and quieting down the opposing side's witches.

I activated the plant monster form, courtesy of Rose, and tried to restrain the drake with my vines. His body flared with heat, withering the vines away almost instantly. I figured that would happen, and that's why I hadn't used this form yet. Still, I was fifteen feet tall with fists the size of tree trunks in this form, and with my bestial blessing still active, I was like a force of nature come to life.

Despite being destroyed, the vines were able to stall the flame drake long enough for me to grab it by its remaining neck. I squeezed a veggie hand around its throat to stop any thought it might have had to blast me with flames. From the corner of my eyes, I saw the bright glow of the fenrir's eyes reaching a climax, and I pulled the flame drake forward as a vine caught the wolf by the neck, ripping its gaze away from me just in time for the light in its eyes to flash, sending the beam blasting through the drake's side. The wound punched a basketball sized hole through the creature's vitals, and it roared in pain as it stumbled to the ground with labored breathing.

Sidestepping the drake, I noticed the fenrir was already mid-pounce and the snake tail coiled tightly, ready to lash out at me. I called vines forth, wrapping them around the snake as

I punched down on the top of the wolf's head before pivoting to its left side. It yelped and crashed to the ground, the vines lifting its rear upward and passing off the snake's neck to my waiting hand. Putting the other hand against the wolf's body, I pulled with all my strength. The wolf howled in agony as I tore the snake from its hindquarters, throwing it off to the side and eliciting more gasps and shocked sounds from the enemy covens'.

Just when I thought the fight was over, a blast of flame connected to my side and I screamed as I felt my flesh boiling. This form was especially weak to fire, and the pain was unimaginable. Before it could do more damage, I picked up the fenrir and spun, putting its body in the path of the flames. The stench of burned hair mingled with the burned flesh, making a torrent of disgust rip through me like I wanted to vomit.

The howl of pain died down as the flames stopped. I swapped back to my celestial form, wishing I could cast a heal, but I could tell I didn't have the magical reserves to do much about the fresh wounds. Dropping the whimpering wolf, I summoned my sword and swiftly beheaded the stunned beast. As if the fenrir shared a voice with the crowd, they too fell silent along with him—well, one side did anyway. My coven, on the other hand, erupted into frenzied cheers.

Staggering past its lifeless corpse, I kept my golden eye fixed on the unsteady flame drake. For the first time, my sword felt heavy, and I could barely hold my shield. The drake was barely standing, and its raspy breaths said it wasn't far from death. This monster would die in minutes if left alone. I don't know how I knew it, maybe it was a Greater Familiar thing, maybe it was just instincts, but I could tell that the drake's pride demanded it go down fighting. I nodded at the creature. "I'm sorry you have to die. You deserved a better master," I said.

There was a glint of recognition in its eye. It was intelligent enough to understand. It lowered its head, giving me a slight nod of acknowledgment before releasing one last roar of defiance. I dropped my shield, letting it dissipate and grabbed my sword's hilt in both hands. Before it finished its final shout, I sliced the neck clean through, the head falling to the ground below. No fire shot out from the wound this time, only blood that pooled beneath the lifeless corpse.

I turned, examining the crowd surrounding me. They were caught in stunned silence. I lifted my sword into the air and my coven erupted into cheers, while the other side started shouting in angered cries of disbelief and confusion.

My inner circle came running toward me while the New Moon and Salem coven leaders began their journey as well. I let the magic go, my arm falling to my side and sword disappearing as I shifted back to my human form. I only had the energy and focus to summon my pants, but that was enough.

Before the girls reached me, I dropped to my knees, unable to stand anymore. From there, the weakness from blood loss became too much, and I collapsed to the ground on my back.

"Logan! Hold on! I'm here! I'm here, baby, just hold on!" Halo shouted with tears in her eyes as she skidded to a stop on her knees next to me, her golden healing magic glowing from her hands as she pressed one to my scorched flesh and the other on the hole in my gut. "You're gonna be okay, you hear me? You're gonna be okay, sweety. I'm here. I've got you now."

The corner of my mouth barely curled into a meager smile as I felt her tears dripping against my skin like a leaky faucet. I offered a barely perceptible nod of acknowledgment. Cherry was there next, cradling my face in her hands and lifting my head into her lap as she knelt behind me. "Hey, you're upside down," I struggled to say.

She was crying too, her tears falling onto my face. "You did it, baby!" she sniffled, and didn't seem to know what she wanted to say. "Yeah, I'm upside down, baby. Sorry about that."

Turning my head, I coughed, a splatter of blood flying from my mouth as Halo continued healing my wounds. I looked back up at Cherry with a bloody smile. "Aww, don't be sorry. It gives me ideas for later." Then I shot her the best wink I could. It wasn't much more than a slow, weak blink of one eye, but she got the picture.

She chuckled through her happy sobs, but didn't have time to reply as the enemy coven leaders interrupted us. That's when I realized why Alpha hadn't tried to greet me yet. She was standing tall, with no tears in her eyes, but there was evidence that there had been some recently. I understood quickly that she had been staying vigilant as our enemies approached. Looking up at Illumina and Demonique, I noticed they both eyed me with furious gazes.

"So. You won. Somehow. Your pet doesn't look like much, but I'll admit that was quite the impressive display," Illumina said. However, her tone still appeared if she was doing me a favor by complimenting me at all.

Demonique's hand took on a deep red glow as she looked down at me, but spoke to Alpha. "Perhaps, with this little toy of yours broken, we should just take what we came here for, anyway. It's not like you could stop us."

Illumina's eyes and wicked smile grew wider. "Oooh, I like the sound of that. Perhaps one of us takes the pet, and the other takes the amulet?"

Alpha smirked and flipped her hair out of her face. "Is that your plan? And just how long do you think you'll last when your entire coven spends the next generation cursed for violating a magically bound contract by attacking a coven in a post-battle grace period? Just how useful will your spoils be when you're weaker with them than you were without them?"

Both coven leaders looked at one another with a grimace. "Fine," Illumina said with disdain. "If we're done here." She lifted her chin and turned to Demonique. "The truce ends tomorrow at midnight. But, perhaps we should discuss an extension," she glanced at Alpha with disdain before turning her attention back to Demonique. "And the possibility for further cooperation." Without waiting for a response, she shot a burst of light at the fenrir corpse, obliterating the remains to dust and walked away.

"Such a petty child," Demonique sneered. "But yes, it seems we have concluded our business here—for now. Enjoy this victory, because it will not happen again." She walked away as well, snapping her fingers and incinerating the corpse of the flame drake.

My wounds slowly closed, but weakness still engulfed my body. Alpha remained still until the last of the enemy witches left. The rest of our coven surrounded us, cheering and clapping. Alpha crouched down, running her fingers through my sweaty hair. "You're such a good boy," she said with a smile.

I rolled my eyes, but grinned. "I'd suggest we party tonight, but I'm pretty tired."

"Golly, baby, don't you worry! Once I get you all patched up I have just the spell to help you feel refreshed. You'll be good as new in a few more minutes. But, wow, you cut it close this time. Don't scare me like that again," Halo said. The warm waves of her healing magic coursed through my body, replenishing lost blood and removing all traces of the injuries that almost killed me.

"You looked badass out there. The way you swapped between your forms and beat the shit out of those two—that was amazing! I didn't know you could fight like that!" Arachna said, her spider legs chittering excitedly.

Vines suddenly lifted several witches and cleared a space near me. "Get out of the freakin' way! Where is he, Logan? Lo—There you are! Holy shit! You were like whoosh! And boom! And 'ay, you fuckin' douchebag!' That was hilarious!" Rose exclaimed, using wild hand motions and sound effects in her abridged retelling of recent events. She didn't even wait for me to respond as she saw Novella and bombarded her with more of her theatrics. For poor Novella's part, she smiled and nodded along, as if she hadn't watched it all happen with the rest of the coven.

Then two light pats on my cheek brought me back to the crimson eyes of my Vampire Witch. My mind recalled when I first noticed those fangs and frighteningly red eyes. It somehow felt like months ago, not weeks. I grinned, glancing from her eyes to her lips. "Hi, you must be Cherry Cola."

She giggled, catching onto my wavelength quickly. "I am. And you must be my professor tonight."

Reaching up, I pulled her in closer. "I guess I am." Our lips met, and I kissed her.

"Hey Logan," Cherry said after the kiss, looking guilty for some reason.

"What?" I asked.

"Before the fight, when the other Greater Familiars came out, I shouted 'size isn't everything.' I'm sorry if I made it sound like your dick wasn't big. It's fucking enormous. Like, it's pretty crazy."

I smiled at her but I had... no idea what she was talking about.

EPILOGUE

Team Building Exercises

Alpha was busy answering questions on the other end of the new rooftop patio after our inaugural coven meeting. We were up to thirty members now. While we were still outnumbered by both the New Moon and the Salem covens nearly two to one, they still needed to find new Greater Familiars soon or they'd lose their respected status. Rumors were already spreading that some of their members were preparing to abandon their sinking ships.

Our growth was the reason we needed to find a new place to live. When discussing options, the girls decided we should find a place with room to expand our inner circle and rooftop access for easier broom travel. That's why we became the new owners of a two-story penthouse apartment in downtown Fresco City.

Digging into our own finances for such a massive expenditure would have left us broke. So, to pay for it, we sent a couple of new members to rob a bank across the border. Imagine my surprise when they returned with millions in hand.

I learned afterward that Novella directed them to target a casino instead of a bank. As it turned out, casinos kept far more money on hand than an average bank did. It seemed to me that she was trying to make her value known fast.

It took a few spells, charms, and a really good accountant named Barry Johnson to wash and deposit it all safely, avoiding all suspicion, but it got done in the end. It helped that we split a large portion of it among our members to finance their living expenses, making it even harder to track. If we'd been good on money before, our coven had nearly secured a lifetime of financial stability now—as long as we weren't wasteful, anyway.

When Alpha was busy, others started coming to me with updates and questions before leaving. Apparently, Alpha and I working together to deal with the coven leaders set a precedent, as if I, a man and familiar, were the unofficial second-in-command. Of course, it was also an excuse for some to get close to me. The whole situation reminded me of the Coven King legend that Rose had mentioned, and I wondered if there might be some truth to it.

"Thank you so much for having me today, Mr. Morrison. I took extensive notes of all the various talking points, including Cherry's demand," Novella said with a smirk as she checked her tablet. "Namely that she is your exclusive oral alarm clock, and she, 'better not find any of you dirty witches poaching on my breakfast.' That was a direct quotation."

"Sounds like her," I laughed, smiling back at her.

Novella stood before me in a women's sports coat, a button-down top with only the top two buttons undone, a business skirt that hugged her hips and thighs, stopping at her shin, and a pair of high heels. Her blonde hair was tied in a tight, high ponytail, and I looked into her green eyes as she pushed up her black-rimmed glasses with one finger at the bridge of her nose.

"I've also compiled a detailed itinerary for each cell of the coven, a road map if you will, to give all members a path to achieve the goals Alpha has set for us. In addition, I've created a sufficient system to determine the proper tithe percentages and collection methods, as well as the distribution of benefits. And I have uploaded all the documents to Alpha's iCloud, along with Cherry's video folder, since it has been declared a 'common good'. I'll have the financial information Alpha requested completed by the morning."

Staring at Novella, my jaw flapped like a dead fish. She quirked an amused brow before closing it with a finger beneath my chin. Leaving it there, she leaned in close. The scent of her intoxicating perfume tickled my senses. "I see the way you look at me, Mr. Morrison. I think I've made it clear to the others what I want. Perhaps you could put in a good word for me as well? I could give you so much more than administrative aid," she said with a throaty purr. Then she closed the distance and pressed her lips to mine, leaving a lingering kiss on my lips before backing away. "I look forward to our next meeting, *Mr. Morrison.*" And before I could say a word, she turned and walked away to the broom pad.

I let out a long, steady breath as Arachna approached me, a fruity drink in hand. "So, what was that about?" she asked before taking a sip from her straw.

"What? Oh!" I chuckled nervously, ruffling my hair. "That? She just wanted to give me an update on itineraries and documents and stuff."

"And—uh, the kiss?" she asked, her cheeks turning a lighter shade of red and her eight eyes focusing on her glass.

"You saw that, did ya?" I sighed. "Yeah, she's hoping I'll put in a good word for her."

"Seems like that's not the only thing she wants you to put in for her," she quipped with a giggle.

I rolled my eyes and reached over to the table, picking up a straw. I stuck it in her glass, leaned forward, and sipped while she was still sipping.

Her eyes widened as she pulled her lips away and gulped. "Hey!"

I let out a refreshed sigh. "Ahhh. What is that? It's delicious."

Arachna's cheeks turned red, and she fluttered her many lashes. "It's moon berry blast. You know, that was kind of... romantic." As if she just realized what she said, her eyes went wide, and she stammered, trying to backtrack.

"Or, well—I mean it could be—but—no, I didn't mean—shit, I'm so bad at this."

Chuckling, I put a hand on her shoulder. "Nah, you're good. That did have some potential for romance."

Arachna's four spider legs on her back began chittering, which I realized was a sign that she was nervous or anxious about something. "Umm, speaking of romantic. I was kinda wondering if maybe you might want to—or maybe not. You totally don't have to decide now, but I just thought that you might want to go on a—"

"Oh my freakin' Gawd, Arachna! Are you about to ask Logan out on a date?!" Rose shouted so loudly that everyone left on the rooftop could hear it. The rest of the girls rushed over to join us, leaving Alpha alone to finish up with the last two witches.

Arachna's poor legs were going even crazier now, and a flush was creeping up her neck. "What? I—uh. Sure, of course I was. Why wouldn't I think I have a chance when he's already got four super hot chicks hanging all over him?" she asked in a sarcastic tone.

I frowned. "For your information, I would be down. I bet you'd have something really awesome planned, too."

Her jaw dropped, and the glass slipped out of her hand. Reacting quickly with my enhanced senses, I caught it and handed it back to her. "Shit! Oh, thanks." She shook her head in disbelief. "You'd really want to go out with me sometime? Like, for real, for real?"

Shrugging, I said, "Why not?"

Halo joined the conversation, her head tilted as she twirled a pigtail around one finger and batted her lashes at me. "Golly gee, we haven't been on a date in a long time. Maybe we can do something a bit more interactive next time? Like maybe take a pottery class? It's cute and lets us express our creativity. Plus, it'll give you something tangible to remember the night by. Doesn't that sound like a swell time?"

Rose crossed her arms. "Pottery? Seriously? Who fucks with pottery anymore?"

Tilting my head, I examined the Flower Witch. "Huh, for some reason, I thought that was something you'd be into."

"Hell to the no!" she said, pointing her index finger up and sliding it from one side of her body to the other. "Screw that shit. I'd take you to a freakin' drag race! We could sit in the front row, where you could smother me in smooches as the engines rev and the vibrations run up my—"

"Boring!" Cherry interjected. "I have the perfect date planned. First, we take a fancy helicopter so we can sip champagne and I can ride you while we look down over the city. Then, we hit up that new taco food truck down the block, where we'll steal glances at each other and sneak off and...from there, you can eat *my* taco," she said, winking at me, and I realized that since we met, her wink timing had drastically improved. "Then, we'll come back home and I'll lead you to your bed that I covered in rose petals—"

Rose snapped her fingers and put a hand on her hip as she jutted it out. "Ex—freakin'—cuse me, witch! You're not using my petals unless I'm there."

"I was talking about regular rose petals, not your petals," Cherry muttered.

"I can see how she got confused," Halo sighed.

Arachna looked down at her shuffling feet. "I was thinking about packing some snacks and maybe doing some star-gazing."

Rolling her eyes, Rose said, "Puh-leez, honey. Like he wants to spend the night with you in a cemetery."

The Arachnid Witch stomped five of her six legs all at once. "Hey! How did you know I was gonna take him there?"

"I think that sounds great, Arachna," I managed to say as Alpha stood up. "I always wanted to fool around in a cemetery."

"F-fool around?!" she gushed, blushing profusely.

Alpha finally joined the conversation. "It doesn't matter where any of you would take him. I've got this," Alpha said, crossing her arms and leaning on me with her shoulder and a confident smile. "You see, Logan needs something more exciting. So I'm thinking of a break from the city. We'll teleport over to a mountain range I've hiked a few times. Targeting sunset for our arrival time, we'll climb to the summit. From there, we'll pop up a tent and a few spells and he can spend the entire night being my good boy with no one around for miles to interfere. In the morning, we'll use the zip-line trail to come back down where I'll ride him for hours. Maybe if you girls behave, I'll send you some pictures."

"Pfft, like your pictures could be better than mine. Look!" Cherry said, pulling out her phone. From there, the conversation devolved into unintelligible shouting as each girl tried to either steal Cherry's phone or talk over the others.

Putting both hands in the air, palms down, and waving them up and down slightly, I shouted, "Whoa! Not all at once! Sheesh. Honestly, I think we might need some team-building exercises like a birthday lineup, escape rooms with no magic, or maybe the mystery taste test game. Something, so we stop arguing so much." Their replies started coming back to back.

"I tried Trust Falls with Cherry and Halo but they just let me hit the ground," Arachna whimpered.

Rose tilted her head. "Is a birthday lineup like something where we line up in our birthday suits?"

I paused. "...Yes, it is. From this day forth."

Halo snickered. "Jeepers Logan, you already did an escape room the day we met you, remember?"

Cherry tongued a fang and winked. "I think I could do better if I tried again. Ain't no way he'd escape this time."

There were many things I wanted to say in response, but I didn't get the chance. Alpha smirked at me, noticing my overwhelmed expression. "I think some team building is exactly what we need, come to think of it. Everyone, head down to the living room, now. That's an order," she barked.

· ♥ · ♥ · ♥ · ♥ · ♥ ·

After only a little bickering, all of us made our way to the spacious living room waiting for Alpha to return from her bedroom. It didn't take long before she came down the steps from the mezzanine holding a box—and completely naked. Unable to help myself, I gawked at her fit, flawless body. "Alright everyone, clothes off, now," she shouted.

I was far too distracted by the sight to notice what she said. Movement caught my eye as the two others on the couch with me, Cherry and Halo, both stripped off their clothes without a second thought. I grinned, seeing the piercings on the crimson-eyed beauty's puffy little pink nipples once again. Looking down, I saw her socks were still on.

"What? My little piggies are cold," she whined, pouting with puffed-up cheeks.

"Nothing, it's fine. Keep them nice and toasty," I said.

"Golly, you and your love for feet," Halo teased me with a giggle.

I rolled my eyes, but couldn't fight off the grin. "Great, now you'll make the new girls think I have a foot fetish."

Turning my head, I noticed the green vine-haired Flower Witch was also already naked, showing off her slightly darker green nipples and shaved mound. She was short, petite, and curvy, a fantastic combination if I ever saw one. Our eyes met, and she bit her lip, catching me staring. "Aww yeah, you can suck my freakin' toesies any time, baby. They taste minty fresh!"

I blinked. "I really don't have a foot fetish."

"It's okay. I don't judge," Arachna said, pulling my gaze toward her with her words. I was going to respond, but as she stood there in nothing but her black bra and panties, I was left speechless. Her spider legs fidgeted nervously and her eight eyes locked on mine.

The Spider Witch's pale skin flushed red from her chest to her ears, but she slowly reached back and unclasped her bra, letting it fall to the floor. Arachna's tits were small, but they were the most perfect smaller tits I'd ever seen. Arachna, like Cherry, had nipple piercings, but Arachna's were rings instead of studs.

My mouth watered as she thumbed her panties, slowly dropping them to the floor. She looked away from me as she meekly stood there, nervously rubbing one arm. I took special note that even her labia had a small ring piercing that pressed a button I didn't know I had.

Gulping, I said, "Damn, Arachna. You look incredible."

She glanced at me shyly. "You think so?"

"Hell yeah, girl!" Rose shouted, crossing her arms with a pout. "I'm jealous."

I chuckled. "Don't be. You've got nothing to be jealous about. You're all so hot in different ways."

Alpha coughed, catching my attention. I looked at her. "Huh?" She pointedly looked down at my body, then back to my face. I followed her gaze, realizing I was the only one still dressed. "Oh! Shit, sorry. I was distracted."

My honesty earned several giggles. I was, admittedly, very eager for whatever Alpha had planned. Rather than slowly undress, I just put all my clothing in my dimensional storage, going from dressed to completely naked in an instant.

Arachna's eyes widened to saucers, and all eight of them focused on my erect member.

"Fuck, way to rip the bandaid off," Cherry joked, playfully slapping me on the arm.

Arachna gulped and nodded at the Vampire Witch's statement, and her spider legs started frantically fidgeting again, but this time, it looked more like anticipation or excitement. It was odd—after I dominated her spider form like I did the others, it seemed like I could read her emotions better thanks to her legs. If not for that, I'd have thought she was panicking by the look on her face.

Eventually, Arachna shook her head, as if coming out of a daze, and she glanced up, seeing me looking at her. Her legs and body tensed and she slowly sat back down in her seat as her spider legs curled around her while she wiped a bit of drool from her lips.

Alpha opened the small box and sat it on the coffee table. "Today we're going to play Adult Truth or Dare: Group Edition. There's going to be some dares that help us ladies get to know each other more intimately. Just keep in mind that this is an extra special reward for our good boy, as he really loves seeing us all playing well together."

Like a ferret hidden in a tightly sealed sack of biscuits, my penis flailed at the promise behind these words.

Halo quickly nodded with a serious expression, and I watched as her pigtails flailed in fervent agreement. "It's true. We found that when we fool around in front of him, it gets him really riled up."

Cherry nodded with uncharacteristic solemnity. "They're right. And if we show enthusiasm when we do it, he pounds us so much harder and can keep going until he's left us all a gooey mess."

Alpha nodded sagely, then she continued. "Each card is a truth or a dare, not both. And I'm going first." She drew a card and read it aloud. "Truth. Tell the person to your right a sexual fantasy you've had about them." Alpha turned her head to the right, where Rose sat and smirked. "I've fantasized about showing Logan how fast my pussy could shut that lippy mouth of yours if I only sat on it."

The plant girl's eyes went wide. "Holy shit! Really? That's so freakin' hot. My turn!" Rose drew a card and cackled maniacally. "Dare. Kiss the person across from you. But it has to be between their legs." She looked up, and straight across from her seat was Halo. Throwing the card in the air, she rushed over and dropped to her knees.

"Cheese n' rice! Can't we talk about this for a sec—ooh my gosh!" Halo's protests ended swiftly as Rose wasted no time shoving her knees apart and diving in.

She gave wet, sloppy kisses, planting her lips on the blonde's sex and massaging her clit. "Mua! Mua! Muaa! Don't I give the best smooches? Mua!"

As I was watching the show, a soft hand wrapped around my hard cock, slowly stroking me, and I shuddered. Well, I shuddered until Alpha smacked Cherry's hand and moved it away. "No cheating," Alpha scolded us. Cherry and I both pouted at that.

Halo Kitty's hands gripped the vines of the Flower Witch, pulling her in tighter. "Holy Gosh! Oh wow! That's not half bad, but Logan's kisses are still my favorite! Ah—oh no no no! Gosh dangit!" she shouted as Rose pulled herself away.

Rose blew a kiss up to Halo. "Maybe you'll get lucky and I'll draw another card for you." Then she scampered back to her seat and away from the now flustered and frustrated angelic woman.

Arachna was breathing heavily after watching the two witches next to her. "M-my turn?" she asked, but didn't wait for an answer as she drew a card. She gulped and her eyes widened as she read it. "Dare. Is there a popsicle to suck nearby? If not, use the closest dick instead." Her gaze shot to me and her breathing quickened. She didn't move, but I saw her legs chittered with more excitement than I'd ever seen before.

"What are you waiting for? Get over here and suck my man's cock," Alpha said plainly.

The goth girl looked from me to Alpha, and then to my firm member. She walked over slowly, almost like she was in a trance. "This is really happening..." she whispered.

The sight of her nude beauty coming closer to me made my cock throb in anticipation. My breath hitched as she dropped to her knees between my legs. Her spider legs extended toward me slowly before the tips rested against my torso and thighs, gently dragging across my flesh. Her head tilted to the side as she sat with shoulders slumped, a stupid smile on her lips as drool slid down the corner of her mouth.

Moving in closer, her eyes closed as she sniffed my shaft. Her tongue lolled out before taking a tentative lick. As soon as she tasted me, her eyes opened wide again and she dove in, her lips and throat rapidly engulfing my girth in one smooth motion. "Mmmm!!" she squealed.

My jaw dropped, and I flexed every muscle in my body as the intoxicating pleasure overwhelmed my senses. The next instant, her hands shot up, gripping the base of my rod and massaging my balls. Her spider legs started practically vibrating against my skin, tapping all over and instantly relaxing my tense muscles, and I leaned back into the couch. Arachna's raven hair flailed while she mercilessly bobbed on my dick, her crossed eyes staring up at me. "Hmmm! Hmmm! Hmmmm! Mmmmm!" she moaned constantly as she worked, and I didn't know how long I could last.

Cherry scooted closer to me, gently running her fingernails through my hair and kissing my neck and ear. "Fuck, respect," she said as she glanced down at the Arachnid Witch going psycho on my entire length. "You like the way she swallows you, baby? Look at her, eight eyes all staring, waiting to see your reaction when you unload that hot stuff into her throat."

"Goodness, I guess I'd better take my turn. It seems like she's not gonna stop anytime soon," Halo said, drawing a card. "Oh my! Dare. Let the second person to your right touch you between the legs. Well...okay!" Halo jumped up, kneeling against Cherry, and pulled my hand from around the Vampire Witch's waist with a lascivious smile. I let her guide me to her folds where I took over, parting them and delving two fingers inside her. "Mmm. Your fingers are magical, baby! Please don't stop."

Alpha passed Cherry a card since she was in no position to get up. "Shit, did someone stack the deck? Dare. Kiss, lick, and stroke the person to your right in any way you want." She shrugged, tossed the card, and started grinding her pussy against my leg as she resumed her kisses and licks.

I opened my mouth to speak, but only a groan of pleasure came out as Arachna's cheeks hollowed and she pulled off my cock, stroking it like her life depended on it. Saliva covered her chin and tits, several strands lingering between my tip and her body. "Am I doing a good job?" she asked, coming out of her trance-like state.

I nodded, trying to explain that yes, she was doing a wonderful job and I would very much appreciate it if she kept going. But before I could, she was back at it, her lips kissing my pelvis with my member down her throat. So I gave up on trying to speak for now and gave her a thumbs up with my free hand before waving for a card. Alpha passed me one. I quirked a brow, suddenly agreeing with Cherry's claims. "Dare. Allow the person to your right to ride your face," I managed after several tries.

Alpha smirked and made her way over. She stood above me, one leg on the cushion below, her knee on the back of the couch. "There we go. Now be a good boy and show me how much you love the taste of your fearless leader's pussy." Lowering herself down, she grabbed my hair in one hand, and the other fondled her breast while she ground her slit against my mouth. I gobbled her pearl between my lips, sucking on the firm nub before peppering it with kisses and licks.

A voice shouted from somewhere in front of me. "Screw the freakin' cards! I'm getting in on this action! Come to mama!" Rose said, and seconds later I felt my only free hand nestled between her thighs. She manually adjusted my hands, directing me exactly as she wanted. "Yeah, right there, wait, a little higher, a little deeper, come this way—OH YES right there, Daddy! Mmm!"

The warmth of Arachna's delightful mouth left my cock, exposing it to the cool air. I felt bad for the poor little guy until I felt two more knees against my thighs and an even hotter, tighter, silkier sensation replaced the warm mouth. "I–I'm gonna fuck you now. Is that okay? Arachna asked nervously.

I did my best to convey the following: *But of course, Arachna, I'd actually really appreciate that. Please, by all means sit on my dick. You have no idea just how much that would hit the spot about now.* However, with Alpha's pussy grinding my face it came out as a series of happy muffles.

"I can't really understand what you're saying, but it sounded like you're fine with it, so I'm just gonna–" Arachna's words cut out as she gradually worked her way down my length, inch by inch until I was all the way inside her. "F—fuck! You're so goddamn deep!" she shouted before she started riding me–nice and slow with long strokes.

The sensation briefly overwhelmed my senses, and I forgot what I was doing. A chorus of whines got me back on track, though. Halo actually slapped my hand. "Fffuck! Don't lollygag! I need more!" she said before I quickly got back to work. "Mmm yes, baby! Ah! that's better!" I quickly got back to work. The rare swear word coming from my sweet Halo sent shivers down my spine.

Cherry's hand reached between Arachna's legs and began massaging my balls. "Do you like this, baby?" She cooed. "Five women all using you to pleasure themselves at once? Can you handle it?"

"Mhmm," I mumbled with Alpha's pussy in my mouth.

"That's our good boy," Alpha chuckled.

Then Cherry slipped out of the pile, and I heard her quietly talking to Arachna. "Use your legs to keep you lifted a little higher. I've got work to do down below." Then I felt her straddle my shin, her pussy grinding against me, and a wet tongue slipped beneath Arachna as Cherry lapped and suckled on my sack.

For a while, all the coordinated movements helped me remain distracted enough to last longer, but the pleasure was overwhelming me. Every lick from Cherry's slick tongue, every time Arachna's pussy gripped tighter on my shaft, milking me, and every moan from all five women was starting to add up.

The game had changed from truth or dare to who would cum last, and we were all destined to be winners. As a squeal of delight came from my right, and a pussy clamped down hard on my fingers, I knew Rose wouldn't be the last witch standing. "Oh god, Daddy! Just like that, just like thaa—AHHH! Yes, yes! I'm Cu—mmmm!" The vast amount of girlcum that soaked my hand spoke to the truth of her words.

Arachna was fighting hard and trying to play dirty. "C'mon! I want to feel you fill this spider pussy up! I want to be so full it comes out of my fucking nose!" Admittedly, the comment was a little weird, but in the heat of the moment, it was working for me. Still, I held strong.

The next to fall was Cherry, who was relentlessly grinding against my leg. But Cherry was a champ and never pulled my balls from her mouth even as she came. "MmmFkLGNAHMPH!" Weird noise aside, I applauded her dedication. Or, I would have if Halo wasn't using my hand to orgasm at that very moment.

"Ah shih tzu, baby! It's so—so—Mmm, I'm so close. I'm—I'm—Ah! Gosh, baby!" My blonde angel's pussy squeezed my fingers so tightly I thought she'd break them as she lost control, her face falling forward against Alpha's thigh as she cried out in ecstasy.

Three down, two to go. You can do this, Logan! I thought. I redoubled my efforts, swirling my tongue in sync with Alpha's grinding. She pulled my hair, pressing herself down against me so hard I thought my lip would bust open. "Fuck yeah, just like that. That's my good boy. Don't stop, don't you fucking dare stop," she demanded. "Yes! You're so good with your tongue–Ffuck! AH!" Alpha cried out, her body shaking as her juices poured into my mouth and down my chin. "Yes, yes, yes, *yes*. Mmm fu—fuck! Logan! Ah!" I was glad I could hold my breath for a while because she had me locked in so tight that I couldn't breathe, and her orgasm lasted for what felt like minutes.

Finally, she gave me the chance to get some air as she threw her head to the sky before dropping lower, straddling my upper body, and kissing me passionately. "I taste so fucking good, don't I? Do you love the way I taste in your mouth, my good boy?"

"Fuck yeah I do," I said between breaths. Alpha started kissing my neck as Rose and Halo kissed my arms, sides, cheeks, anything they could. Finally, I had my first view of Arachna's flawless body as she continued to ride my dick. Her petite breasts bounced while she played with her nipples, tugging on the rings that hung from them.

"I bet you like this fucking pussy, too, don't you!" Arachna taunted me as Cherry popped my balls out of her mouth.

With Cherry safely out of the way, my hot perky-tittied goth leaned forward, pressing herself against Alpha's back and looked at me over her shoulder. "Now I'm gonna show you what this spider pussy can really do." Then sent her hips into overdrive. Arachna's ass slapped against my thighs over and over as the other girls all egged me on, trying to help their coven sister win the non-existent contest.

"Come on, baby. Don't you want to just explode into her and fill her womb up?" Halo prodded.

Rose giggled. "That's right. Give in and flood her with your warm seed and make her your little slut forever."

Cherry had moved around, standing above me, her upside-down face staring down at me and shooting me a wink. "C'mon, baby. The faster you cum, the faster you can fill my tight little pussy, too." Then she lowered herself, resting her breasts atop my head, slowly rubbing them against me while she played with her nipple studs.

Arachna cried out, and I could feel her pussy clenching. She was fighting off her orgasm as hard as she could, but I knew I had her right where I wanted her. My hips started bucking, matching her pace. I slammed my cock deep inside every time her ass came down. Her eyes widened. "Oh shh-it! Logan! You're gonna make me—"

As she was screaming my name, Alpha cooed into my ear and ran her fingers through my hair on the side of my head. "Mmm, look at you. So good. That's it, be Mommy's good boy. Cum inside her. Fill her. *Breed* her." She said it knowing full well we still didn't have a Fertility Witch on hand, but that didn't seem to matter much to my dick.

Her words struck me deep, hitting something primal inside of me. What was a sure victory became a photo finish in an instant. Arachna's walls clenched down hard at the same time that my cock thickened and prepared to burst.

Arachna stated the obvious as her juices coated me, and I painted her insides white. "I'm–Ah-cumming Oh! Fuck! Nyahh!" Our bodies spasmed as the girls all cooed and praised us. I almost couldn't stop cumming for thirty seconds, pulse after pulse erupting from my cock, overflowing her pussy.

Things finally calmed down and Alpha pulled one leg over me, stealing Rose's place at my side. She didn't seem to mind and scooted over, snuggling up against Alpha's back.

Arachna sat up and looked down, rubbing her stomach. "Holy fuck, I really do feel so full," she groaned.

She wasn't kidding. My cum had clearly been leaking out of her for a while. As Arachna started pulling off my cock, Rose and Halo instantly hopped off the couch and onto their knees. As my half erect cock fell out of Arachna's overstuffed pussy, more juices poured out, coating it further.

Rose and Halo both licked, sucked, and drank up our combined juices. "Mmm! Gosh! Your dick is so yummy!" Halo said between licks.

Arachna took Halo's former spot at my left side and snuggled up against me as she placed gentle kisses along my shoulder and arm as she panted, still trying to catch her breath.

Halo took my length into her mouth. She desperately sucked and cleaned it, making me groan in delight. She moaned with a happy giggle as my cock twitched in her mouth. "MmmMMmm!"

When Rose saw Halo had the prize, she slid past her and spread the Arachnid witch's legs apart. "Open up, Spidey! I need more of Daddy's freakin' cream!" she shouted before diving forward.

"Rose, what are you—oh shit! Ahmm!" Before Arachna could protest, Rose's long tongue was lapping at her pussy, eagerly accepting all the juicy leftovers.

Fuck, is this my life now? I never expected things to turn out like this, but I sure as hell didn't regret the development. As I lay there, my cock slowly returning to full mast from Halo's tender administrations, Alpha began running her hand through my hair. "Mmm. Four more rounds to go." She kissed me on my cheek. "How's my good boy feeling now?"

I turned, smiling at her. Then, I kissed my redheaded lover. "I feel like a fucking king."

COVEN KING 1

Cherry giggled, pecking me on the forehead. She winked at me. "All hail the Coven King."

LINKS TO FOLLOW

First of all, this is a new author debut, <u>so PLEASE leave a review</u>! Edgar Riggs did a huge portion of the drafting on this (80% or more), with Virgil mainly providing the bulk of the plot, handling the editing and some prose rewrites, and helping to avoid pitfalls. By the time this book is out, we should already be knee deep in book 2, but it sure would help morale if this one got some positive feedback! Thanks!

For more Harem Lit and Monster Girl content check out the following:

https://www.facebook.com/groups/haremlit
https://www.facebook.com/groups/haremlitaudiobooks
https://www.facebook.com/groups/haremlitbooks/
https://www.facebook.com/groups/monstergirllovers
https://www.facebook.com/groups/dukesofharem
https://www.facebook.com/groups/MonsterGirlFiction/
https://www.facebook.com/groups/1324476308314052
https://www.facebook.com/groups/404822691240858
https://www.facebook.com/RoyalGuard2020
https://www.royalguardpublishing.com
Virgil's Patreon:
https://www.patreon.com/virgilknightley

Printed in Great Britain
by Amazon